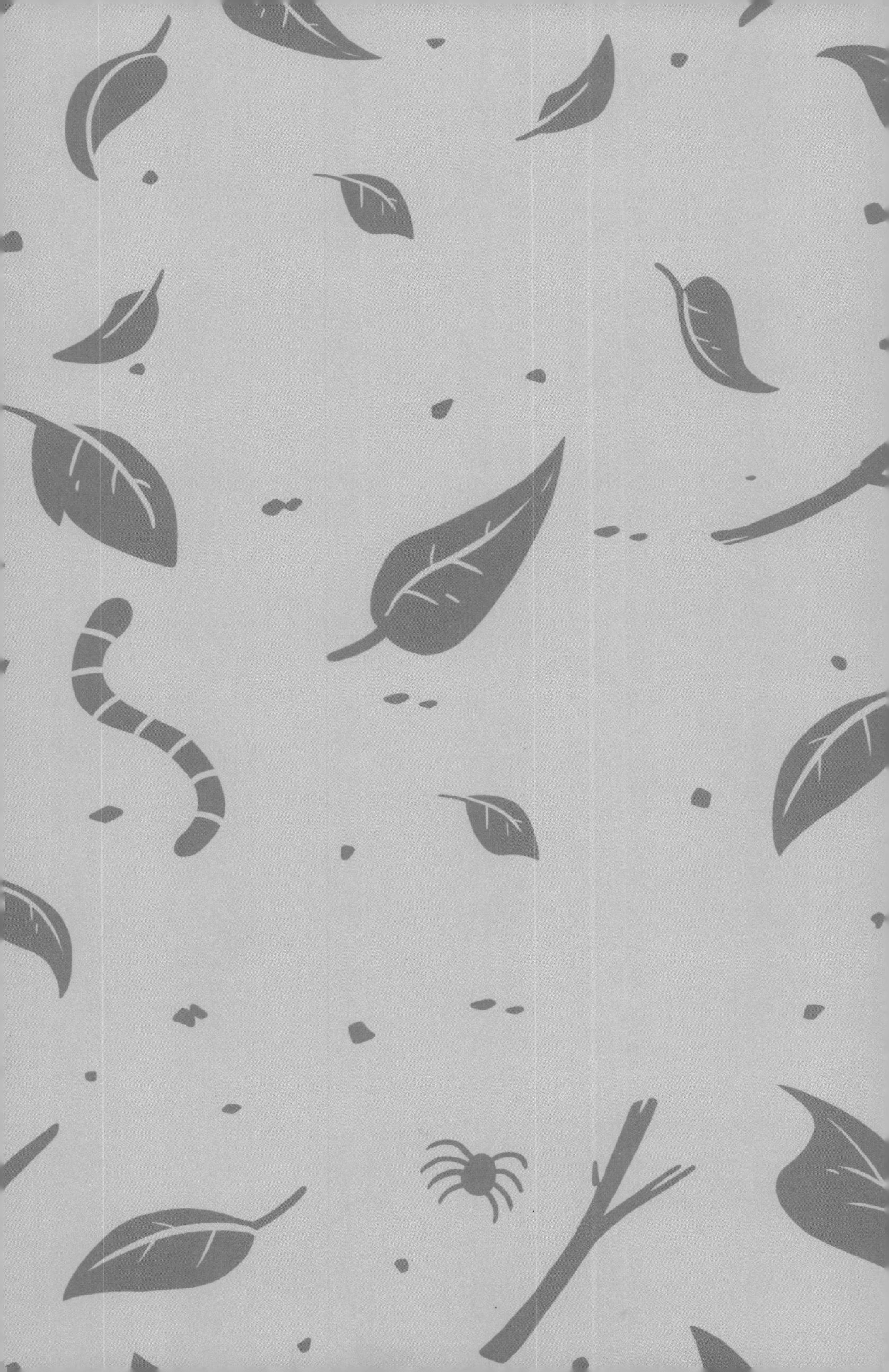

Acclaim for Kean Soo's

"A simply wonderful tale of friendship and whimsy,
masterfully constructed with depth and moxie."
–Kirkus Reviews

"Sophisticated and thoughtful,
this comic also has plenty of child appeal."
–School Library Journal

"I'm addicted to Jellaby! Kean Soo's
storytelling is irresistable."
–Scott McCloud, author of *Understanding Comics*

"Jellaby will win your heart."
–Jeff Smith, creator of *Bone*

Eisner Award nominee
for Best Digital Comic

Joe Shuster Award winner
for Best Comic for Kids

JELLABY

The Lost Monster

Kean Soo

Stone Arch Books
a capstone imprint

Acknowledgements:
Special thanks to Calista Brill, Roberta Pressel,
Judy Hansen, Hope Larson, David & Nicolas Seigneret, Ben
Hu, Jason Turner, Clio Chiang, Kazu Kibuishi, and of course,
all my friends and family for their love and support
over the years. A very special thank-you to the Canada
Council for the Arts for their support of this work.

Jellaby is published by Stone Arch Books
a Capstone imprint
1710 Roe Crest Drive
North Mankato, Minnesota 56003
www.capstonepub.com

Text © Kean Soo 2014
Illustrations © Kean Soo 2014

Cataloging-in-Publication Data is available on the Library of Congress website.
ISBN: 978-1-4342-9195-0 (Library Binding)

Summary:
After moving to a new neighborhood, ten-year-old Portia Bennett
finds a new best friend -- a huge purple monster behind her house!
Convinced the sweet, silent creature is lost, Portia decides to help
Jellaby find his way home. Together, these new friends embark
on a mysterious and extraordinary adventure.

Cover Design: Kean Soo & Kazu Kibuishi

Printed in the United States of America in North Mankato, Minnesota.
032015   008793R

Foreword

When Kean asked me to help him redesign the cover for this new edition of *Jellaby* you are now holding in your hands, I accepted enthusiastically, of course. Kean and I actually go way back. He was one of the first friends I made through email exchanges while drawing webcomics. At the time, Kean was drawing one of the best journal comics on the Internet. It was often highlighted by Scott McCloud -- our mentor and the driving inspiration for the creation of webcomics. During the long drawing sessions that often lasted through the night, Kean and I would chat and encourage each other as we worked.

It was a great, formative time in our careers. Soon, we collaborated on the *Flight* anthology, and Kean was one of its first contributors, but he also served as its assistant editor, having been there from the moment of its creation. He is uncle to my kids, he is a close friend, and his work is an inspiration to all those who know him.

We often bonded over a shared love of the work of Hayao Miyazaki, Bill Watterson, Jeff Smith, Osamu Tezuka, and other masters. This love is something I feel is clearly evident in the pages of *Jellaby*. Kean is working to carry on the tradition of great comic strip storytelling, and he does it while exhibiting the warmth and empathy that he himself carries with him. This is the quiet, introspective, cautious, and caring Kean. These are the first steps in a promising career of a great modern cartoonist. Someday people will also see the goofy, jolly, belly-laughing Kean that so many of us know in person. When the poop jokes start flying, I have a feeling that the readers will be in for quite a wild ride.

In the meantime, I encourage everyone to read and enjoy this wonderful story, as I think it is one of the greatest comics written for all ages, and I hope *Jellaby* continues to walk, or shuffle, among us for many years to come.

~ Kazu Kibuishi,
creator of the bestselling
Amulet series

CHAPTER ONE

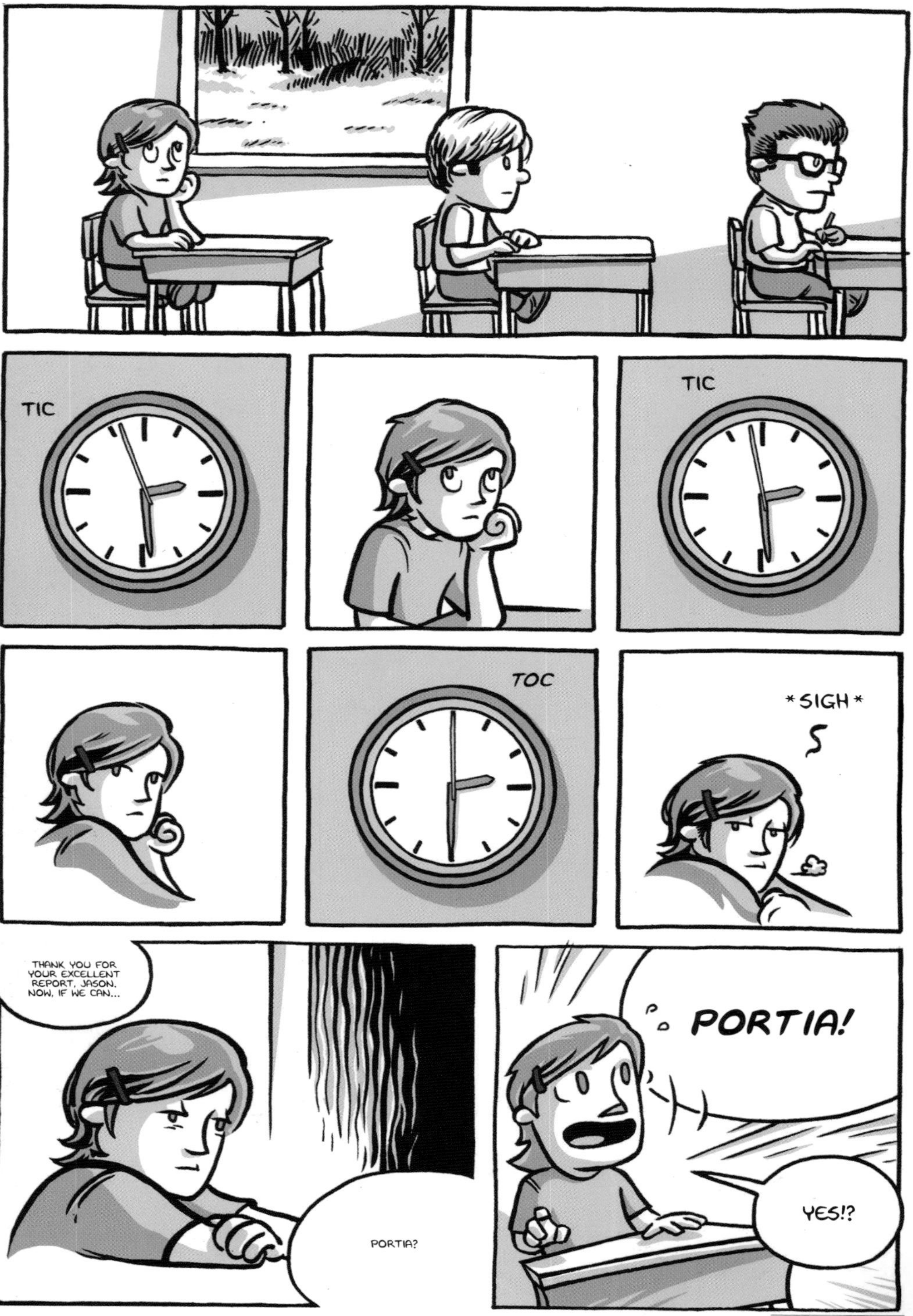
TIC
TIC
TOC
SIGH
THANK YOU FOR YOUR EXCELLENT REPORT, JASON. NOW, IF WE CAN...
PORTIA?
PORTIA!
YES!?

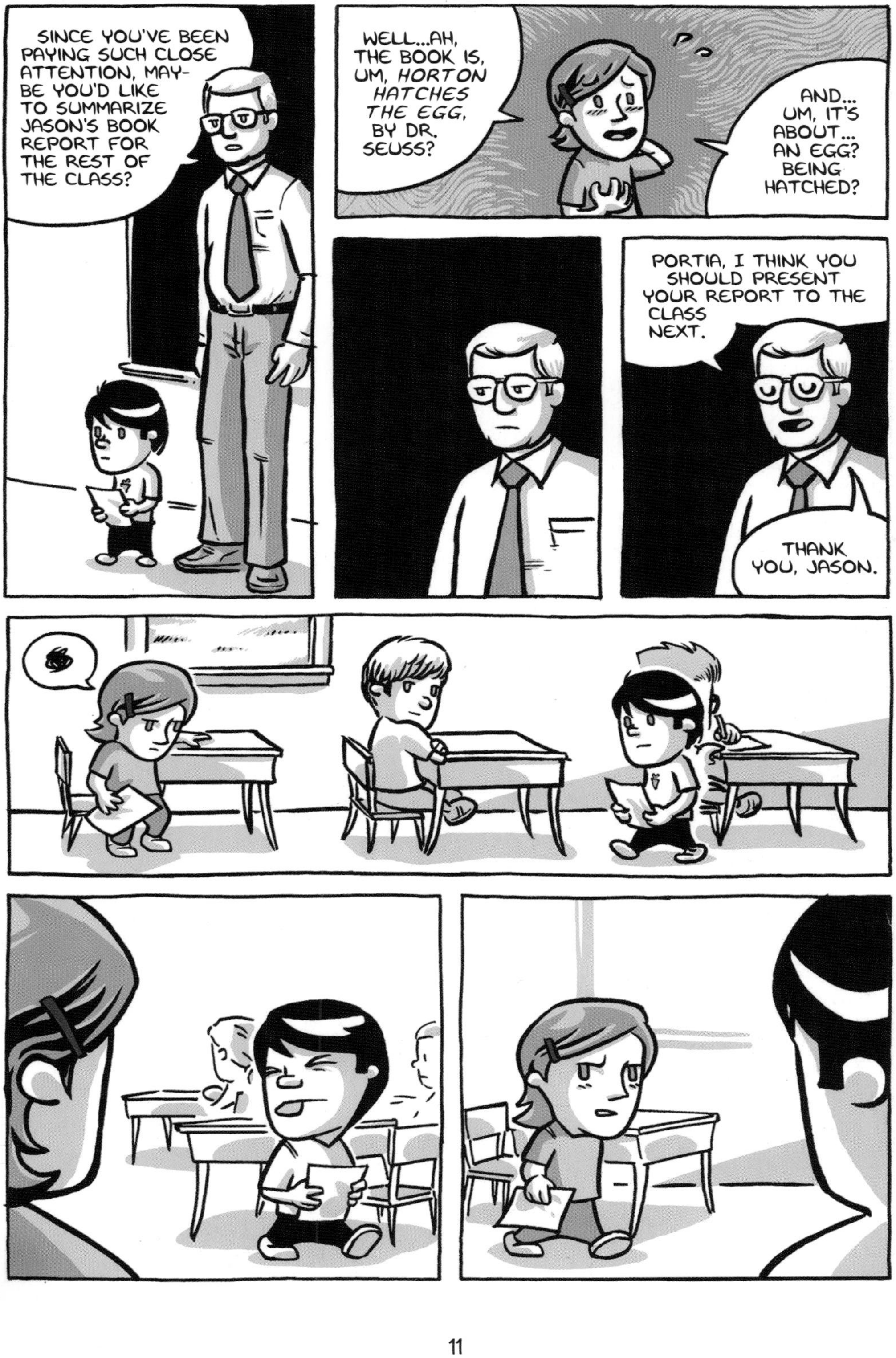
SINCE YOU'VE BEEN PAYING SUCH CLOSE ATTENTION, MAYBE YOU'D LIKE TO SUMMARIZE JASON'S BOOK REPORT FOR THE REST OF THE CLASS?
WELL...AH, THE BOOK IS, UM, *HORTON HATCHES THE EGG*, BY DR. SEUSS?
AND... UM, IT'S ABOUT... AN EGG? BEING HATCHED?
PORTIA, I THINK YOU SHOULD PRESENT YOUR REPORT TO THE CLASS NEXT.
THANK YOU, JASON.

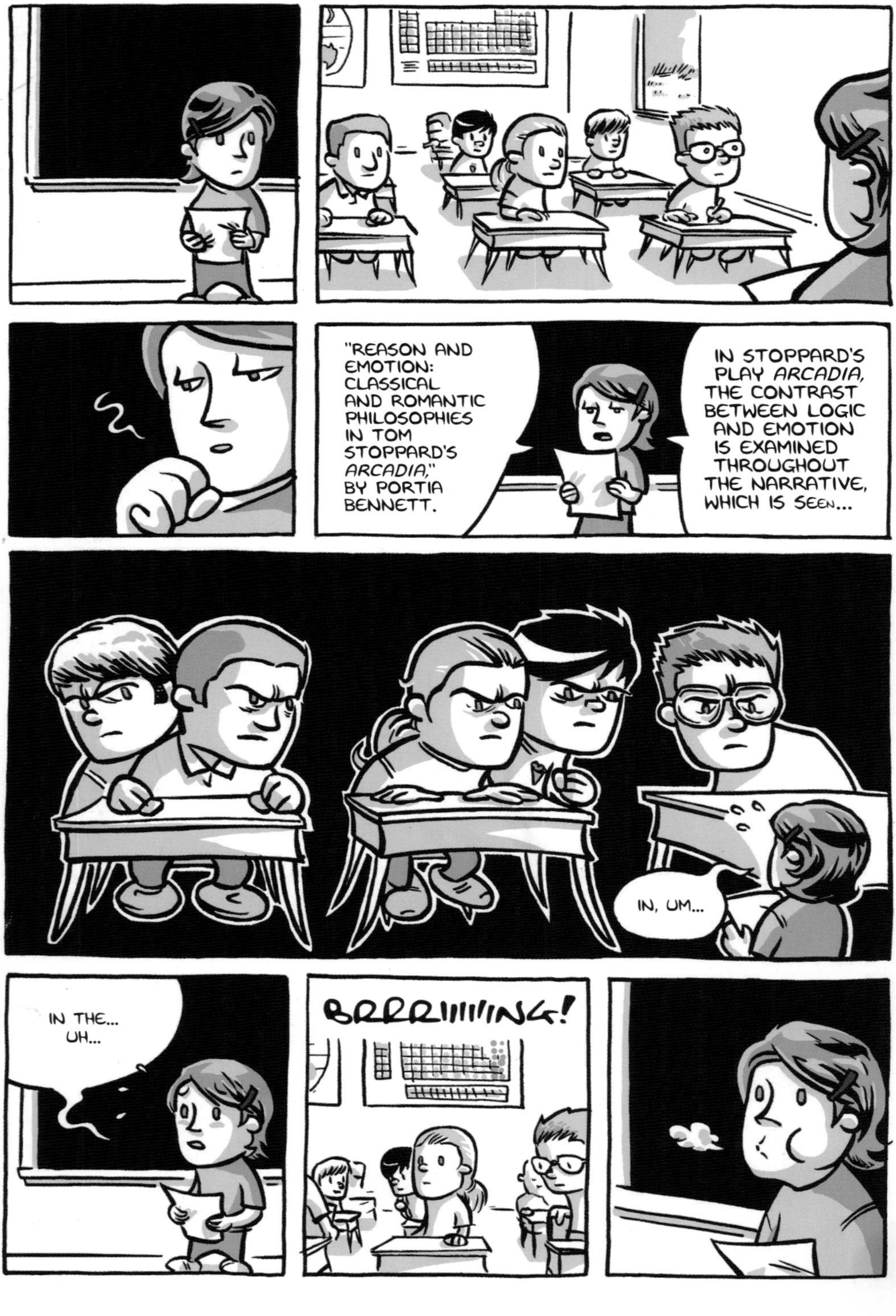
"REASON AND EMOTION: CLASSICAL AND ROMANTIC PHILOSOPHIES IN TOM STOPPARD'S *ARCADIA*," BY PORTIA BENNETT.
IN STOPPARD'S PLAY *ARCADIA*, THE CONTRAST BETWEEN LOGIC AND EMOTION IS EXAMINED THROUGHOUT THE NARRATIVE, WHICH IS SEEN...
IN, UM...
IN THE... UH...
BRRRIIIIIING!

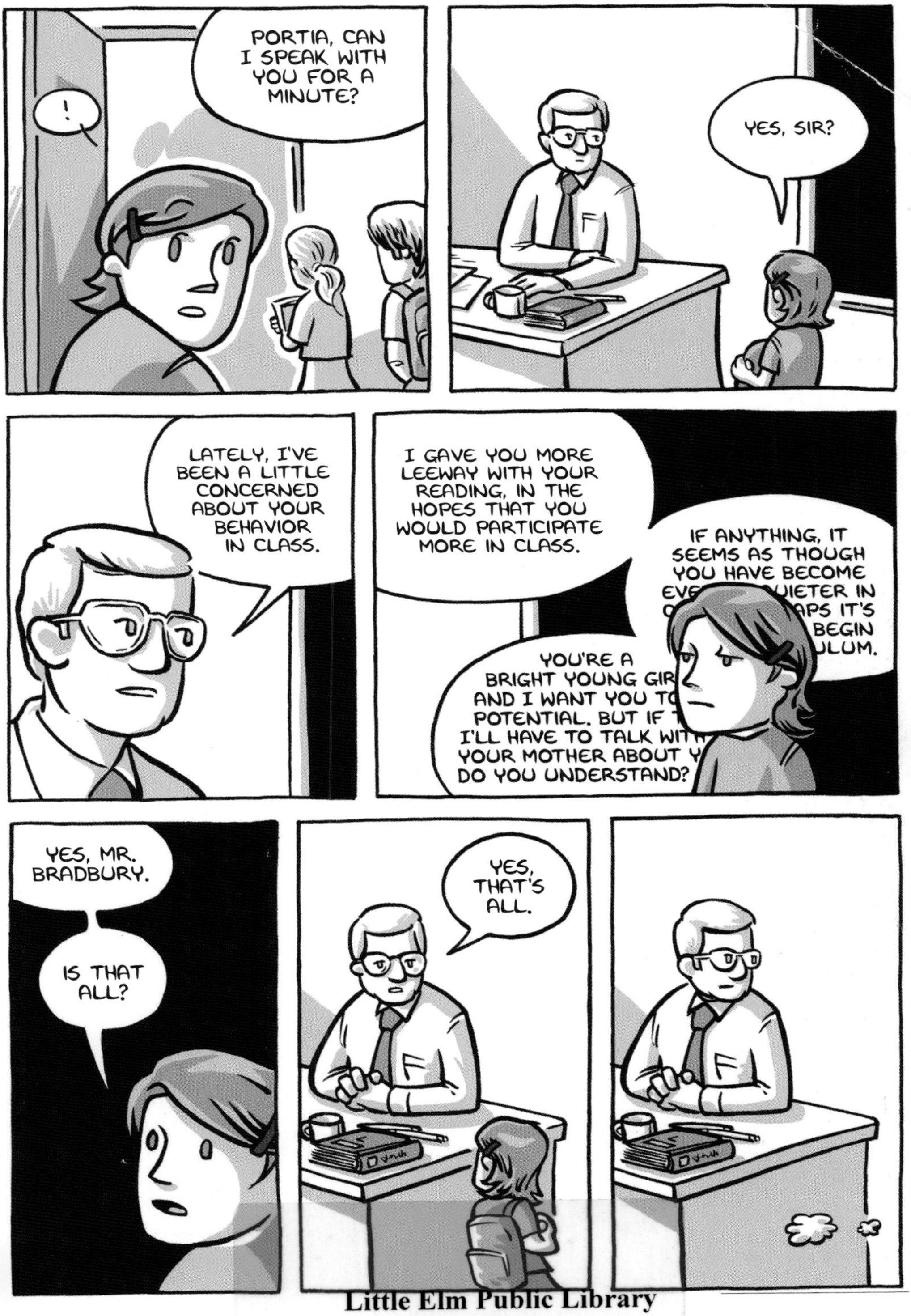
!
PORTIA, CAN I SPEAK WITH YOU FOR A MINUTE?
YES, SIR?
LATELY, I'VE BEEN A LITTLE CONCERNED ABOUT YOUR BEHAVIOR IN CLASS.
I GAVE YOU MORE LEEWAY WITH YOUR READING, IN THE HOPES THAT YOU WOULD PARTICIPATE MORE IN CLASS.
IF ANYTHING, IT SEEMS AS THOUGH YOU HAVE BECOME EVE UIETER IN C APS IT'S BEGIN ULUM.
YOU'RE A BRIGHT YOUNG GIR AND I WANT YOU TO POTENTIAL. BUT IF T I'LL HAVE TO TALK WIT YOUR MOTHER ABOUT Y DO YOU UNDERSTAND?
YES, MR. BRADBURY.
IS THAT ALL?
YES, THAT'S ALL.

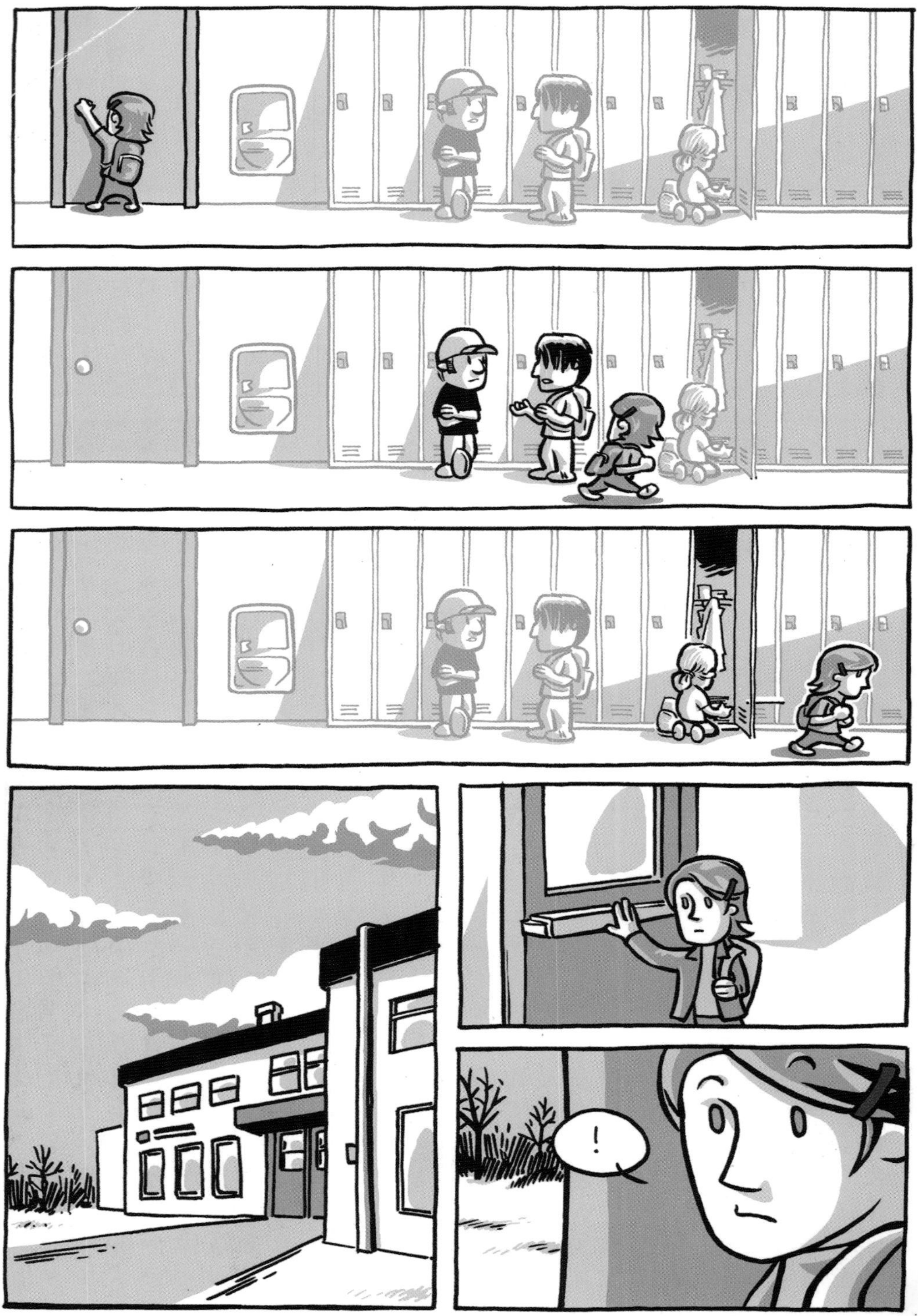
!

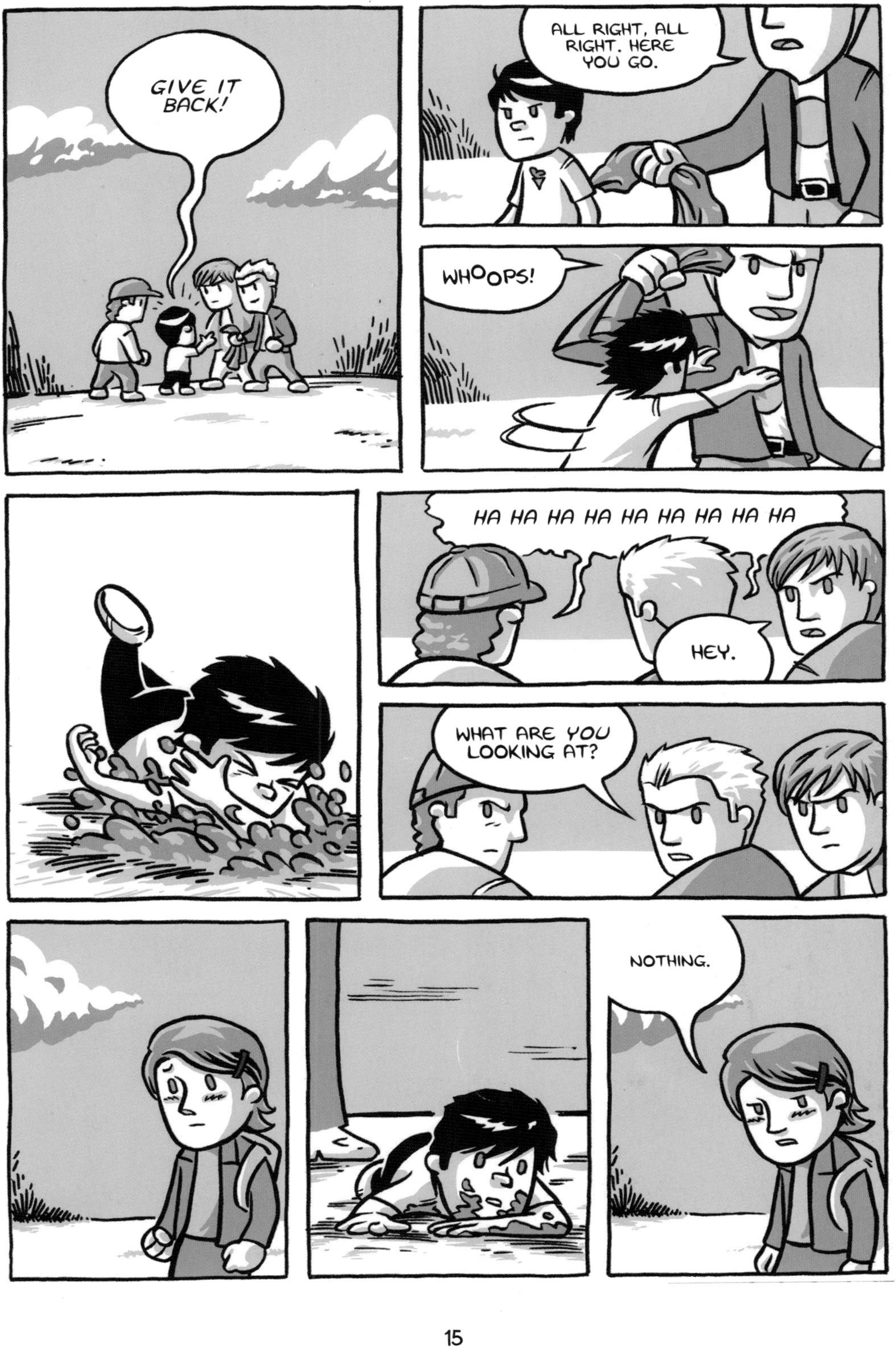
GIVE IT BACK!
ALL RIGHT, ALL RIGHT. HERE YOU GO.
WHOOPS!
HA HA HA HA HA HA HA HA HA
HEY.
WHAT ARE YOU LOOKING AT?
NOTHING.

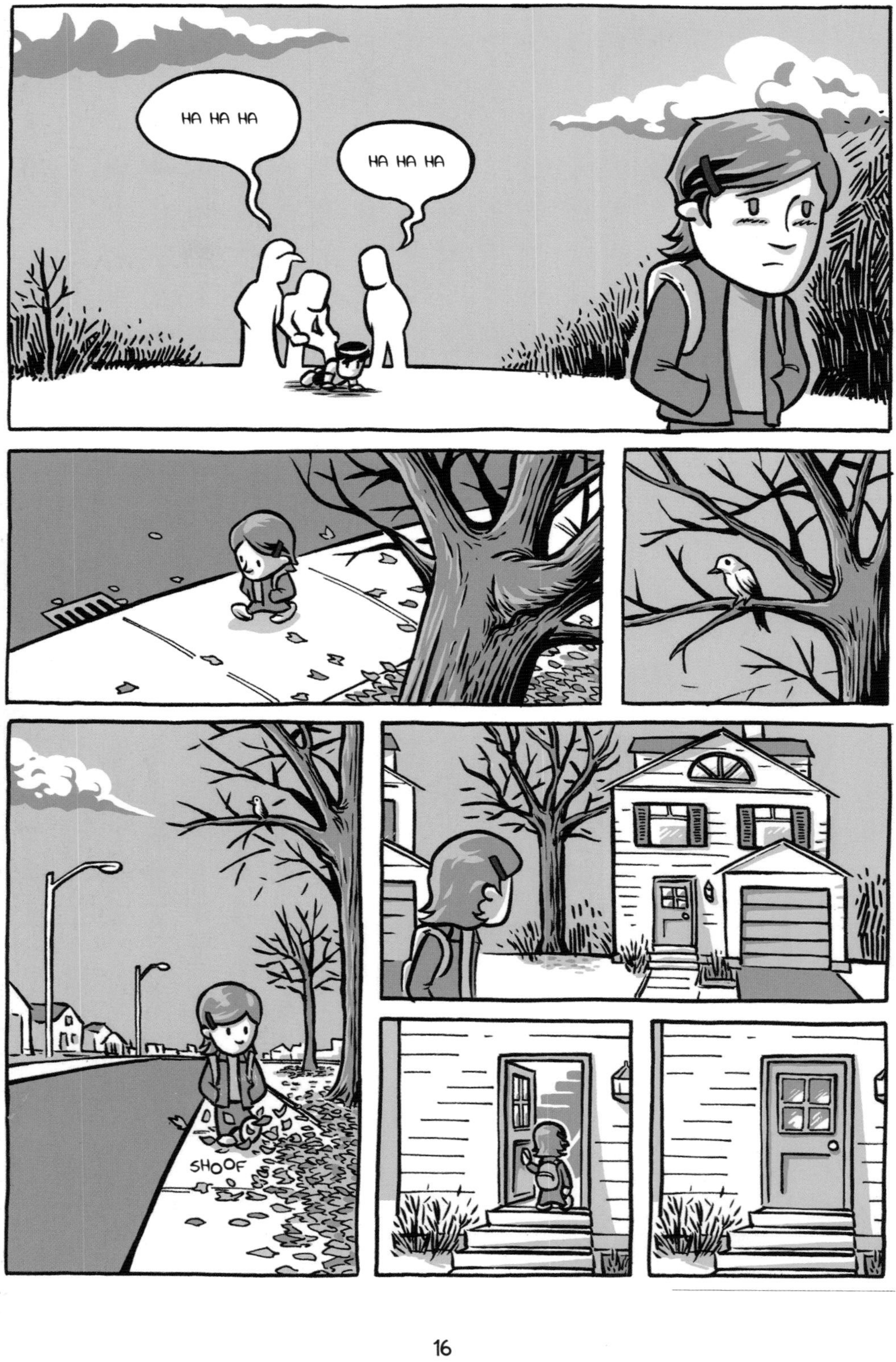
HA HA HA
HA HA HA
SHOOF

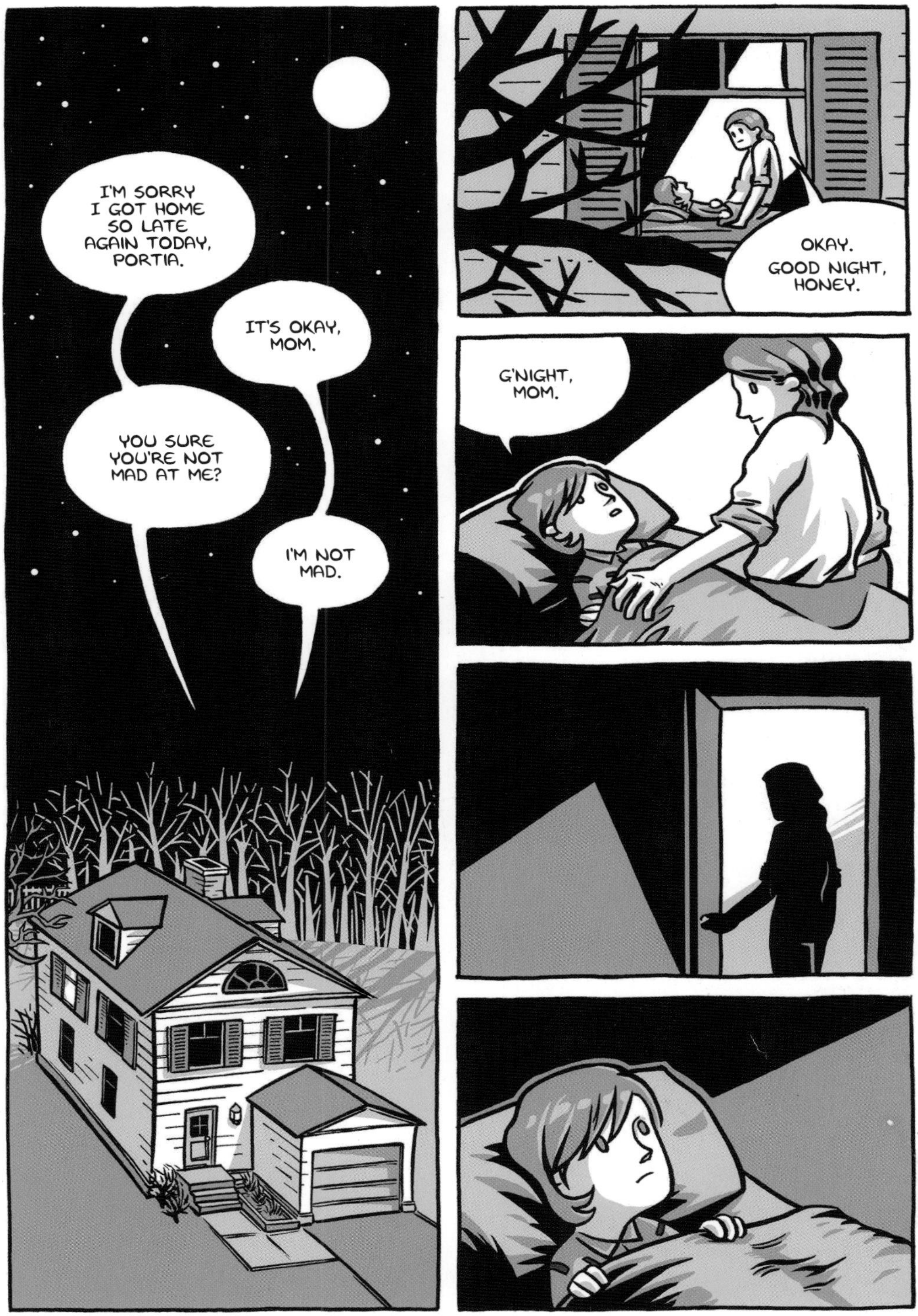
I'M SORRY I GOT HOME SO LATE AGAIN TODAY, PORTIA.
IT'S OKAY, MOM.
YOU SURE YOU'RE NOT MAD AT ME?
I'M NOT MAD.
OKAY. GOOD NIGHT, HONEY.
G'NIGHT, MOM.

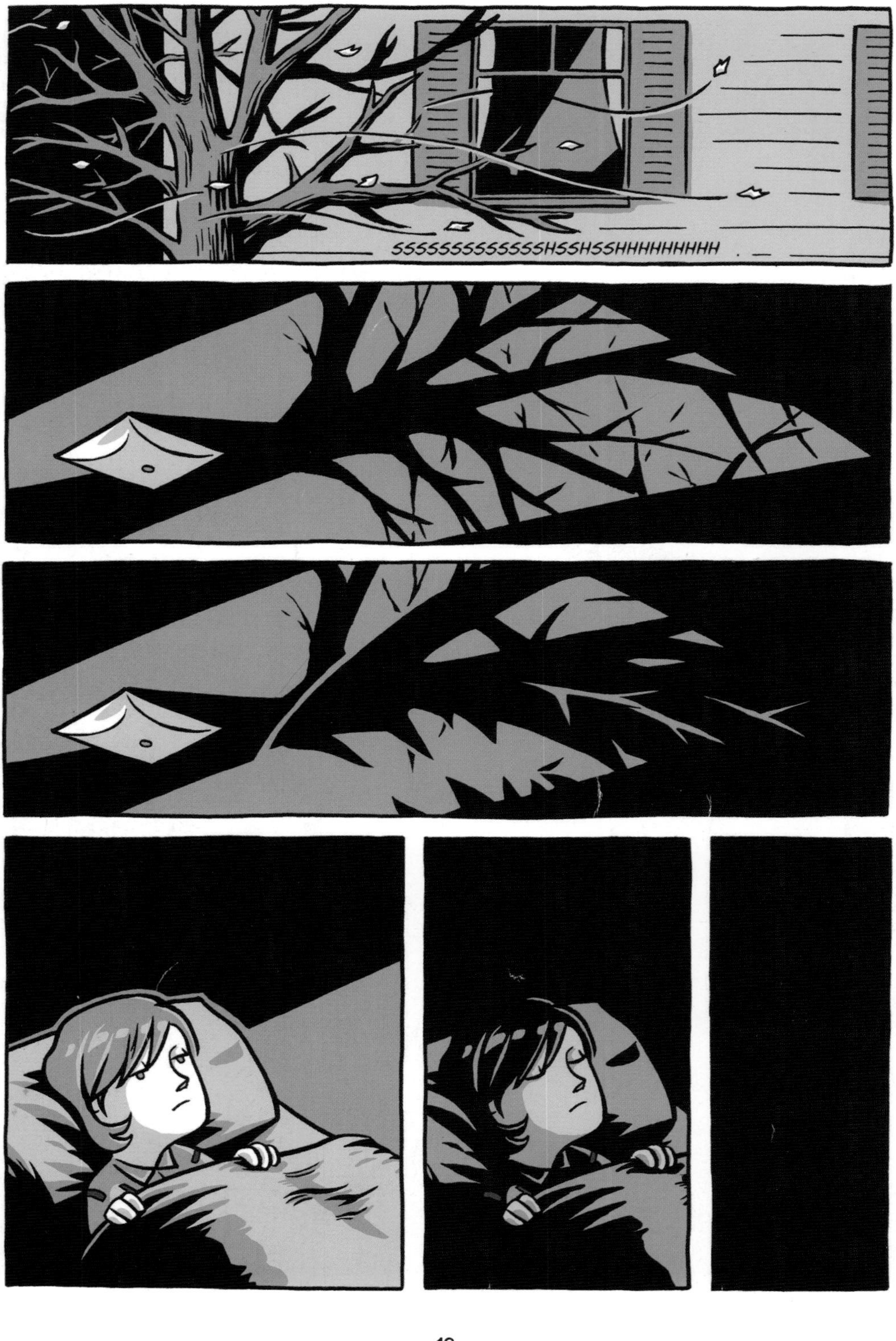
SSSSSSSSSSSSSHSSHSSHHHHHHHHH

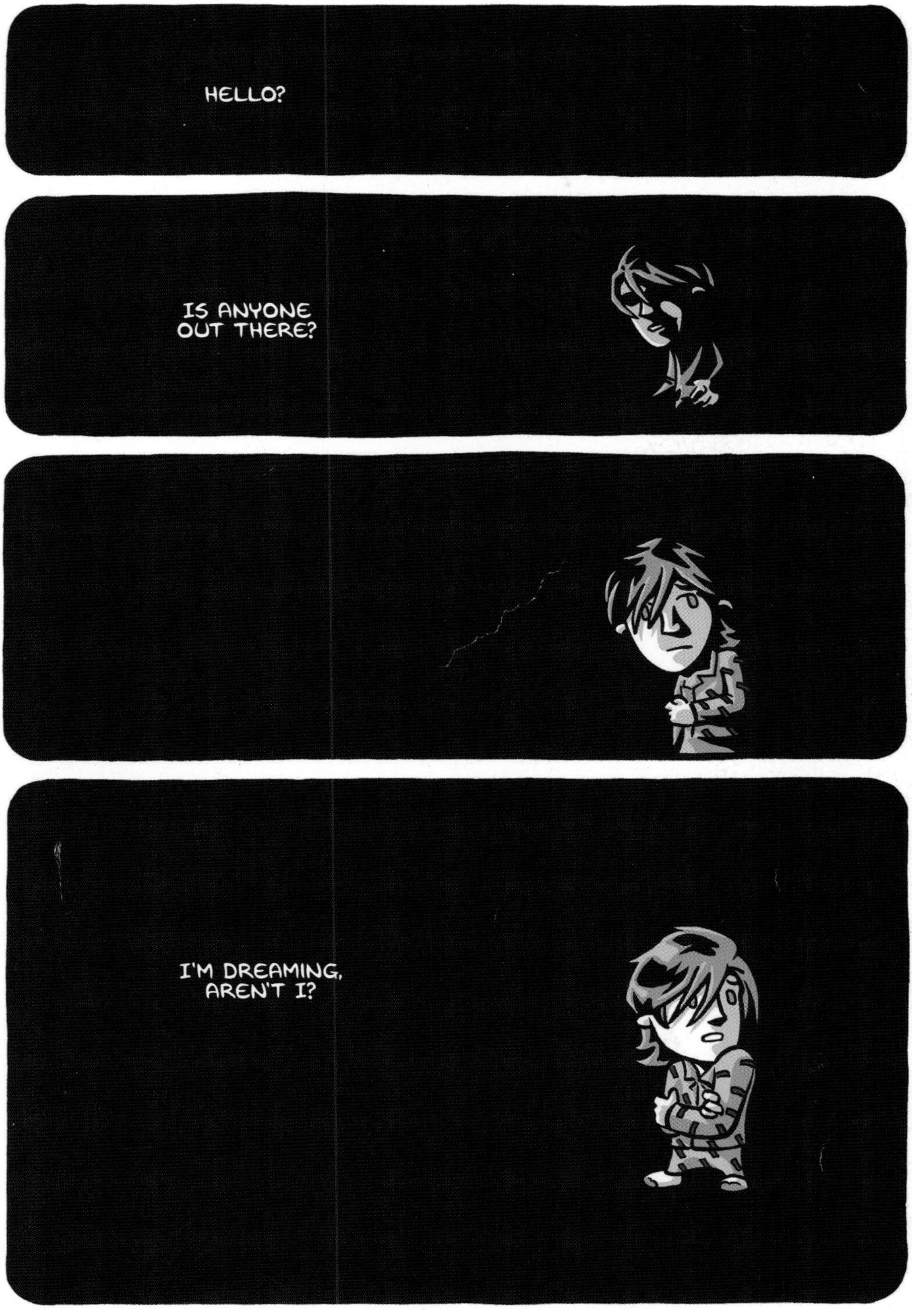
HELLO?
IS ANYONE OUT THERE?
I'M DREAMING, AREN'T I?

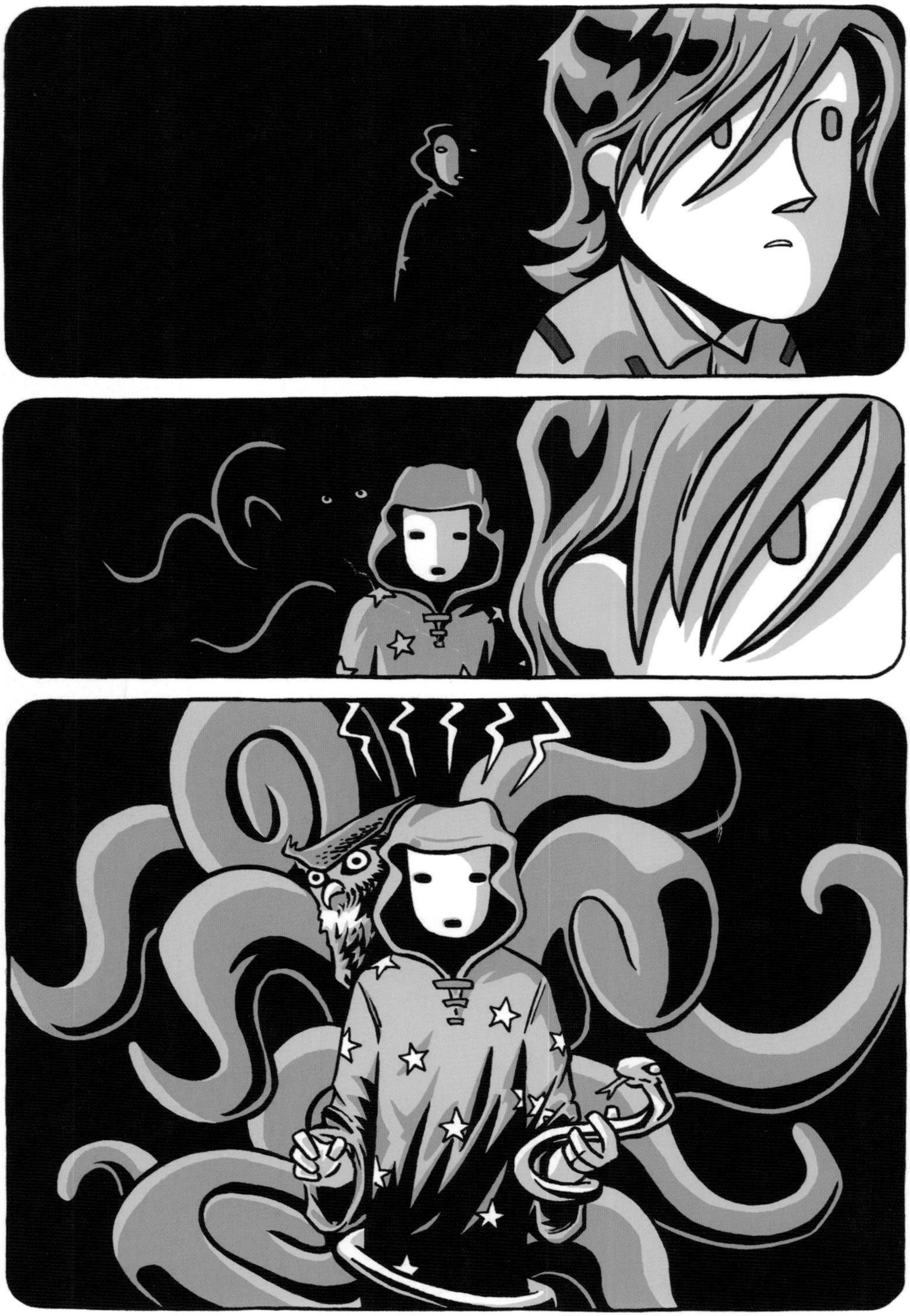

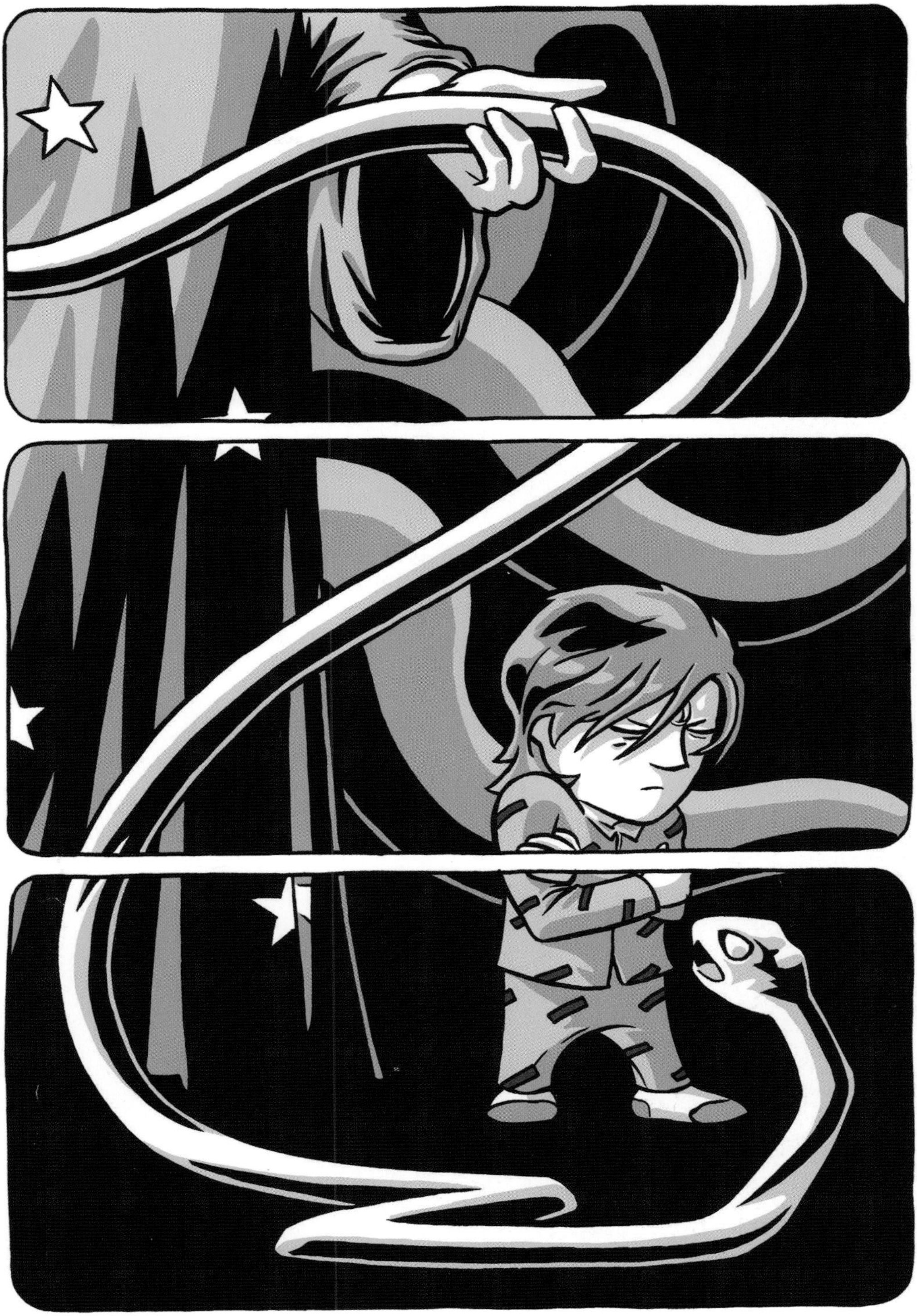

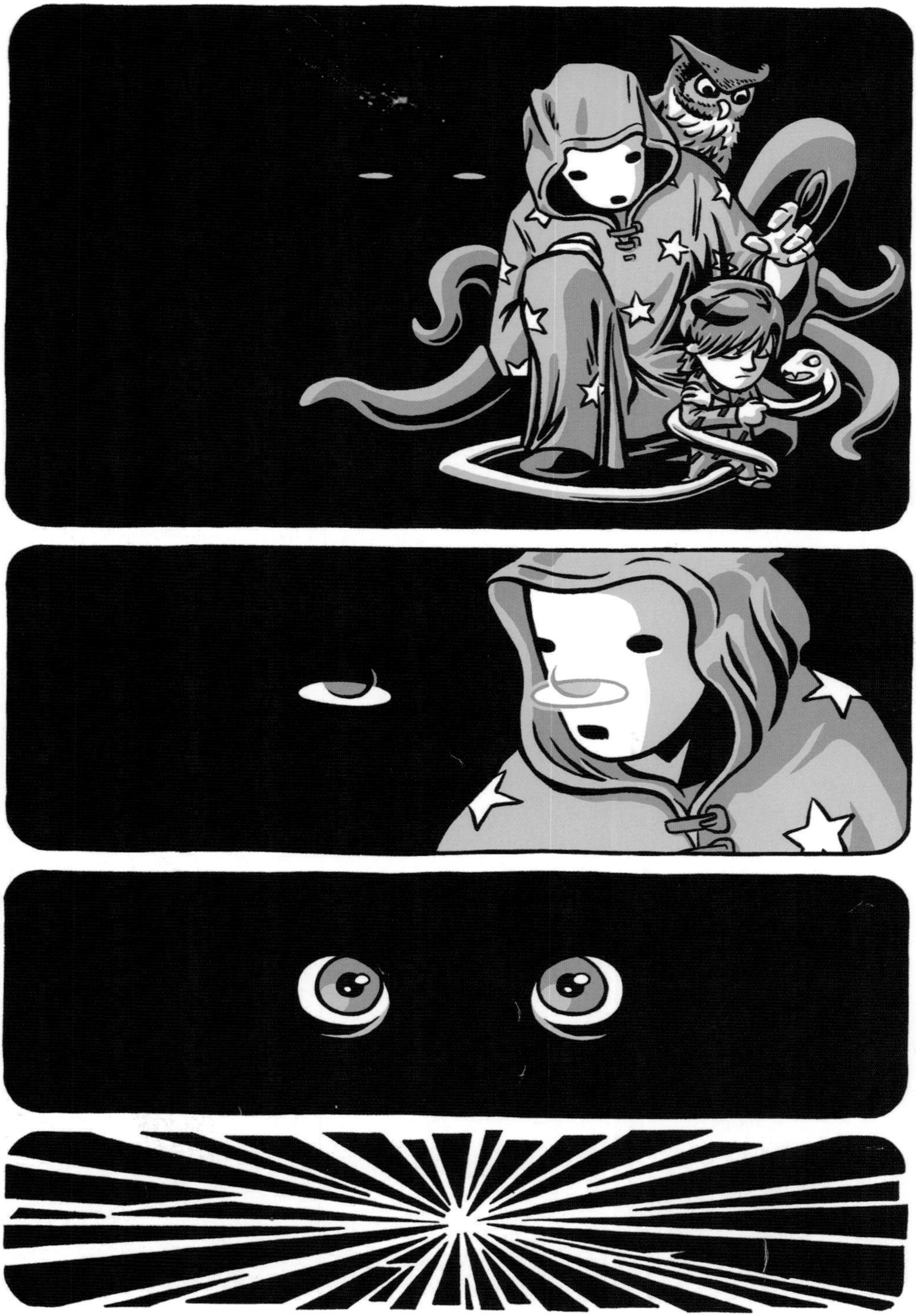

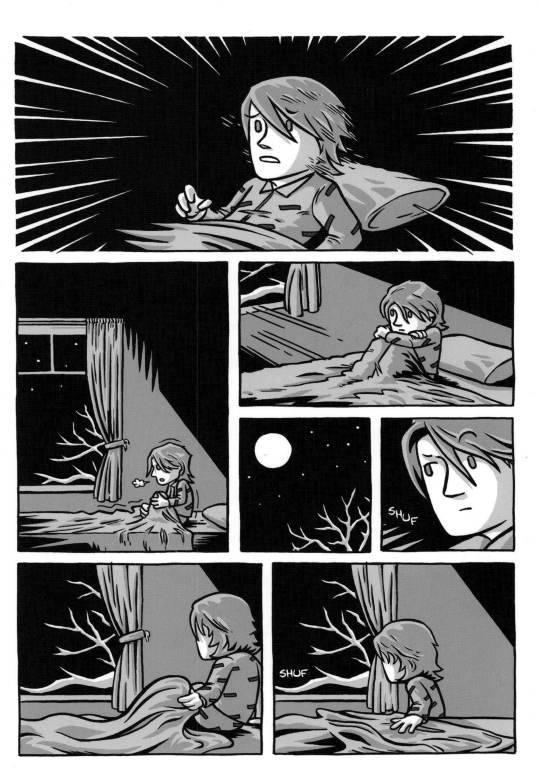

SHUF

SHUF

23

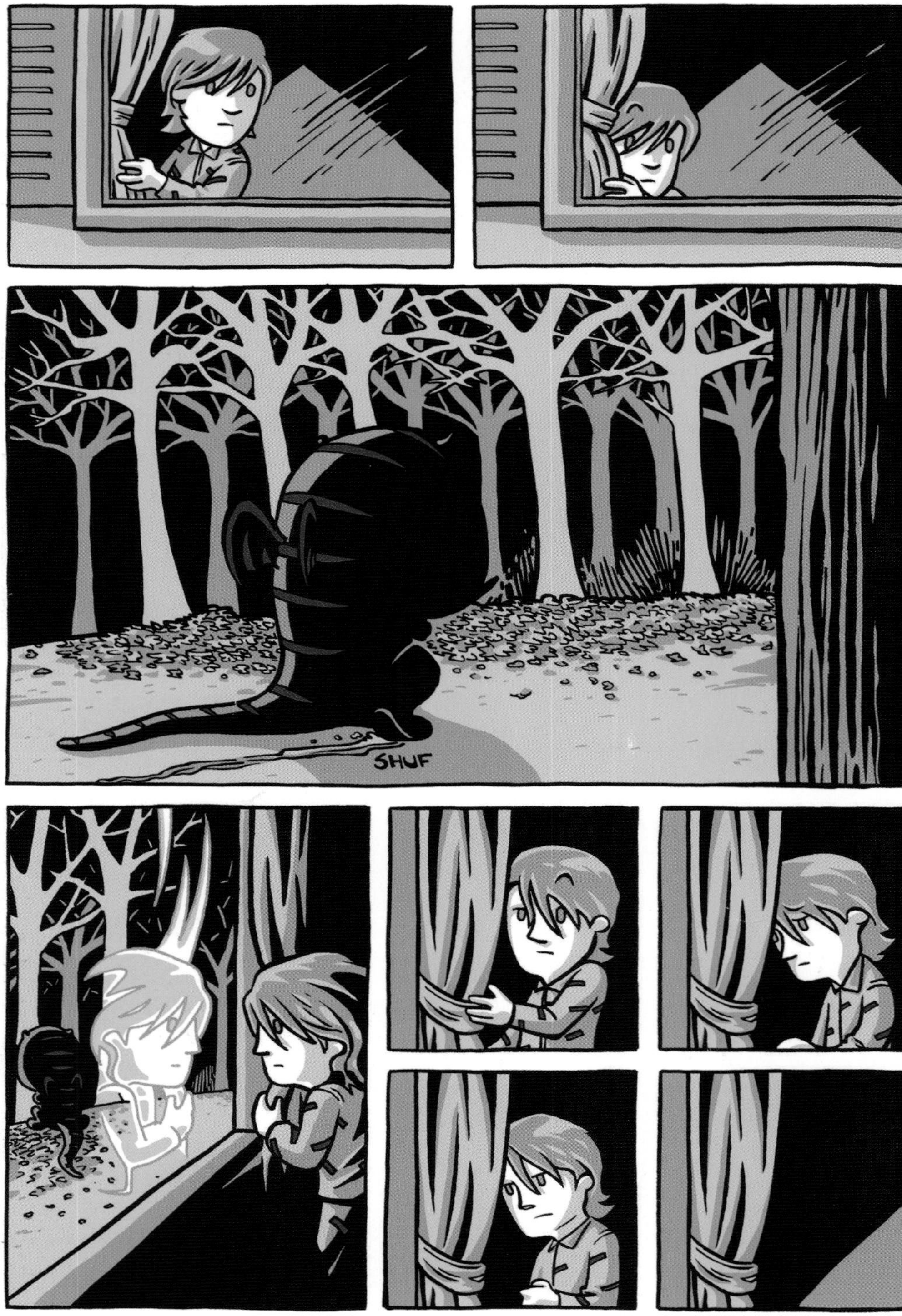
SHUF

CREEEEEE...

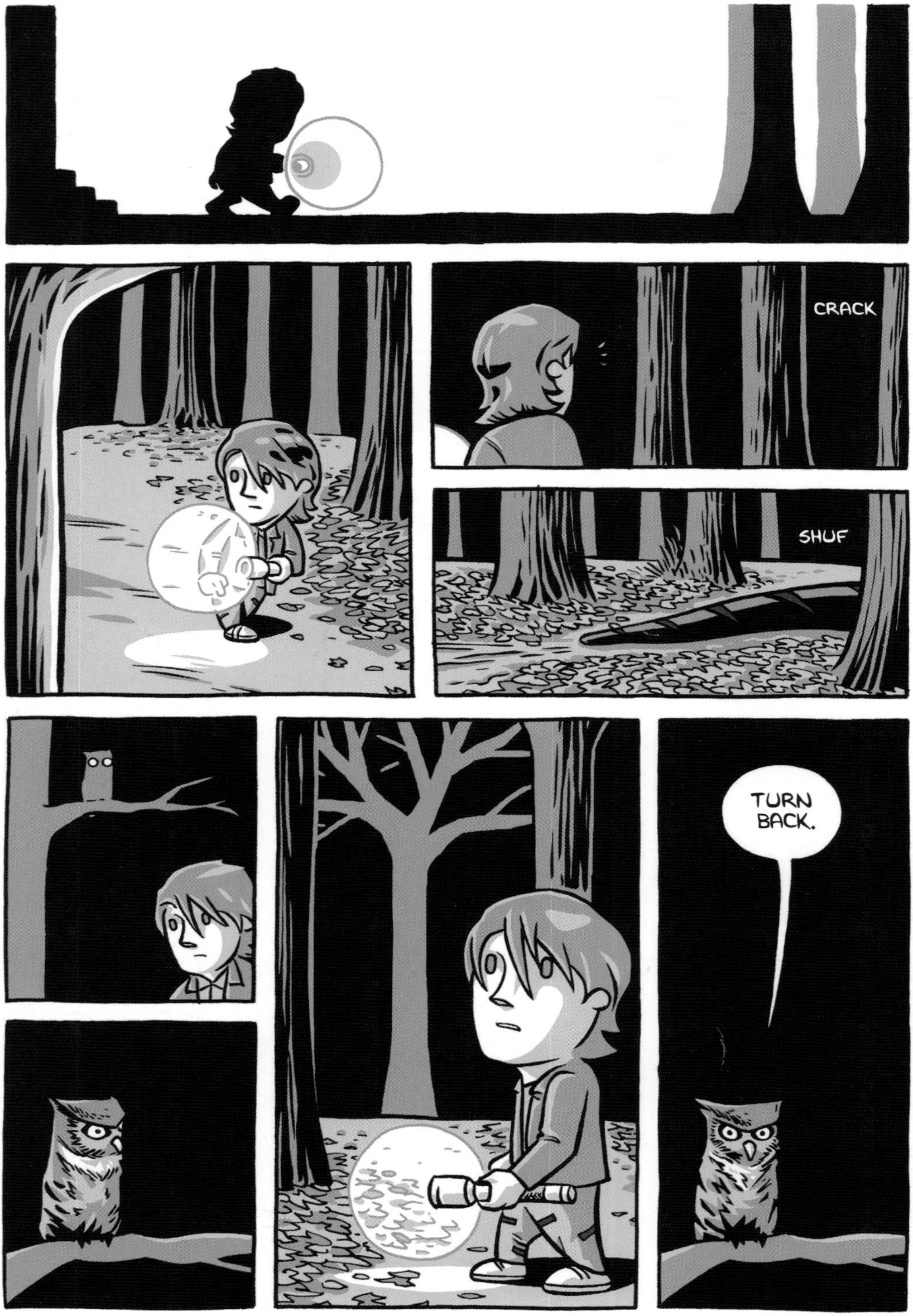
CRACK
SHUF
TURN BACK.

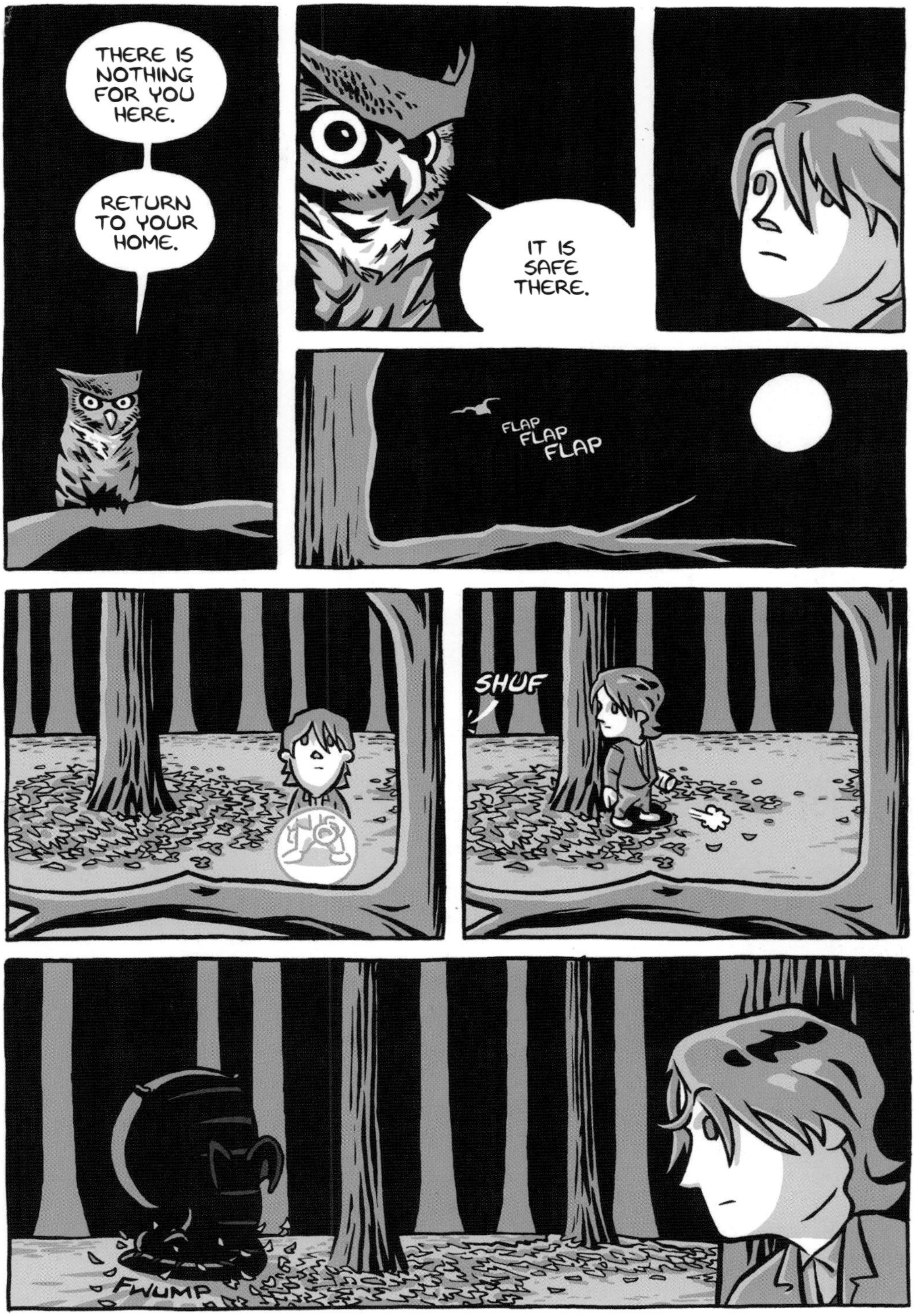
THERE IS NOTHING FOR YOU HERE.
RETURN TO YOUR HOME.
IT IS SAFE THERE.
FLAP FLAP FLAP
SHUF
FWUMP

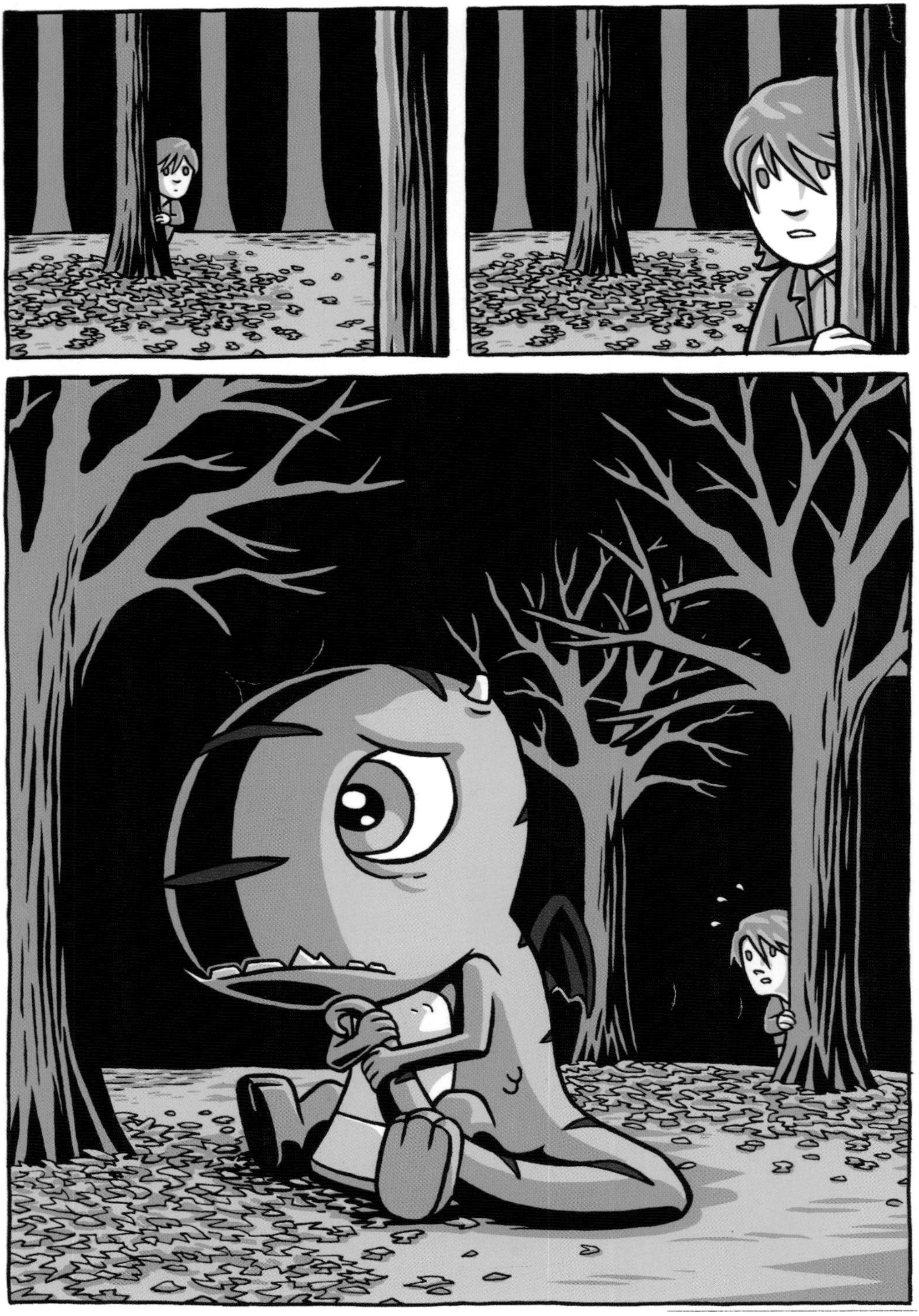

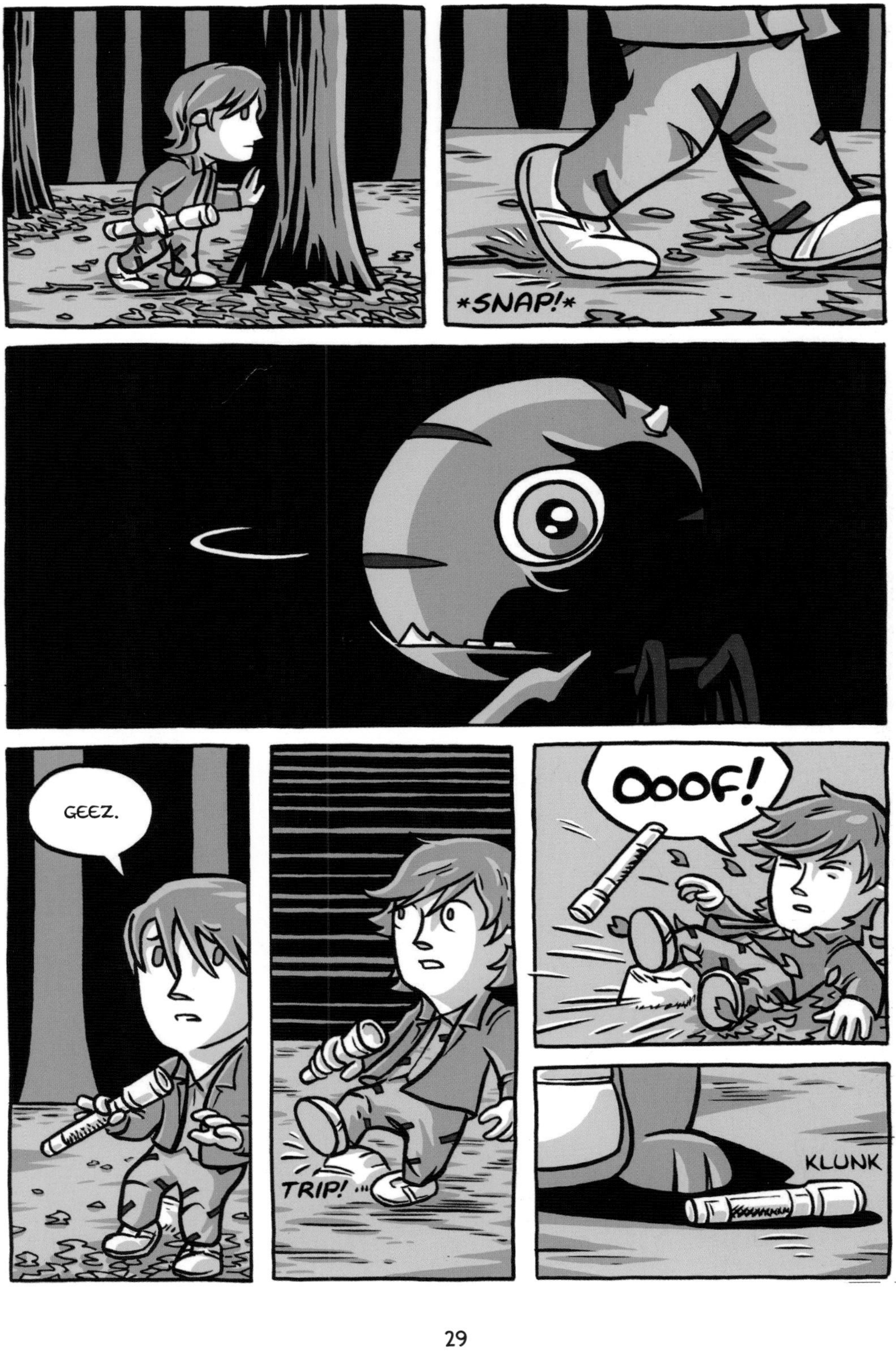
SNAP!
GEEZ.
TRIP!
OOOF!
KLUNK

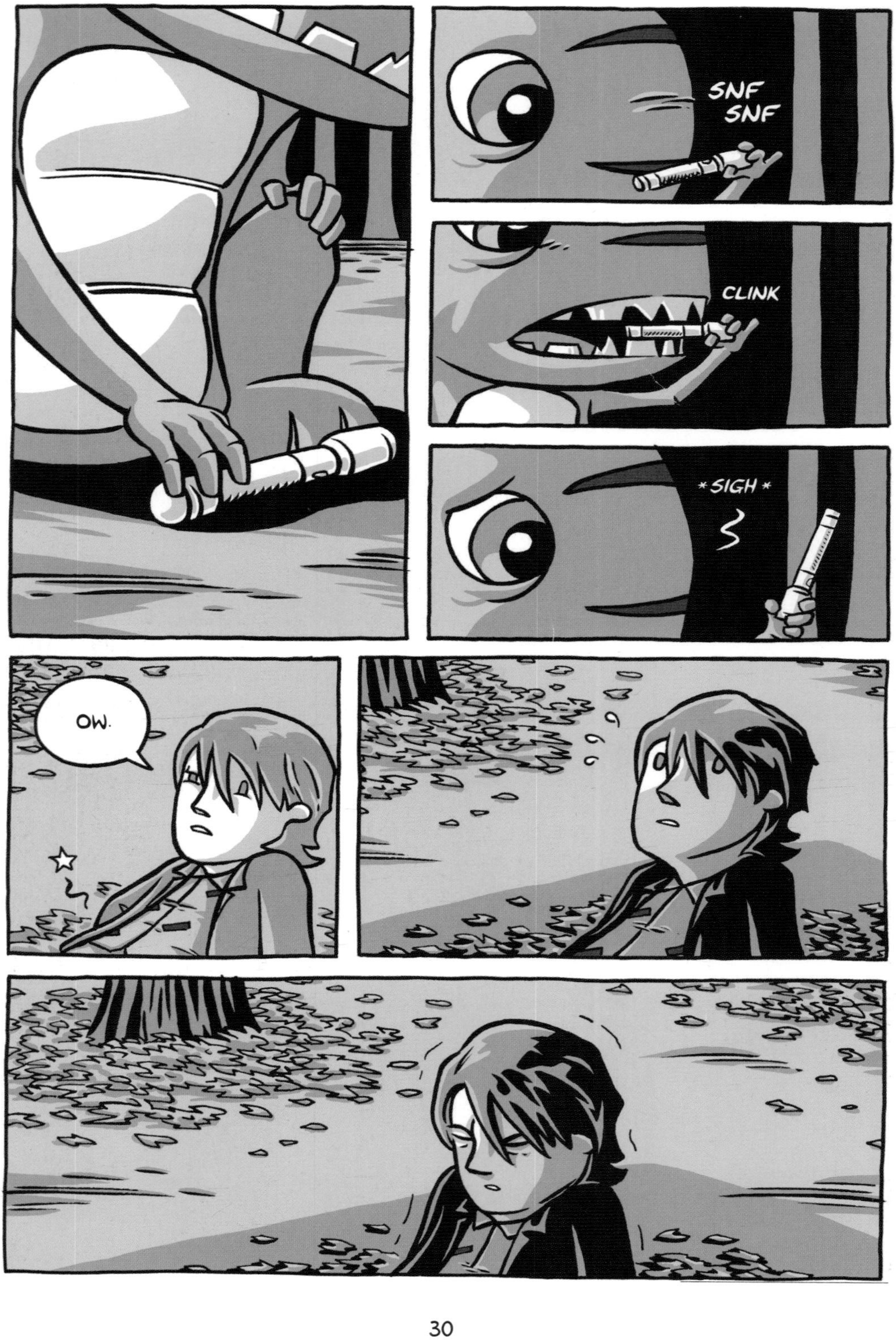
SNF
SNF
CLINK
SIGH
OW.

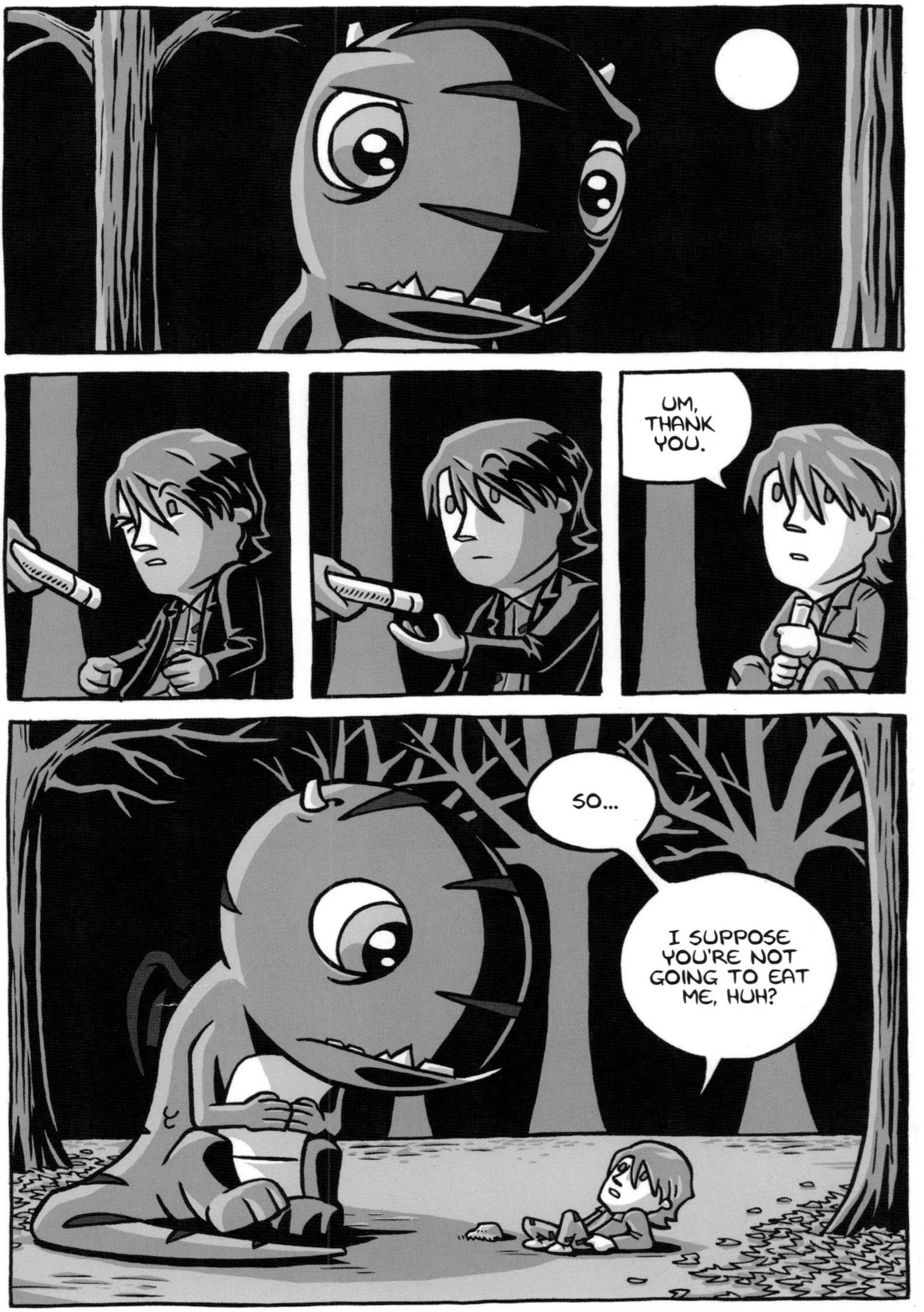
UM, THANK YOU.
SO...
I SUPPOSE YOU'RE NOT GOING TO EAT ME, HUH?

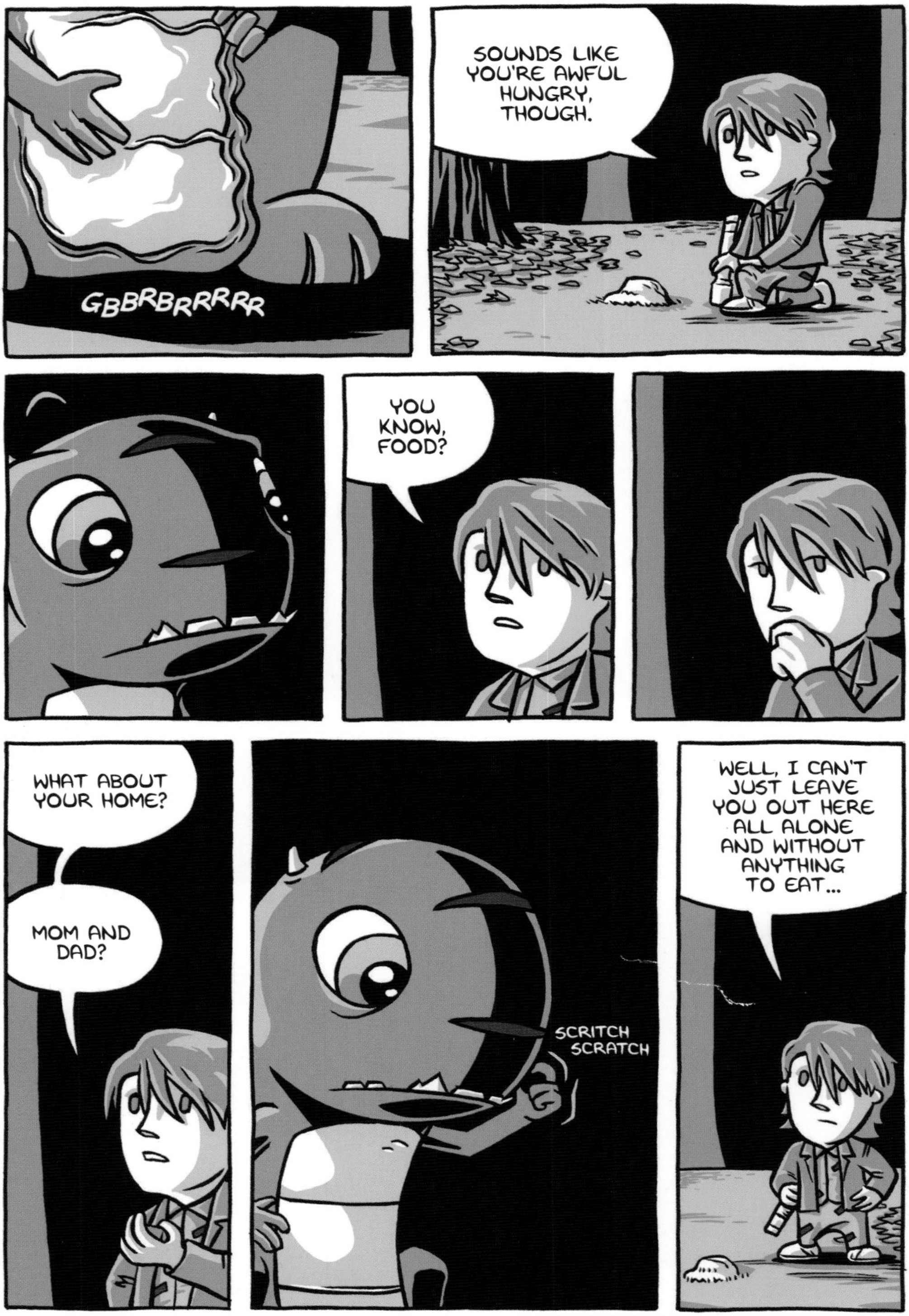
GBBRBRRRRR
SOUNDS LIKE YOU'RE AWFUL HUNGRY, THOUGH.
YOU KNOW, FOOD?
WHAT ABOUT YOUR HOME?
MOM AND DAD?
SCRITCH SCRATCH
WELL, I CAN'T JUST LEAVE YOU OUT HERE ALL ALONE AND WITHOUT ANYTHING TO EAT...

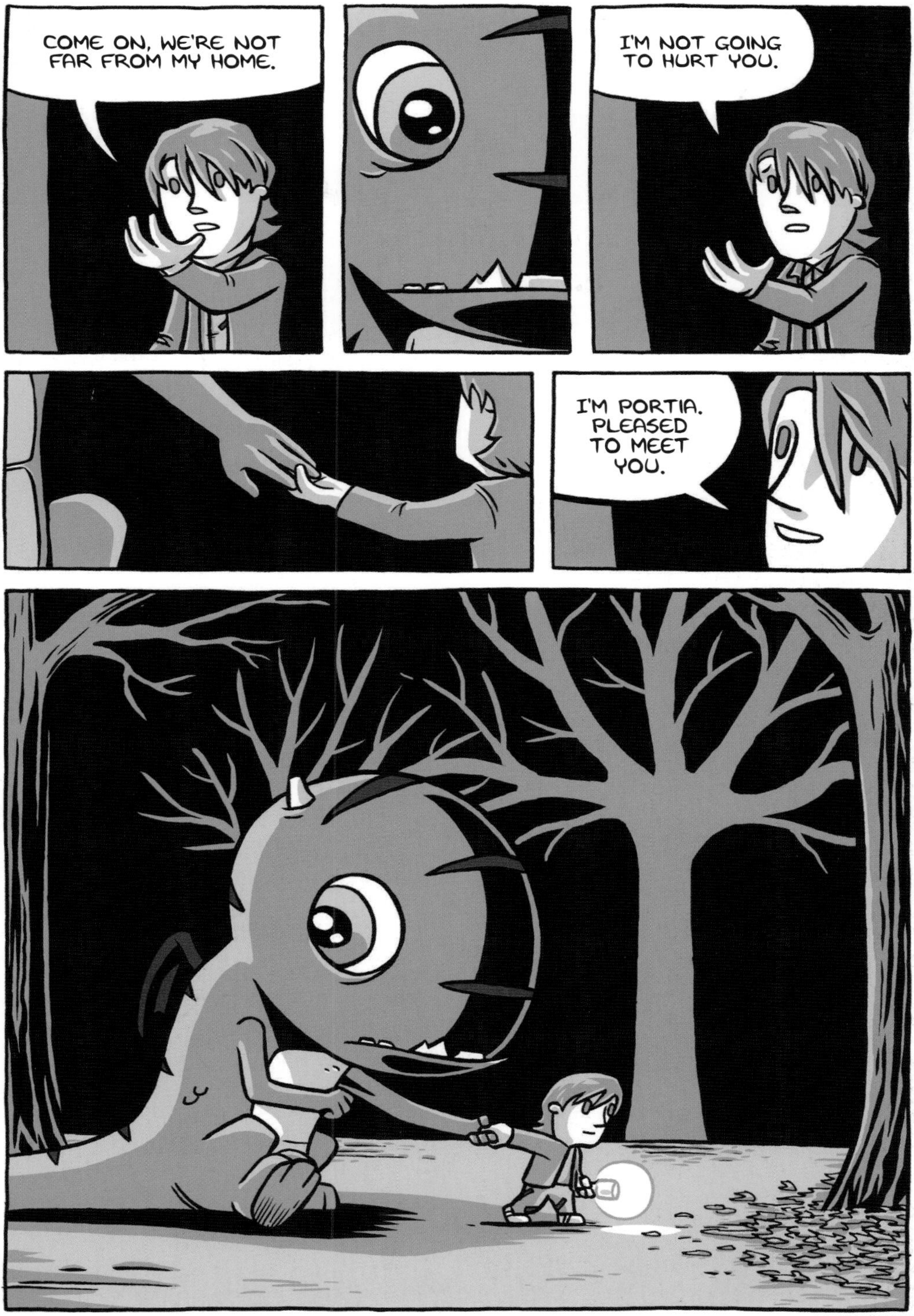
COME ON, WE'RE NOT FAR FROM MY HOME.
I'M NOT GOING TO HURT YOU.
I'M PORTIA. PLEASED TO MEET YOU.

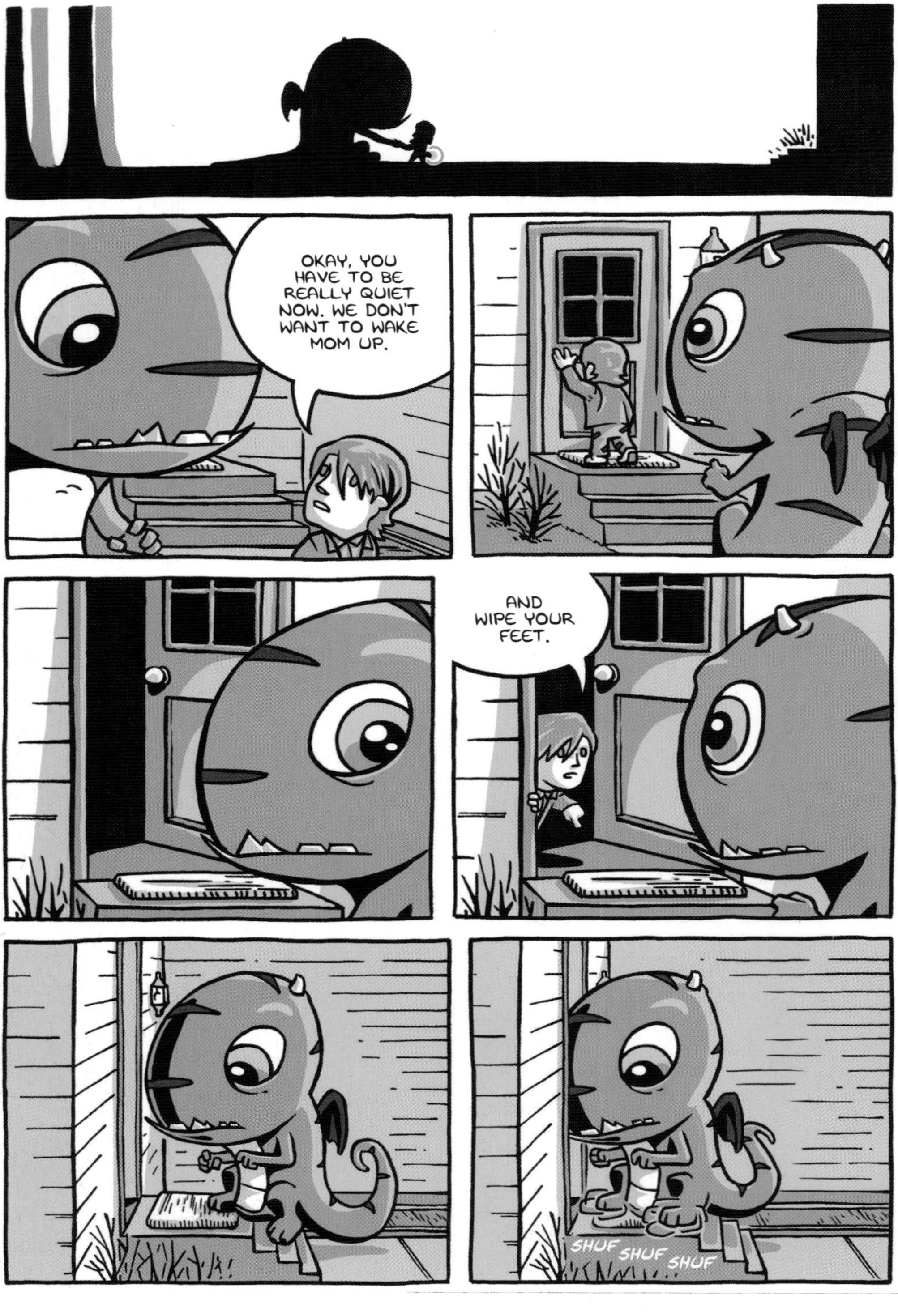
OKAY, YOU HAVE TO BE REALLY QUIET NOW. WE DON'T WANT TO WAKE MOM UP.
AND WIPE YOUR FEET.
SHUF SHUF SHUF

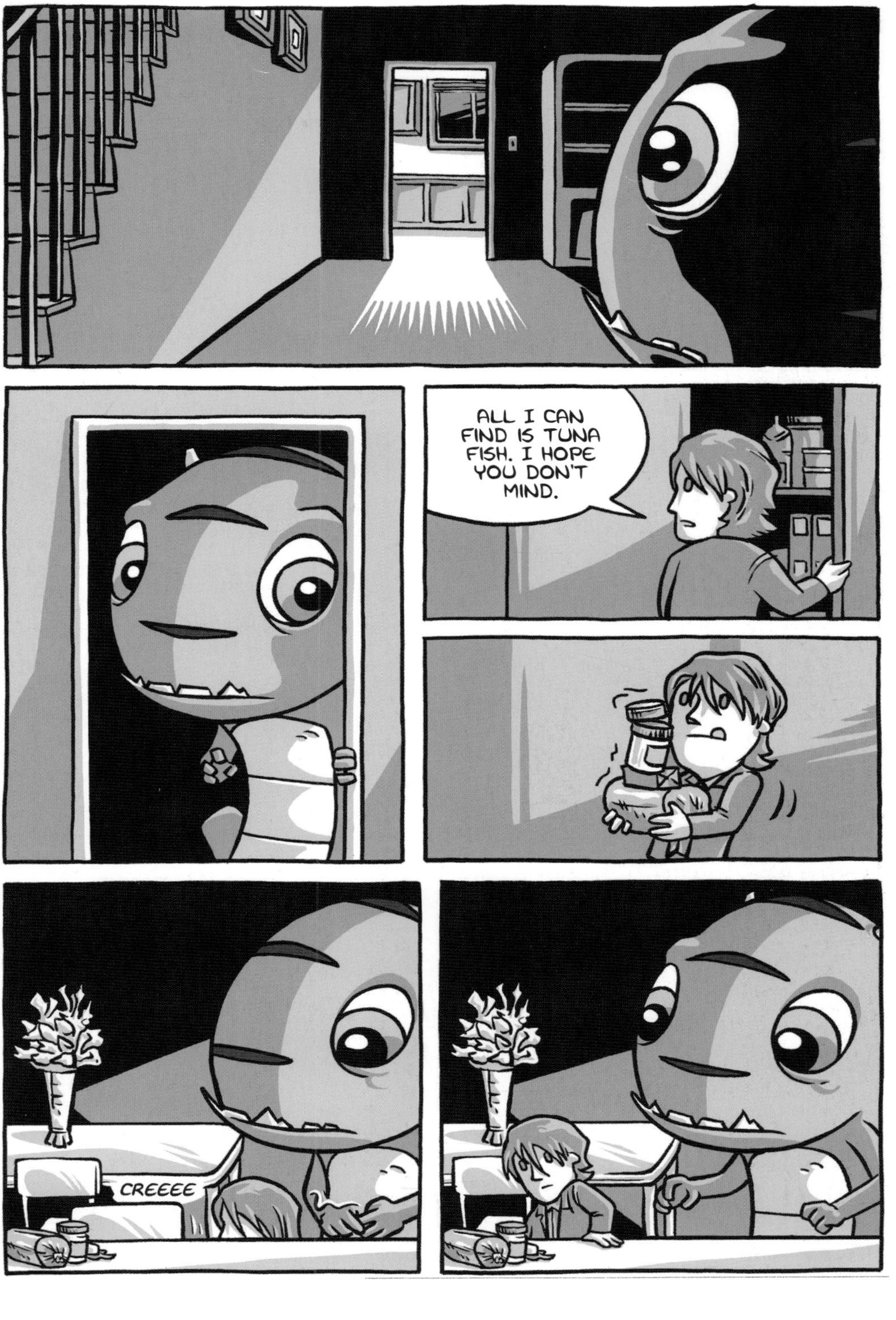
ALL I CAN FIND IS TUNA FISH. I HOPE YOU DON'T MIND.
CREEEE

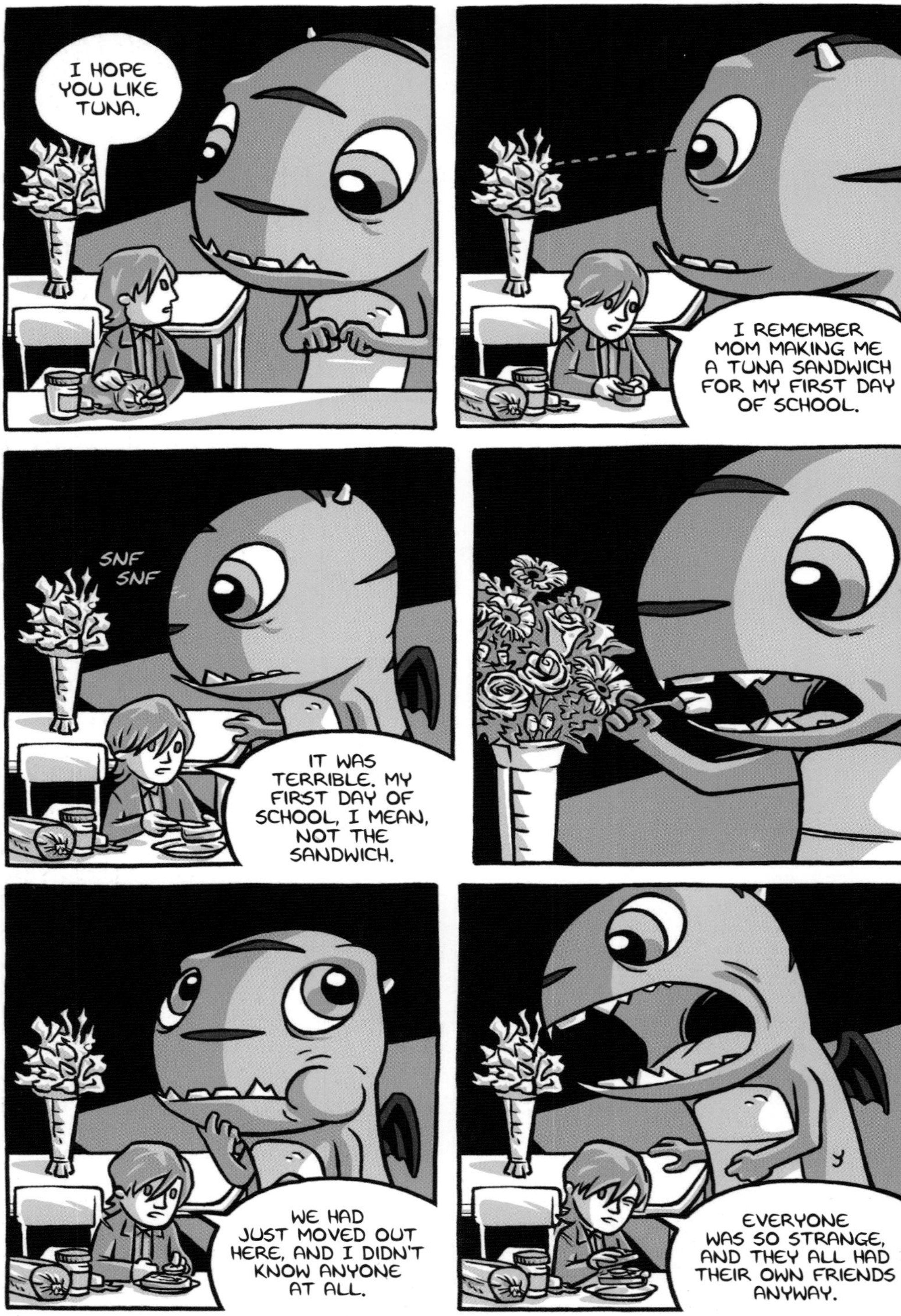
I HOPE YOU LIKE TUNA.
I REMEMBER MOM MAKING ME A TUNA SANDWICH FOR MY FIRST DAY OF SCHOOL.
SNF SNF
IT WAS TERRIBLE. MY FIRST DAY OF SCHOOL, I MEAN, NOT THE SANDWICH.
WE HAD JUST MOVED OUT HERE, AND I DIDN'T KNOW ANYONE AT ALL.
EVERYONE WAS SO STRANGE, AND THEY ALL HAD THEIR OWN FRIENDS ANYWAY.

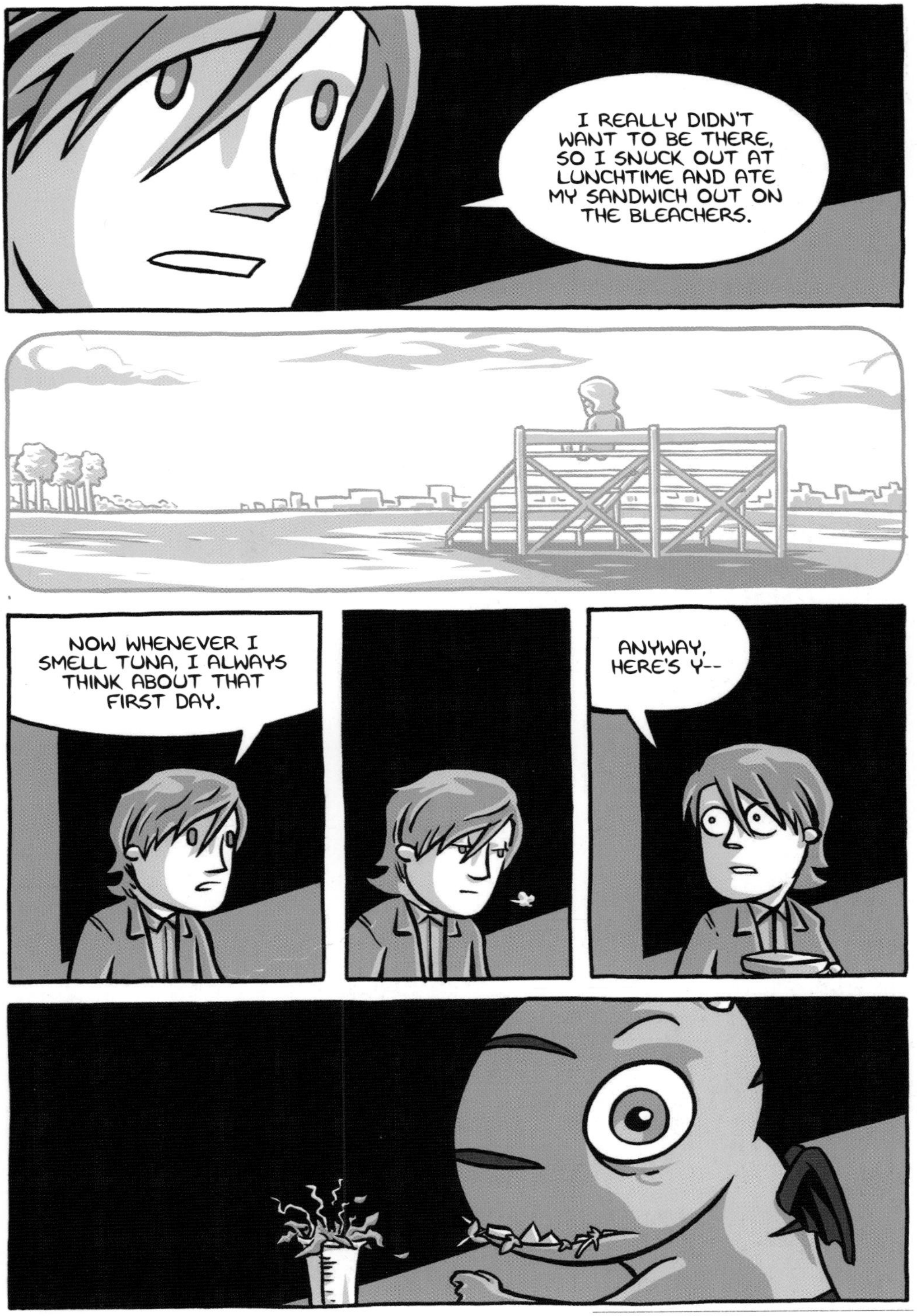
I REALLY DIDN'T WANT TO BE THERE, SO I SNUCK OUT AT LUNCHTIME AND ATE MY SANDWICH OUT ON THE BLEACHERS.
NOW WHENEVER I SMELL TUNA, I ALWAYS THINK ABOUT THAT FIRST DAY.
ANYWAY, HERE'S Y--

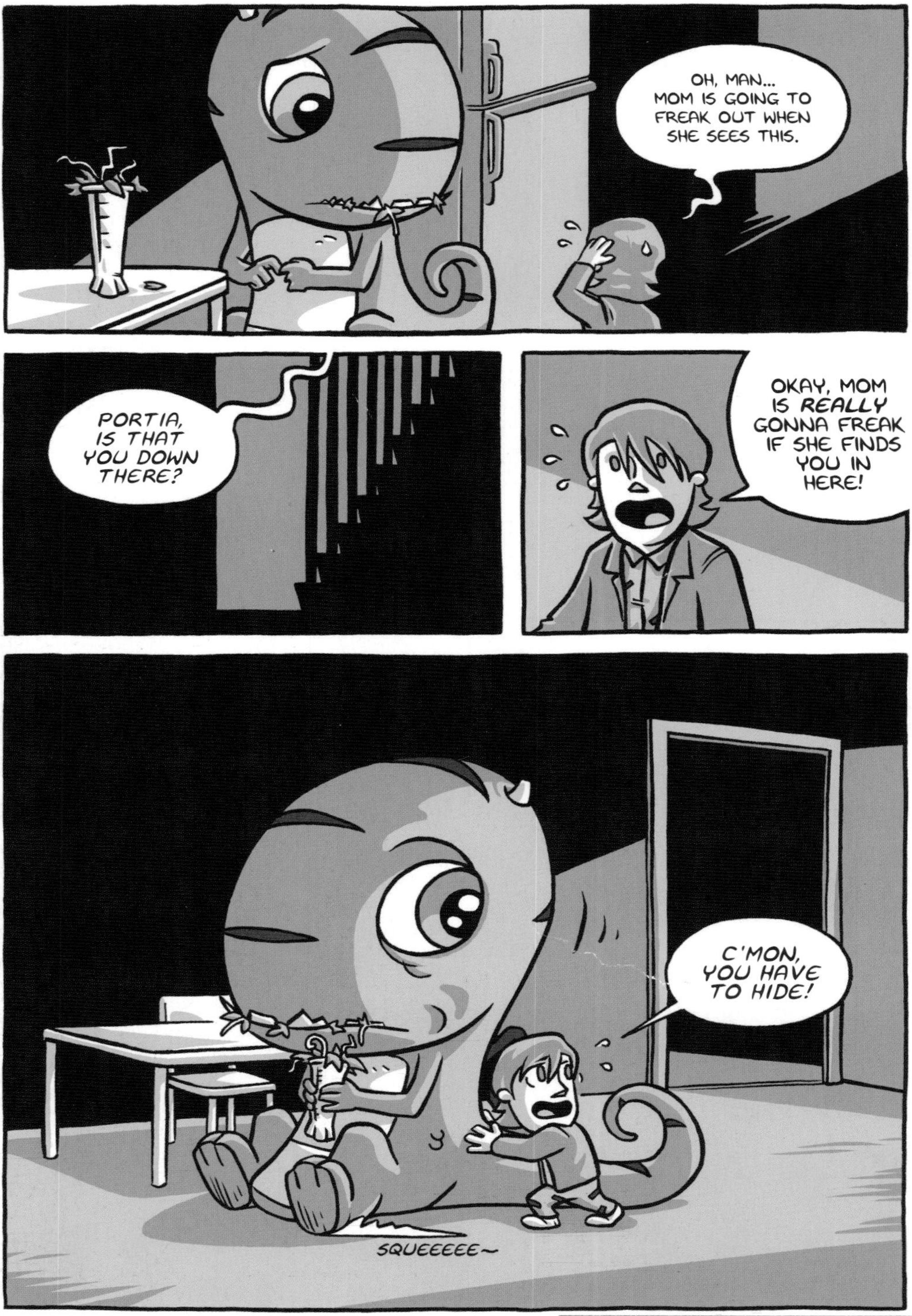
OH, MAN... MOM IS GOING TO FREAK OUT WHEN SHE SEES THIS.
PORTIA, IS THAT YOU DOWN THERE?
OKAY, MOM IS *REALLY* GONNA FREAK IF SHE FINDS YOU IN HERE!
C'MON, YOU HAVE TO HIDE!
SQUEEEEEE~

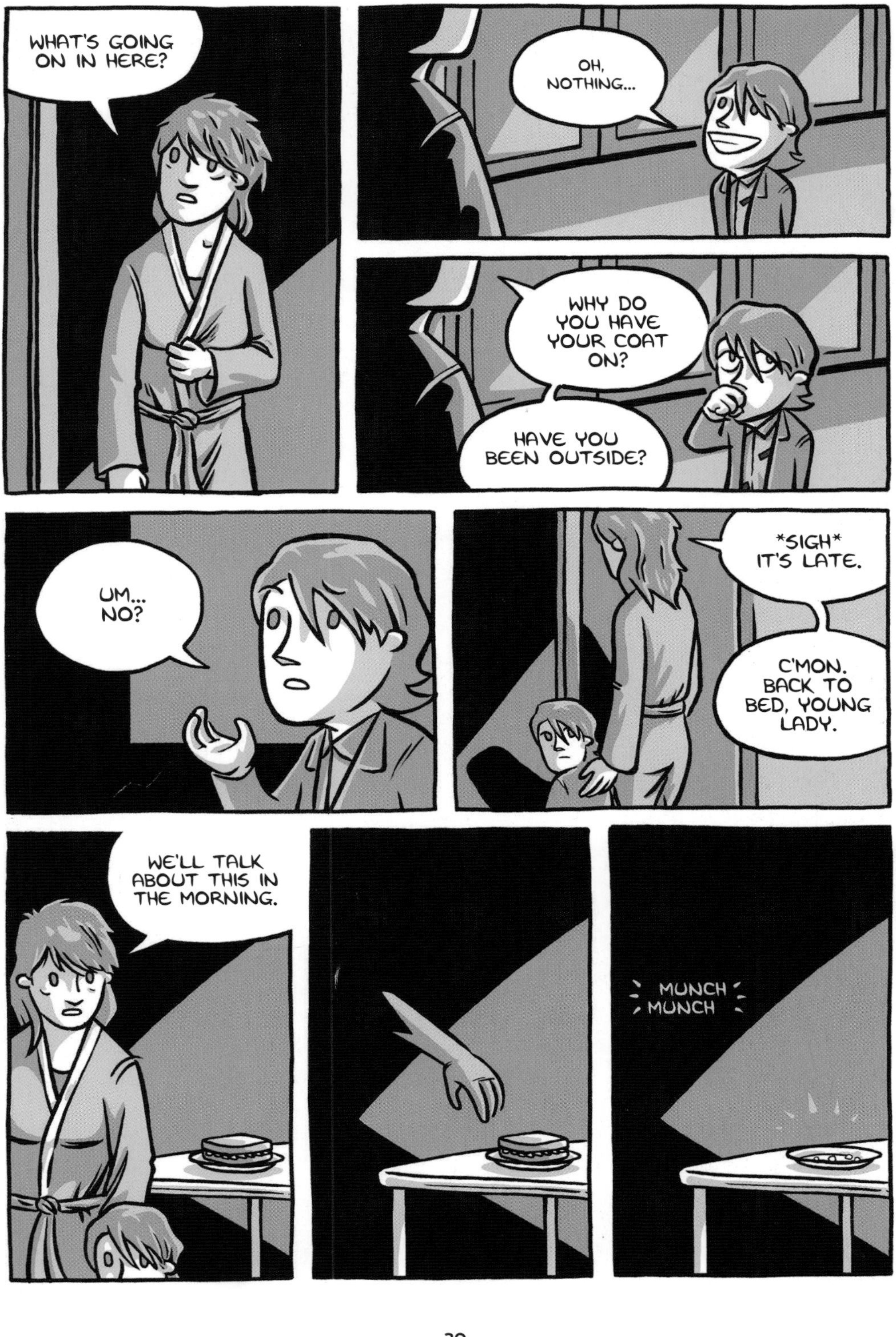
WHAT'S GOING ON IN HERE?
OH, NOTHING...
WHY DO YOU HAVE YOUR COAT ON?
HAVE YOU BEEN OUTSIDE?
UM... NO?
SIGH IT'S LATE.
C'MON. BACK TO BED, YOUNG LADY.
WE'LL TALK ABOUT THIS IN THE MORNING.
MUNCH MUNCH

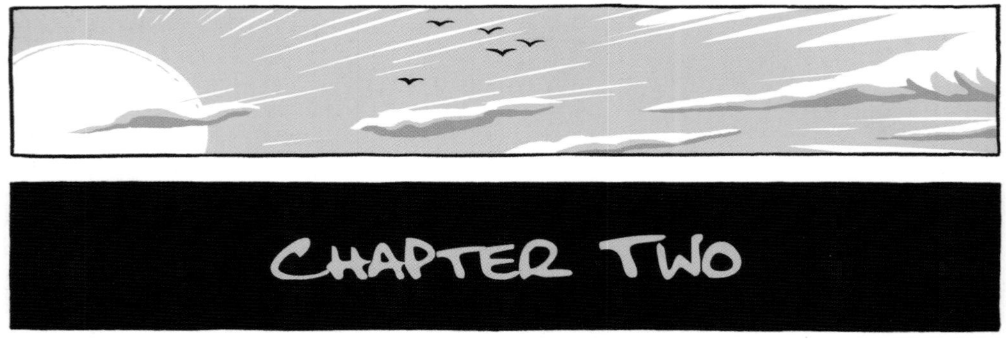

CHAPTER TWO

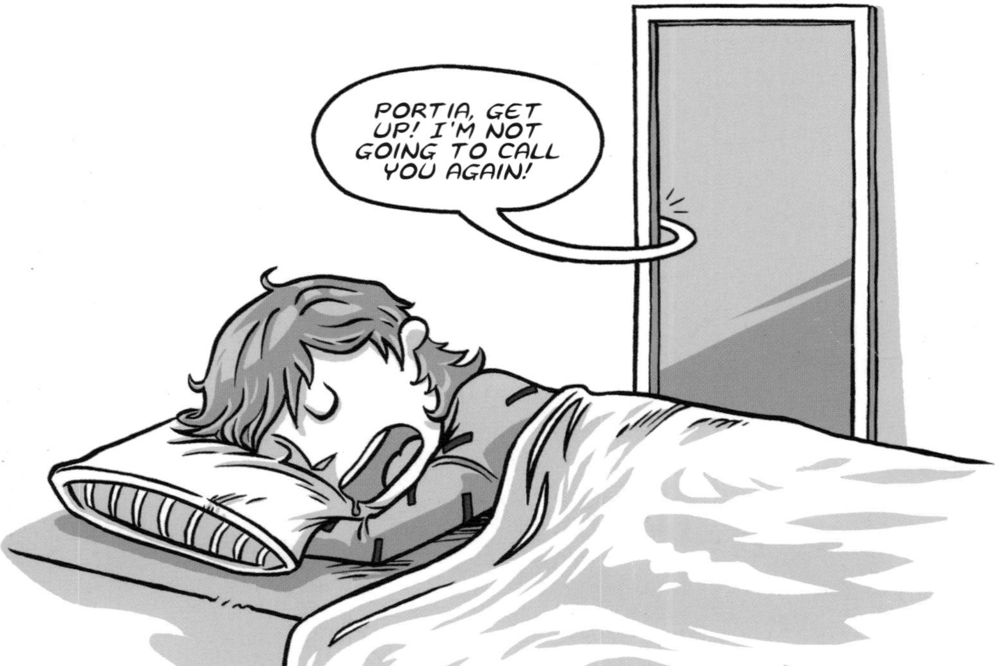
PORTIA, GET UP! I'M NOT GOING TO CALL YOU AGAIN!

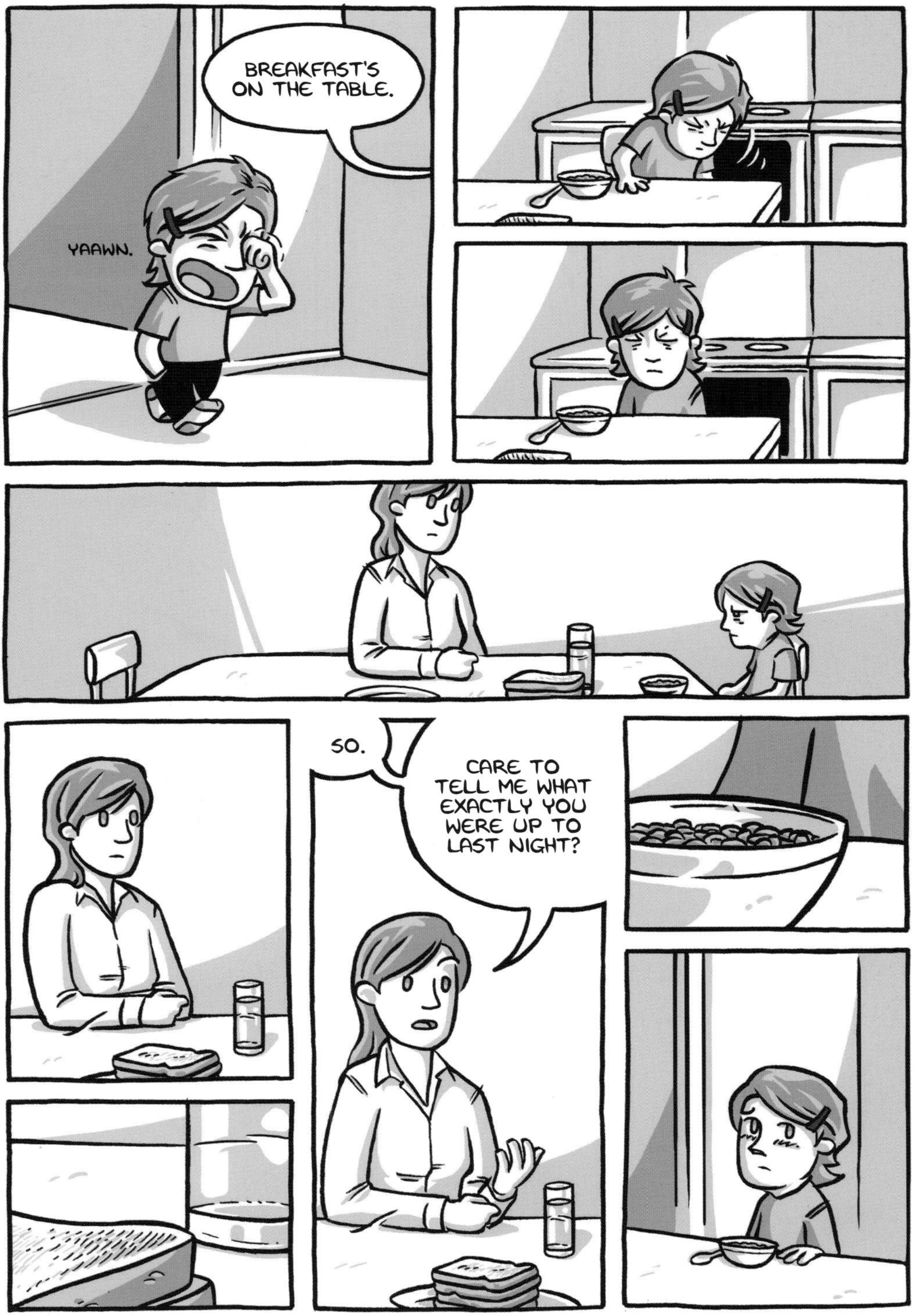
BREAKFAST'S ON THE TABLE.
YAAWN.
SO.
CARE TO TELL ME WHAT EXACTLY YOU WERE UP TO LAST NIGHT?

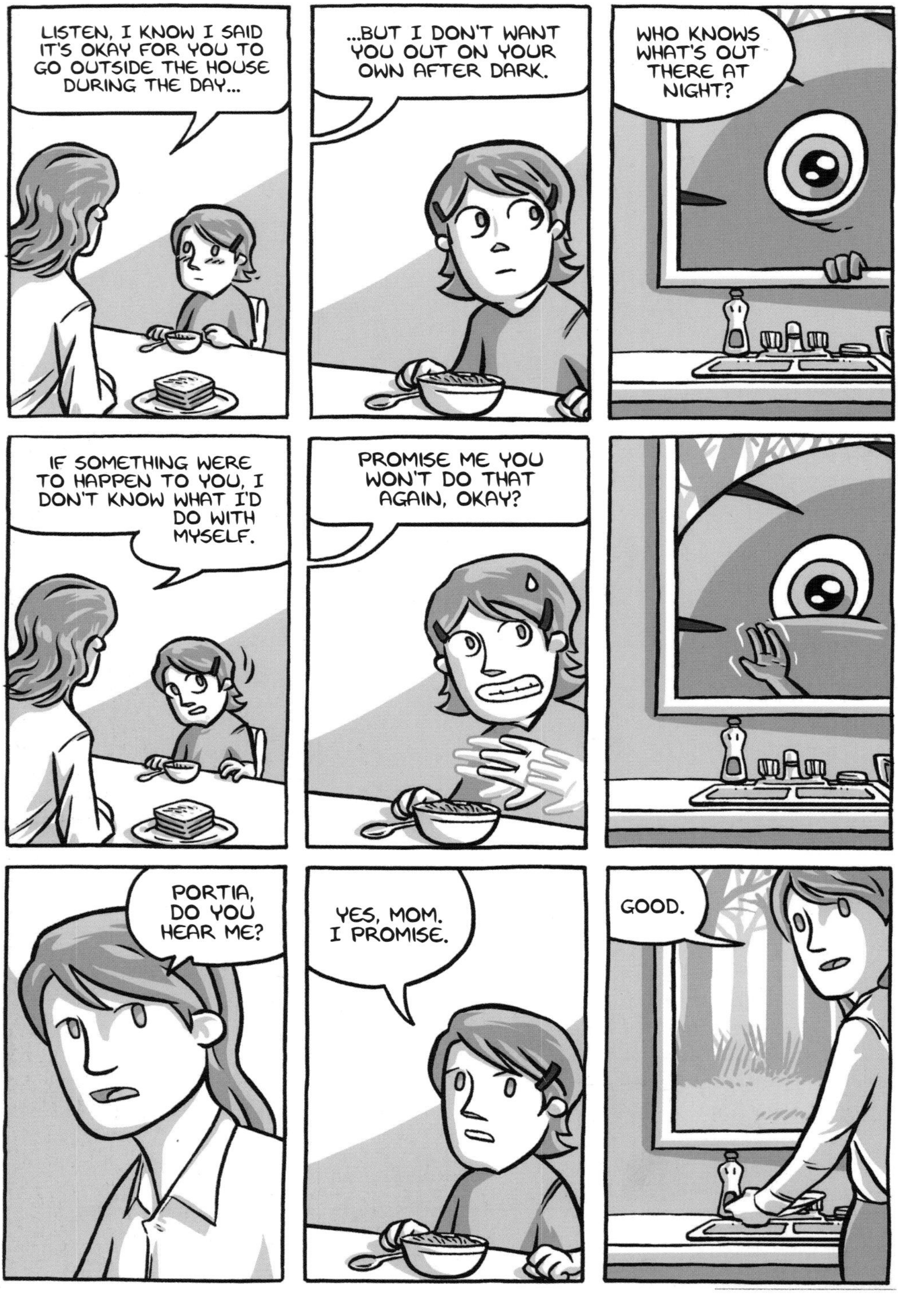
LISTEN, I KNOW I SAID IT'S OKAY FOR YOU TO GO OUTSIDE THE HOUSE DURING THE DAY...
...BUT I DON'T WANT YOU OUT ON YOUR OWN AFTER DARK.
WHO KNOWS WHAT'S OUT THERE AT NIGHT?
IF SOMETHING WERE TO HAPPEN TO YOU, I DON'T KNOW WHAT I'D DO WITH MYSELF.
PROMISE ME YOU WON'T DO THAT AGAIN, OKAY?
PORTIA, DO YOU HEAR ME?
YES, MOM. I PROMISE.
GOOD.

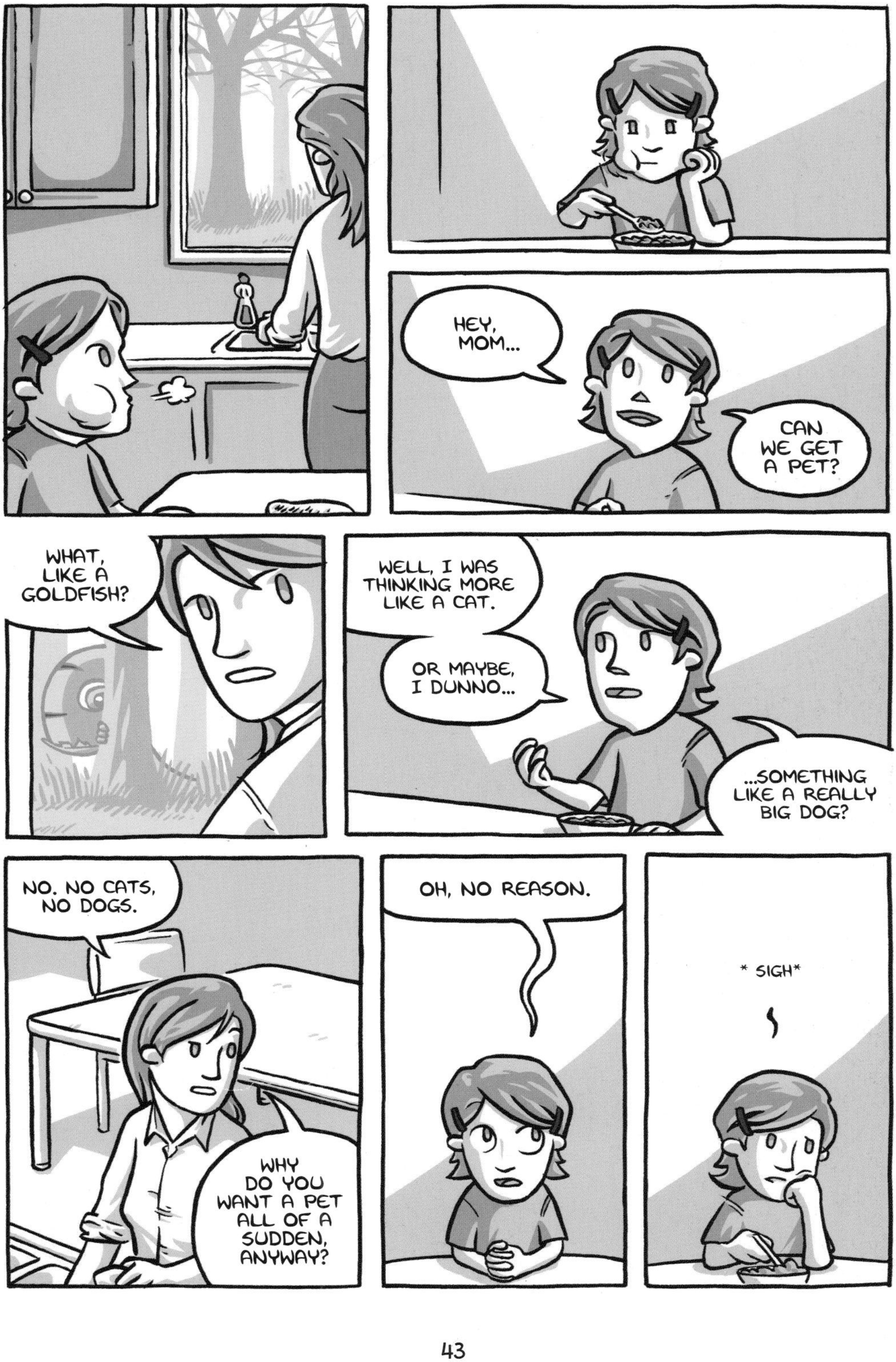
HEY, MOM...
CAN WE GET A PET?
WHAT, LIKE A GOLDFISH?
WELL, I WAS THINKING MORE LIKE A CAT.
OR MAYBE, I DUNNO...
...SOMETHING LIKE A REALLY BIG DOG?
NO. NO CATS, NO DOGS.
WHY DO YOU WANT A PET ALL OF A SUDDEN, ANYWAY?
OH, NO REASON.
* SIGH*

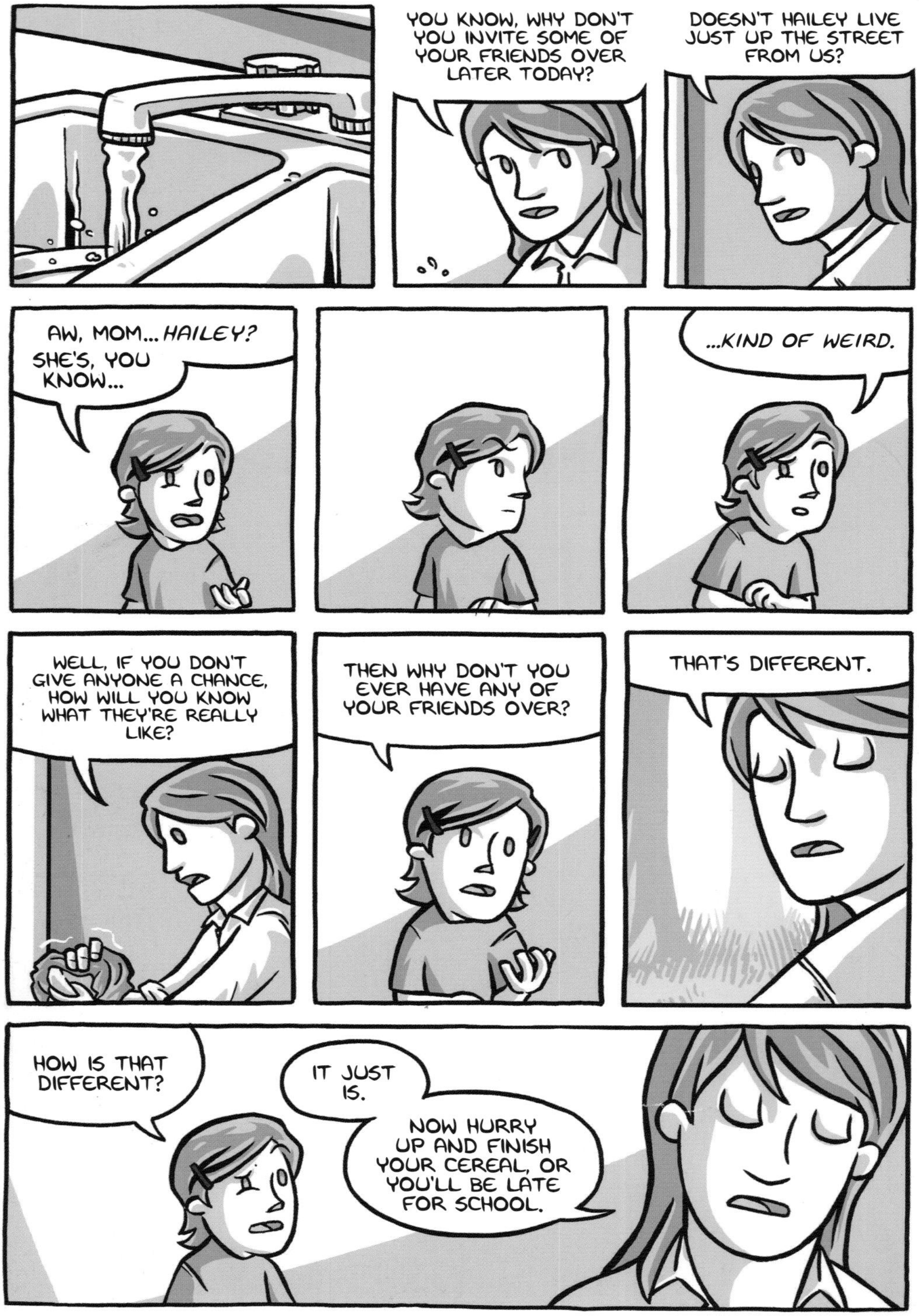
YOU KNOW, WHY DON'T YOU INVITE SOME OF YOUR FRIENDS OVER LATER TODAY?
DOESN'T HAILEY LIVE JUST UP THE STREET FROM US?
AW, MOM... *HAILEY?* SHE'S, YOU KNOW...
...KIND OF WEIRD.
WELL, IF YOU DON'T GIVE ANYONE A CHANCE, HOW WILL YOU KNOW WHAT THEY'RE REALLY LIKE?
THEN WHY DON'T YOU EVER HAVE ANY OF YOUR FRIENDS OVER?
THAT'S DIFFERENT.
HOW IS THAT DIFFERENT?
IT JUST IS.
NOW HURRY UP AND FINISH YOUR CEREAL, OR YOU'LL BE LATE FOR SCHOOL.

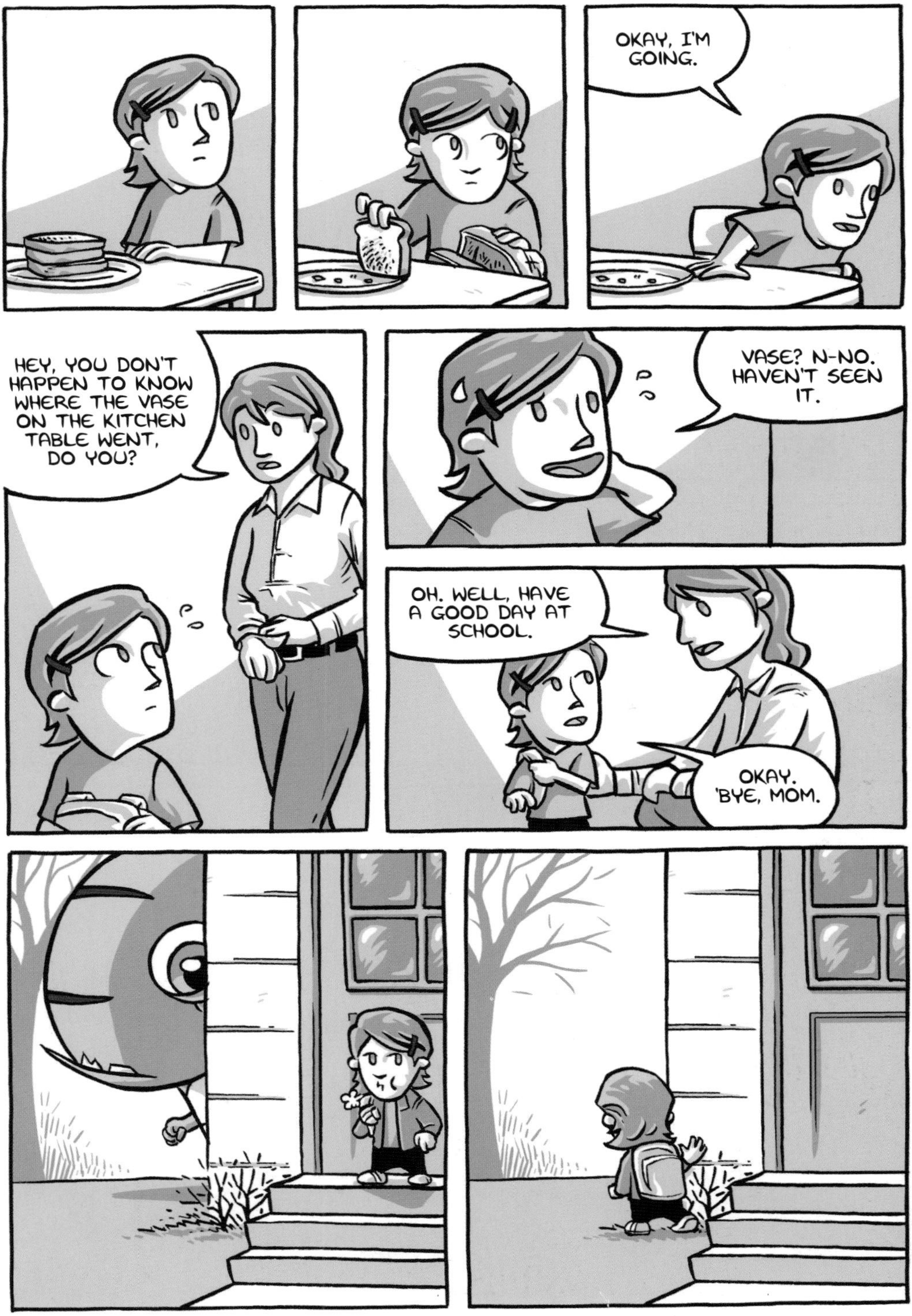
OKAY, I'M GOING.
HEY, YOU DON'T HAPPEN TO KNOW WHERE THE VASE ON THE KITCHEN TABLE WENT, DO YOU?
VASE? N-NO. HAVEN'T SEEN IT.
OH. WELL, HAVE A GOOD DAY AT SCHOOL.
OKAY. 'BYE, MOM.

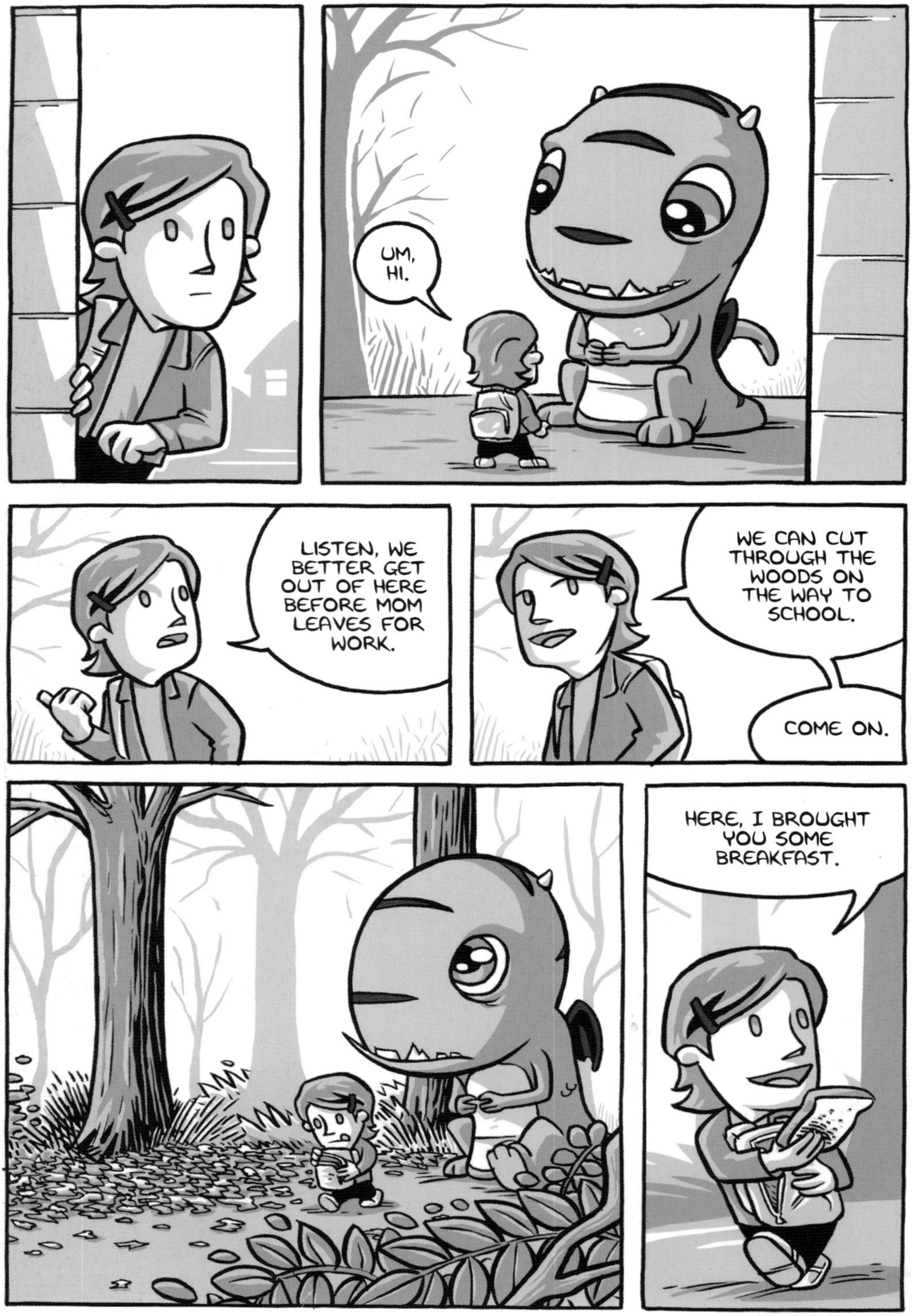
UM, HI.
LISTEN, WE BETTER GET OUT OF HERE BEFORE MOM LEAVES FOR WORK.
WE CAN CUT THROUGH THE WOODS ON THE WAY TO SCHOOL.
COME ON.
HERE, I BROUGHT YOU SOME BREAKFAST.

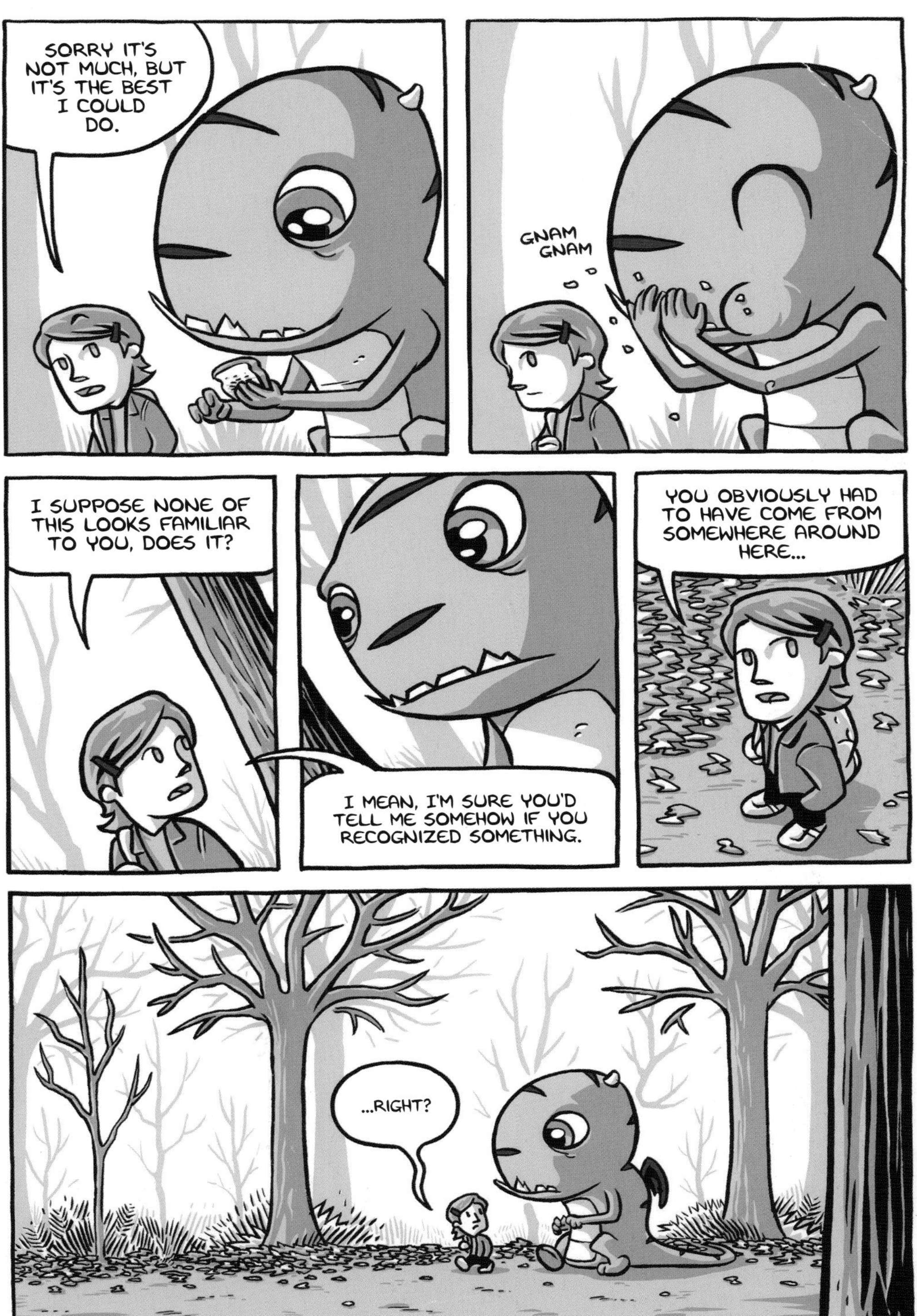
SORRY IT'S NOT MUCH, BUT IT'S THE BEST I COULD DO.
GNAM GNAM
I SUPPOSE NONE OF THIS LOOKS FAMILIAR TO YOU, DOES IT?
I MEAN, I'M SURE YOU'D TELL ME SOMEHOW IF YOU RECOGNIZED SOMETHING.
YOU OBVIOUSLY HAD TO HAVE COME FROM SOMEWHERE AROUND HERE...
...RIGHT?

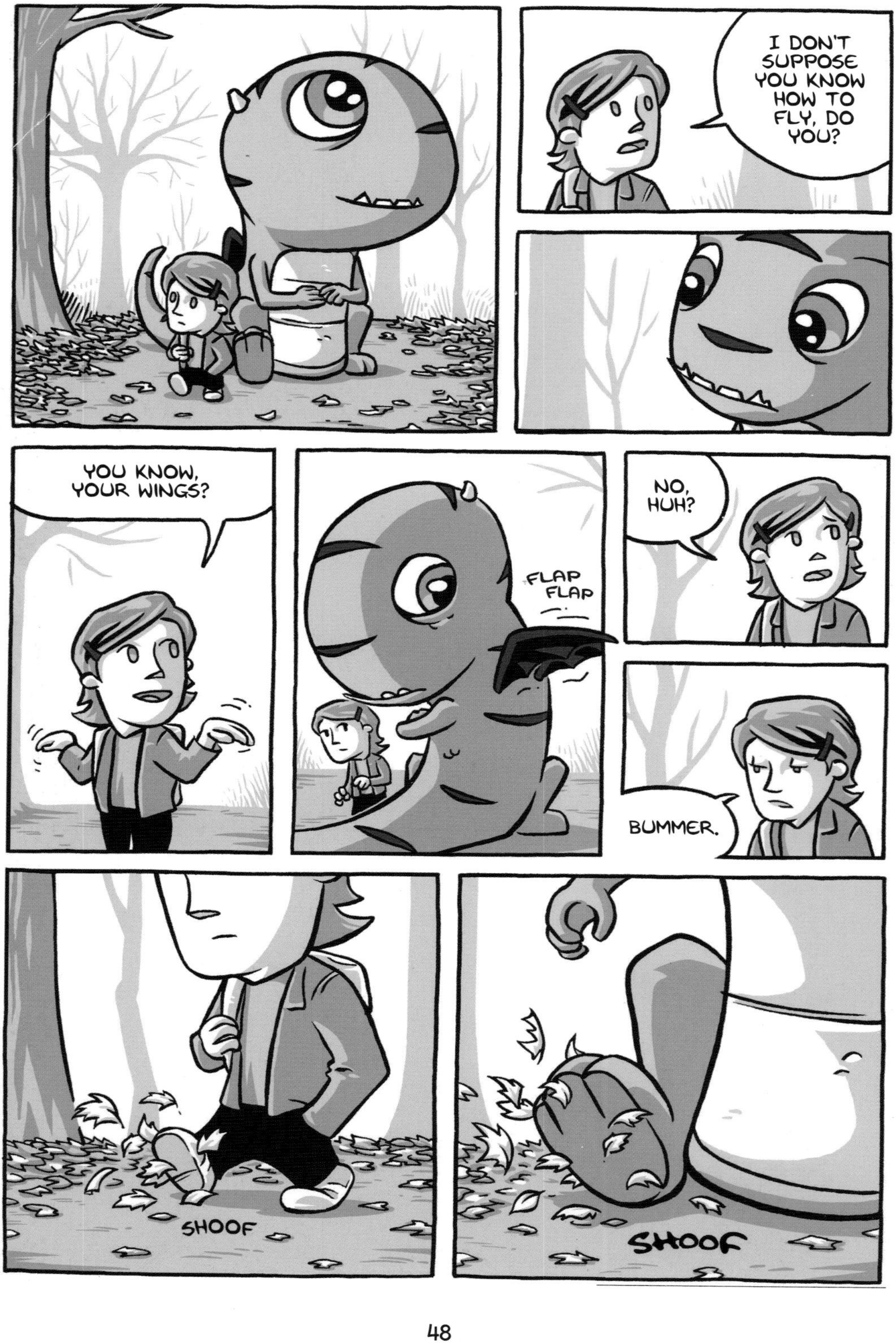
I DON'T SUPPOSE YOU KNOW HOW TO FLY, DO YOU?
YOU KNOW, YOUR WINGS?
FLAP FLAP
NO, HUH?
BUMMER.
SHOOF
SHOOF

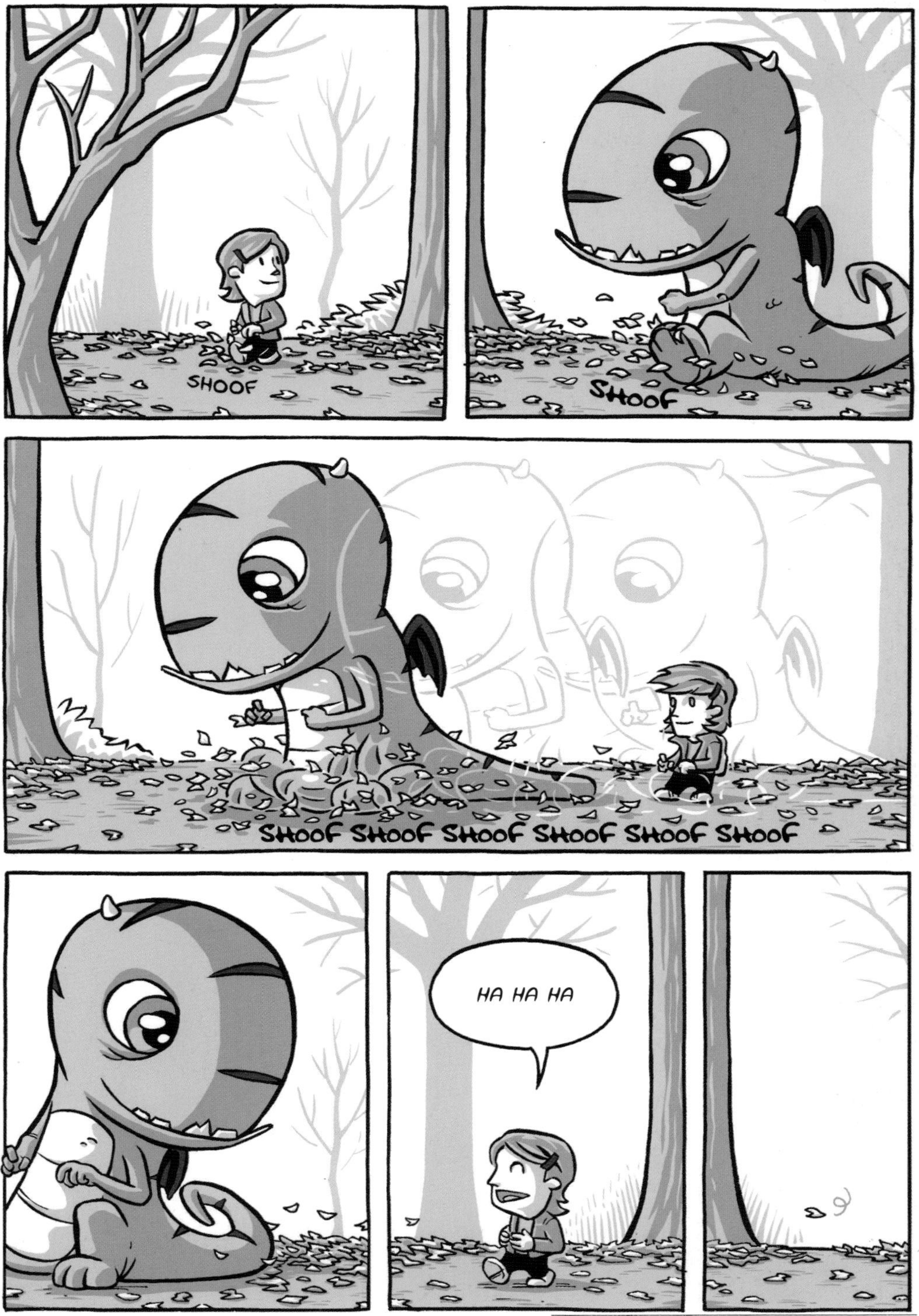
SHOOF
SHOOF
SHOOF SHOOF SHOOF SHOOF SHOOF SHOOF
HA HA HA

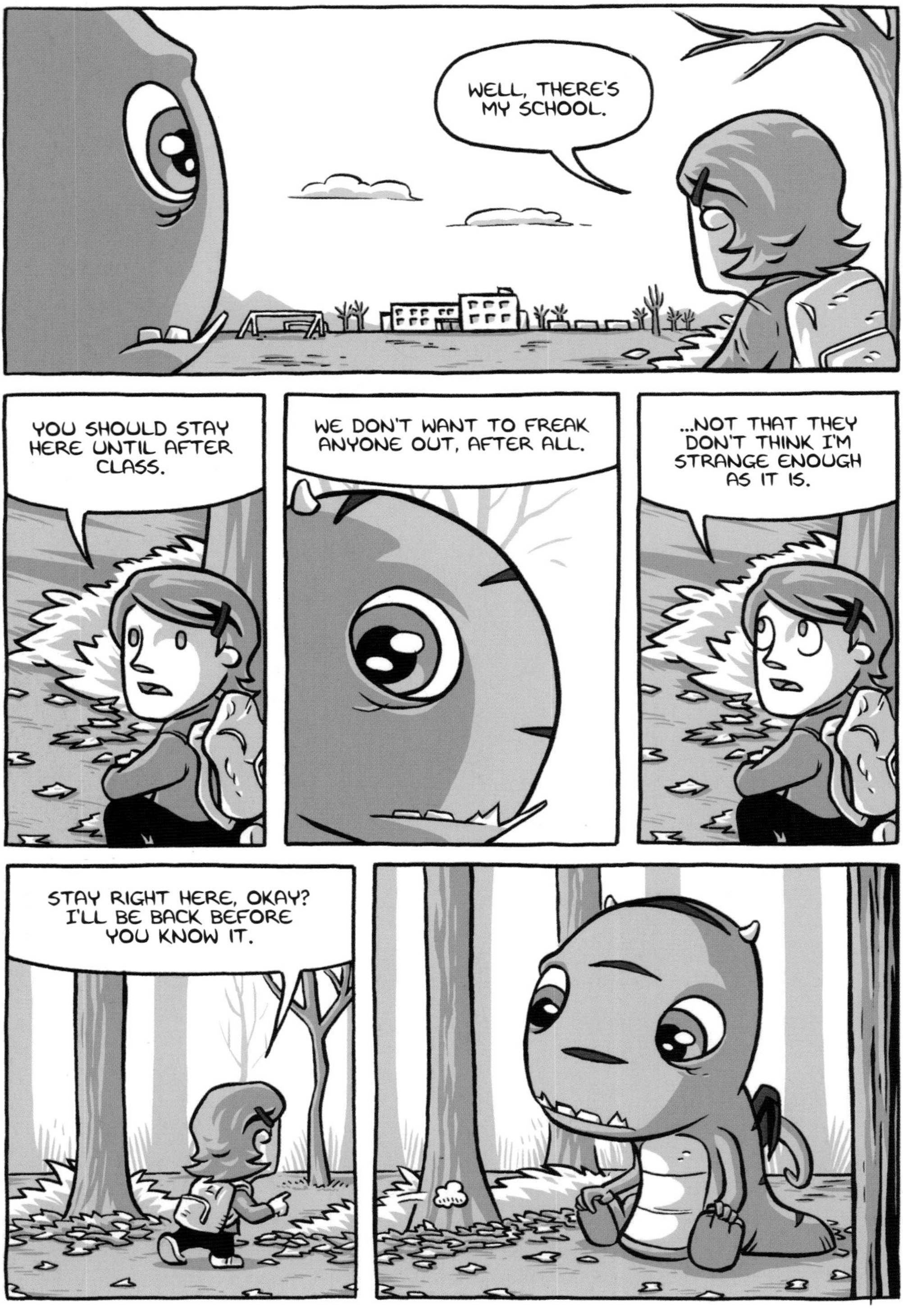
WELL, THERE'S MY SCHOOL.
YOU SHOULD STAY HERE UNTIL AFTER CLASS.
WE DON'T WANT TO FREAK ANYONE OUT, AFTER ALL.
...NOT THAT THEY DON'T THINK I'M STRANGE ENOUGH AS IT IS.
STAY RIGHT HERE, OKAY? I'LL BE BACK BEFORE YOU KNOW IT.

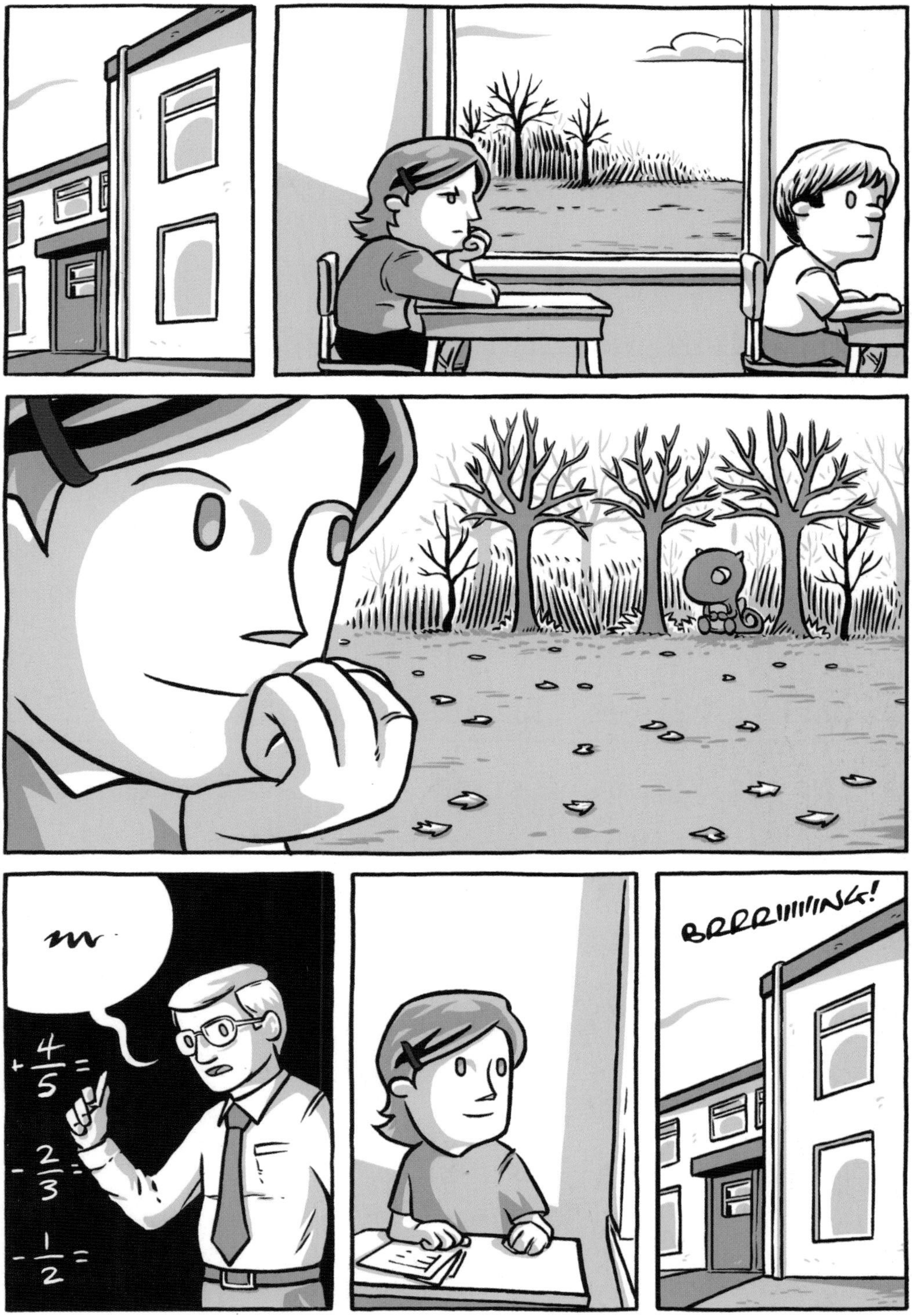
BRRRIIIIIING!

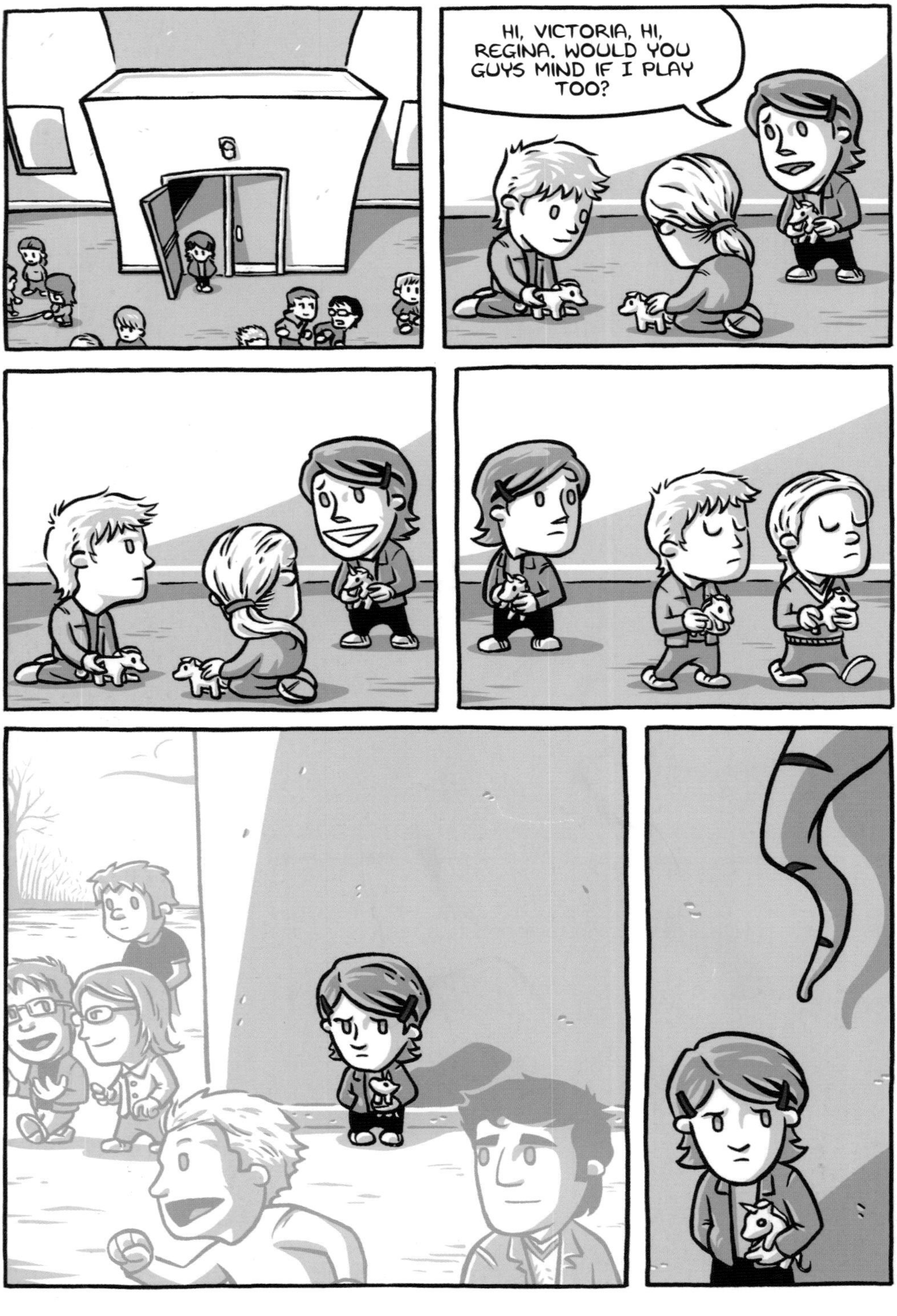
HI, VICTORIA, HI, REGINA. WOULD YOU GUYS MIND IF I PLAY TOO?

!
TAP
TAP
TAP
WHAT ARE YOU DOING UP THERE?! DIDN'T I TELL YOU TO WAIT FOR ME IN THE WOODS? SOMEONE'S GOING TO SPOT YOU FOR SURE!
GIMME A HAND.

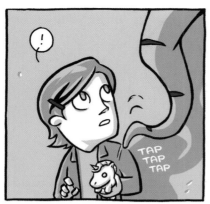

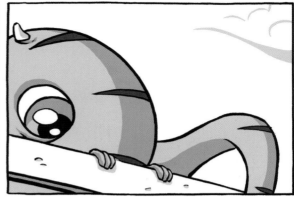

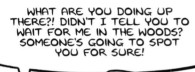

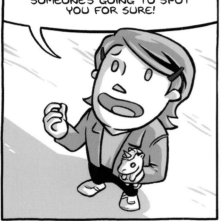

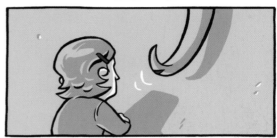

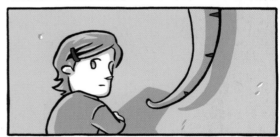

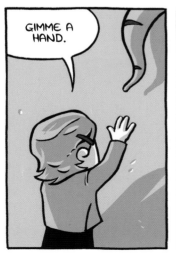

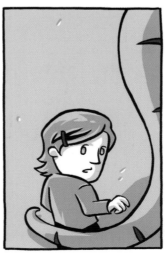

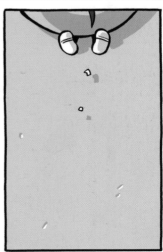

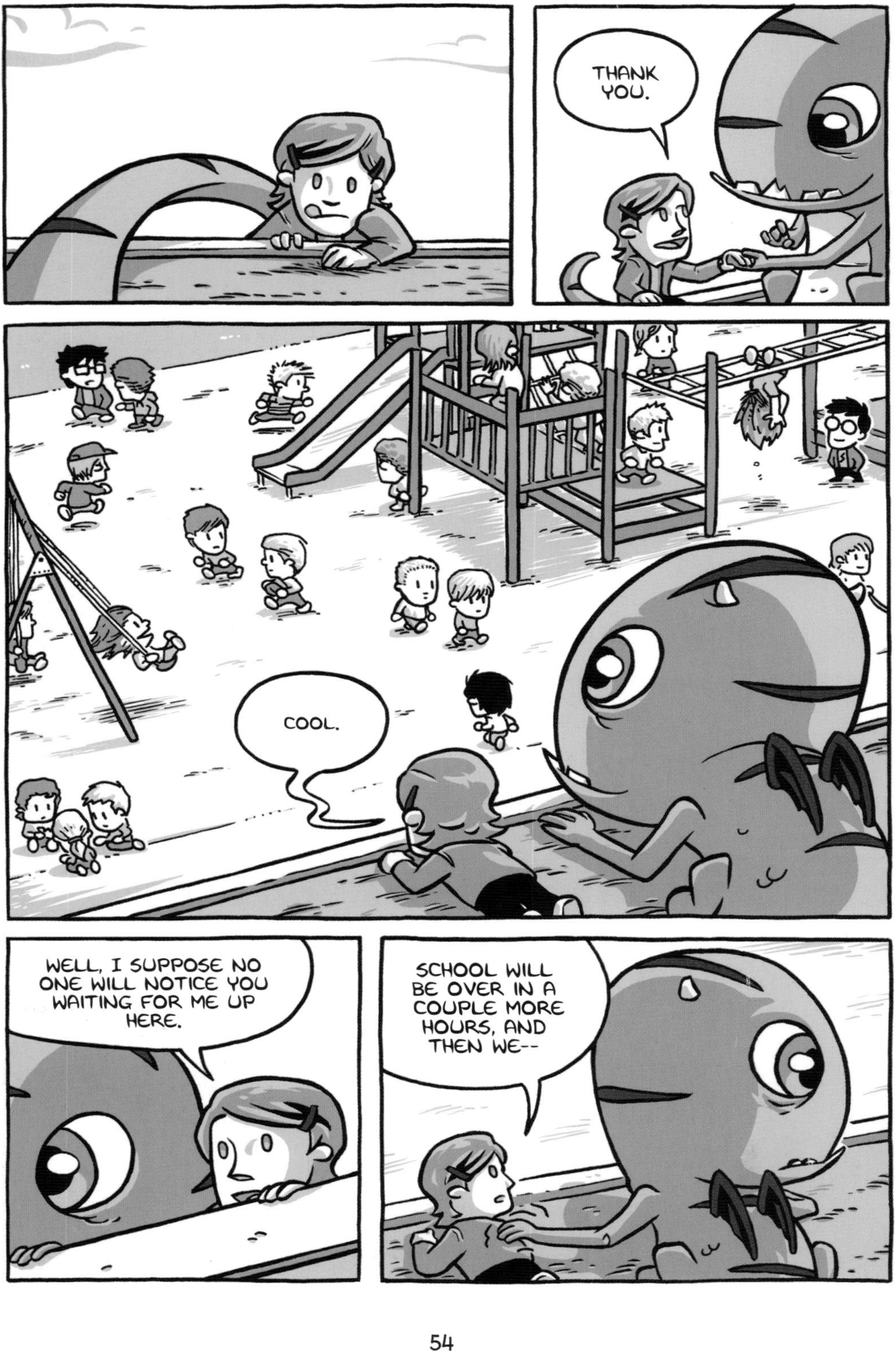
THANK YOU.
COOL.
WELL, I SUPPOSE NO ONE WILL NOTICE YOU WAITING FOR ME UP HERE.
SCHOOL WILL BE OVER IN A COUPLE MORE HOURS, AND THEN WE--

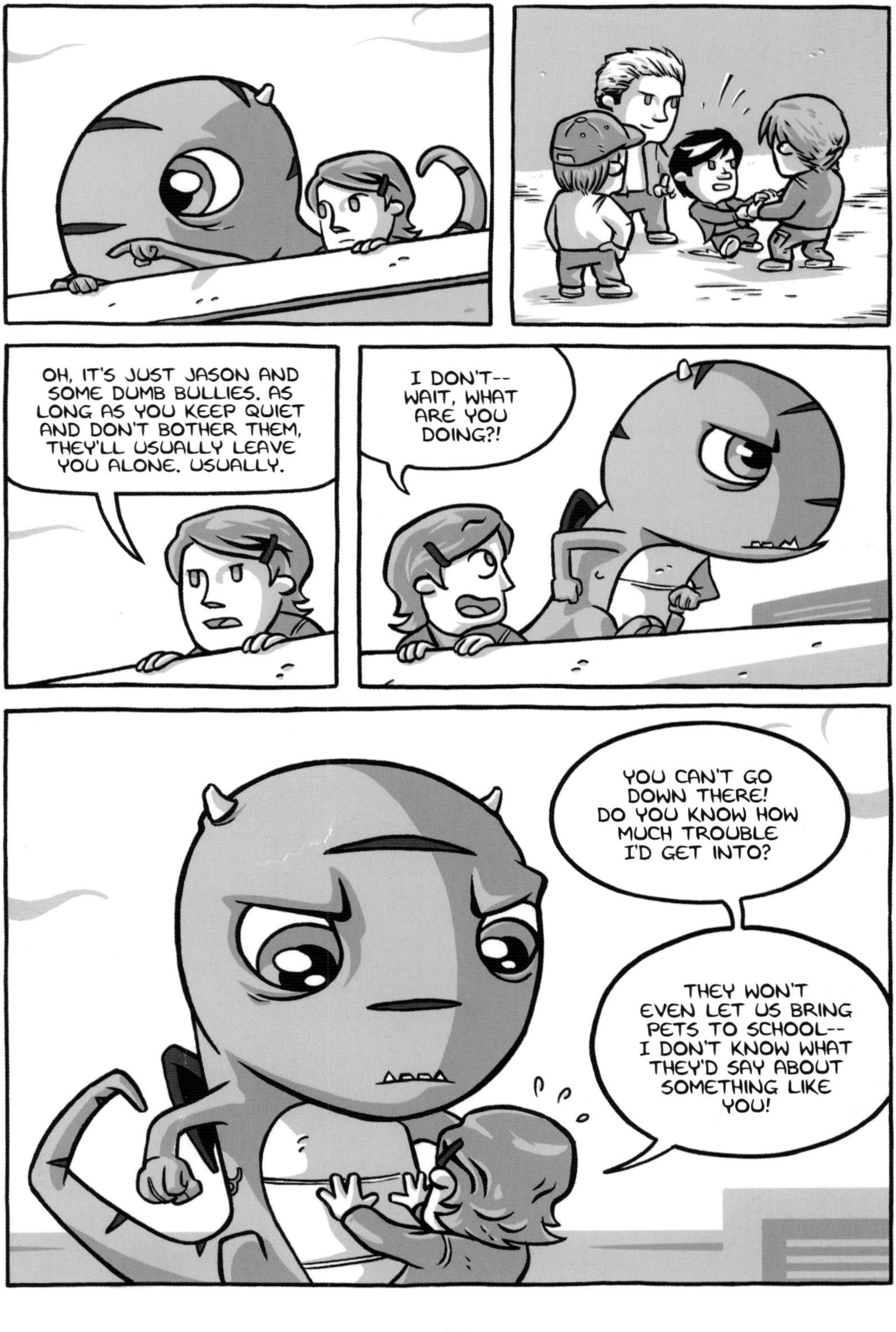
OH, IT'S JUST JASON AND SOME DUMB BULLIES. AS LONG AS YOU KEEP QUIET AND DON'T BOTHER THEM, THEY'LL USUALLY LEAVE YOU ALONE. USUALLY.
I DON'T-- WAIT, WHAT ARE YOU DOING?!
YOU CAN'T GO DOWN THERE! DO YOU KNOW HOW MUCH TROUBLE I'D GET INTO?
THEY WON'T EVEN LET US BRING PETS TO SCHOOL-- I DON'T KNOW WHAT THEY'D SAY ABOUT SOMETHING LIKE YOU!

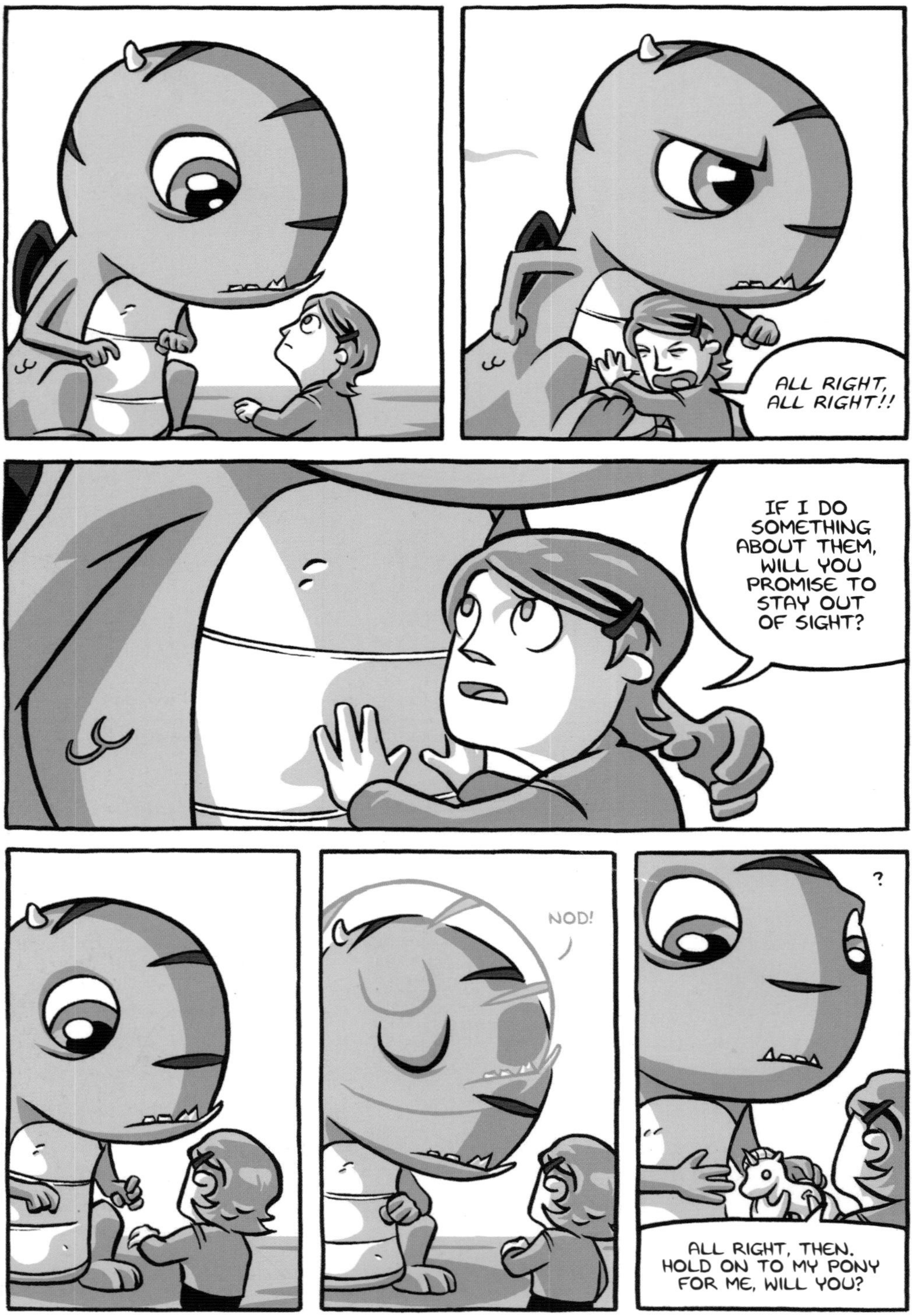
ALL RIGHT,
ALL RIGHT!!
IF I DO SOMETHING ABOUT THEM, WILL YOU PROMISE TO STAY OUT OF SIGHT?
NOD!
?
ALL RIGHT, THEN. HOLD ON TO MY PONY FOR ME, WILL YOU?

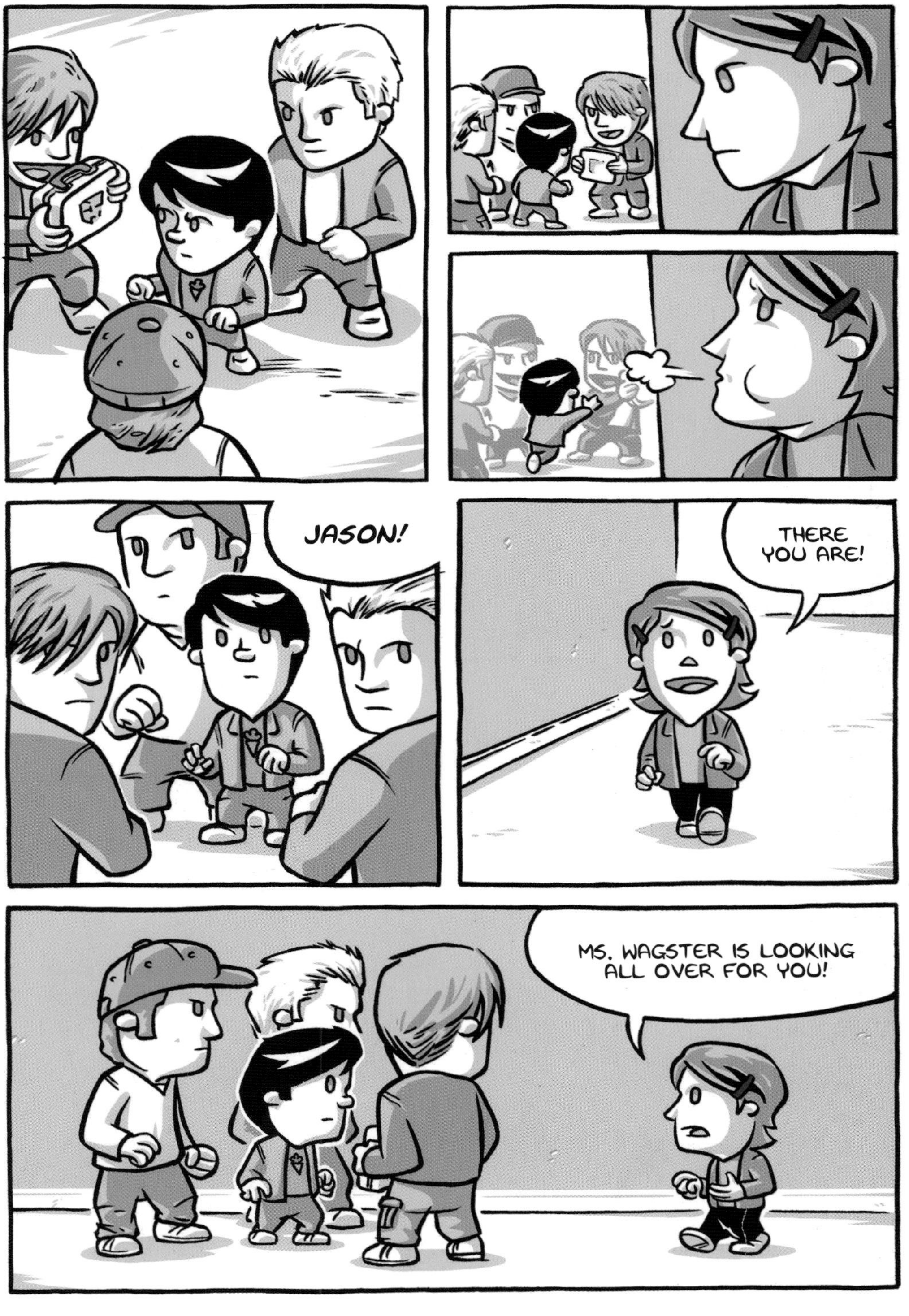
JASON!
THERE YOU ARE!
MS. WAGSTER IS LOOKING ALL OVER FOR YOU!

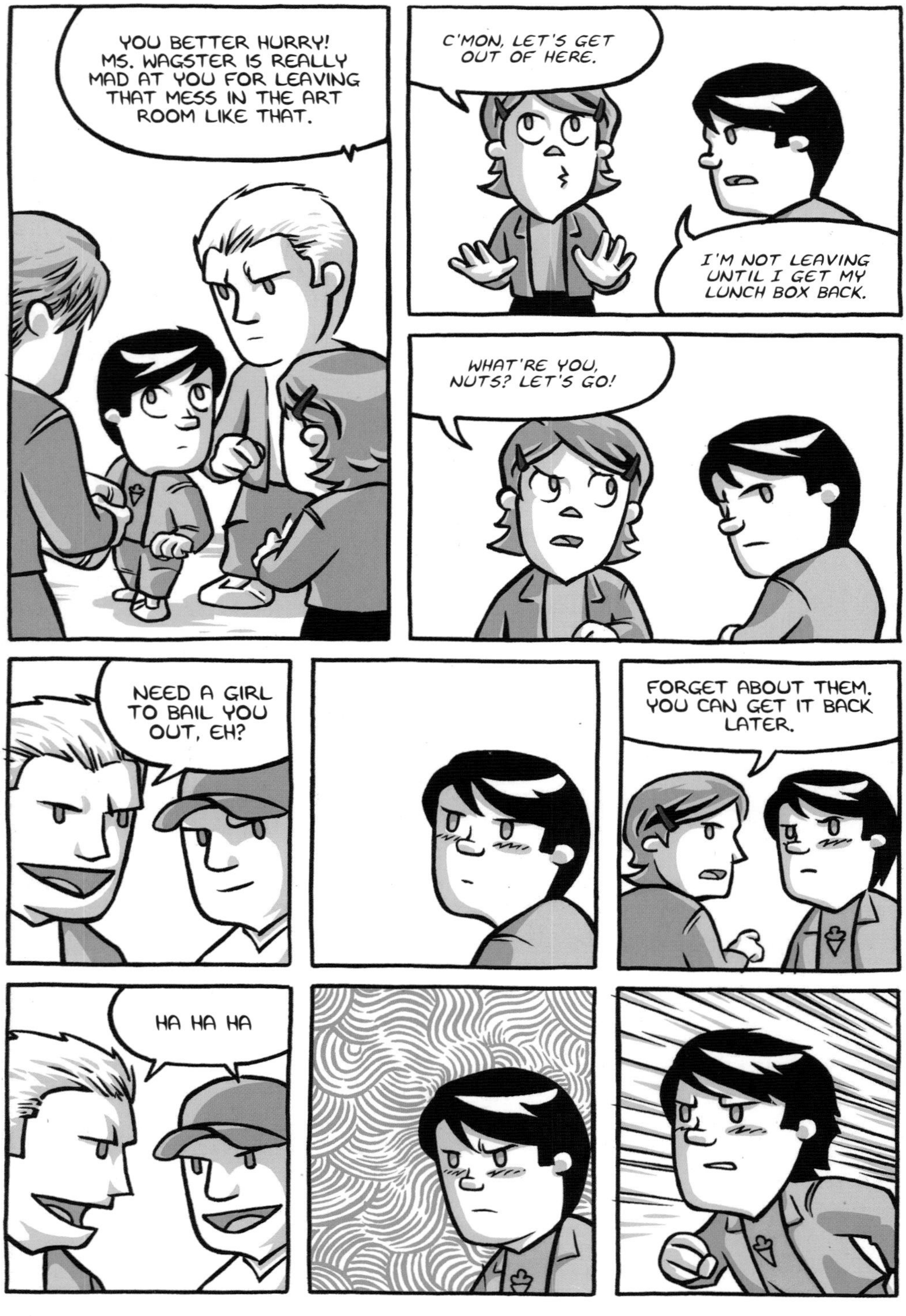
YOU BETTER HURRY! MS. WAGSTER IS REALLY MAD AT YOU FOR LEAVING THAT MESS IN THE ART ROOM LIKE THAT.
C'MON, LET'S GET OUT OF HERE.
I'M NOT LEAVING UNTIL I GET MY LUNCH BOX BACK.
WHAT'RE YOU, NUTS? LET'S GO!
NEED A GIRL TO BAIL YOU OUT, EH?
FORGET ABOUT THEM. YOU CAN GET IT BACK LATER.
HA HA HA

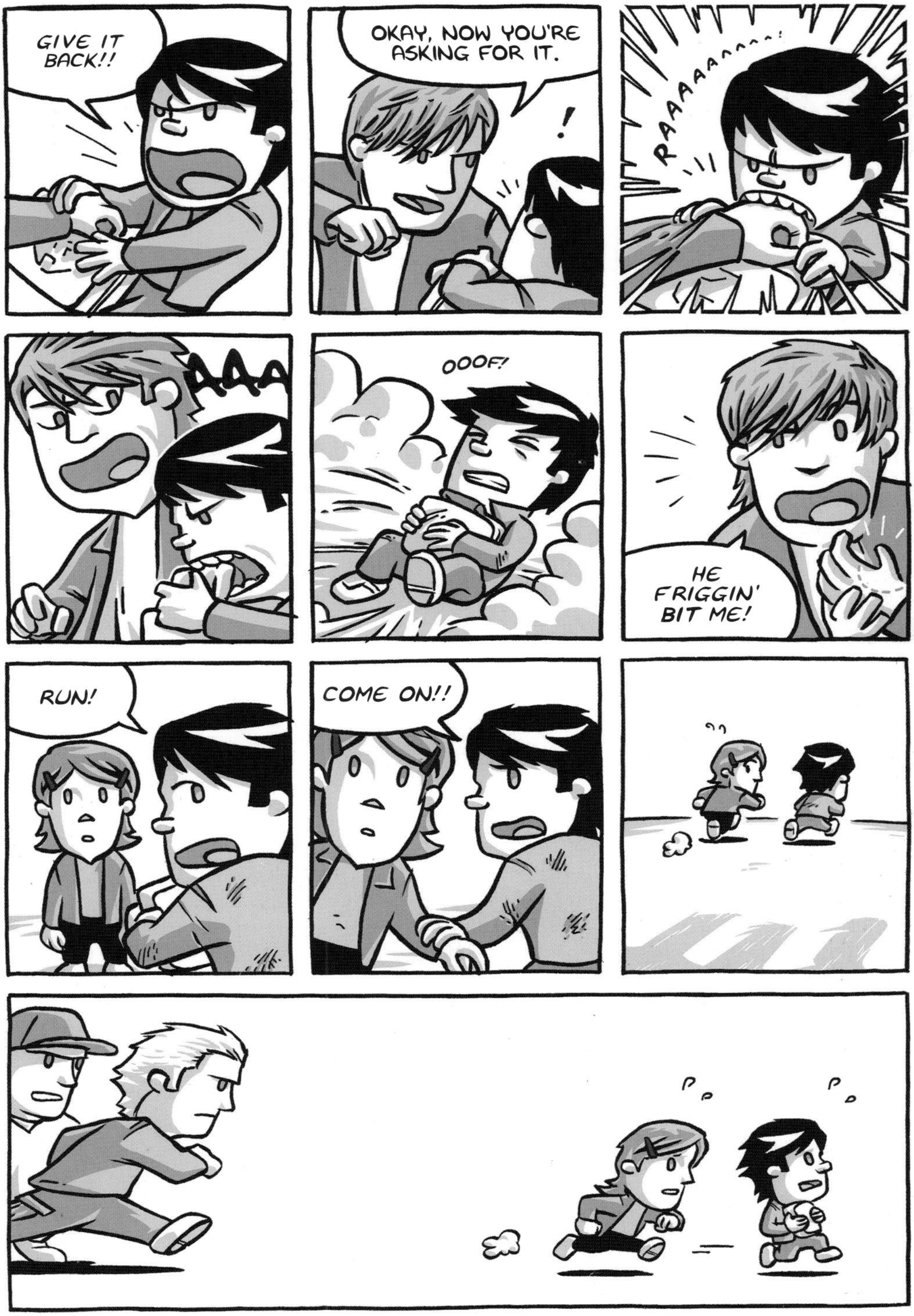
GIVE IT BACK!!
OKAY, NOW YOU'RE ASKING FOR IT.
!
RAAAAAAAAA!
AAA
OOOF!
HE FRIGGIN' BIT ME!
RUN!
COME ON!!

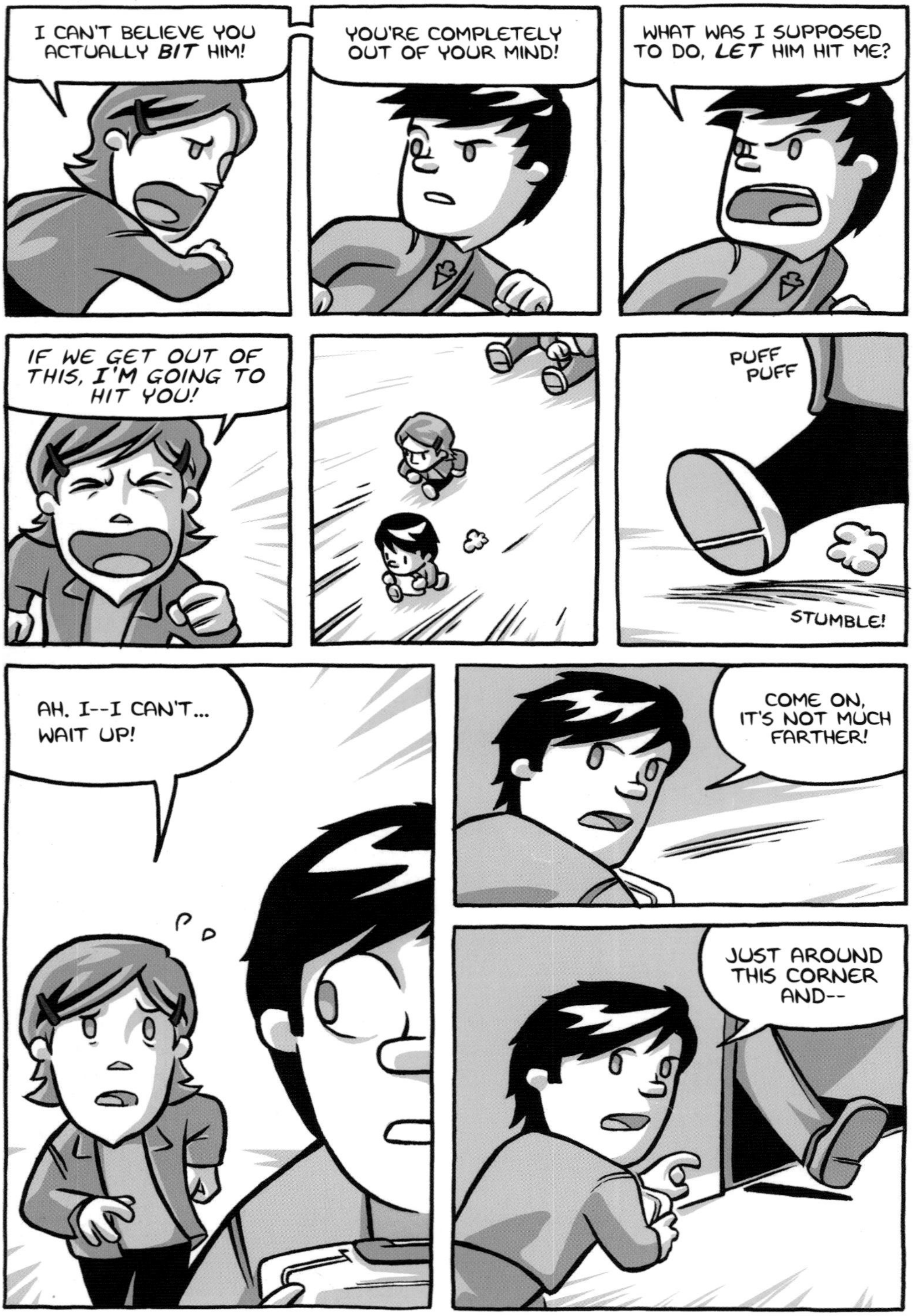
I CAN'T BELIEVE YOU ACTUALLY *BIT* HIM!
YOU'RE COMPLETELY OUT OF YOUR MIND!
WHAT WAS I SUPPOSED TO DO, *LET* HIM HIT ME?
IF WE GET OUT OF THIS, I'M GOING TO HIT YOU!
PUFF PUFF
STUMBLE!
AH. I--I CAN'T... WAIT UP!
COME ON, IT'S NOT MUCH FARTHER!
JUST AROUND THIS CORNER AND--

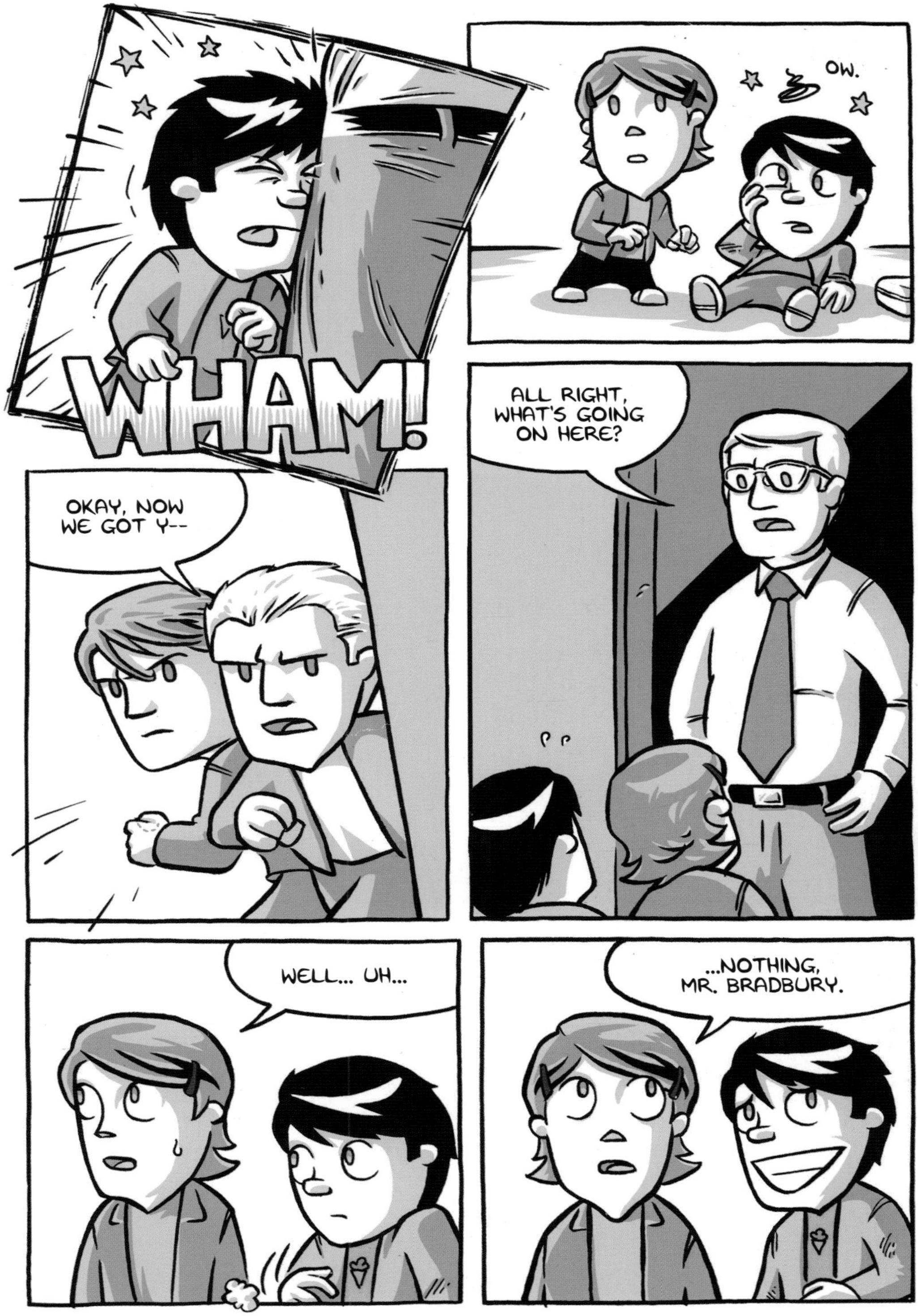
WHAM!
OW.
OKAY, NOW WE GOT Y--
ALL RIGHT, WHAT'S GOING ON HERE?
WELL... UH...
...NOTHING, MR. BRADBURY.

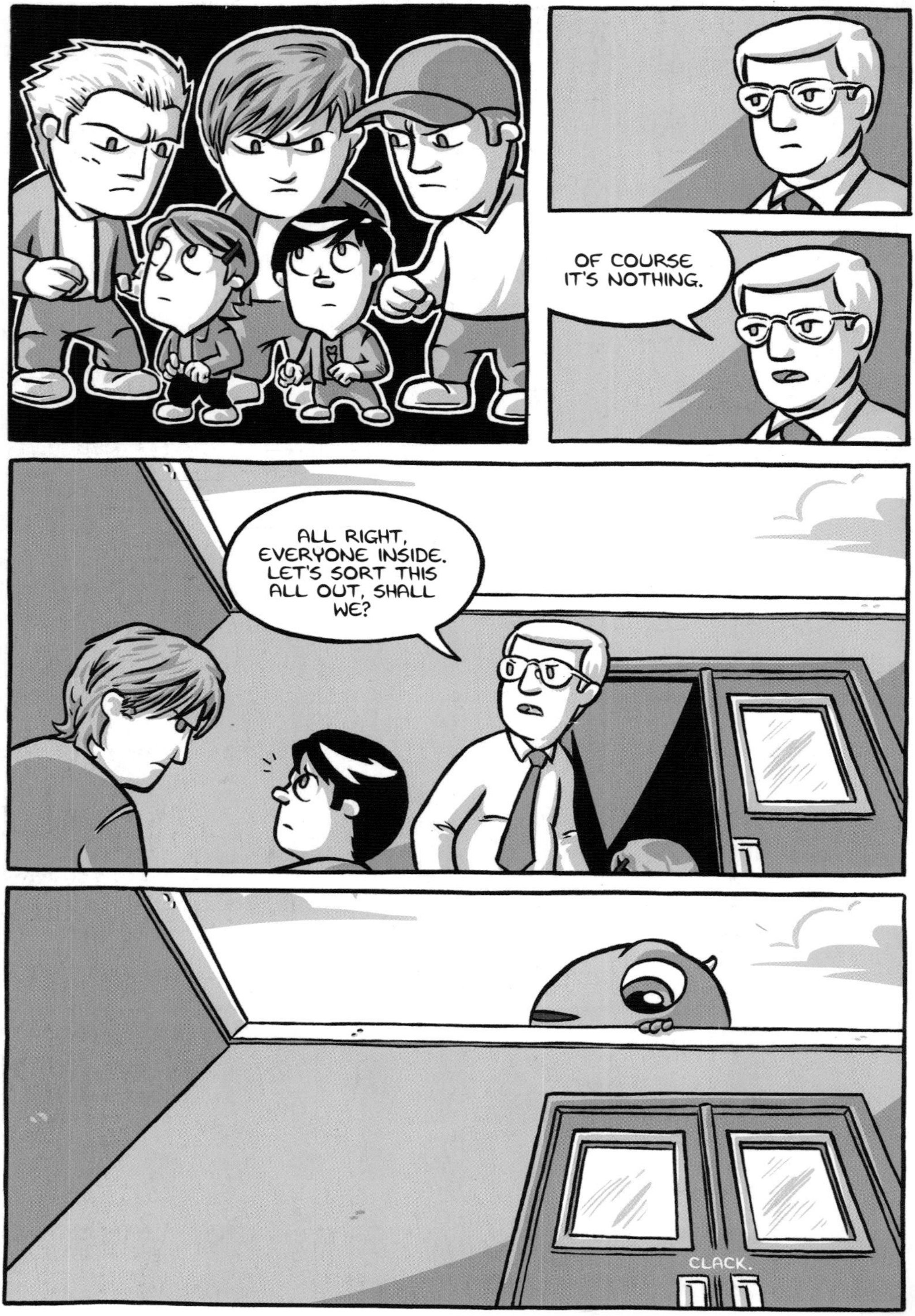
OF COURSE IT'S NOTHING.
ALL RIGHT, EVERYONE INSIDE. LET'S SORT THIS ALL OUT, SHALL WE?
CLACK.

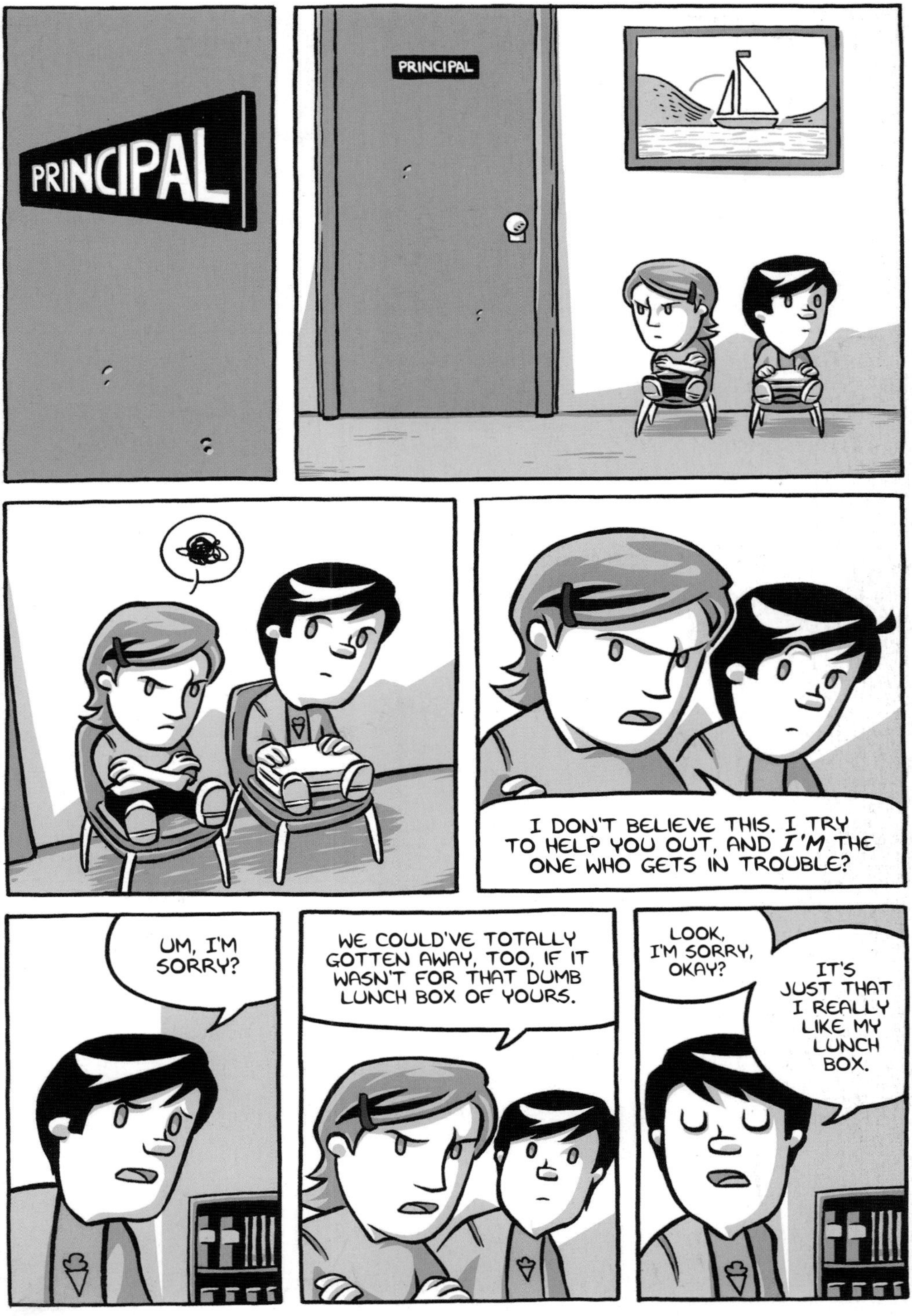
PRINCIPAL
PRINCIPAL
I DON'T BELIEVE THIS. I TRY TO HELP YOU OUT, AND *I'M* THE ONE WHO GETS IN TROUBLE?
UM, I'M SORRY?
WE COULD'VE TOTALLY GOTTEN AWAY, TOO, IF IT WASN'T FOR THAT DUMB LUNCH BOX OF YOURS.
LOOK, I'M SORRY, OKAY?
IT'S JUST THAT I REALLY LIKE MY LUNCH BOX.

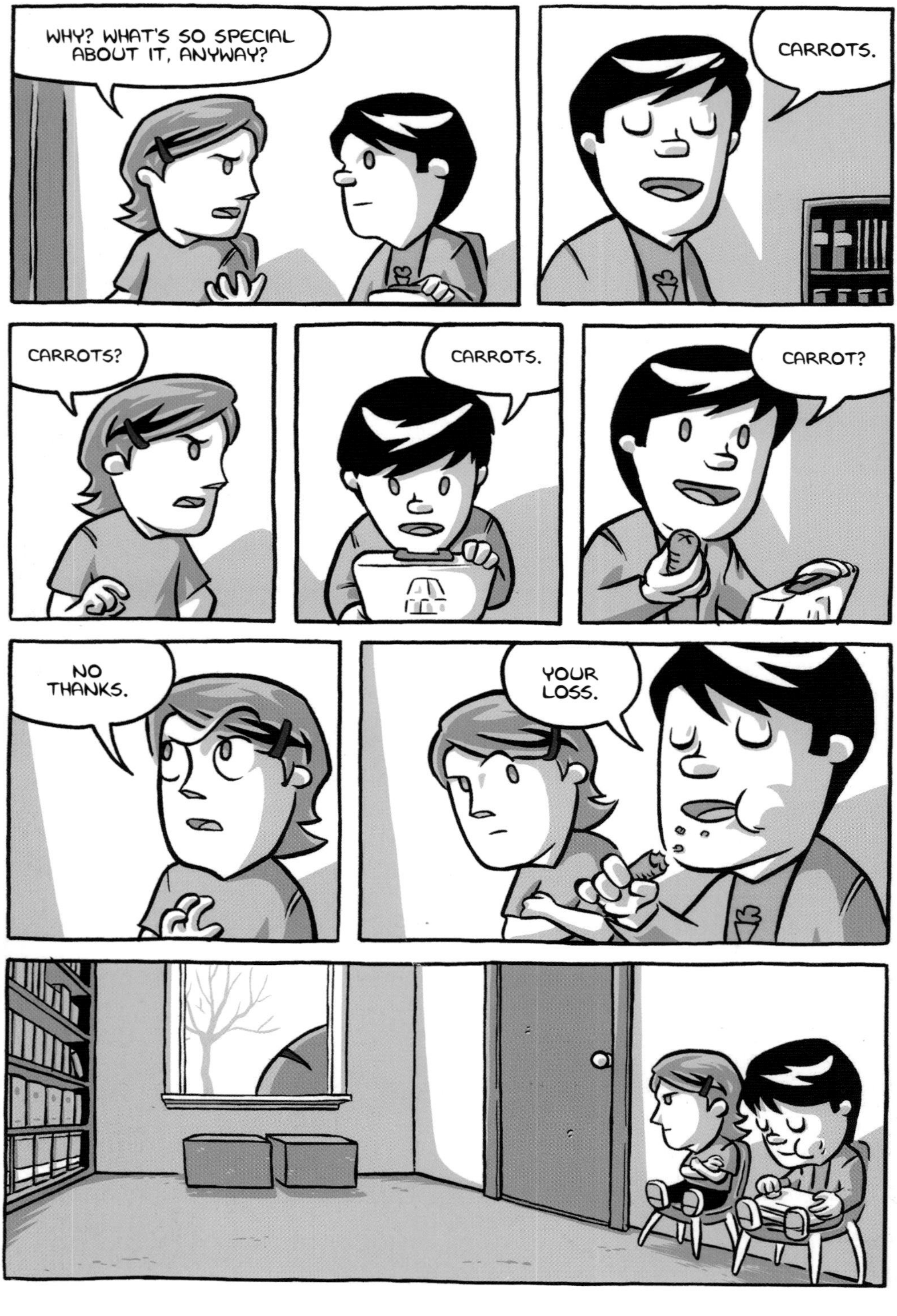
WHY? WHAT'S SO SPECIAL ABOUT IT, ANYWAY?
CARROTS.
CARROTS?
CARROTS.
CARROT?
NO THANKS.
YOUR LOSS.

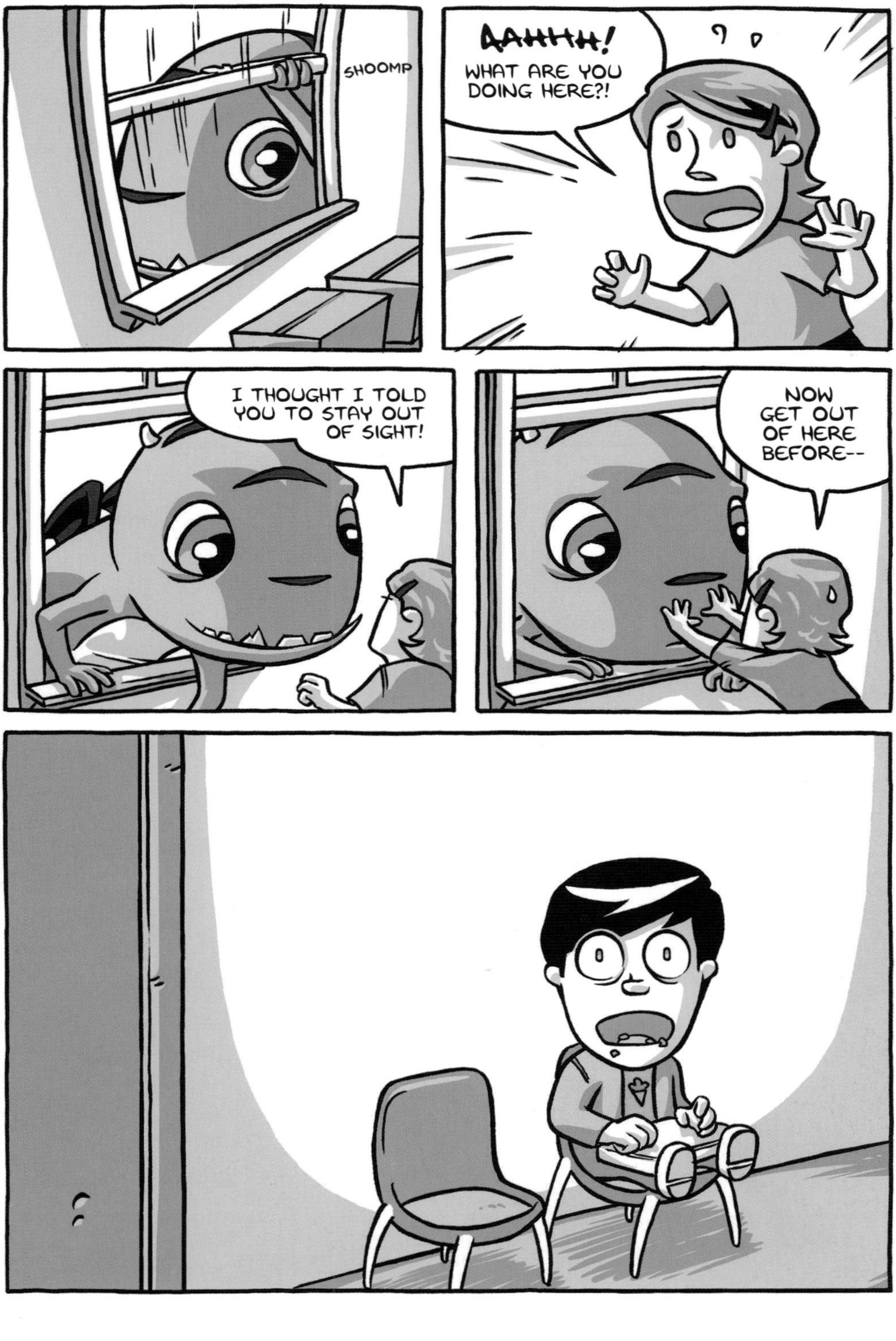
SHOOMP
AAHHH!
WHAT ARE YOU DOING HERE?!
I THOUGHT I TOLD YOU TO STAY OUT OF SIGHT!
NOW GET OUT OF HERE BEFORE--

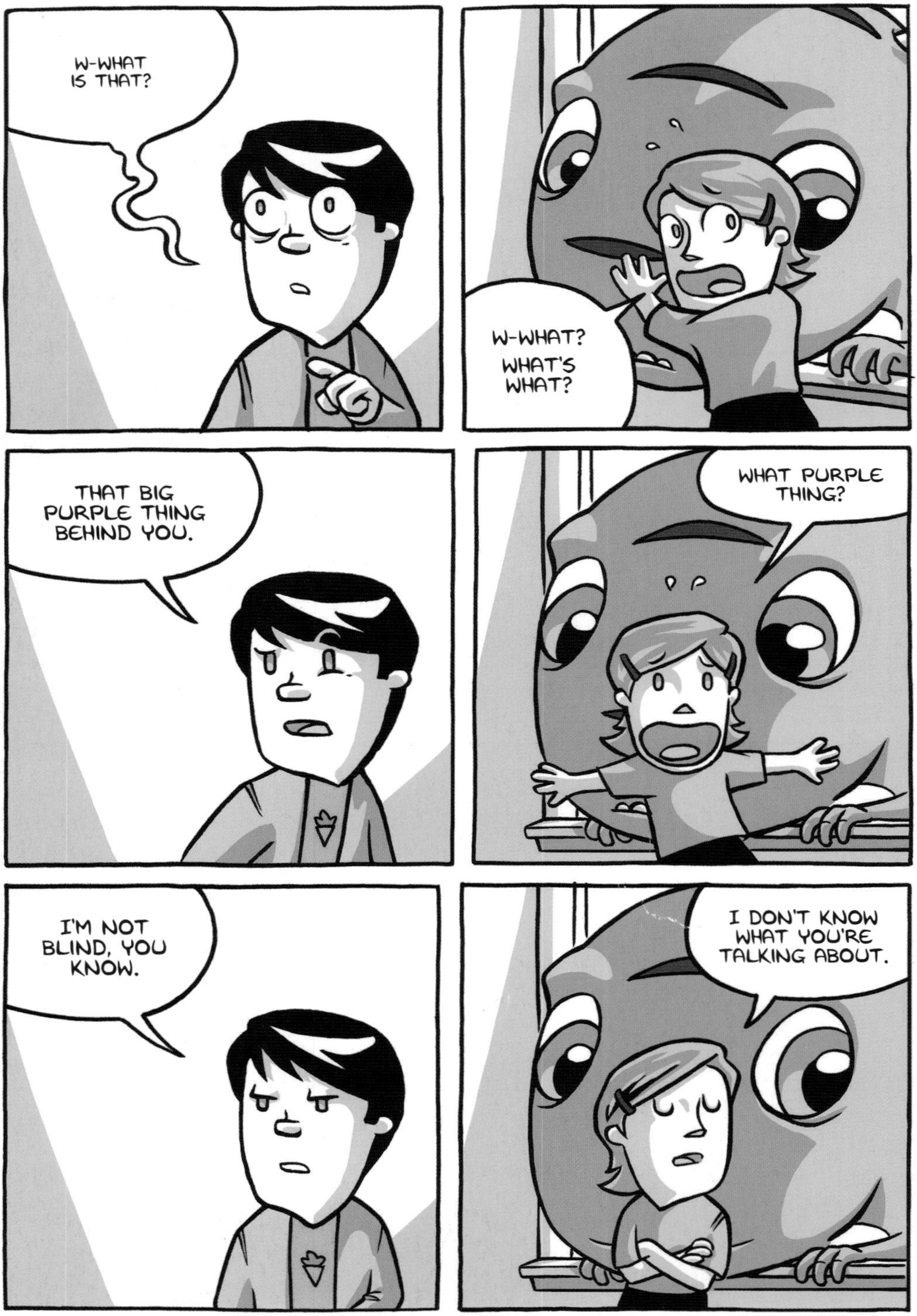
W-WHAT IS THAT?
W-WHAT? WHAT'S WHAT?
THAT BIG PURPLE THING BEHIND YOU.
WHAT PURPLE THING?
I'M NOT BLIND, YOU KNOW.
I DON'T KNOW WHAT YOU'RE TALKING ABOUT.

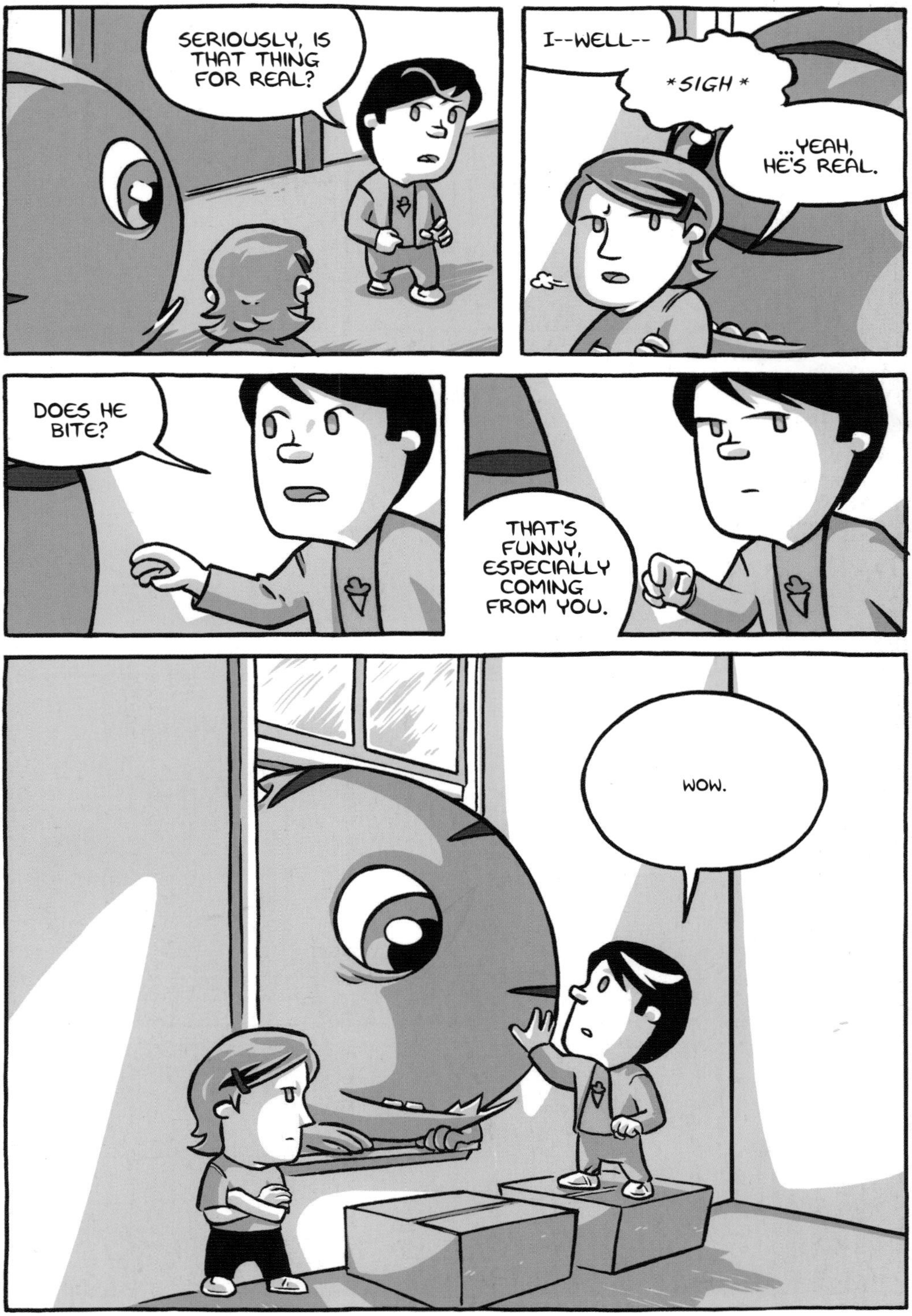
SERIOUSLY, IS THAT THING FOR REAL?
I--WELL--
SIGH
...YEAH, HE'S REAL.
DOES HE BITE?
THAT'S FUNNY, ESPECIALLY COMING FROM YOU.
WOW.

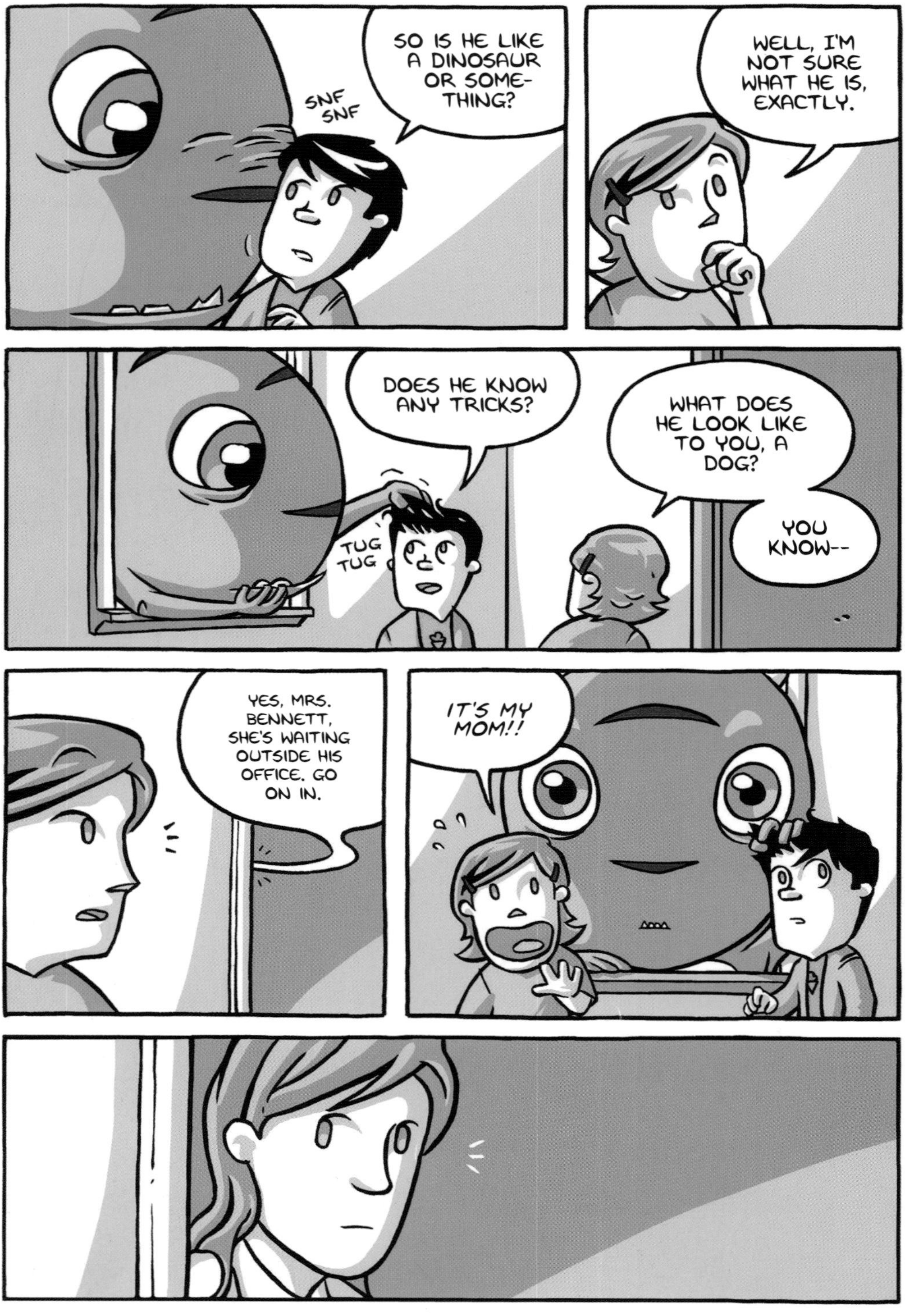
SNF SNF
SO IS HE LIKE A DINOSAUR OR SOME-THING?
WELL, I'M NOT SURE WHAT HE IS, EXACTLY.
DOES HE KNOW ANY TRICKS?
TUG TUG
WHAT DOES HE LOOK LIKE TO YOU, A DOG?
YOU KNOW--
YES, MRS. BENNETT, SHE'S WAITING OUTSIDE HIS OFFICE. GO ON IN.
IT'S MY MOM!!

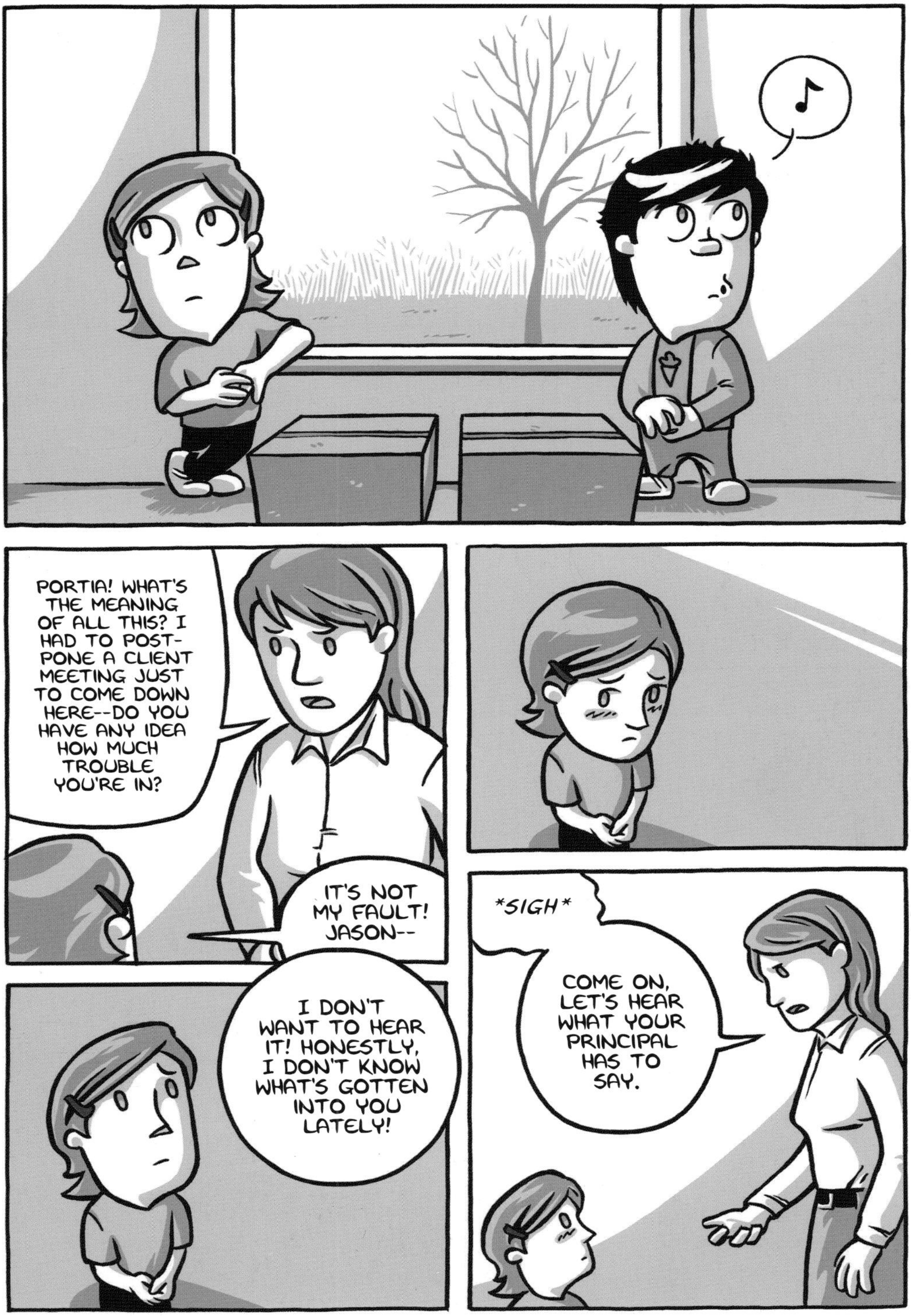
♪
PORTIA! WHAT'S THE MEANING OF ALL THIS? I HAD TO POST-PONE A CLIENT MEETING JUST TO COME DOWN HERE--DO YOU HAVE ANY IDEA HOW MUCH TROUBLE YOU'RE IN?
IT'S NOT MY FAULT! JASON--
I DON'T WANT TO HEAR IT! HONESTLY, I DON'T KNOW WHAT'S GOTTEN INTO YOU LATELY!
SIGH
COME ON, LET'S HEAR WHAT YOUR PRINCIPAL HAS TO SAY.

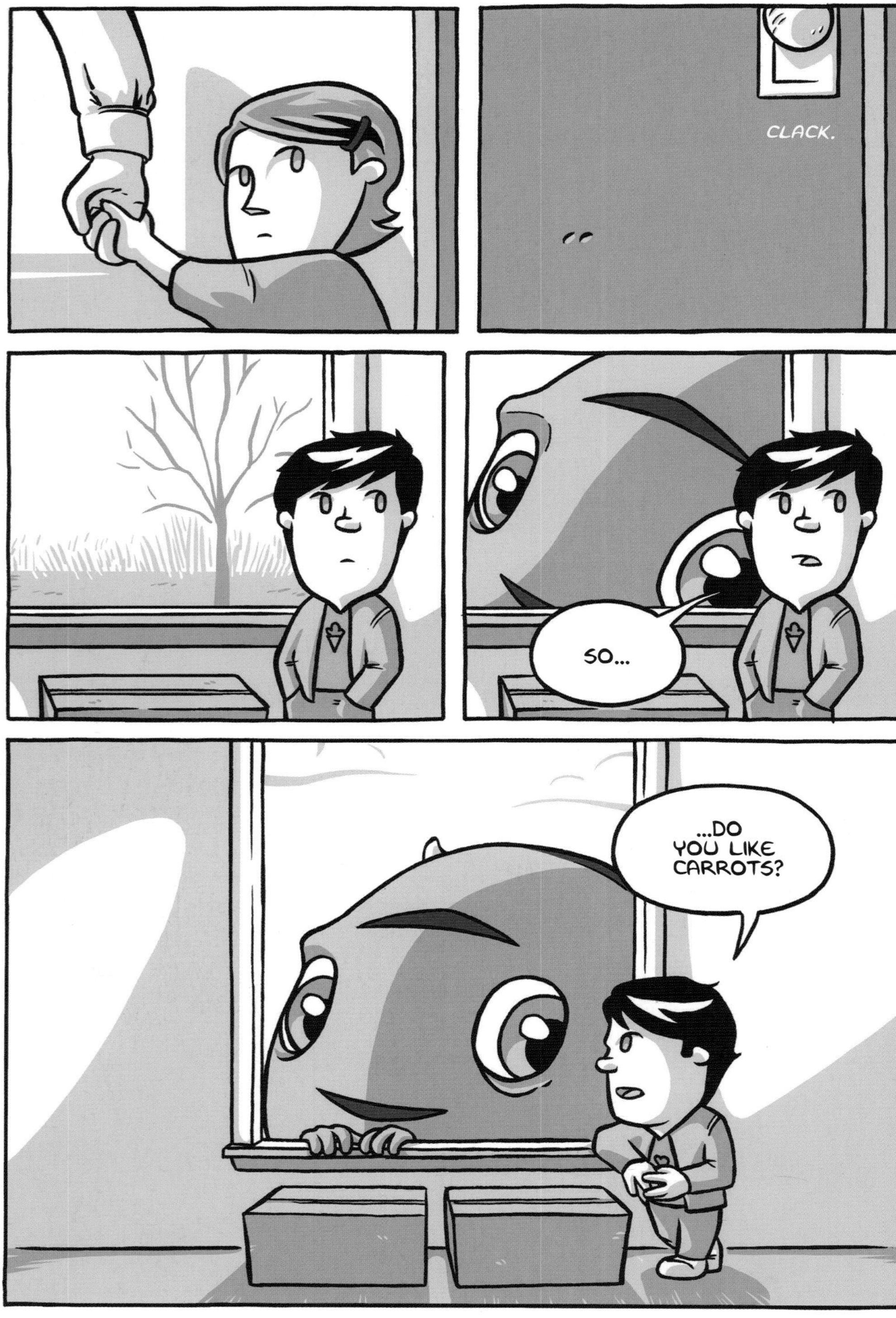
CLACK.
SO...
...DO YOU LIKE CARROTS?

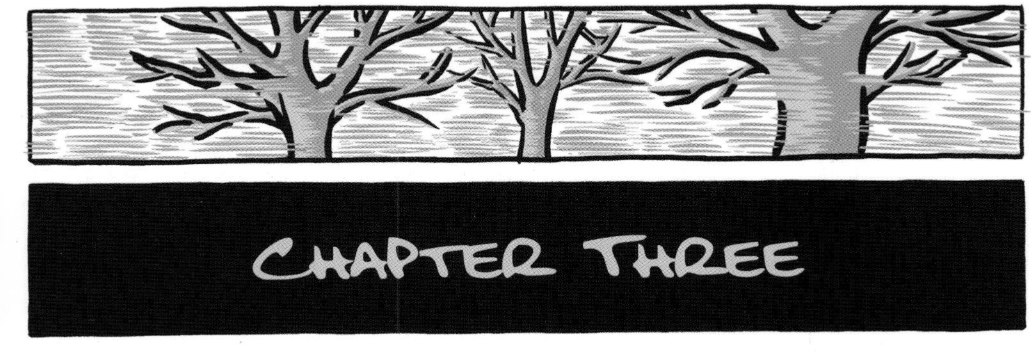

CHAPTER THREE

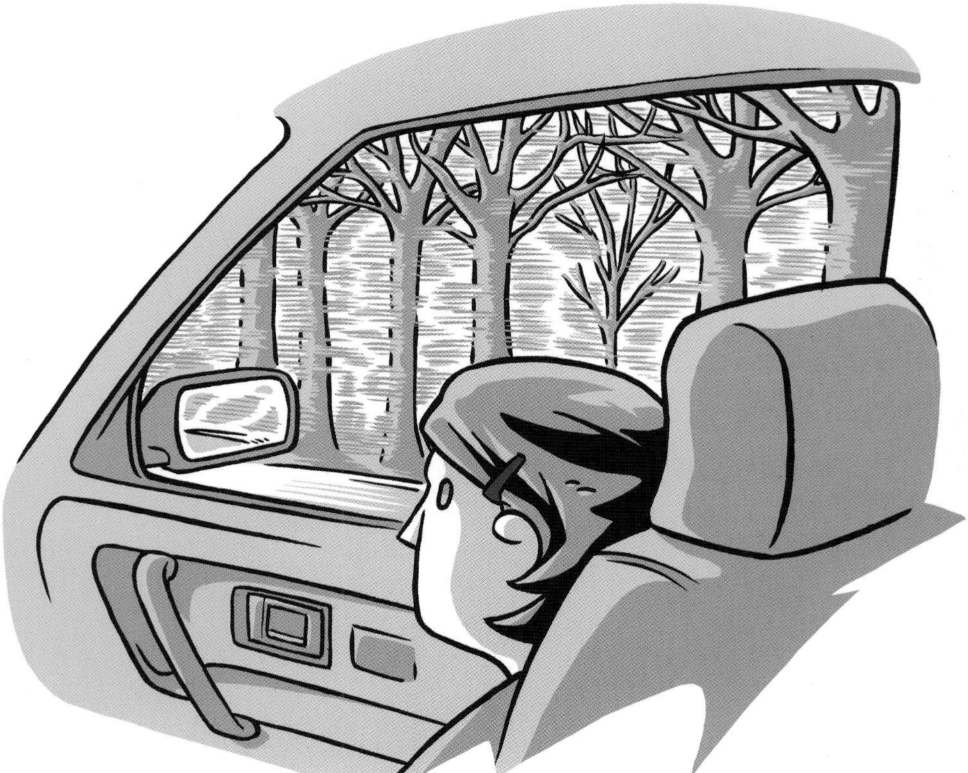

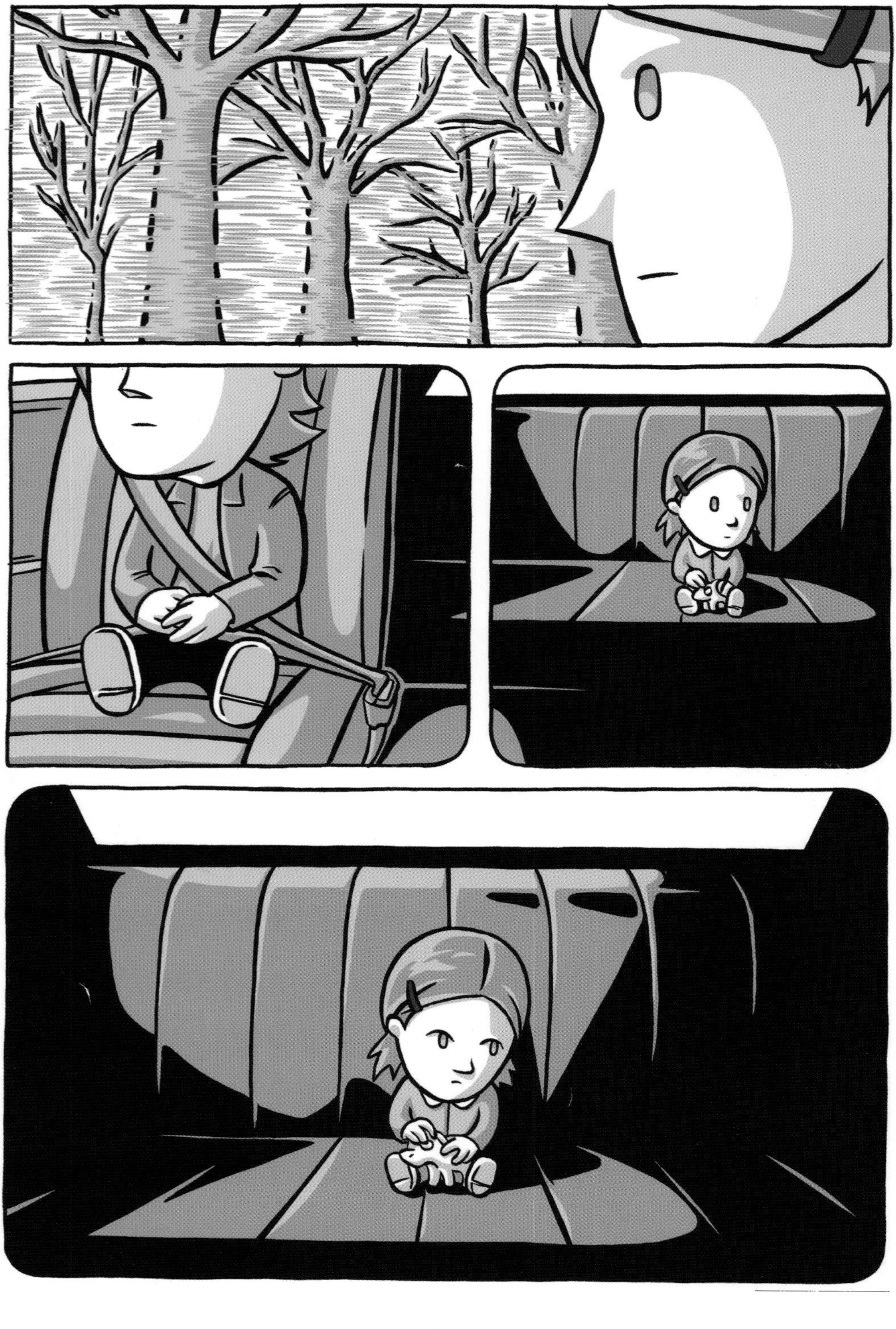

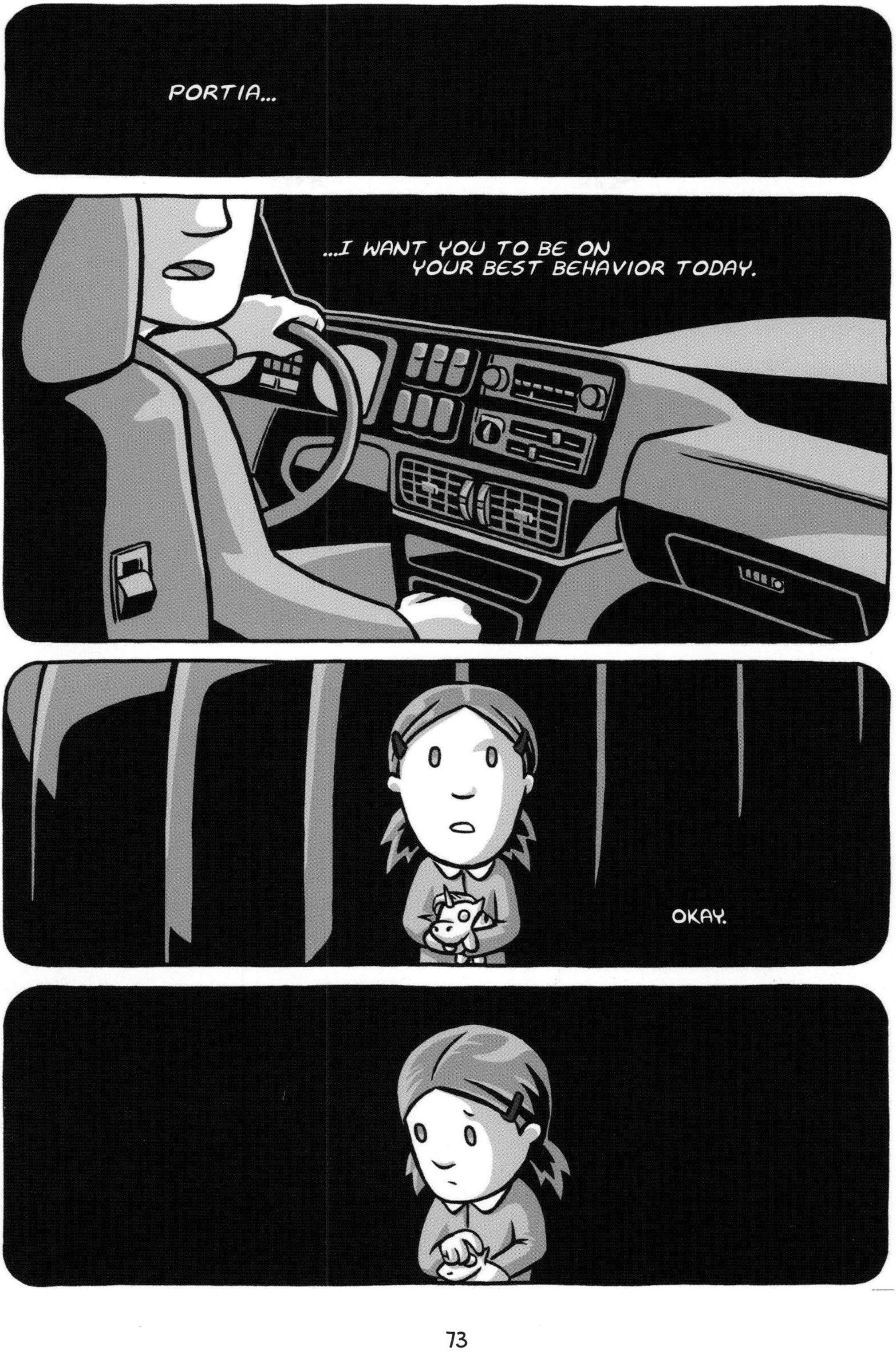
PORTIA...
...I WANT YOU TO BE ON YOUR BEST BEHAVIOR TODAY.
OKAY.

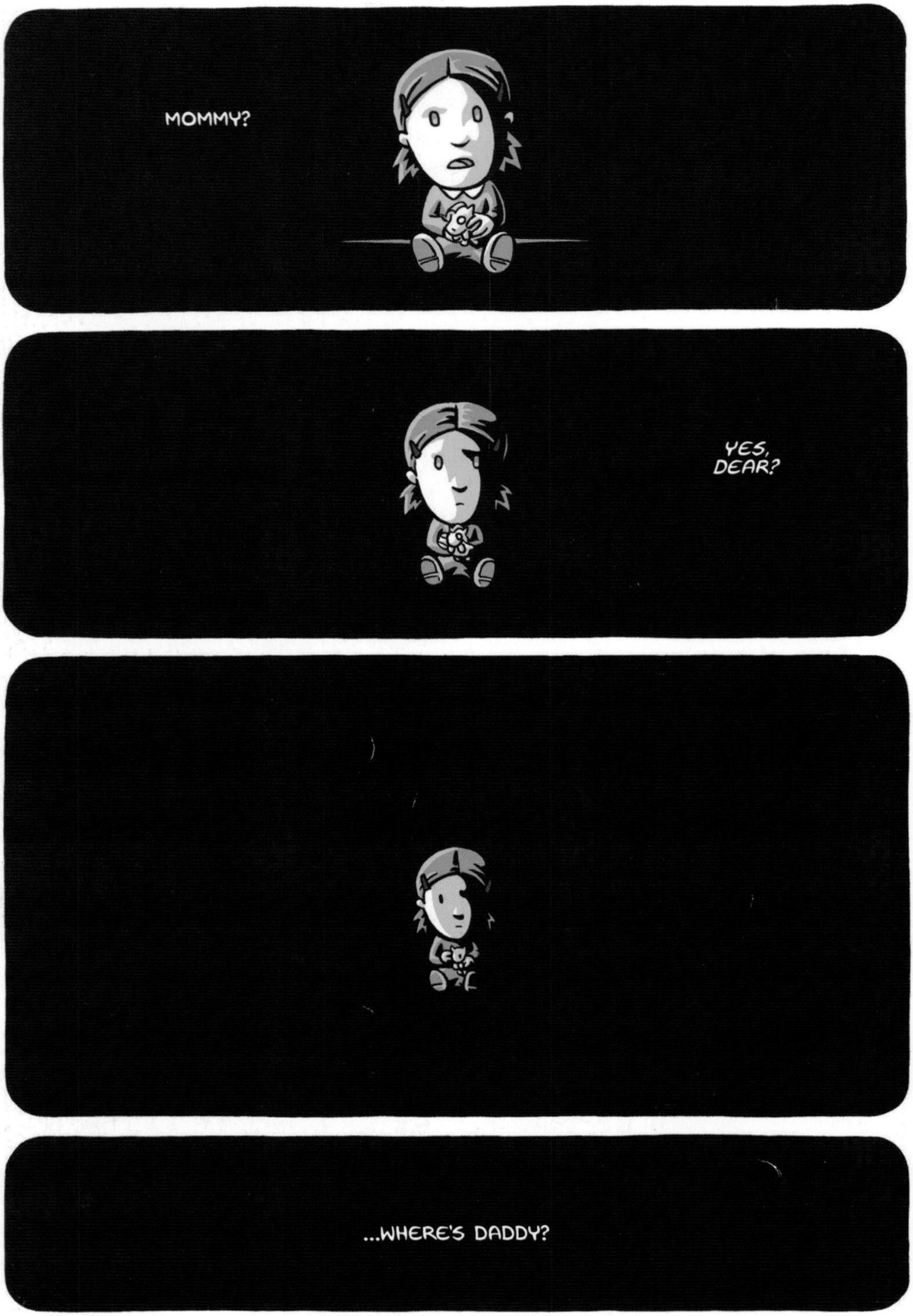
MOMMY?
YES, DEAR?
...WHERE'S DADDY?

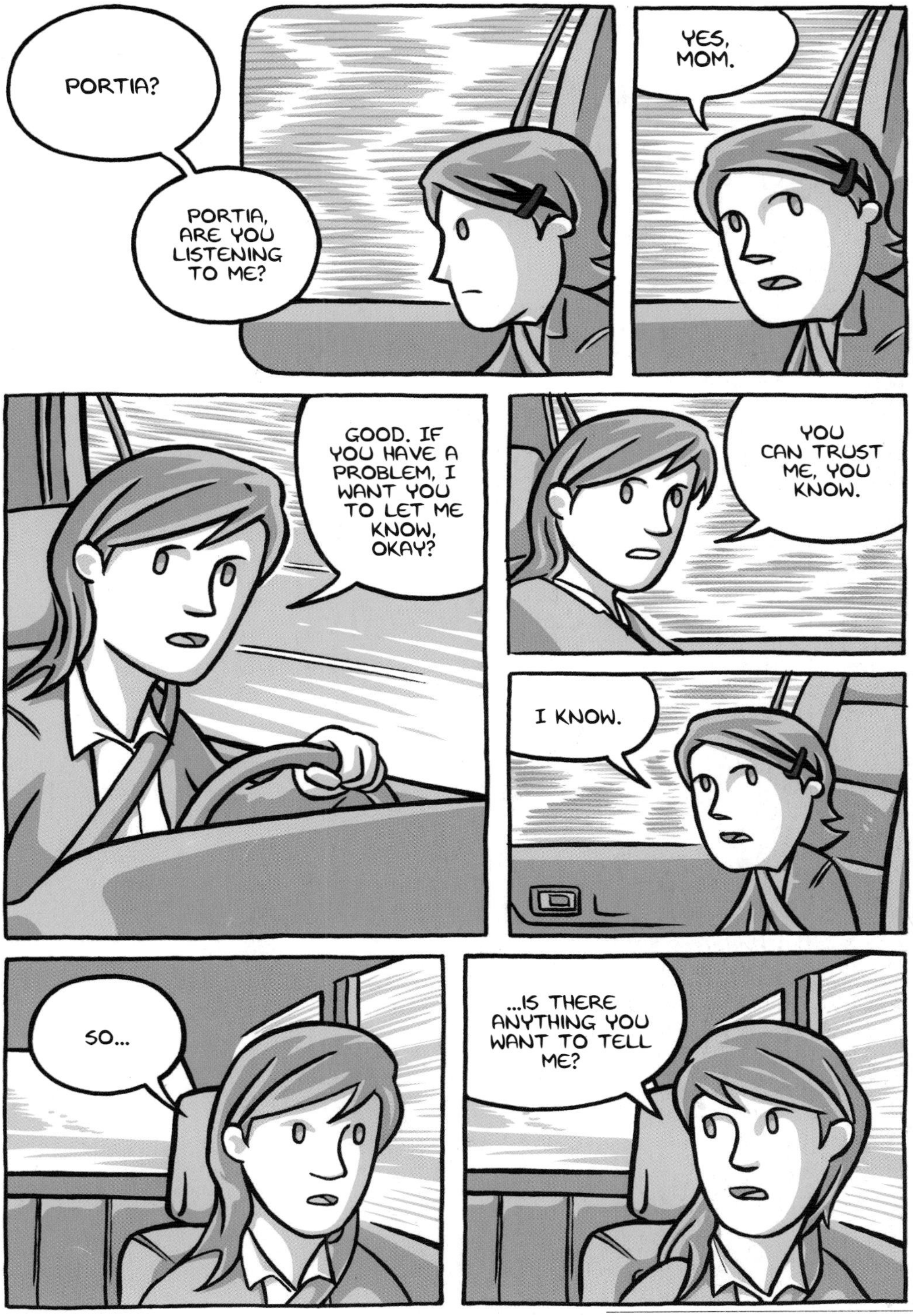
PORTIA?
PORTIA, ARE YOU LISTENING TO ME?
YES, MOM.
GOOD. IF YOU HAVE A PROBLEM, I WANT YOU TO LET ME KNOW, OKAY?
YOU CAN TRUST ME, YOU KNOW.
I KNOW.
SO...
...IS THERE ANYTHING YOU WANT TO TELL ME?

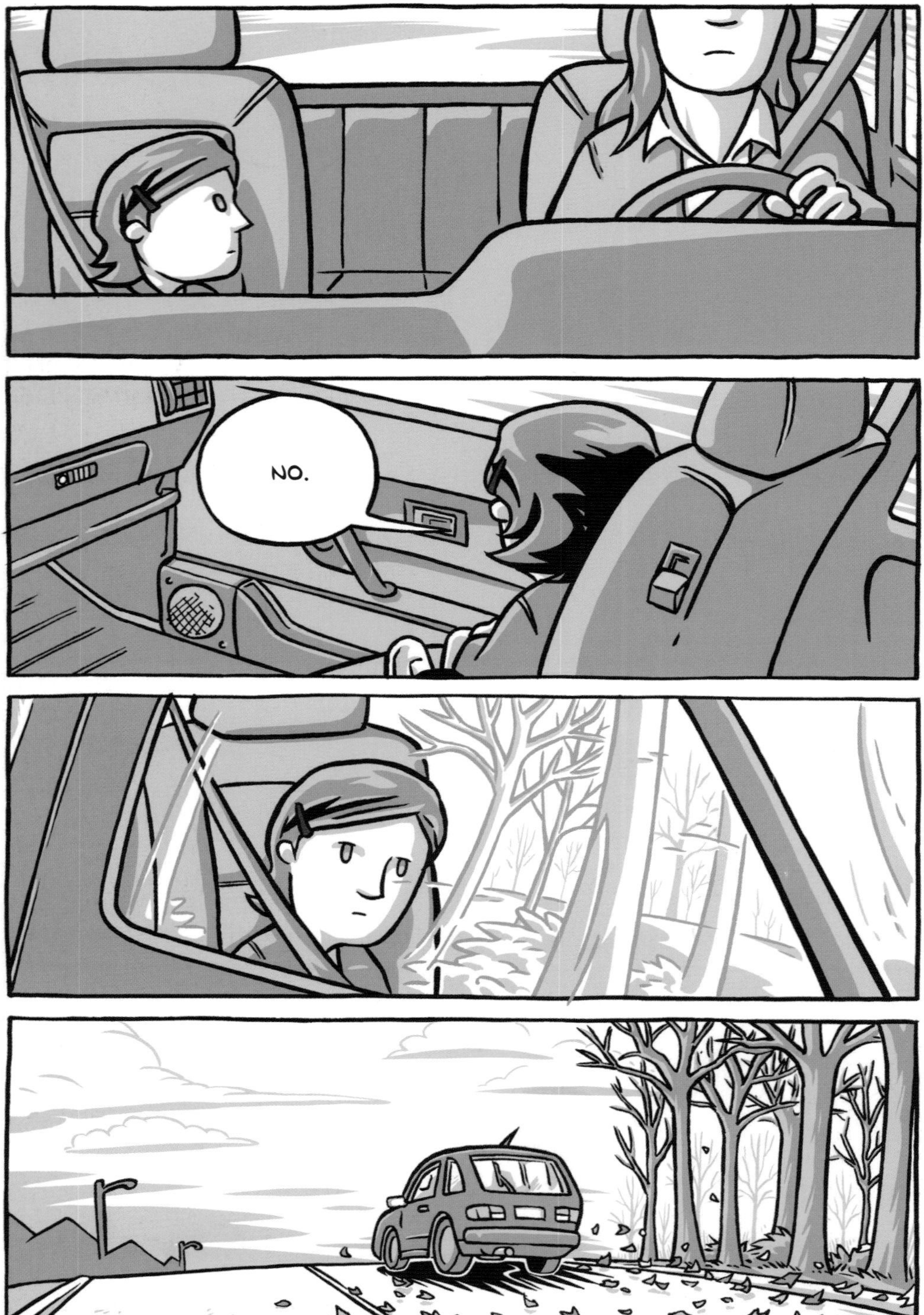
NO.

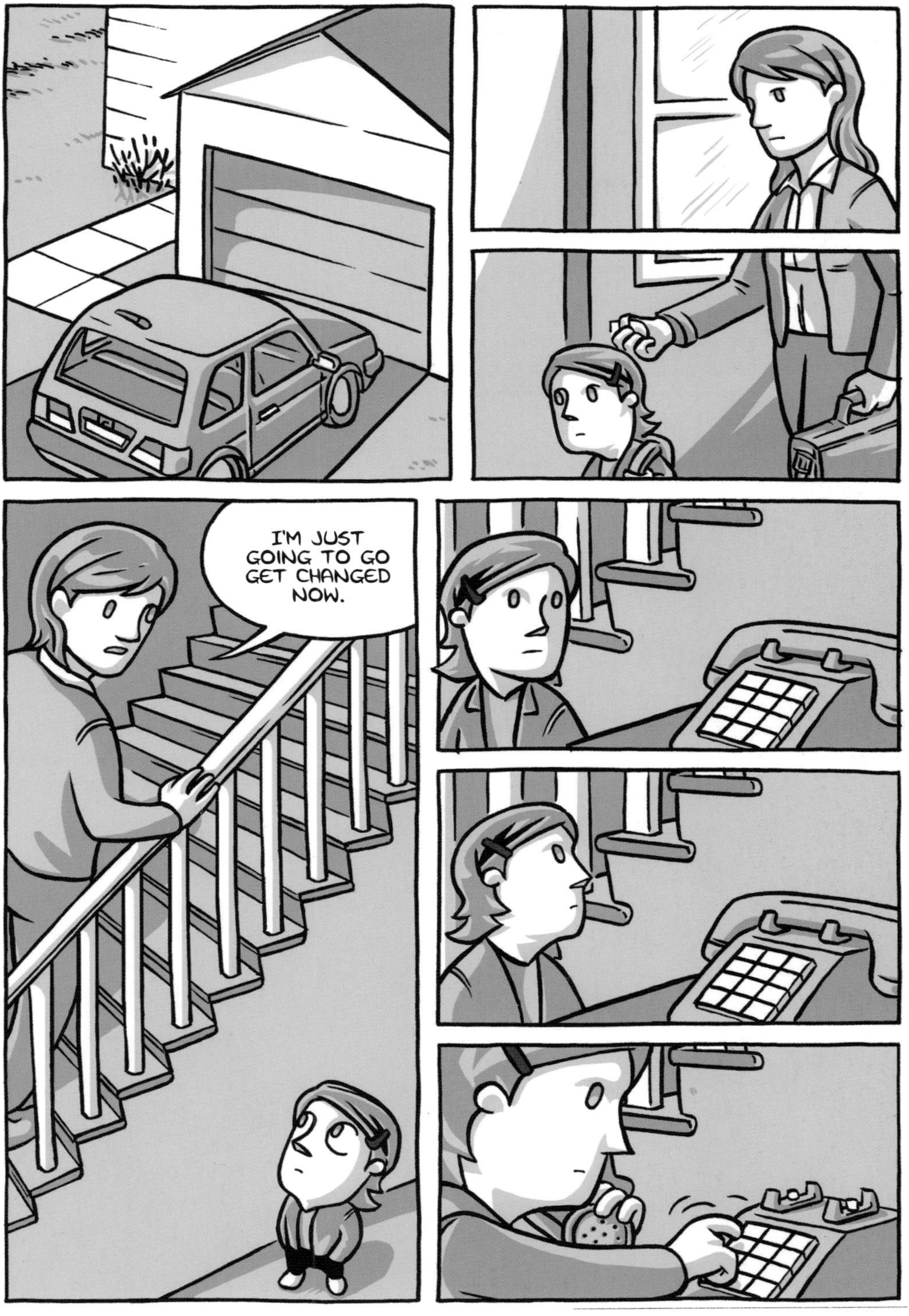
I'M JUST GOING TO GO GET CHANGED NOW.

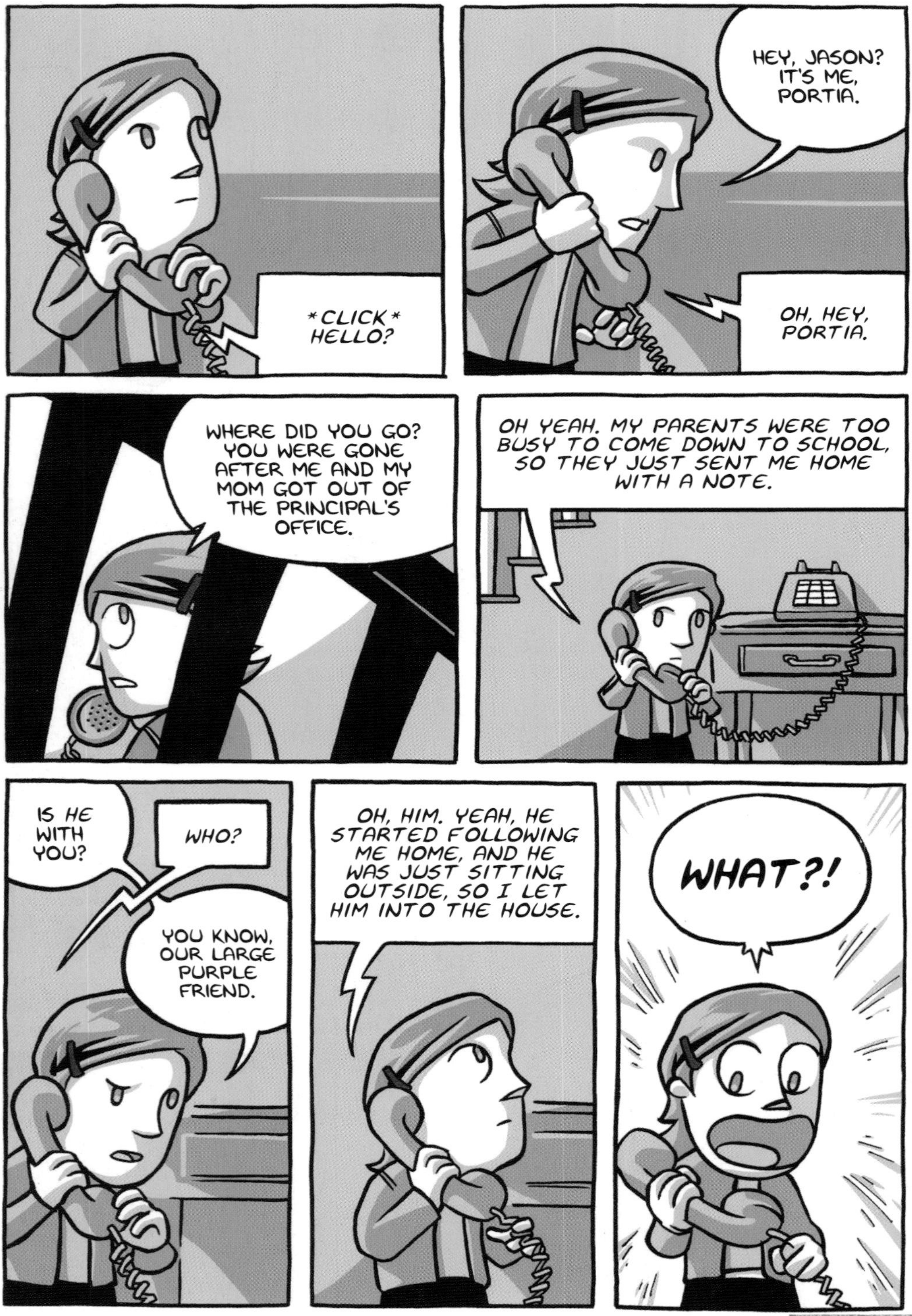
CLICK HELLO?
HEY, JASON? IT'S ME, PORTIA.
OH, HEY, PORTIA.
WHERE DID YOU GO? YOU WERE GONE AFTER ME AND MY MOM GOT OUT OF THE PRINCIPAL'S OFFICE.
OH YEAH. MY PARENTS WERE TOO BUSY TO COME DOWN TO SCHOOL, SO THEY JUST SENT ME HOME WITH A NOTE.
IS HE WITH YOU?
WHO?
YOU KNOW, OUR LARGE PURPLE FRIEND.
OH, HIM. YEAH, HE STARTED FOLLOWING ME HOME, AND HE WAS JUST SITTING OUTSIDE, SO I LET HIM INTO THE HOUSE.
WHAT?!

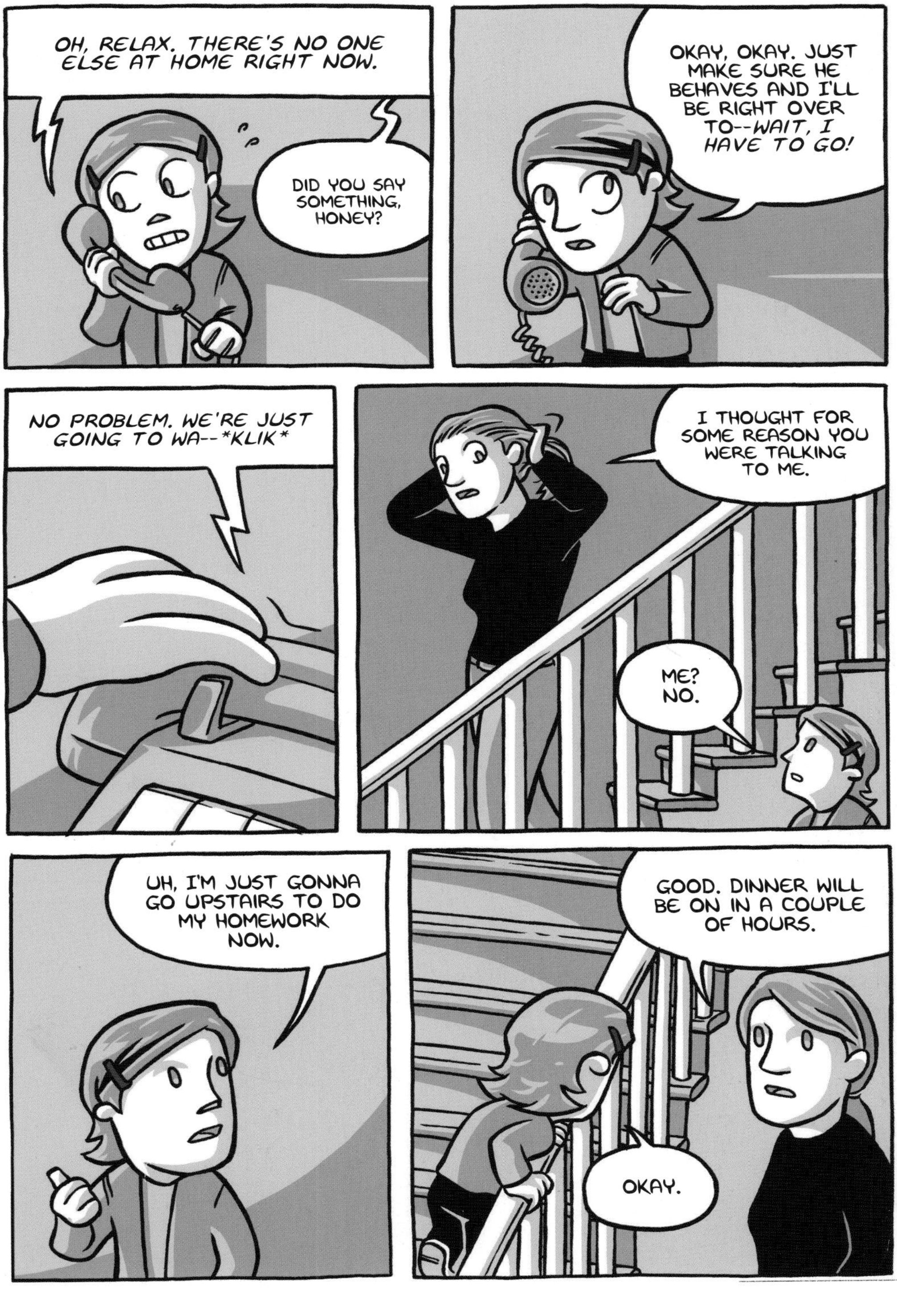
OH, RELAX. THERE'S NO ONE ELSE AT HOME RIGHT NOW.
DID YOU SAY SOMETHING, HONEY?
OKAY, OKAY. JUST MAKE SURE HE BEHAVES AND I'LL BE RIGHT OVER TO--WAIT, I HAVE TO GO!
NO PROBLEM. WE'RE JUST GOING TO WA--*KLIK*
I THOUGHT FOR SOME REASON YOU WERE TALKING TO ME.
ME? NO.
UH, I'M JUST GONNA GO UPSTAIRS TO DO MY HOMEWORK NOW.
GOOD. DINNER WILL BE ON IN A COUPLE OF HOURS.
OKAY.

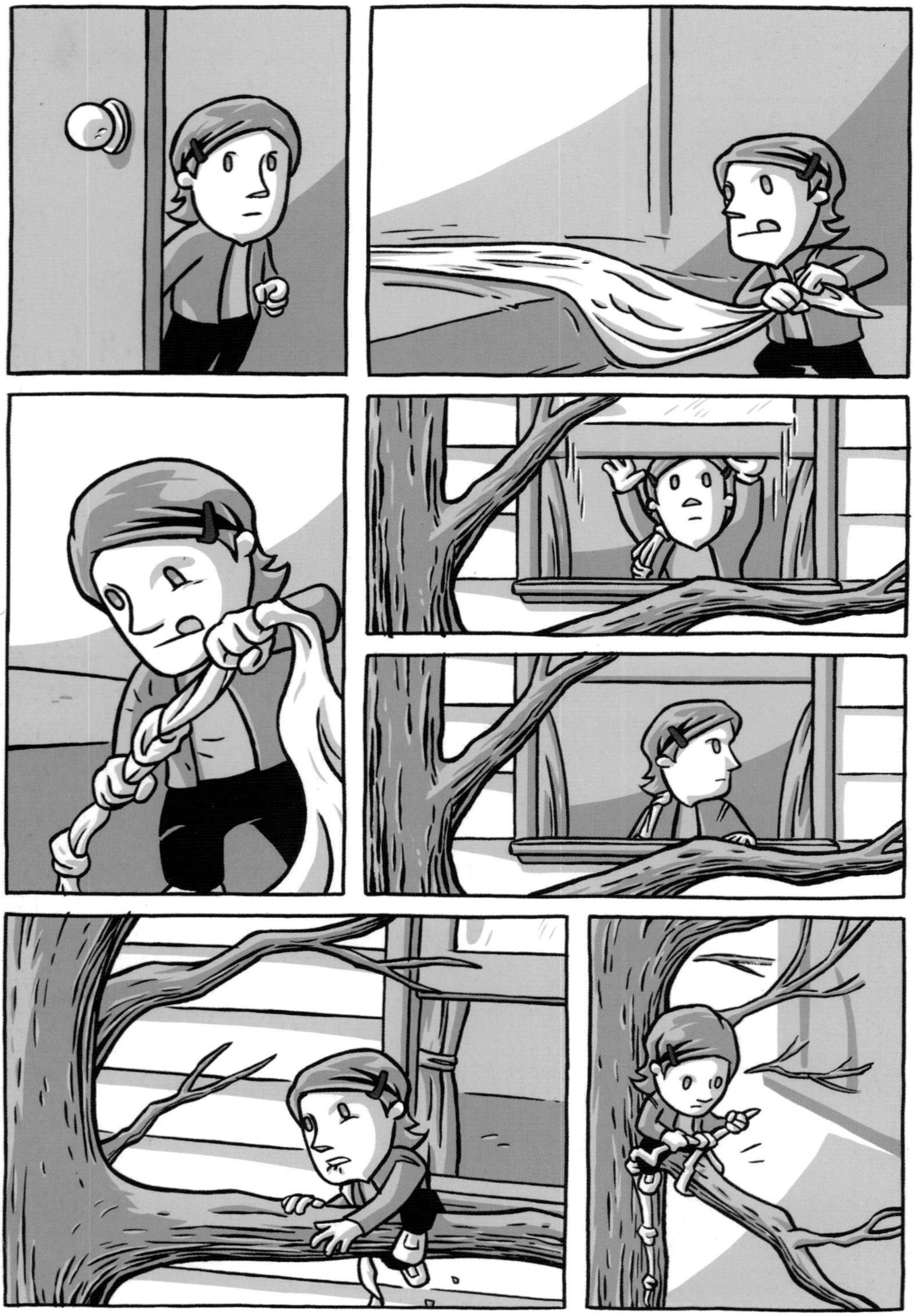

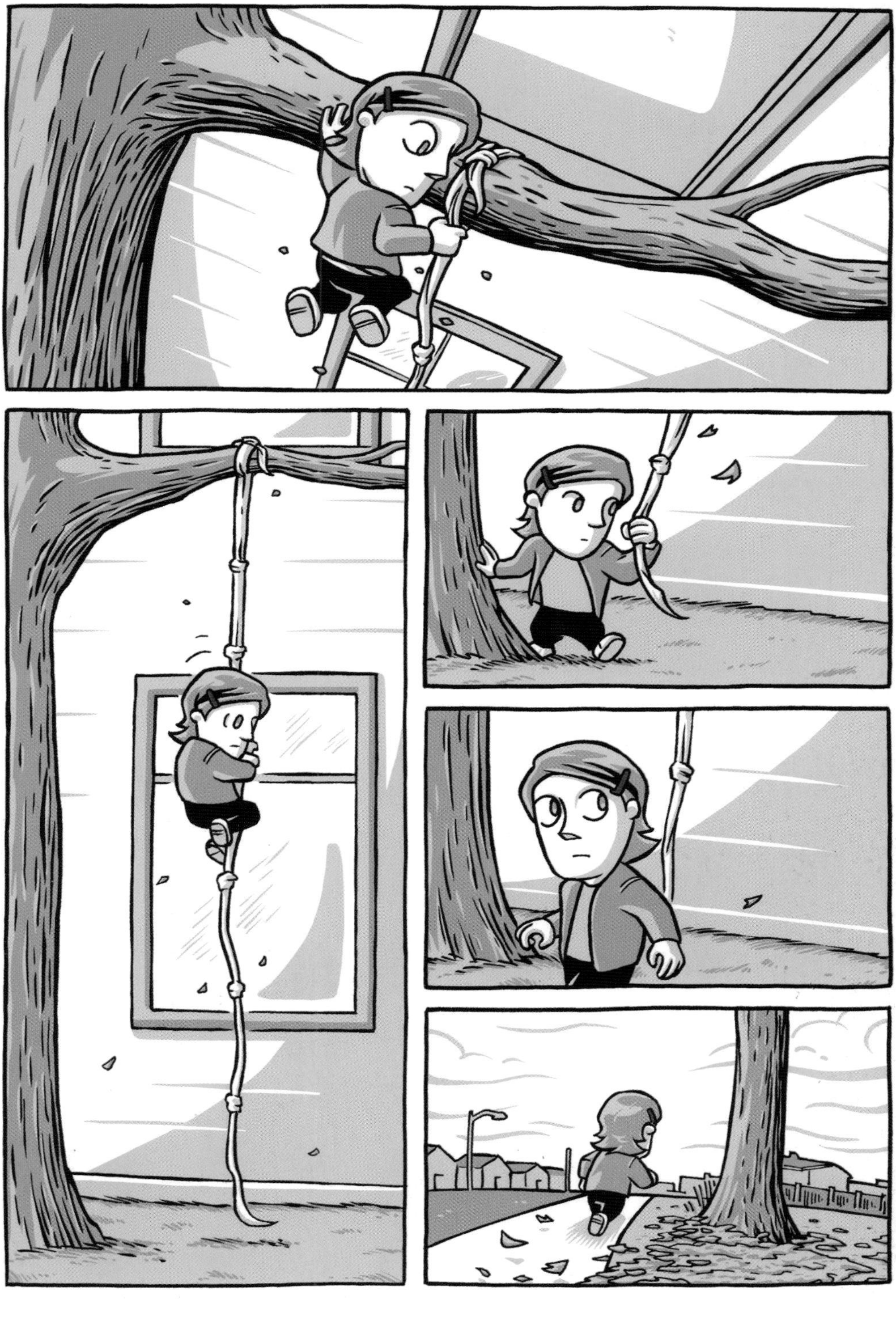

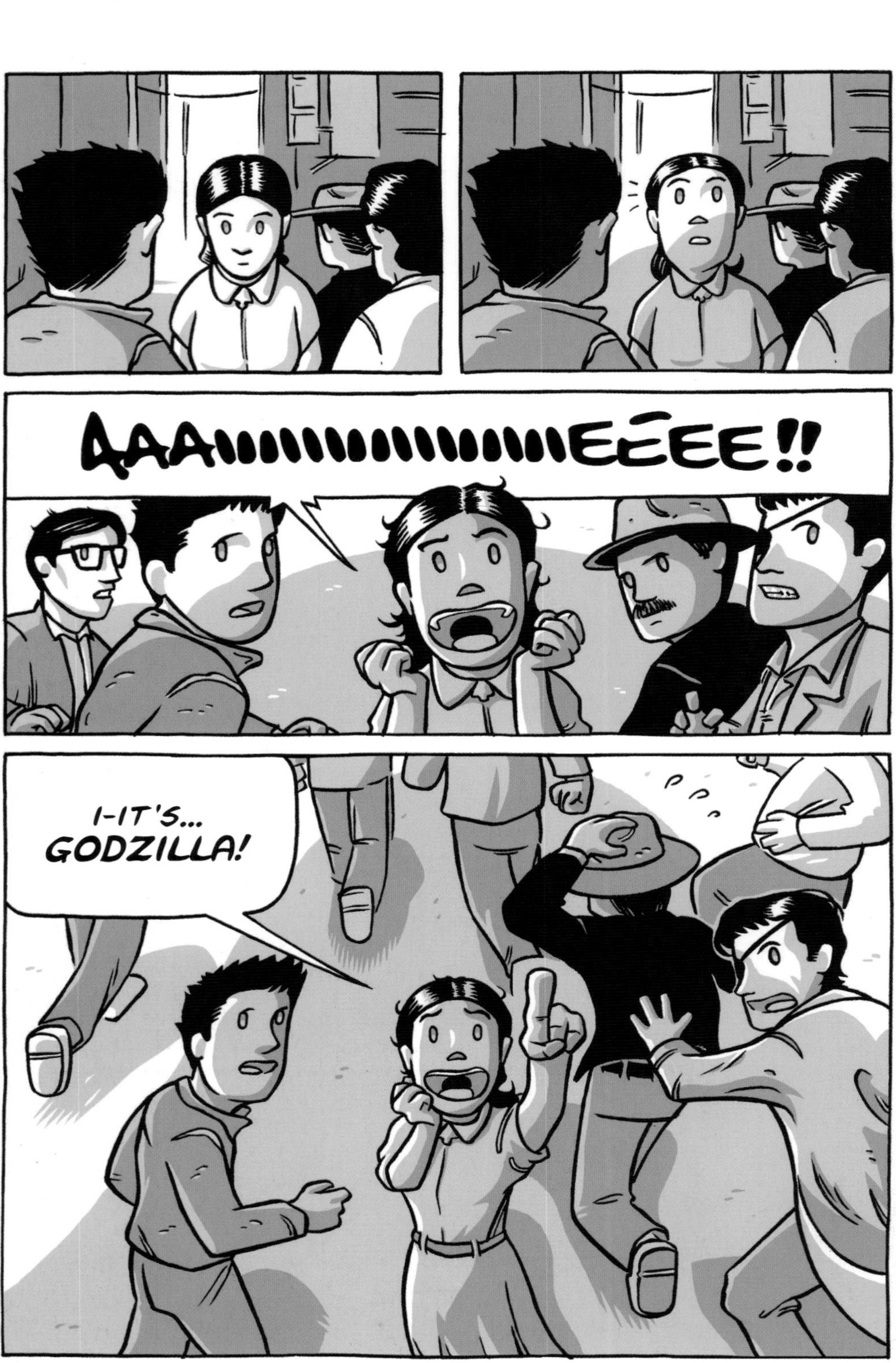
AAAIIIIIIIIIIIIIIIIIEEEEE!!
I-IT'S... GODZILLA!

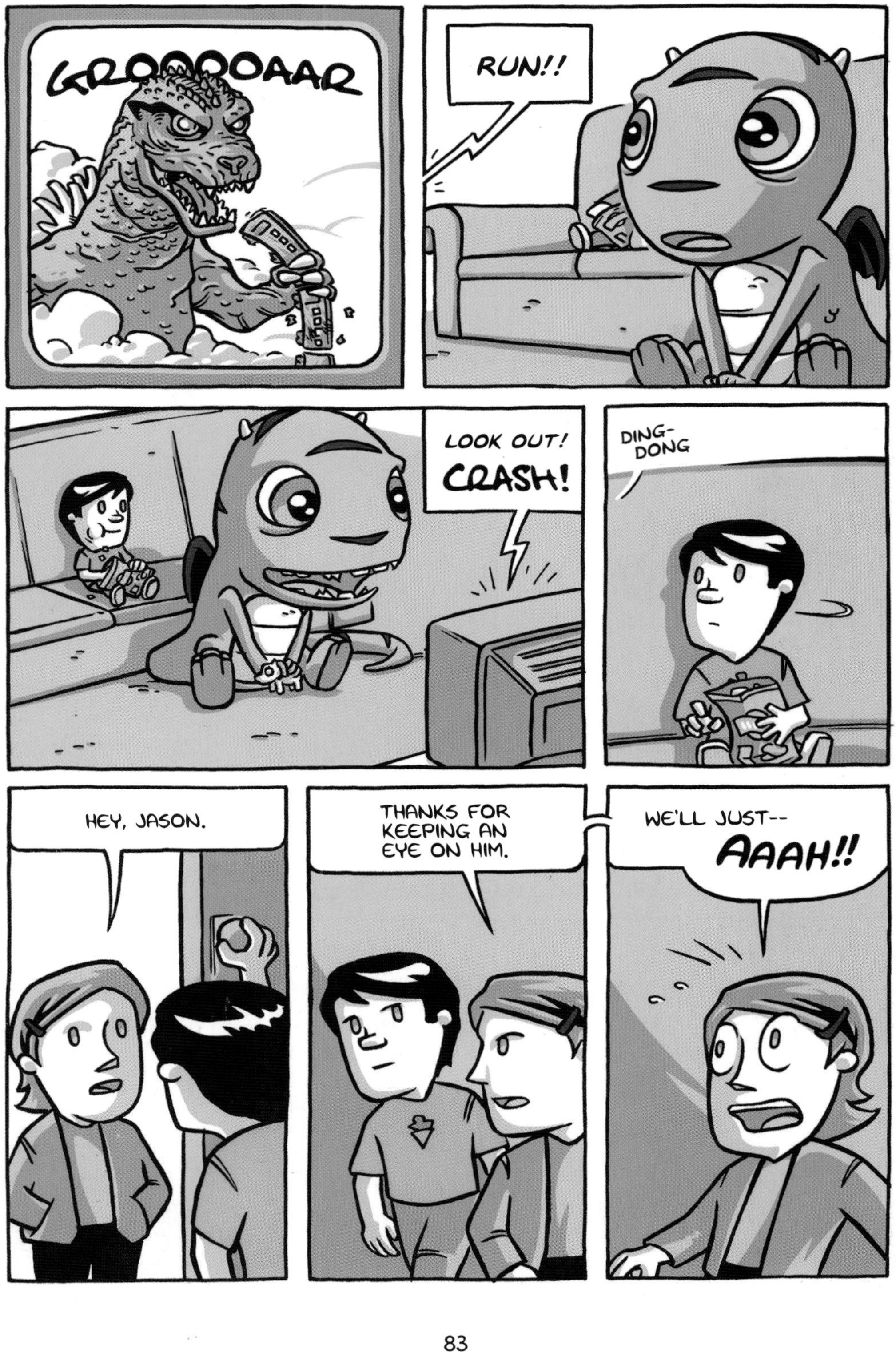
GROOOOAAR
RUN!!
LOOK OUT!
CRASH!
DING-
DONG
HEY, JASON.
THANKS FOR KEEPING AN EYE ON HIM.
WE'LL JUST--
AAAH!!

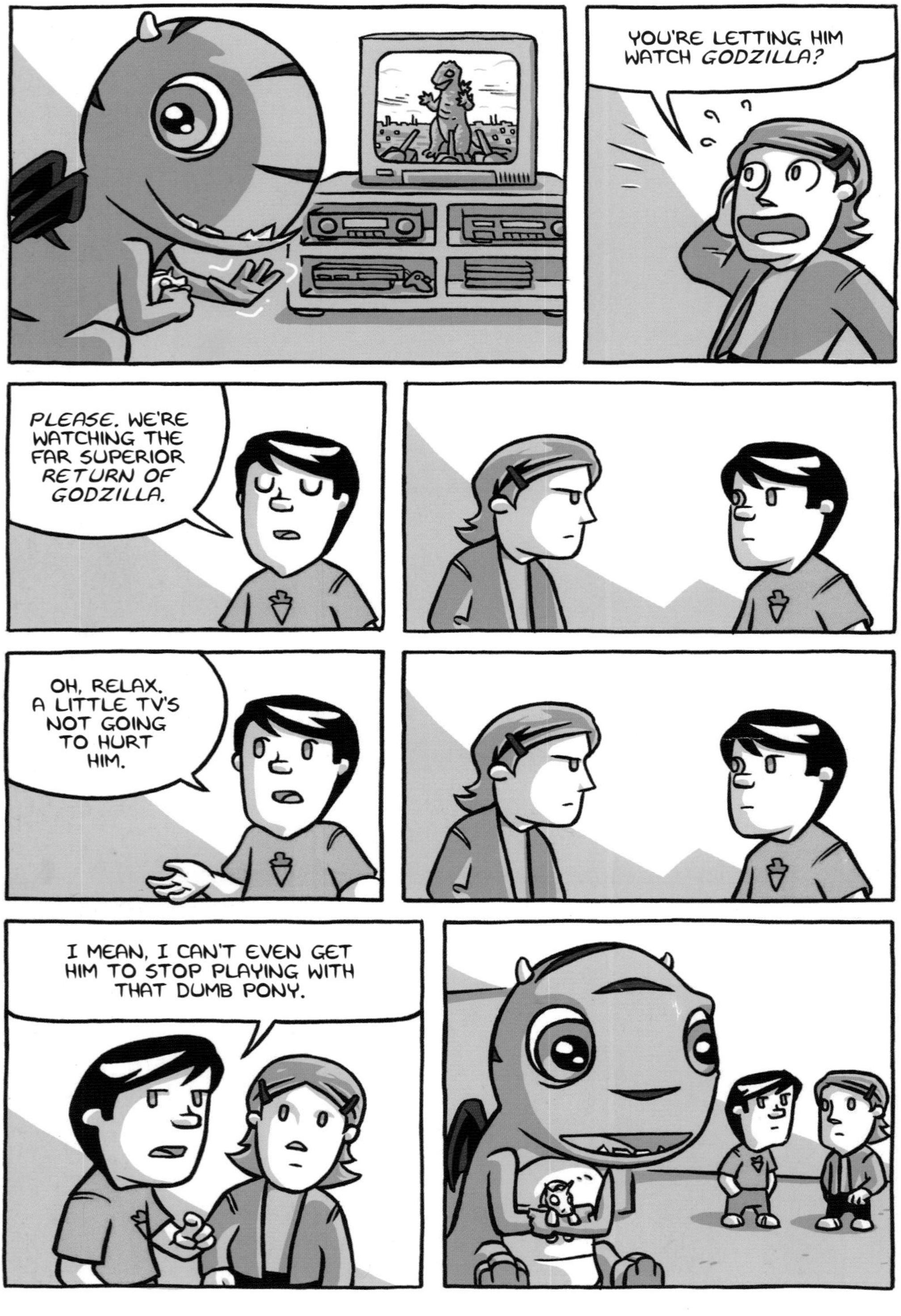
YOU'RE LETTING HIM WATCH *GODZILLA?*
PLEASE. WE'RE WATCHING THE FAR SUPERIOR *RETURN OF GODZILLA.*
OH, RELAX. A LITTLE TV'S NOT GOING TO HURT HIM.
I MEAN, I CAN'T EVEN GET HIM TO STOP PLAYING WITH THAT DUMB PONY.

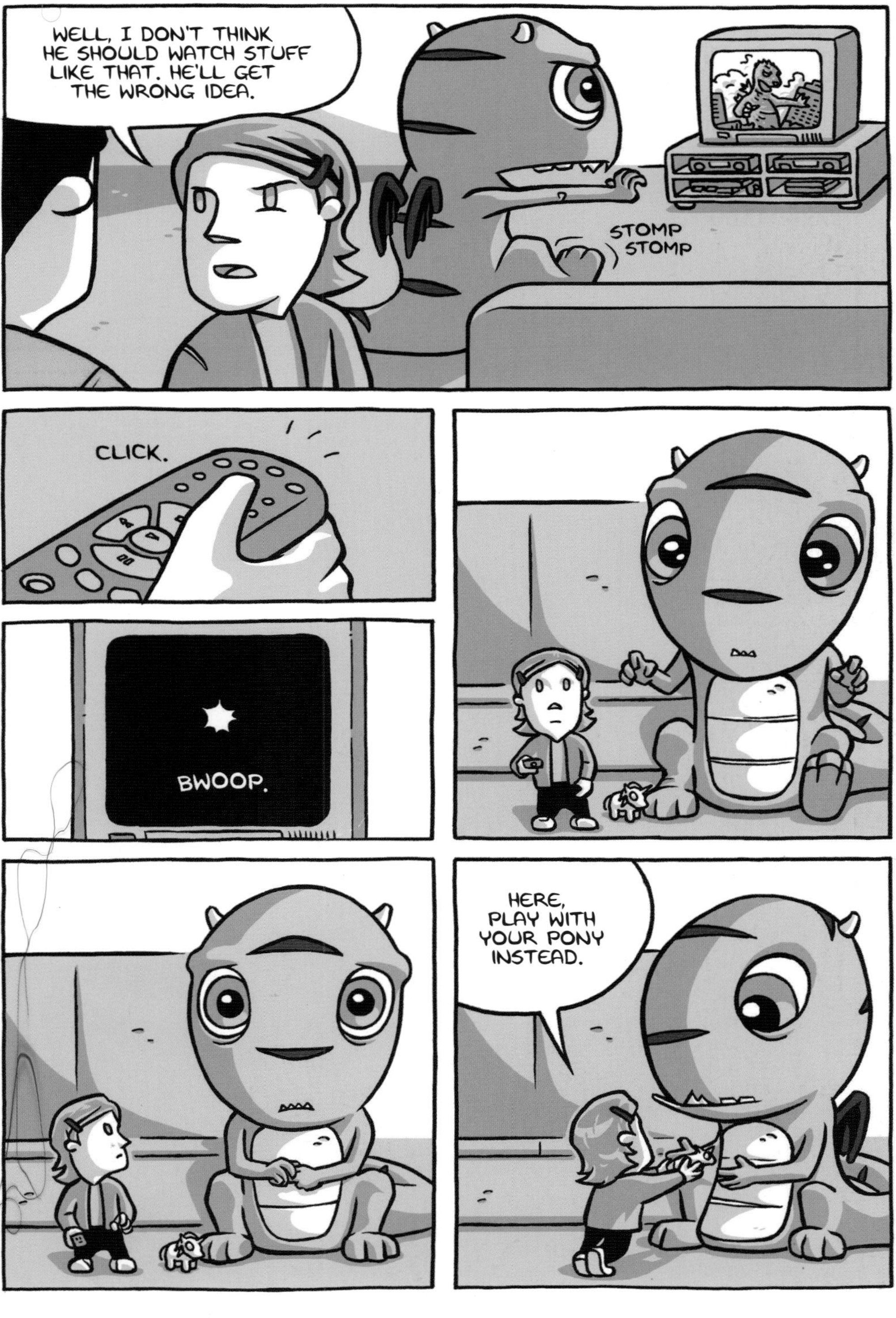
WELL, I DON'T THINK HE SHOULD WATCH STUFF LIKE THAT. HE'LL GET THE WRONG IDEA.
STOMP STOMP
CLICK.
BWOOP.
HERE, PLAY WITH YOUR PONY INSTEAD.

WHAT IS WRONG WITH YOU? MONSTERS AREN'T SUPPOSED TO PLAY WITH PONIES! THEY--

FWEE

UH, HANG ON JUST ONE SEC.

FWEEEE

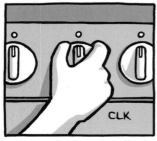

CLK

WHAT ARE YOU DOING?

JUST MAKING SOME CUP RAMEN. WANT SOME?

CUP RAMEN? WHAT'S THAT?

OH, IT'S JUST NOODLES, REALLY.

86

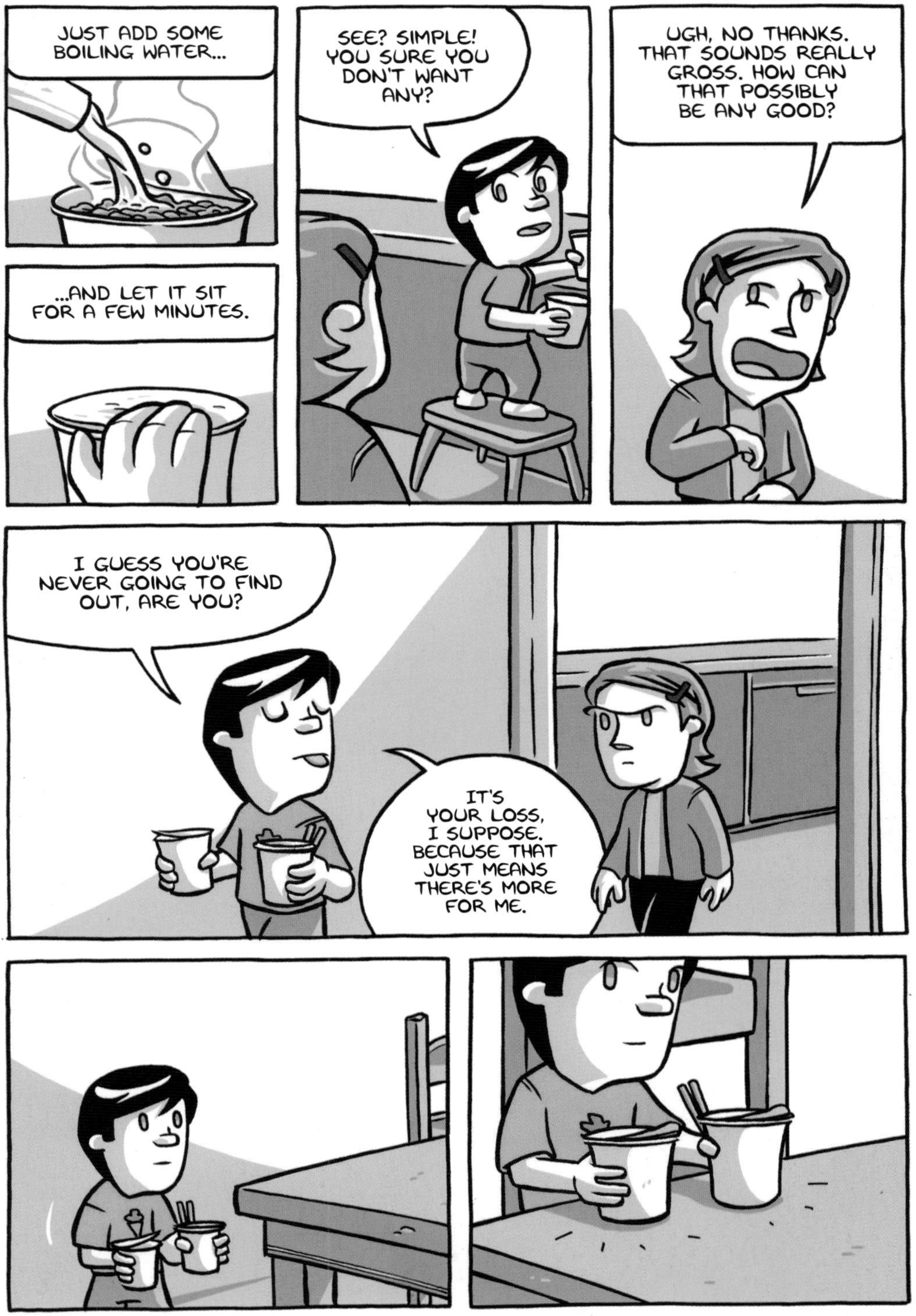
JUST ADD SOME BOILING WATER...
...AND LET IT SIT FOR A FEW MINUTES.
SEE? SIMPLE! YOU SURE YOU DON'T WANT ANY?
UGH, NO THANKS. THAT SOUNDS REALLY GROSS. HOW CAN THAT POSSIBLY BE ANY GOOD?
I GUESS YOU'RE NEVER GOING TO FIND OUT, ARE YOU?
IT'S YOUR LOSS, I SUPPOSE. BECAUSE THAT JUST MEANS THERE'S MORE FOR ME.

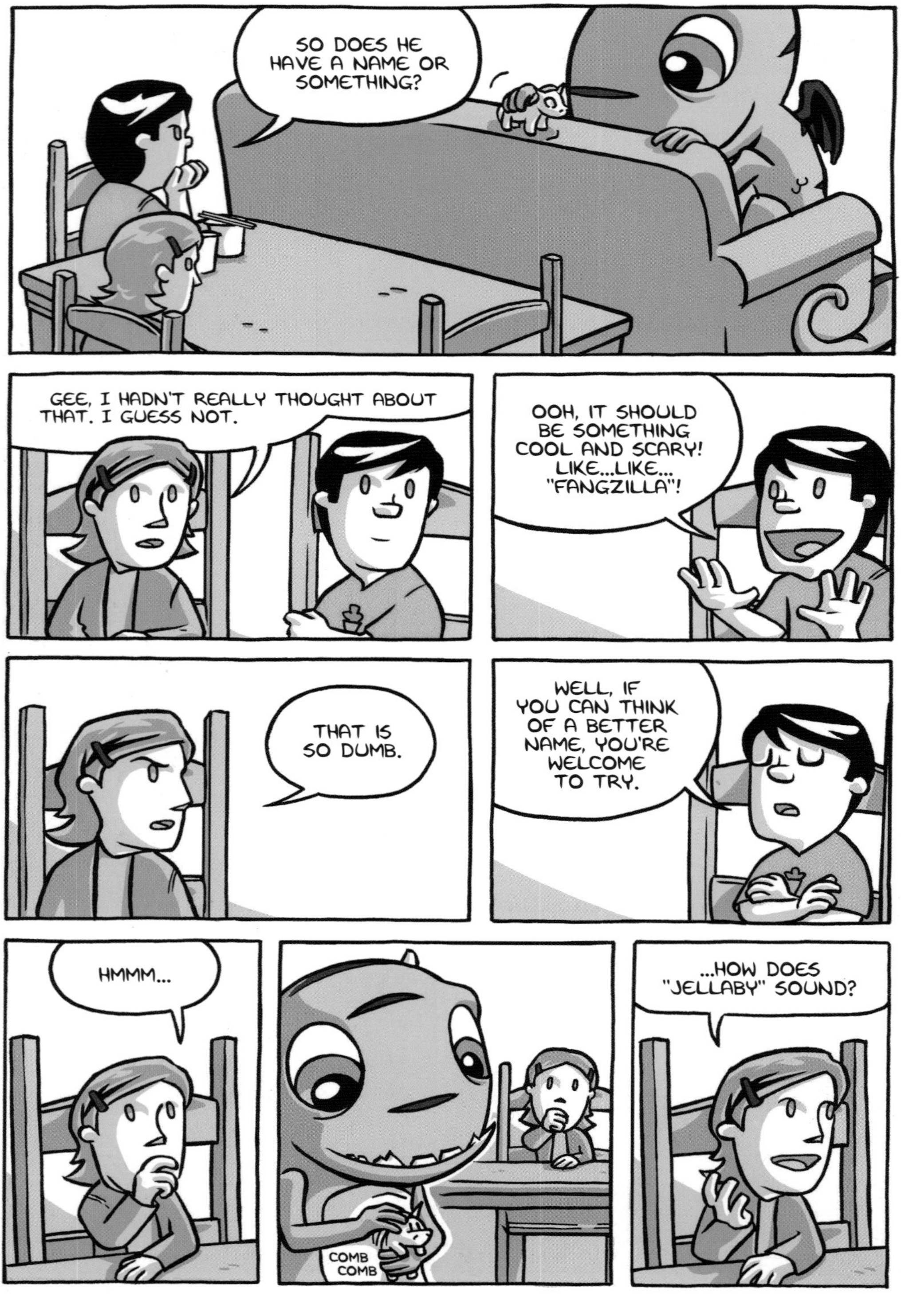
SO DOES HE HAVE A NAME OR SOMETHING?
GEE, I HADN'T REALLY THOUGHT ABOUT THAT. I GUESS NOT.
OOH, IT SHOULD BE SOMETHING COOL AND SCARY! LIKE...LIKE... "FANGZILLA"!
THAT IS SO DUMB.
WELL, IF YOU CAN THINK OF A BETTER NAME, YOU'RE WELCOME TO TRY.
HMMM...
COMB COMB
...HOW DOES "JELLABY" SOUND?

RIIIGHT. LIKE THAT'S ANY BETTER.

WELL WHY DON'T WE ASK HIM AND FIND OUT WHAT HE THINKS?

HEY, COME HERE FOR A SECOND!

?

SO WHICH OF THESE NAMES DO YOU LIKE MORE?

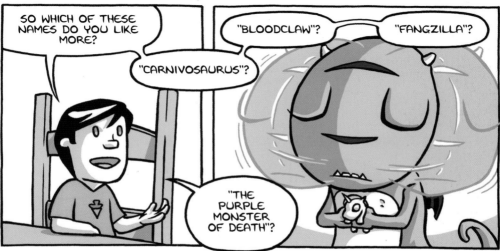

"BLOODCLAW"?

"FANGZILLA"?

"CARNIVOSAURUS"?

"THE PURPLE MONSTER OF DEATH"?

WHAT ABOUT "JELLABY"?

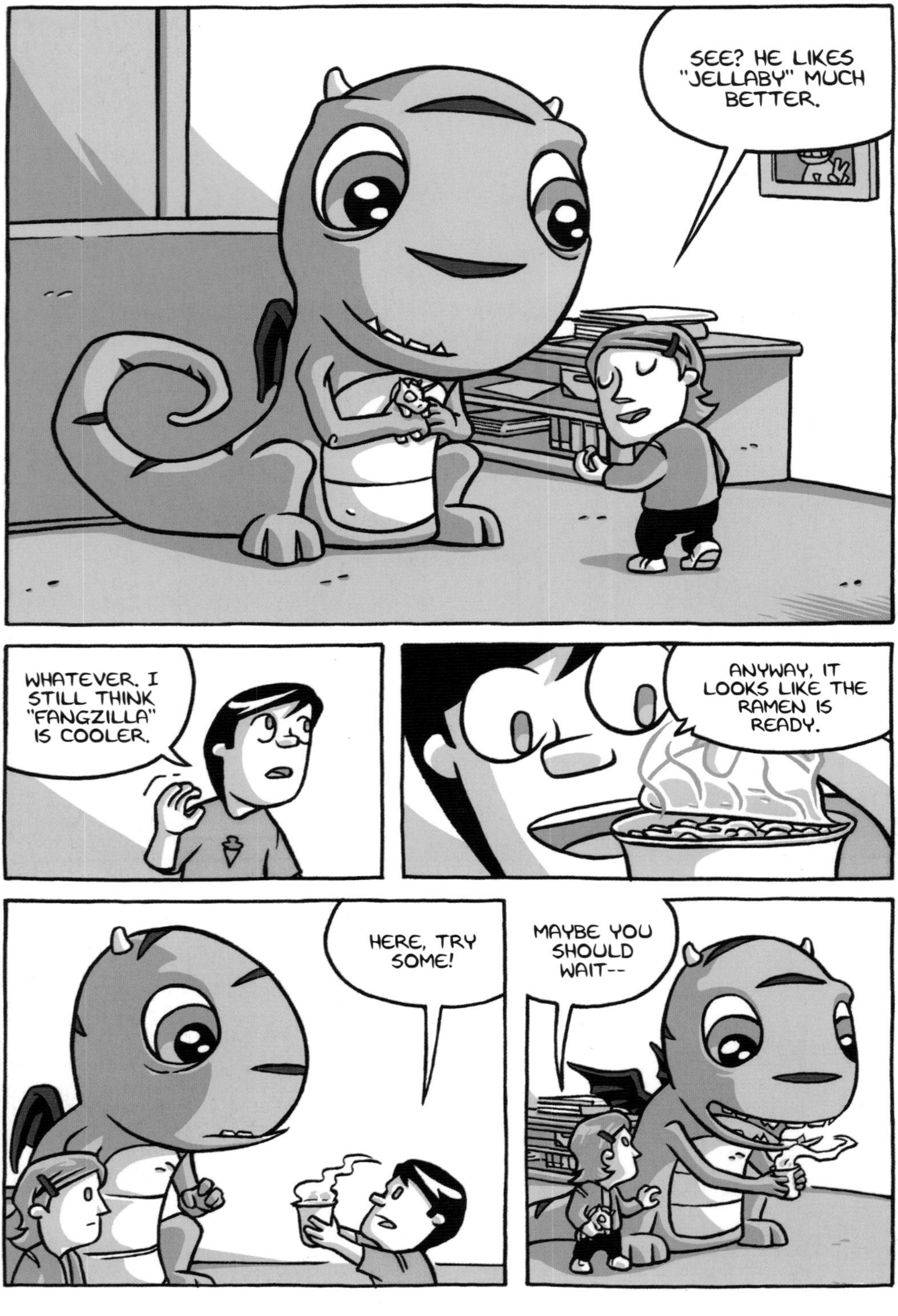
SEE? HE LIKES "JELLABY" MUCH BETTER.
WHATEVER. I STILL THINK "FANGZILLA" IS COOLER.
ANYWAY, IT LOOKS LIKE THE RAMEN IS READY.
HERE, TRY SOME!
MAYBE YOU SHOULD WAIT--

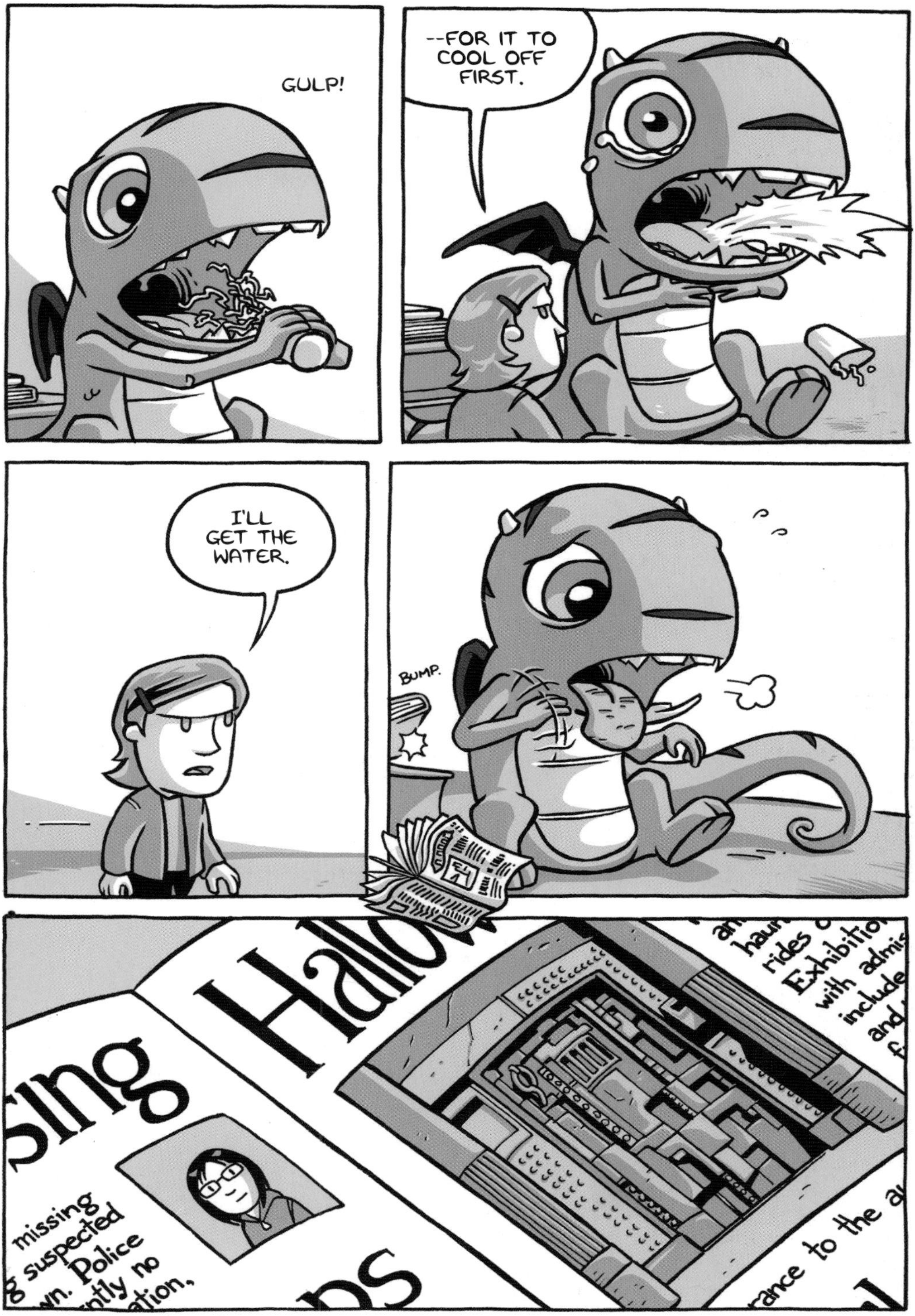
GULP!
--FOR IT TO COOL OFF FIRST.
I'LL GET THE WATER.
BUMP.
missing
g suspected
wn. Police
ntly no
ation.
rance to the a

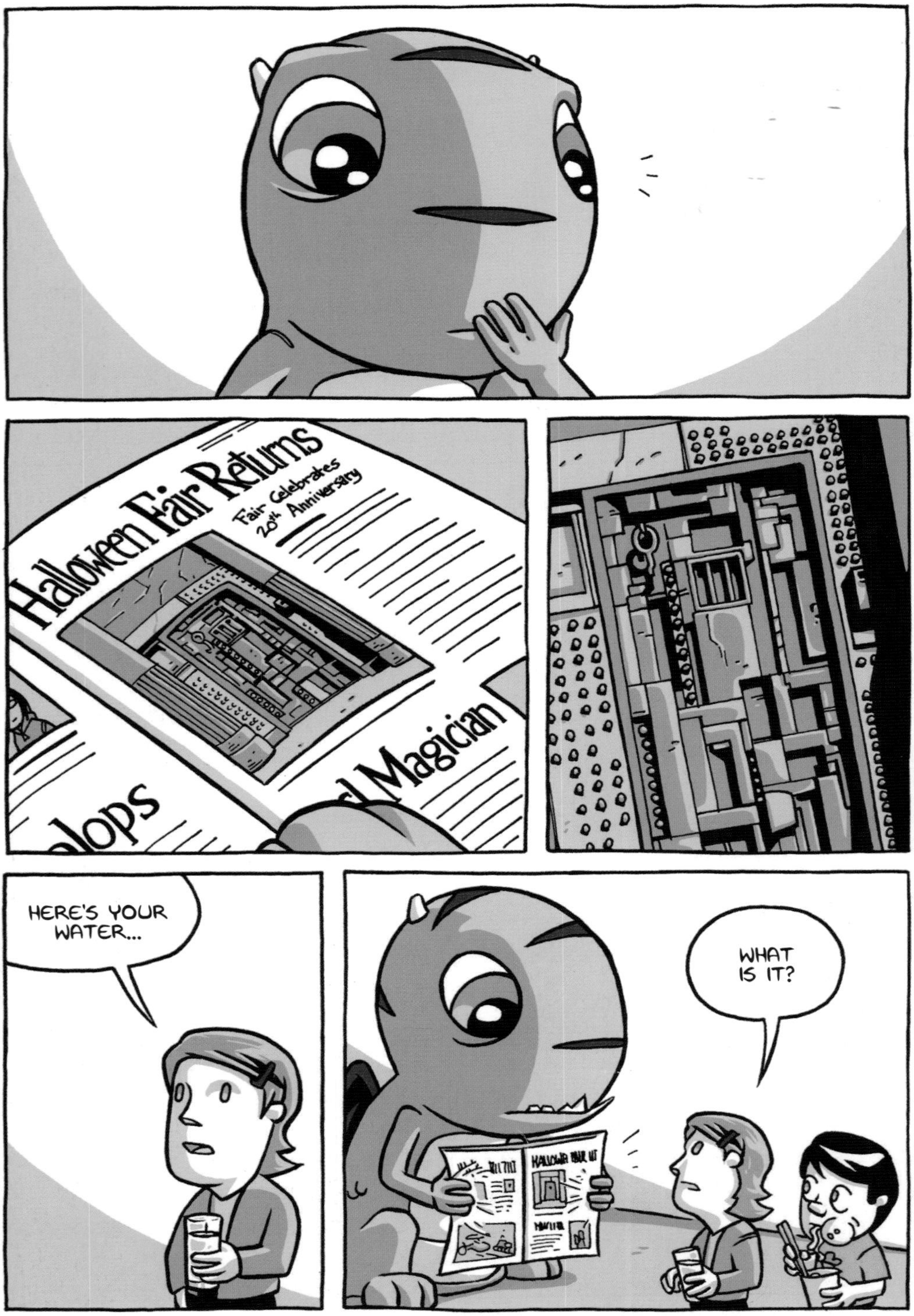
Halloween Fair Returns
Fair Celebrates 20th Anniversary
Magician
HERE'S YOUR WATER...
WHAT IS IT?

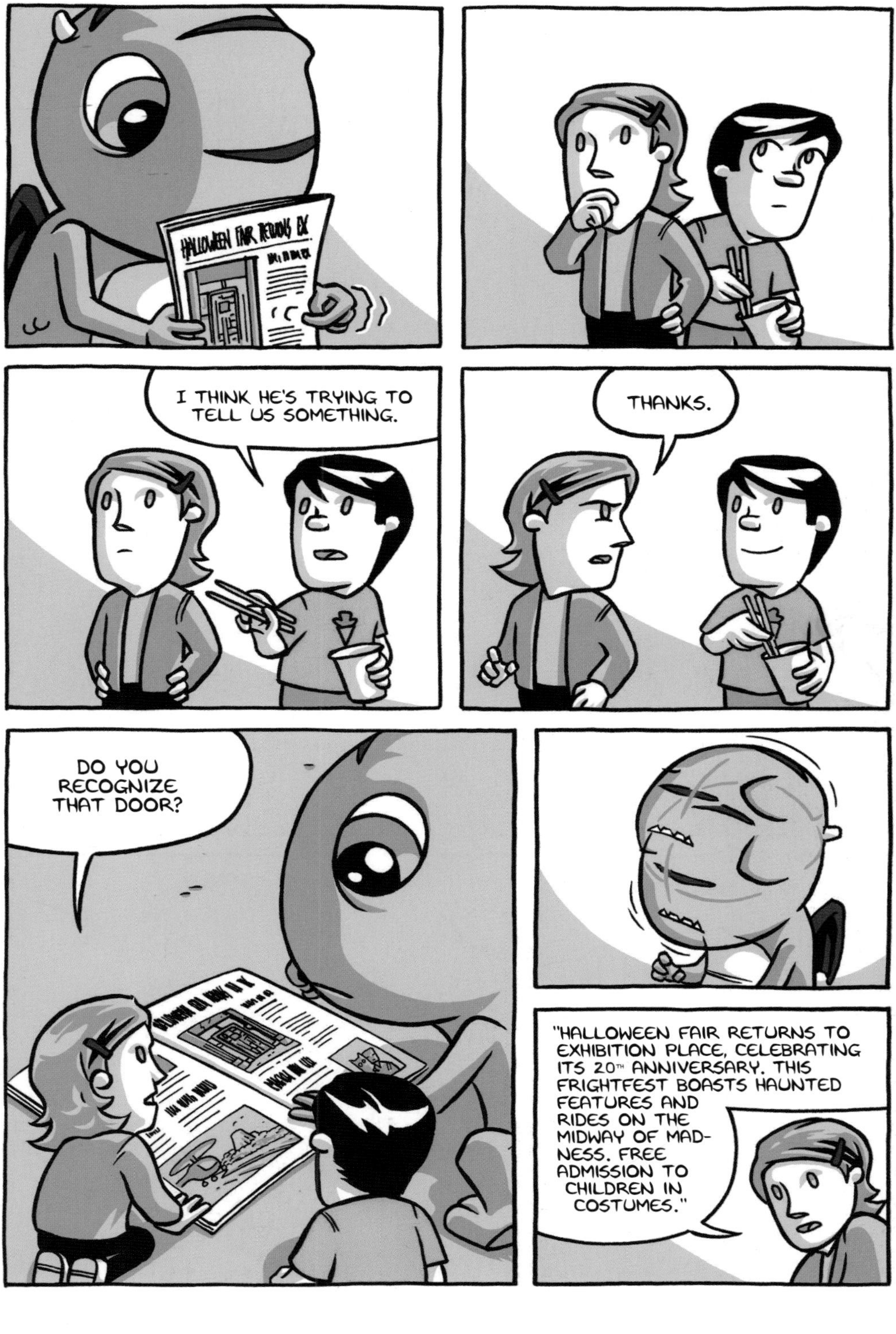
HALLOWEEN FAIR RETURNS EX
I THINK HE'S TRYING TO TELL US SOMETHING.
THANKS.
DO YOU RECOGNIZE THAT DOOR?
"HALLOWEEN FAIR RETURNS TO EXHIBITION PLACE, CELEBRATING ITS 20TH ANNIVERSARY. THIS FRIGHTFEST BOASTS HAUNTED FEATURES AND RIDES ON THE MIDWAY OF MADNESS. FREE ADMISSION TO CHILDREN IN COSTUMES."

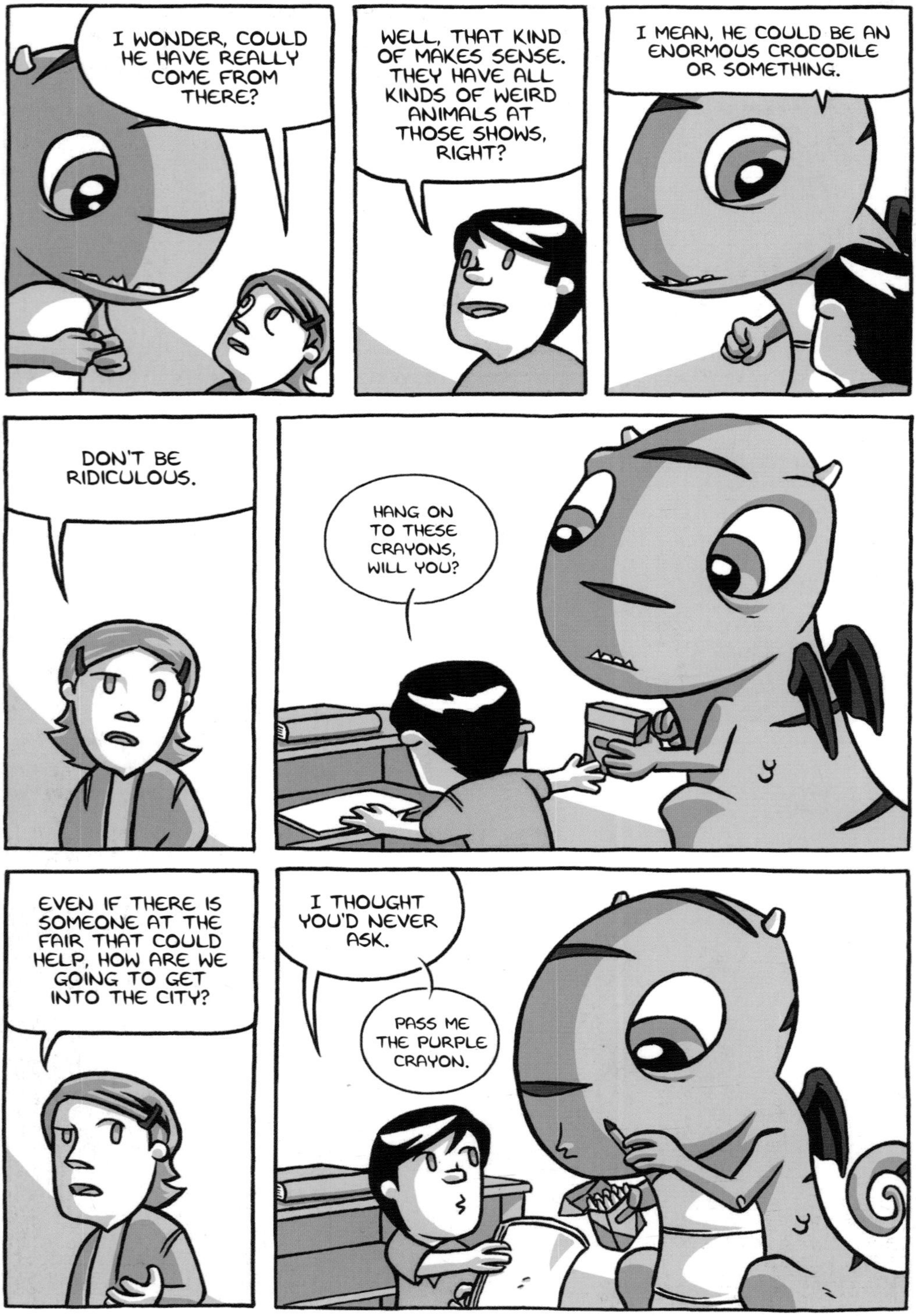
I WONDER, COULD HE HAVE REALLY COME FROM THERE?
WELL, THAT KIND OF MAKES SENSE. THEY HAVE ALL KINDS OF WEIRD ANIMALS AT THOSE SHOWS, RIGHT?
I MEAN, HE COULD BE AN ENORMOUS CROCODILE OR SOMETHING.
DON'T BE RIDICULOUS.
HANG ON TO THESE CRAYONS, WILL YOU?
EVEN IF THERE IS SOMEONE AT THE FAIR THAT COULD HELP, HOW ARE WE GOING TO GET INTO THE CITY?
I THOUGHT YOU'D NEVER ASK.
PASS ME THE PURPLE CRAYON.

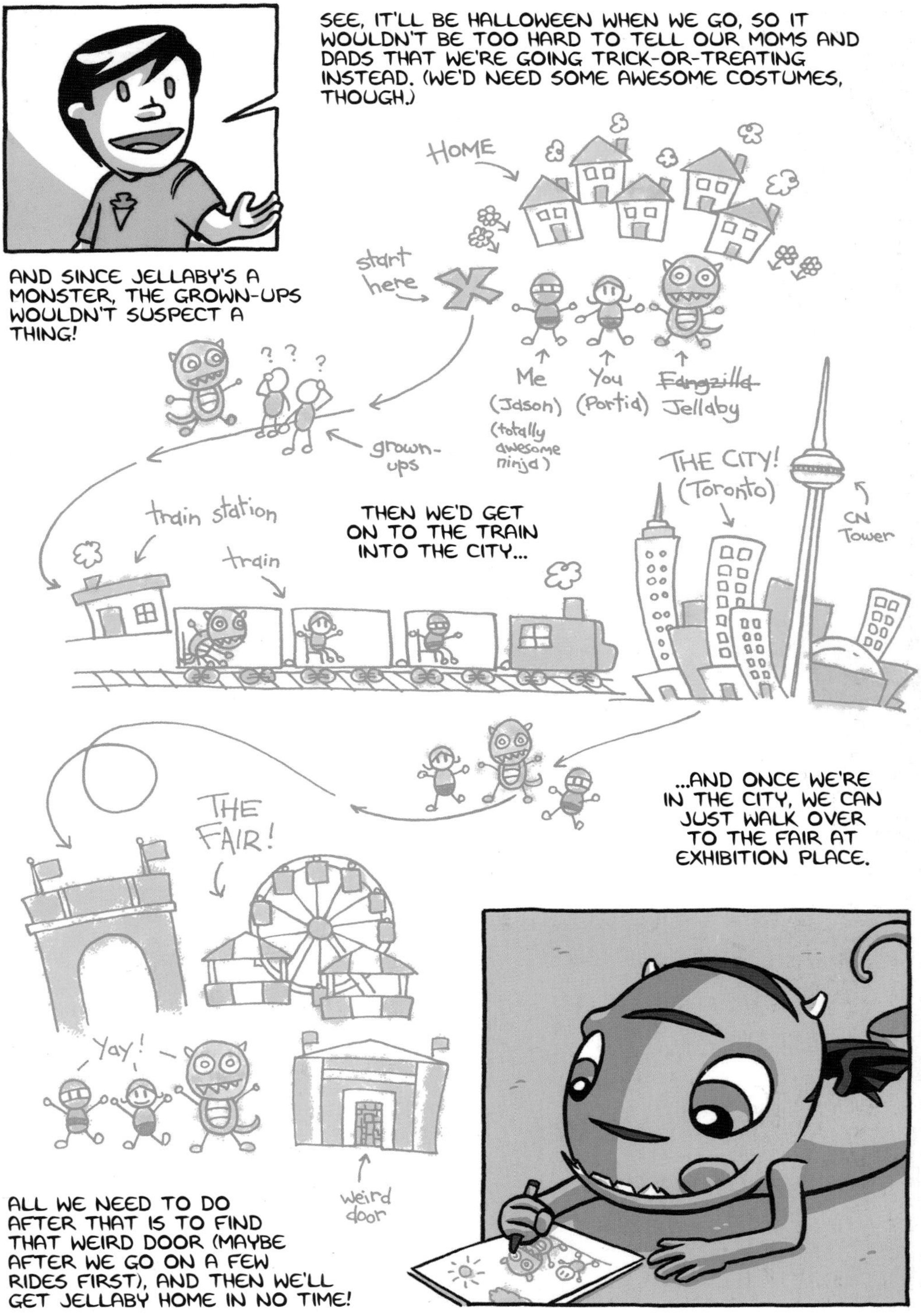

SEE, IT'LL BE HALLOWEEN WHEN WE GO, SO IT WOULDN'T BE TOO HARD TO TELL OUR MOMS AND DADS THAT WE'RE GOING TRICK-OR-TREATING INSTEAD. (WE'D NEED SOME AWESOME COSTUMES, THOUGH.)
HOME
AND SINCE JELLABY'S A MONSTER, THE GROWN-UPS WOULDN'T SUSPECT A THING!
start here
Me (Jason) (totally awesome ninja)
You (Portia)
Fangzilla Jellaby
? ? ?
grown-ups
THE CITY! (Toronto)
CN Tower
train station
train
THEN WE'D GET ON TO THE TRAIN INTO THE CITY...
...AND ONCE WE'RE IN THE CITY, WE CAN JUST WALK OVER TO THE FAIR AT EXHIBITION PLACE.
THE FAIR!
Yay!
weird door
ALL WE NEED TO DO AFTER THAT IS TO FIND THAT WEIRD DOOR (MAYBE AFTER WE GO ON A FEW RIDES FIRST), AND THEN WE'LL GET JELLABY HOME IN NO TIME!

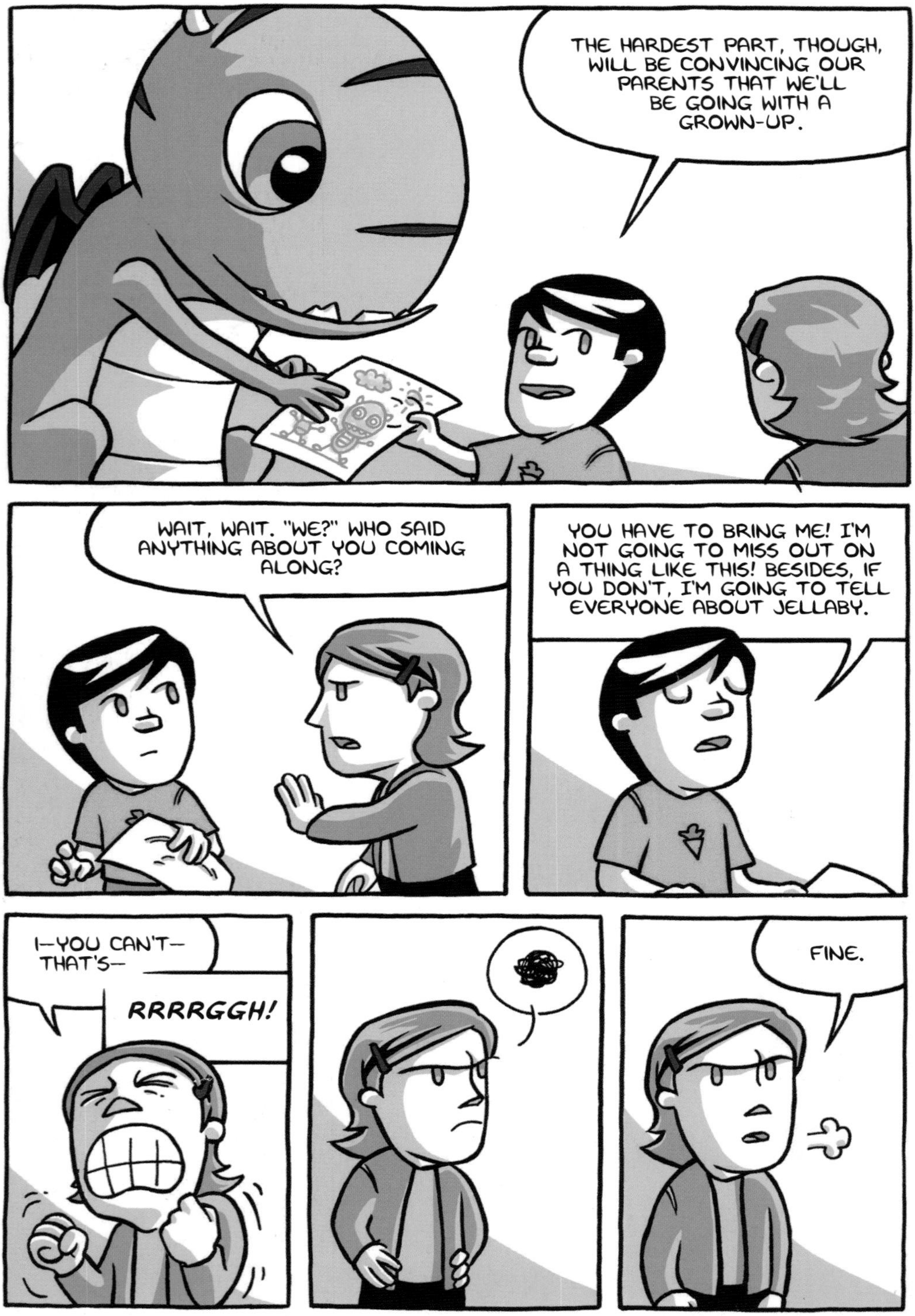

THE HARDEST PART, THOUGH, WILL BE CONVINCING OUR PARENTS THAT WE'LL BE GOING WITH A GROWN-UP.
WAIT, WAIT. "WE?" WHO SAID ANYTHING ABOUT YOU COMING ALONG?
YOU HAVE TO BRING ME! I'M NOT GOING TO MISS OUT ON A THING LIKE THIS! BESIDES, IF YOU DON'T, I'M GOING TO TELL EVERYONE ABOUT JELLABY.
I—YOU CAN'T— THAT'S—
RRRRGGH!
FINE.

SNF
SNF

DON'T EAT THE CRAYONS.

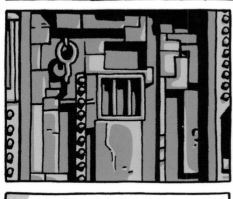

HMM?

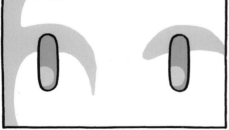

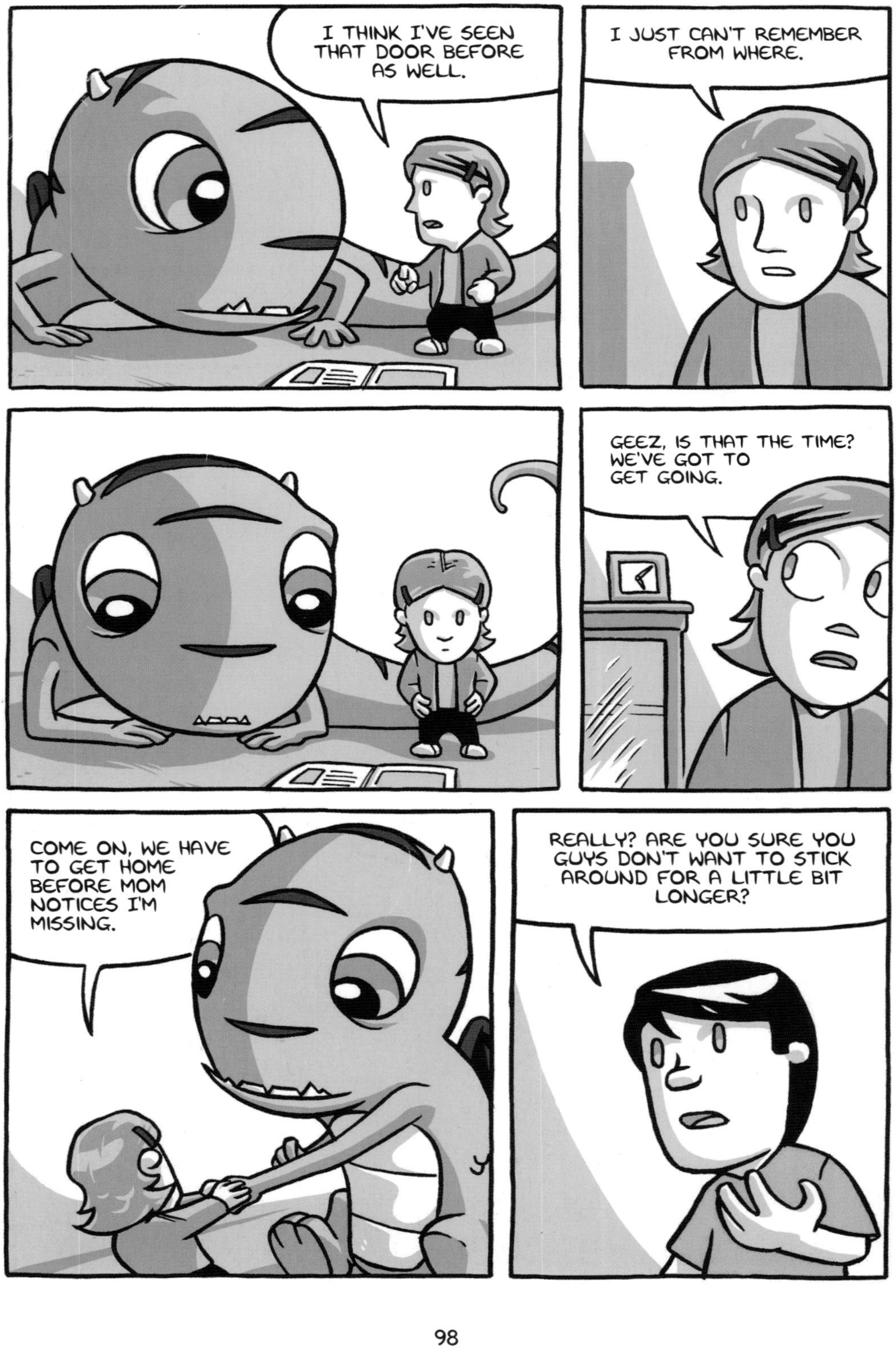

I THINK I'VE SEEN THAT DOOR BEFORE AS WELL.
I JUST CAN'T REMEMBER FROM WHERE.
GEEZ, IS THAT THE TIME? WE'VE GOT TO GET GOING.
COME ON, WE HAVE TO GET HOME BEFORE MOM NOTICES I'M MISSING.
REALLY? ARE YOU SURE YOU GUYS DON'T WANT TO STICK AROUND FOR A LITTLE BIT LONGER?

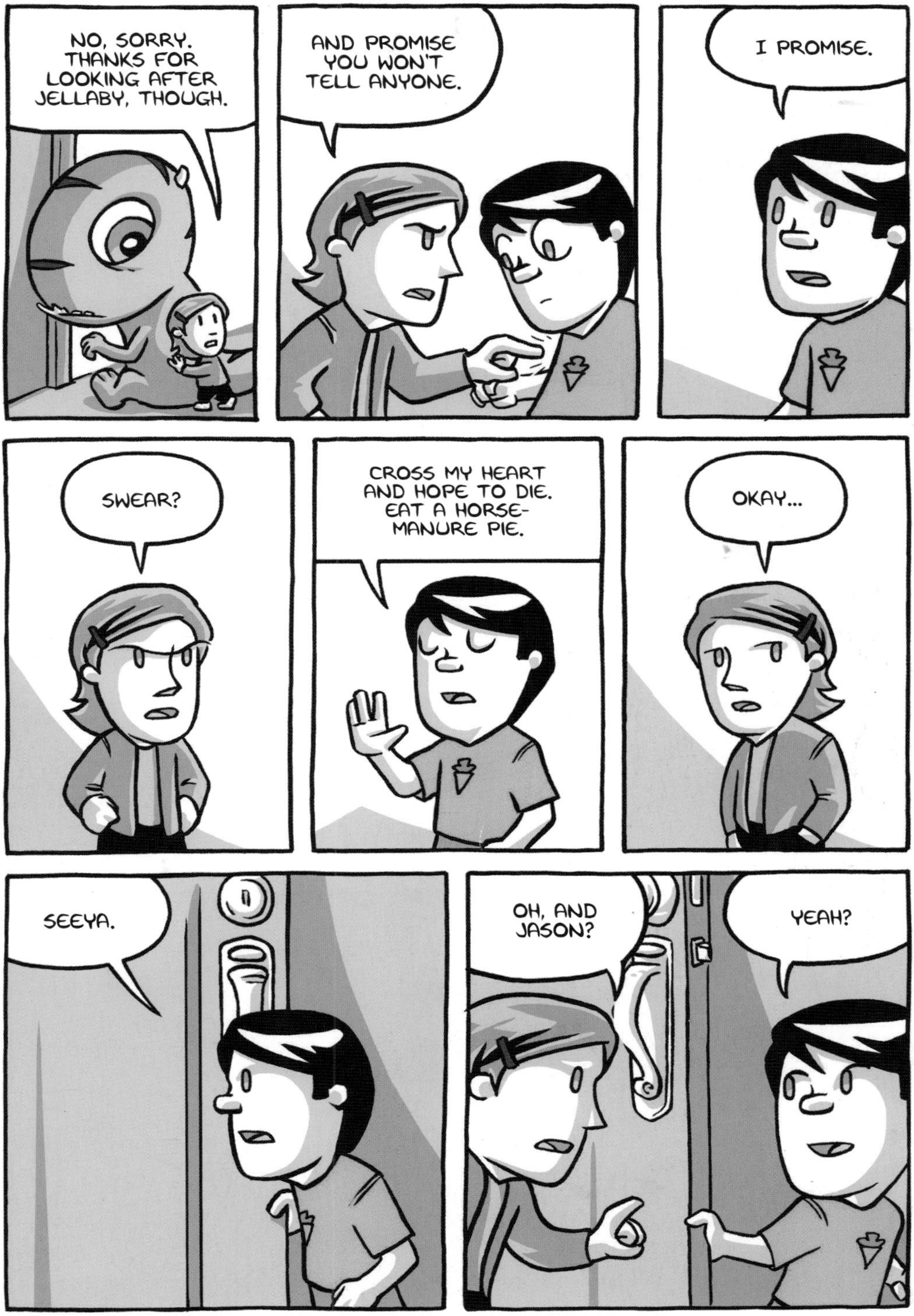
NO, SORRY. THANKS FOR LOOKING AFTER JELLABY, THOUGH.
AND PROMISE YOU WON'T TELL ANYONE.
I PROMISE.
SWEAR?
CROSS MY HEART AND HOPE TO DIE. EAT A HORSE-MANURE PIE.
OKAY...
SEEYA.
OH, AND JASON?
YEAH?

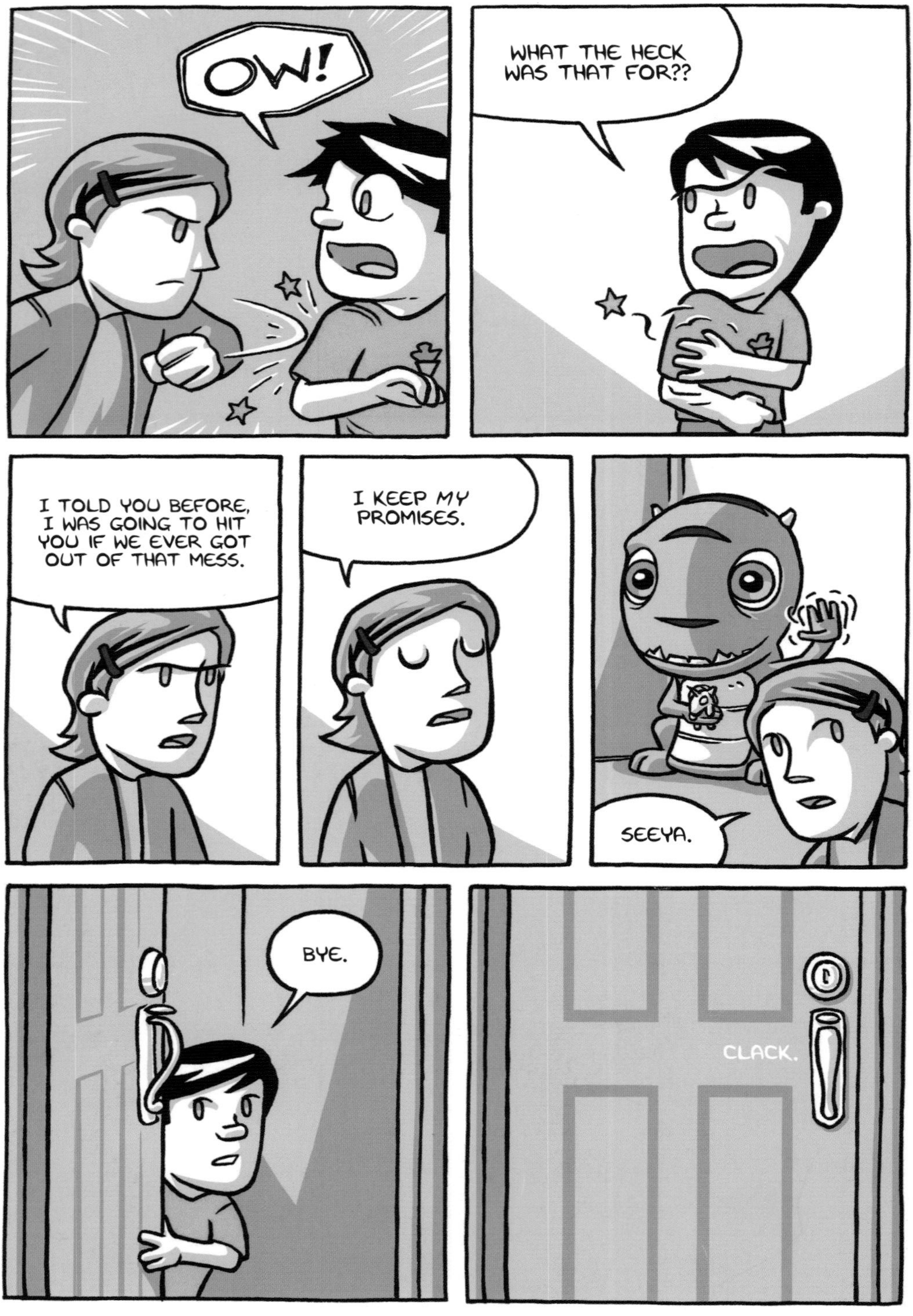
OW!
WHAT THE HECK WAS THAT FOR??
I TOLD YOU BEFORE, I WAS GOING TO HIT YOU IF WE EVER GOT OUT OF THAT MESS.
I KEEP MY PROMISES.
SEEYA.
BYE.
CLACK.

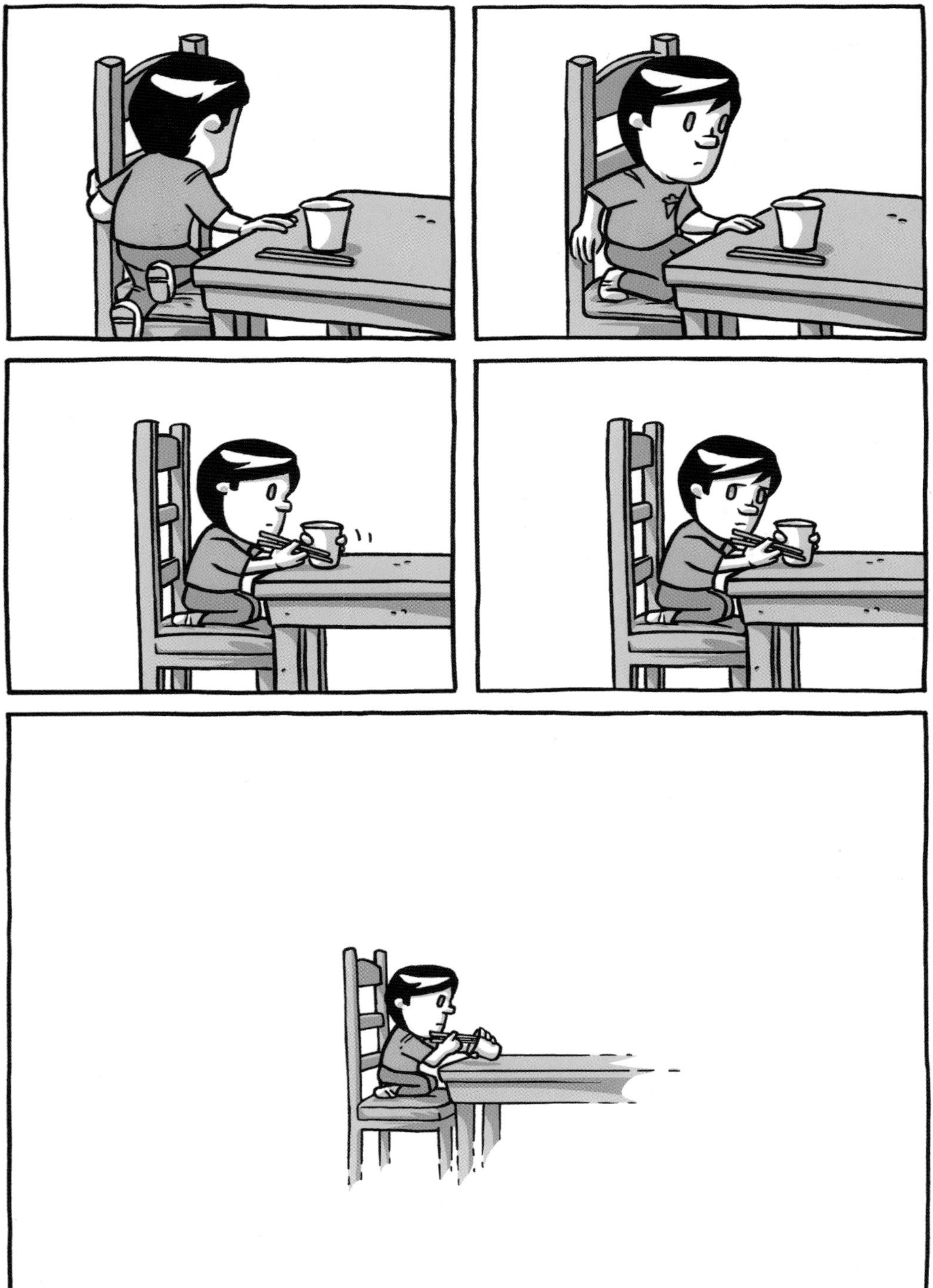

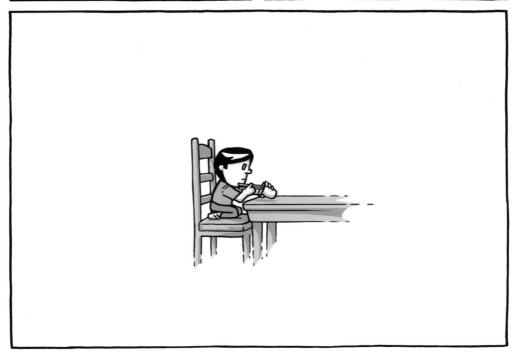

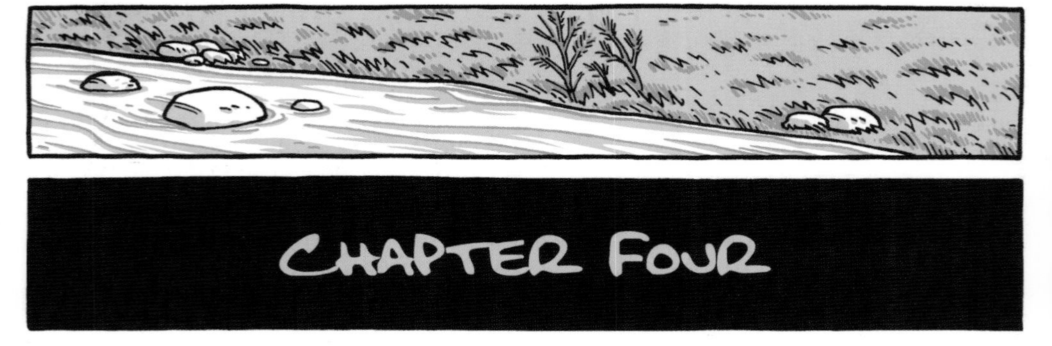

CHAPTER FOUR

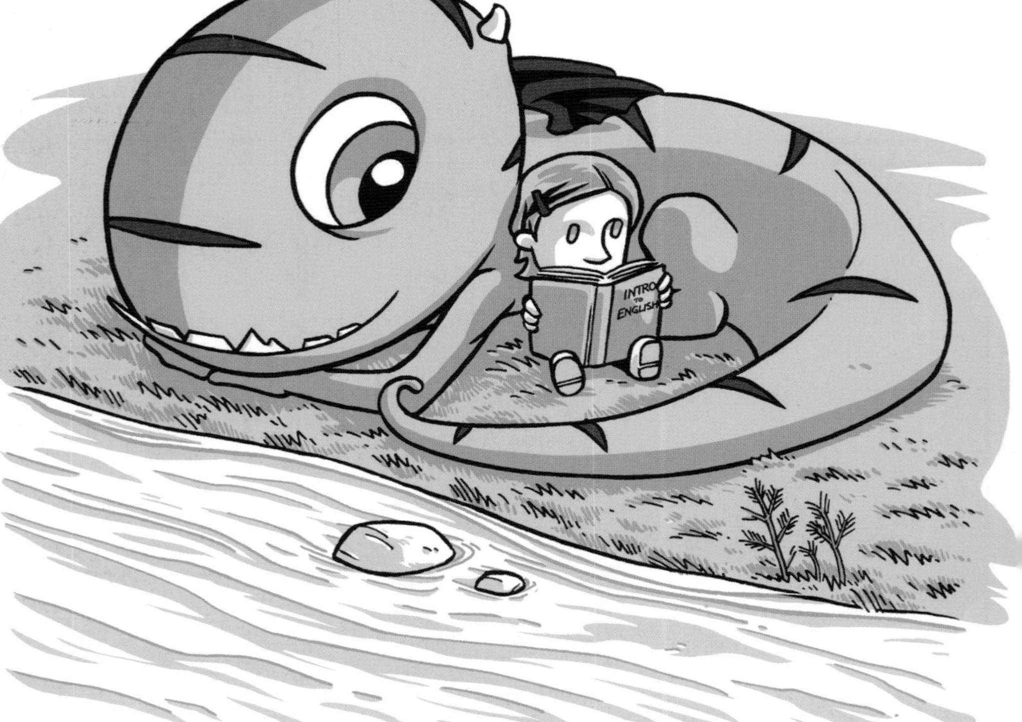
INTRO TO ENGLISH

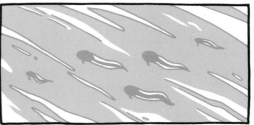

THAT'S ENOUGH FOR TODAY, I GUESS.

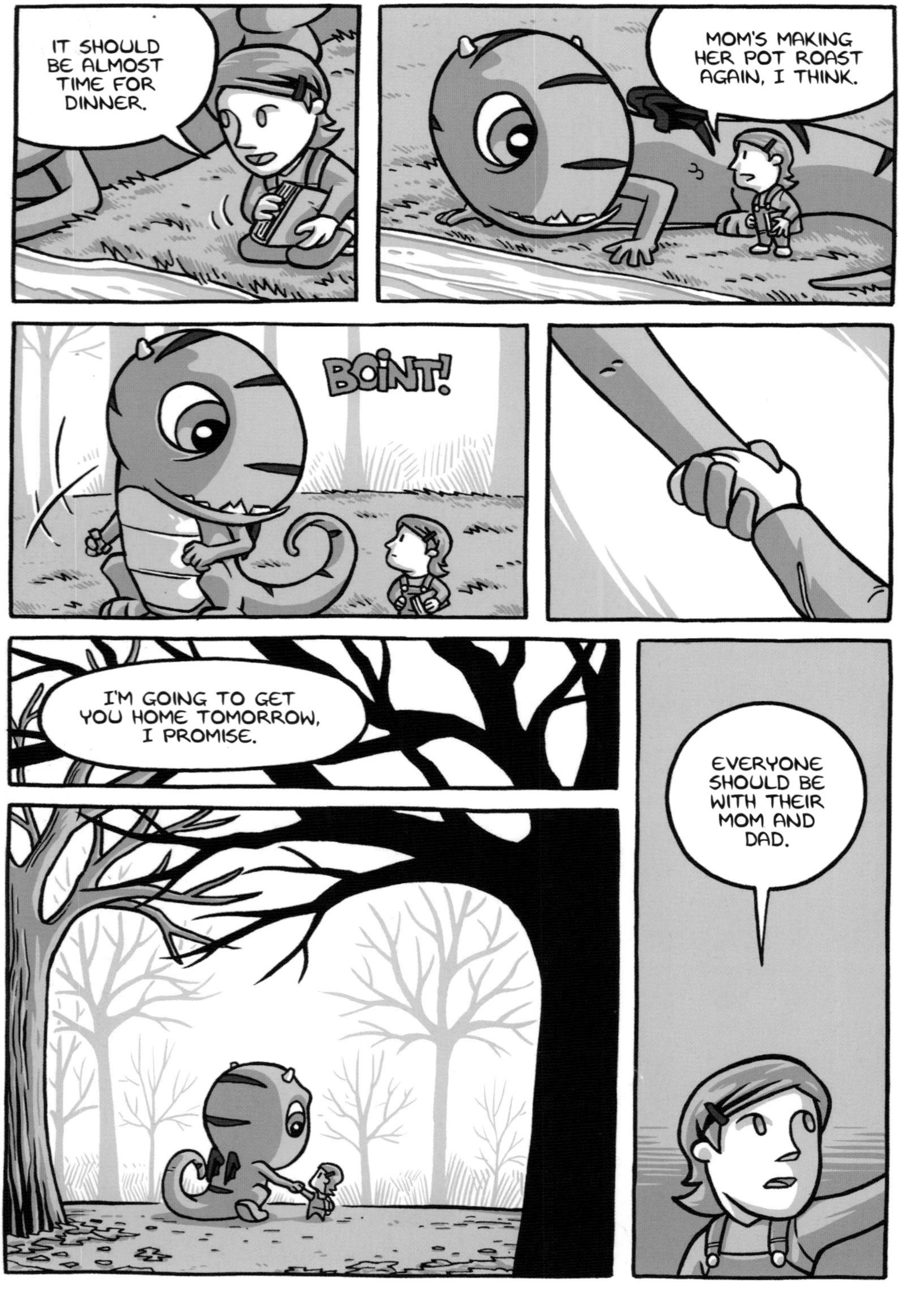
IT SHOULD BE ALMOST TIME FOR DINNER.
MOM'S MAKING HER POT ROAST AGAIN, I THINK.
BOINT!
I'M GOING TO GET YOU HOME TOMORROW, I PROMISE.
EVERYONE SHOULD BE WITH THEIR MOM AND DAD.

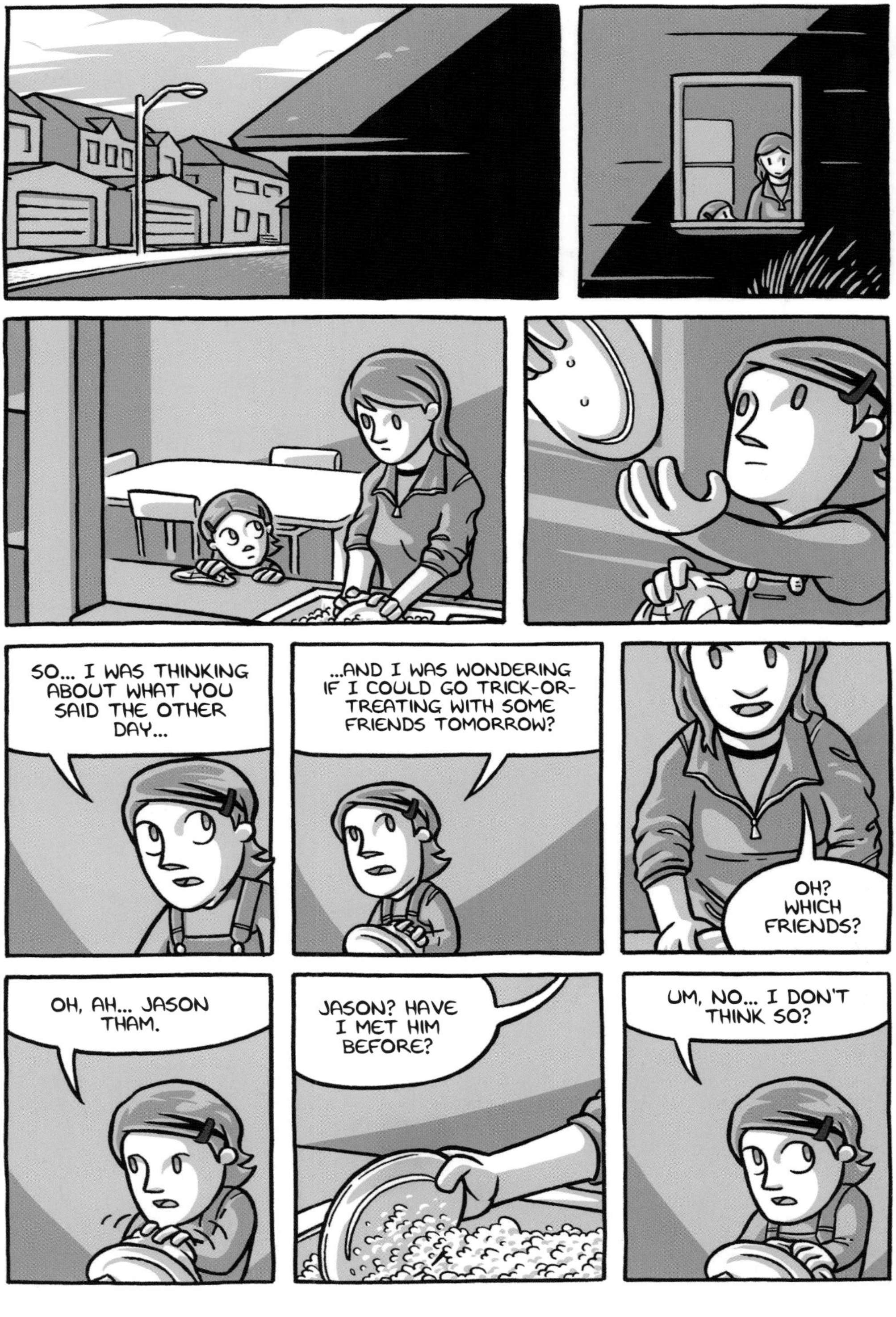
SO... I WAS THINKING ABOUT WHAT YOU SAID THE OTHER DAY...
...AND I WAS WONDERING IF I COULD GO TRICK-OR-TREATING WITH SOME FRIENDS TOMORROW?
OH? WHICH FRIENDS?
OH, AH... JASON THAM.
JASON? HAVE I MET HIM BEFORE?
UM, NO... I DON'T THINK SO?

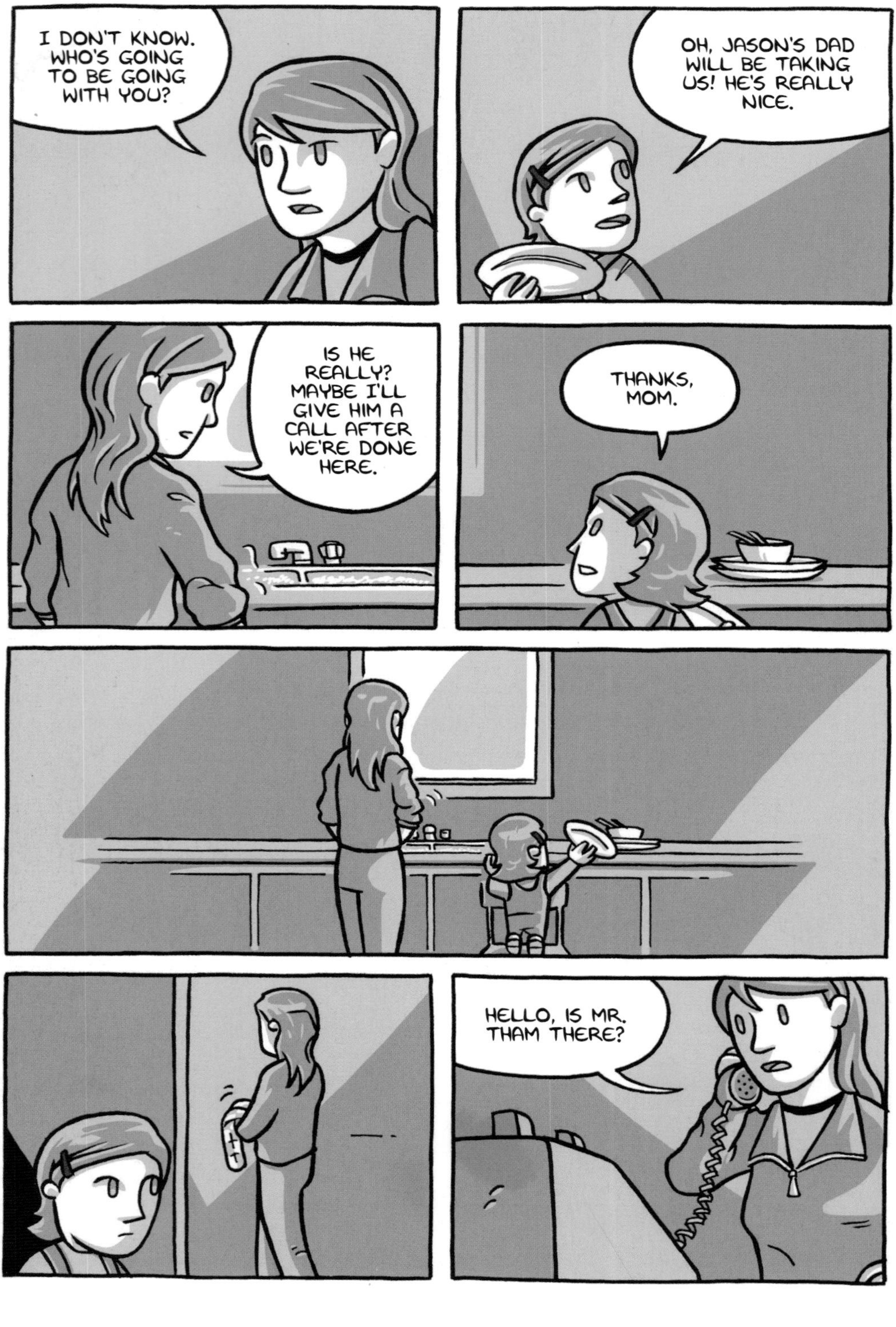
I DON'T KNOW. WHO'S GOING TO BE GOING WITH YOU?
OH, JASON'S DAD WILL BE TAKING US! HE'S REALLY NICE.
IS HE REALLY? MAYBE I'LL GIVE HIM A CALL AFTER WE'RE DONE HERE.
THANKS, MOM.
HELLO, IS MR. THAM THERE?

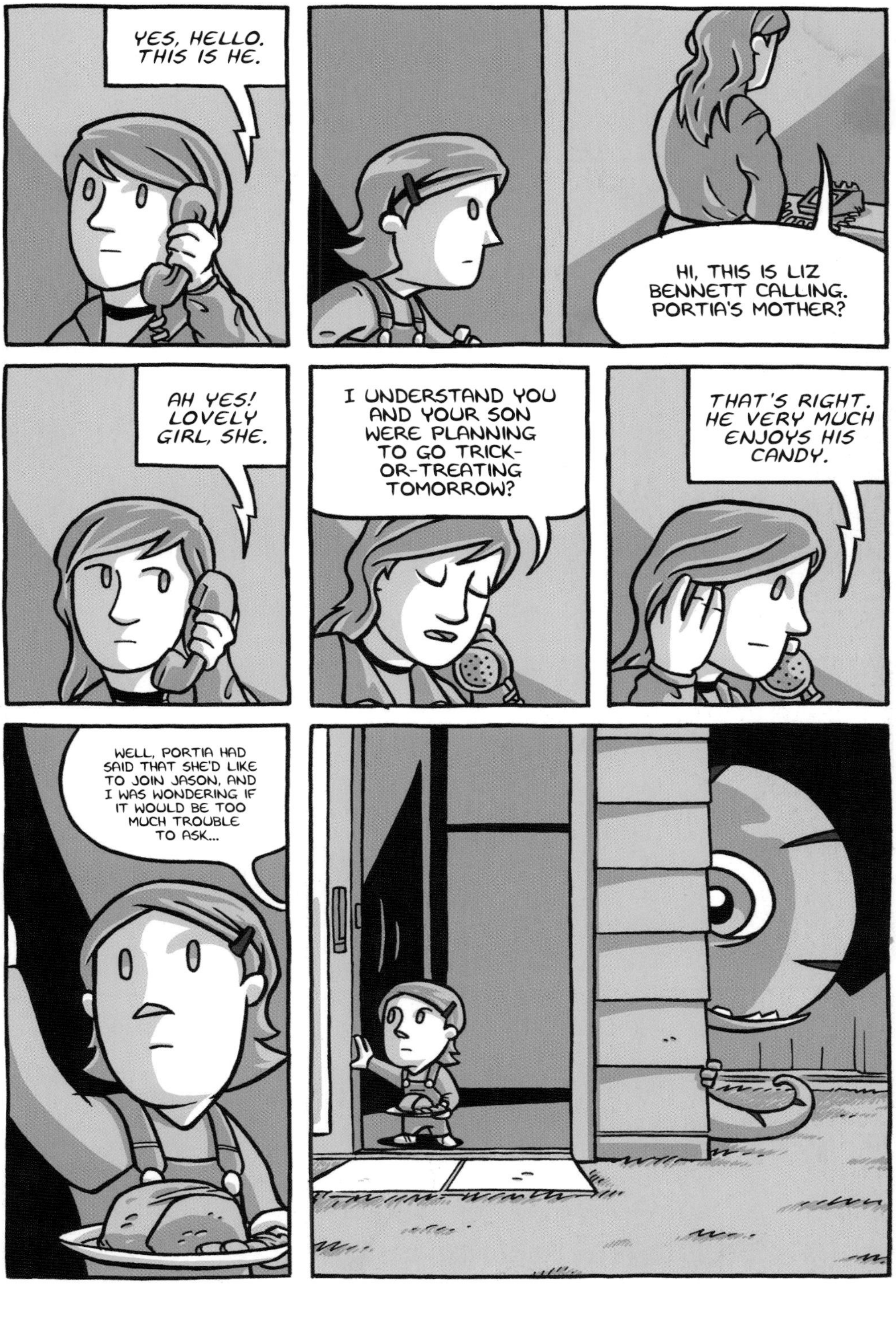
YES, HELLO. THIS IS HE.
HI, THIS IS LIZ BENNETT CALLING. PORTIA'S MOTHER?
AH YES! LOVELY GIRL, SHE.
I UNDERSTAND YOU AND YOUR SON WERE PLANNING TO GO TRICK-OR-TREATING TOMORROW?
THAT'S RIGHT. HE VERY MUCH ENJOYS HIS CANDY.
WELL, PORTIA HAD SAID THAT SHE'D LIKE TO JOIN JASON, AND I WAS WONDERING IF IT WOULD BE TOO MUCH TROUBLE TO ASK...

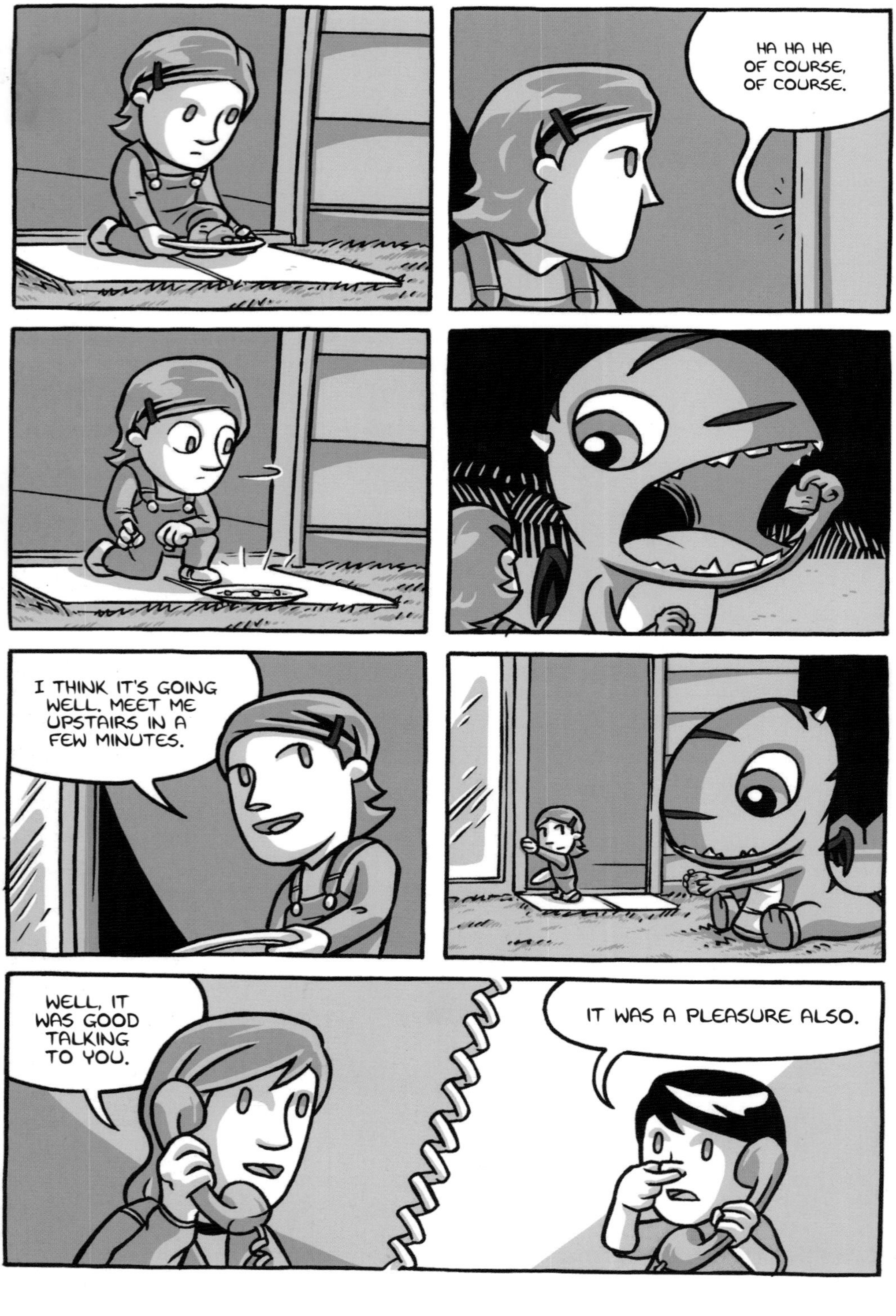
HA HA HA
OF COURSE,
OF COURSE.
I THINK IT'S GOING WELL. MEET ME UPSTAIRS IN A FEW MINUTES.
WELL, IT WAS GOOD TALKING TO YOU.
IT WAS A PLEASURE ALSO.

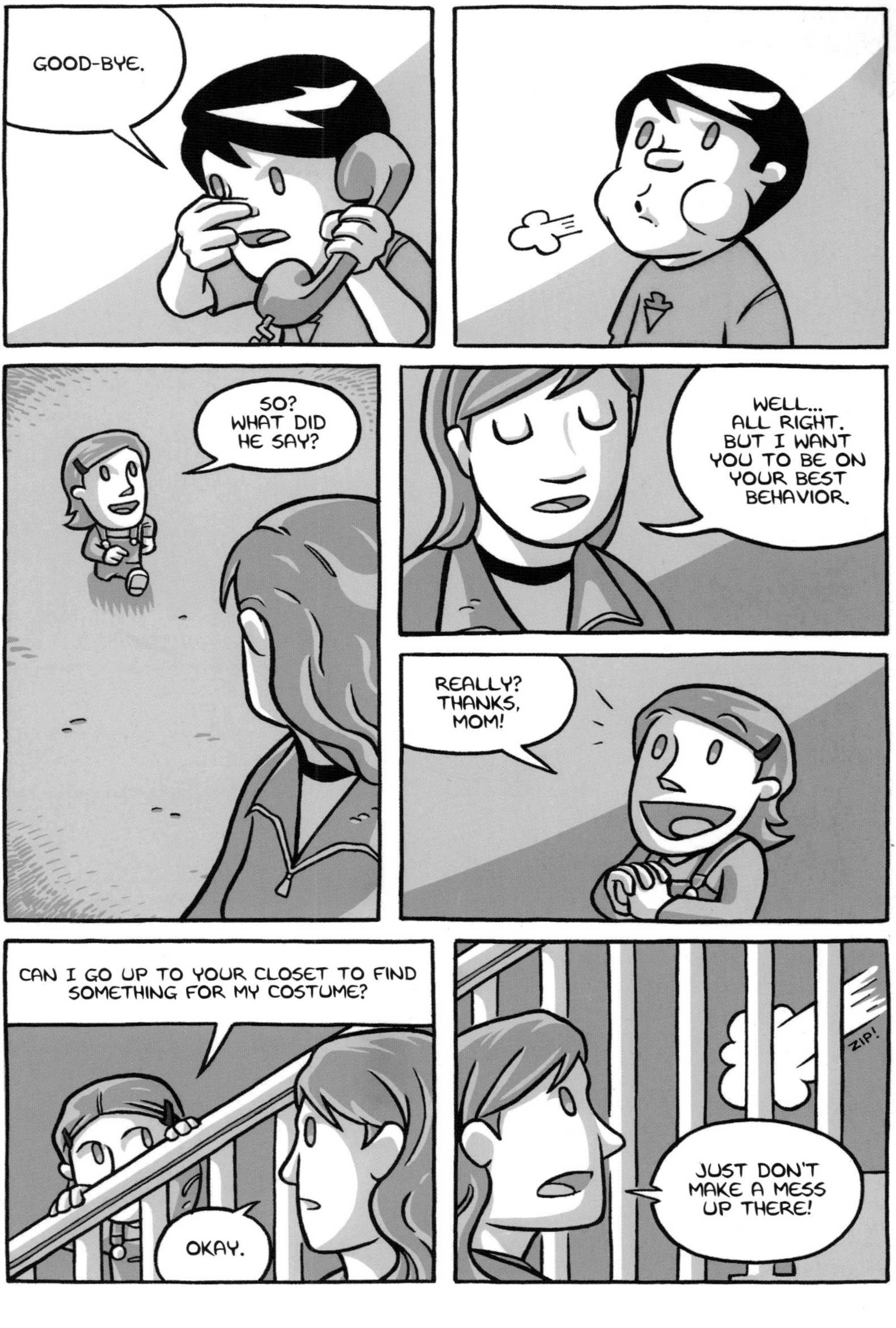
GOOD-BYE.
SO? WHAT DID HE SAY?
WELL... ALL RIGHT. BUT I WANT YOU TO BE ON YOUR BEST BEHAVIOR.
REALLY? THANKS, MOM!
CAN I GO UP TO YOUR CLOSET TO FIND SOMETHING FOR MY COSTUME?
OKAY.
ZIP!
JUST DON'T MAKE A MESS UP THERE!

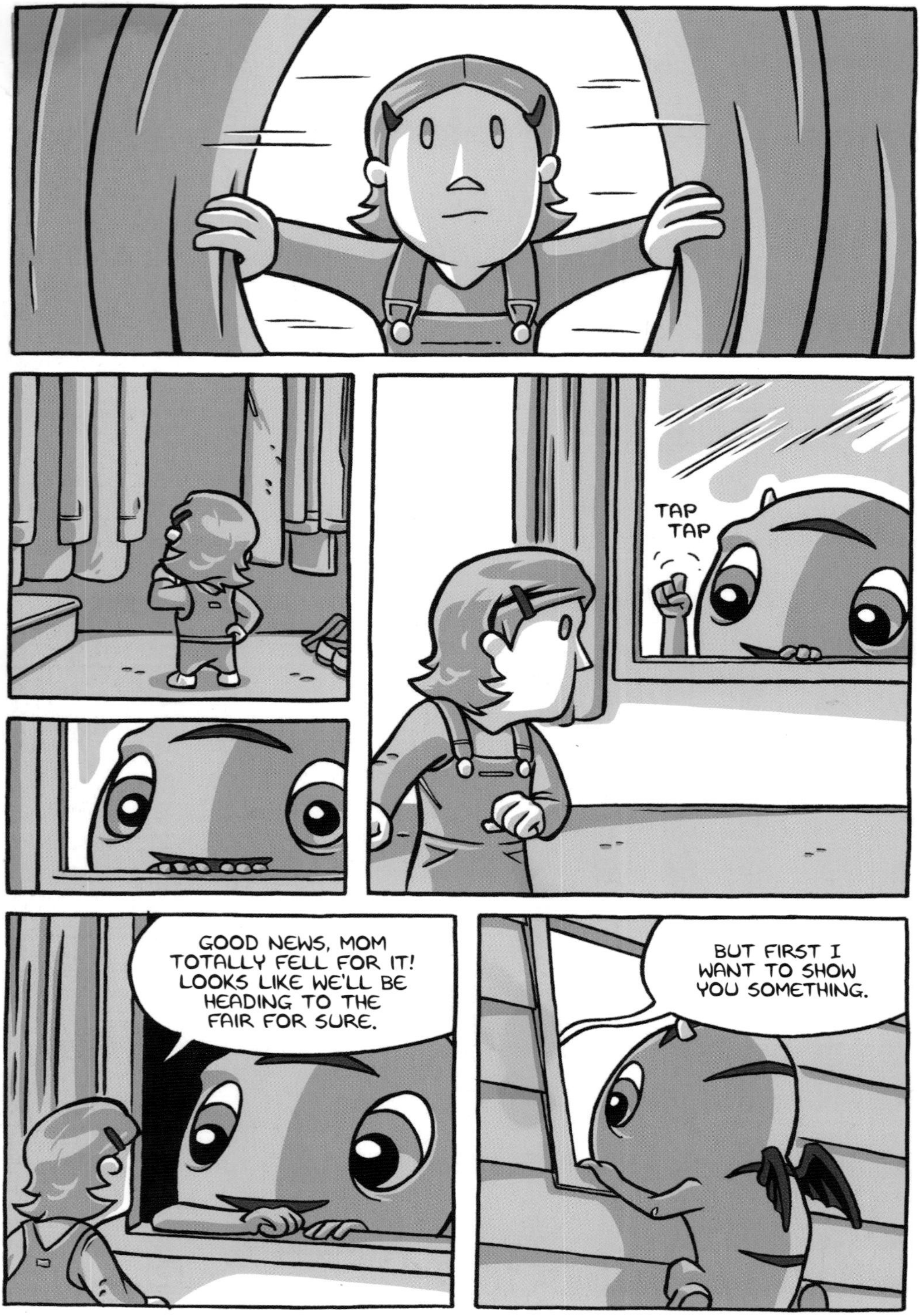
TAP
TAP
GOOD NEWS, MOM TOTALLY FELL FOR IT! LOOKS LIKE WE'LL BE HEADING TO THE FAIR FOR SURE.
BUT FIRST I WANT TO SHOW YOU SOMETHING.

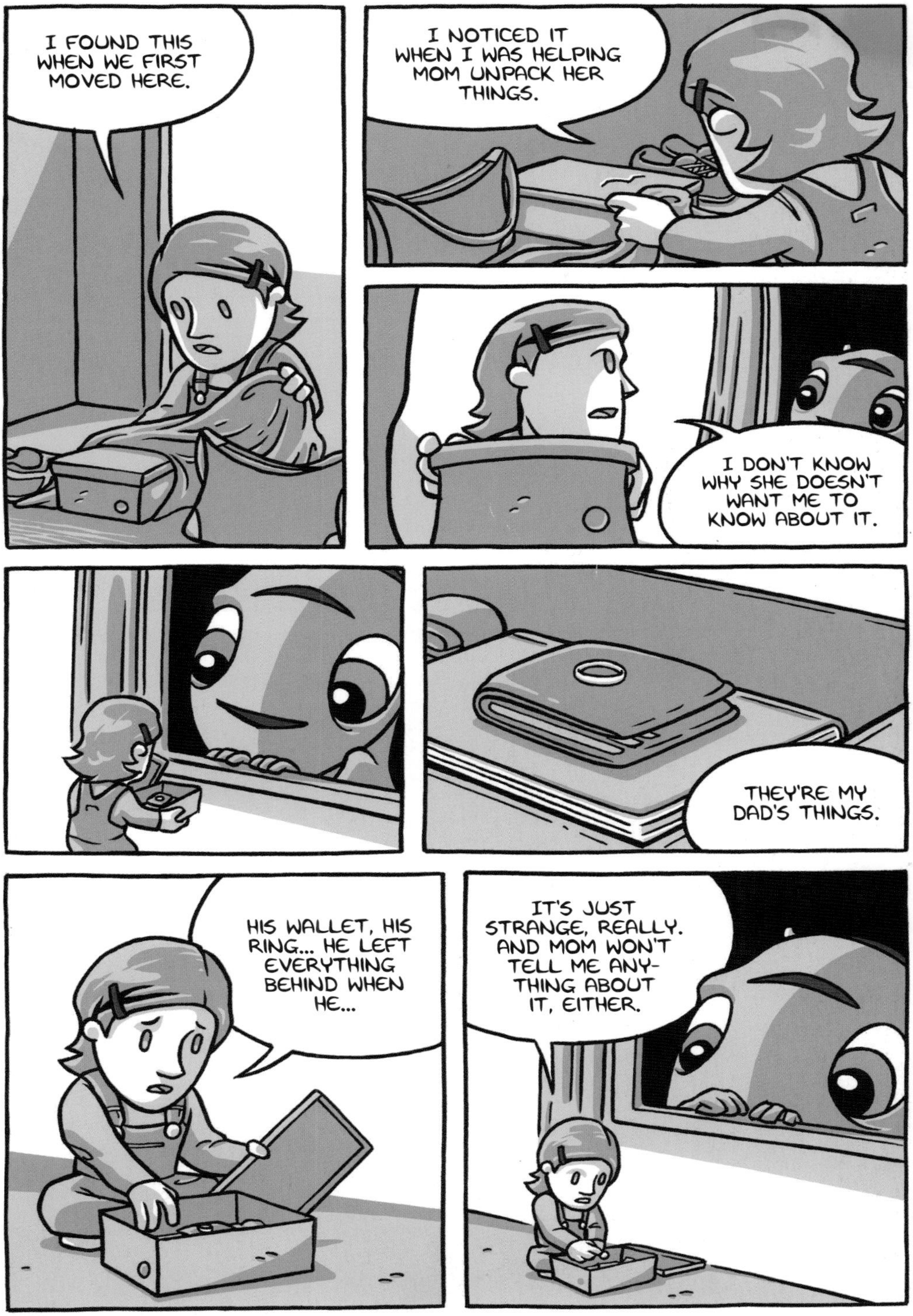
I FOUND THIS WHEN WE FIRST MOVED HERE.
I NOTICED IT WHEN I WAS HELPING MOM UNPACK HER THINGS.
I DON'T KNOW WHY SHE DOESN'T WANT ME TO KNOW ABOUT IT.
THEY'RE MY DAD'S THINGS.
HIS WALLET, HIS RING... HE LEFT EVERYTHING BEHIND WHEN HE...
IT'S JUST STRANGE, REALLY. AND MOM WON'T TELL ME ANY-THING ABOUT IT, EITHER.

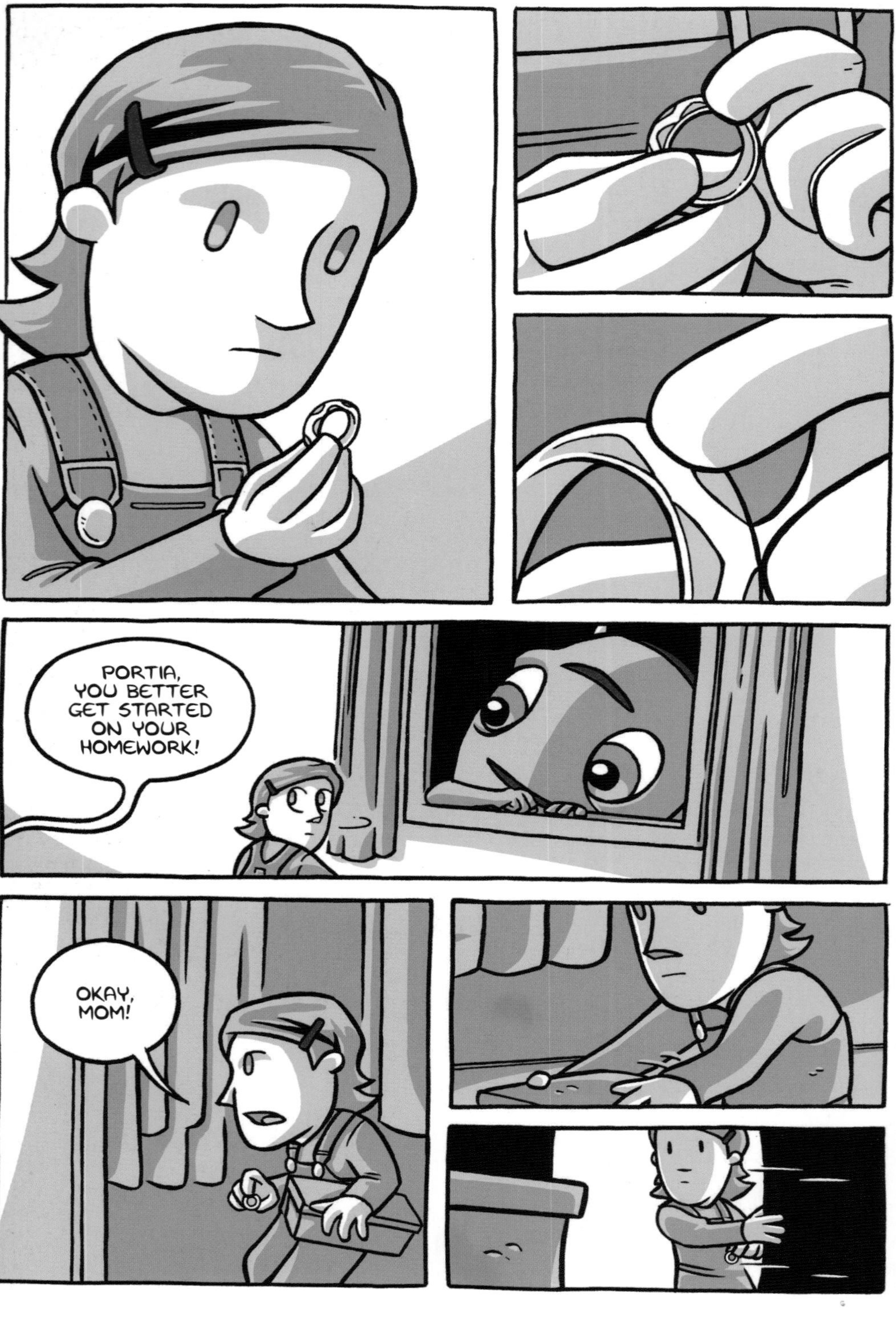
PORTIA, YOU BETTER GET STARTED ON YOUR HOMEWORK!
OKAY, MOM!

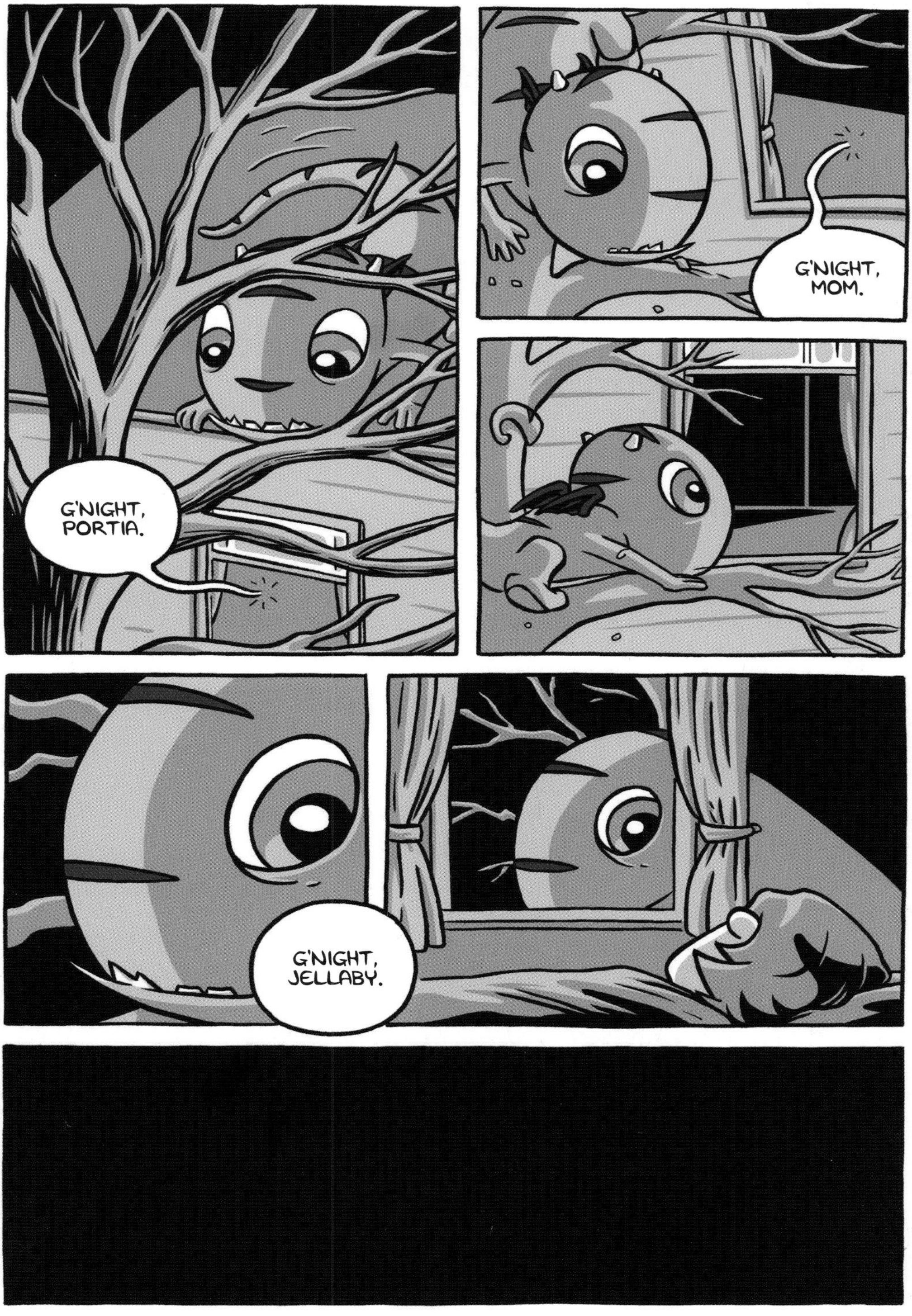
G'NIGHT, PORTIA.
G'NIGHT, MOM.
G'NIGHT, JELLABY.

I KNOW THINGS
I KNOW THINGS
I, UHM, NEED TO FILE A MISSING PERSONS REPORT.

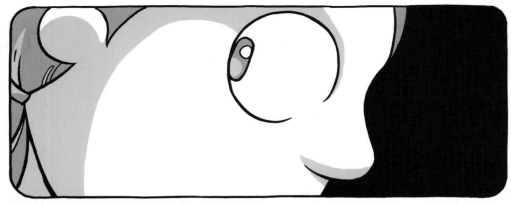

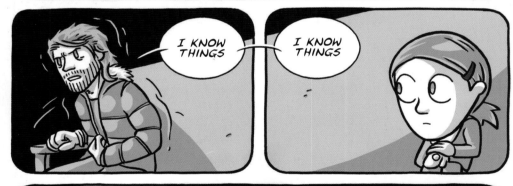

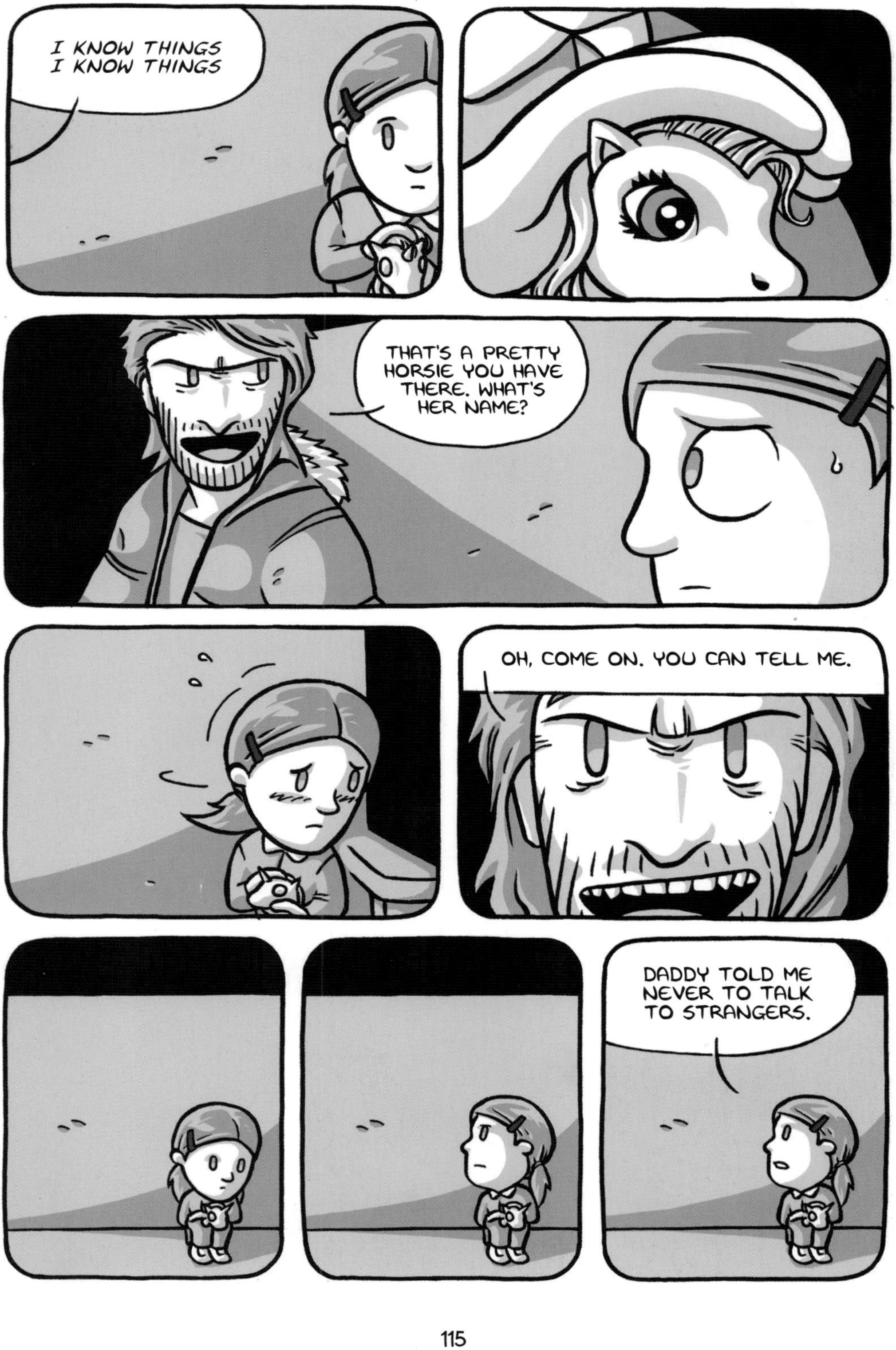
I KNOW THINGS
I KNOW THINGS
THAT'S A PRETTY HORSIE YOU HAVE THERE. WHAT'S HER NAME?
OH, COME ON. YOU CAN TELL ME.
DADDY TOLD ME NEVER TO TALK TO STRANGERS.

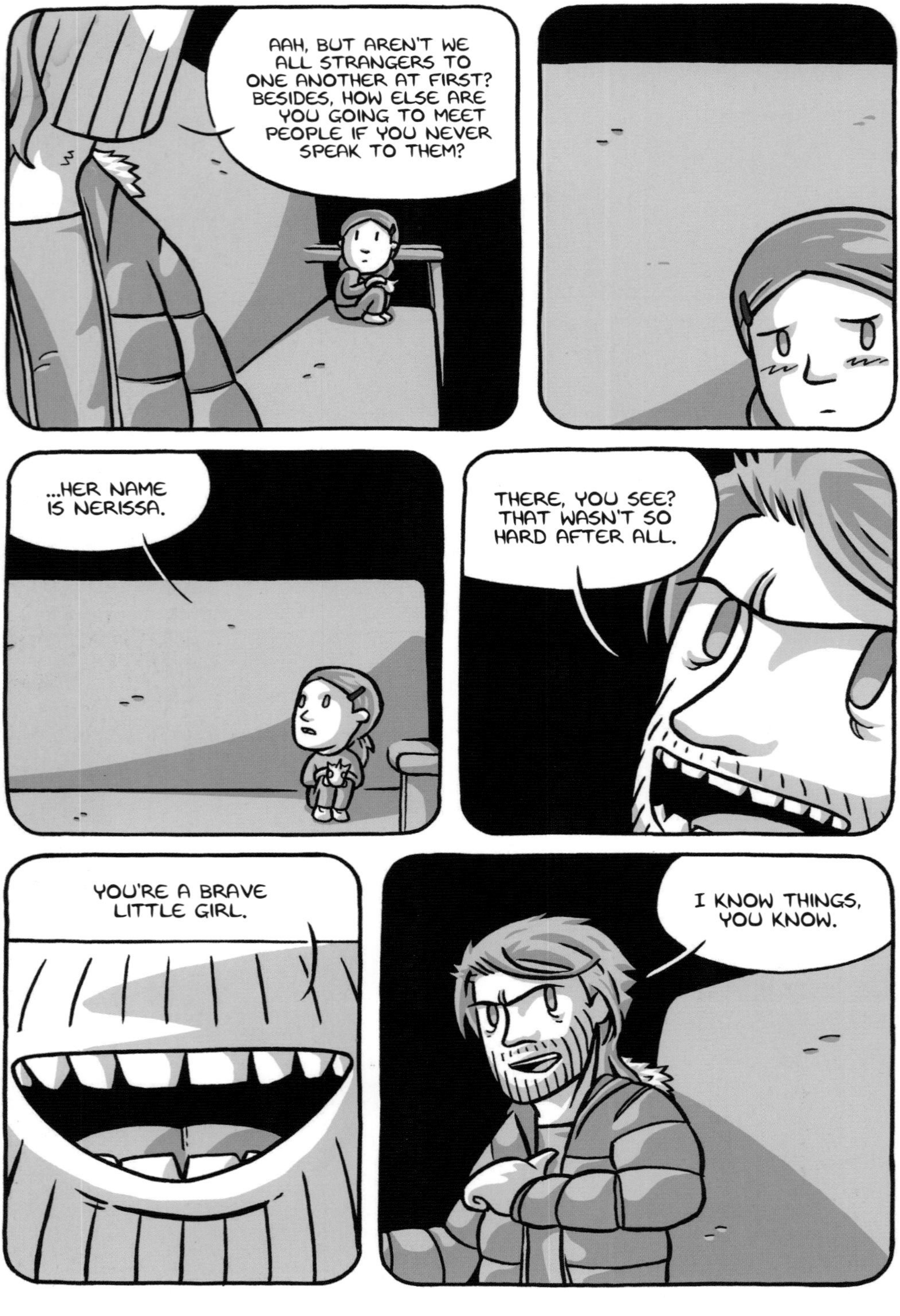
AAH, BUT AREN'T WE ALL STRANGERS TO ONE ANOTHER AT FIRST? BESIDES, HOW ELSE ARE YOU GOING TO MEET PEOPLE IF YOU NEVER SPEAK TO THEM?
...HER NAME IS NERISSA.
THERE, YOU SEE? THAT WASN'T SO HARD AFTER ALL.
YOU'RE A BRAVE LITTLE GIRL.
I KNOW THINGS, YOU KNOW.

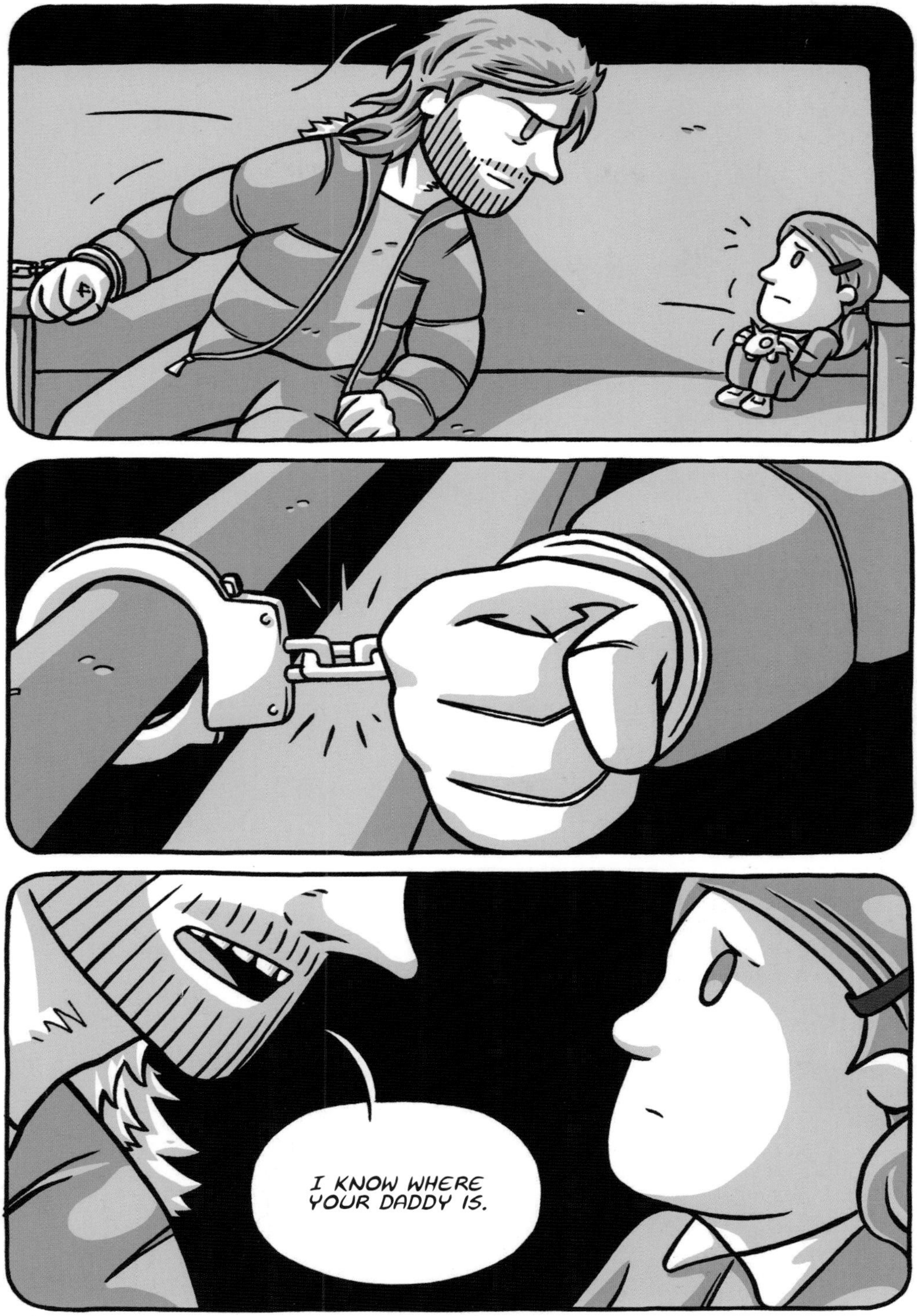
I KNOW WHERE
YOUR DADDY IS.

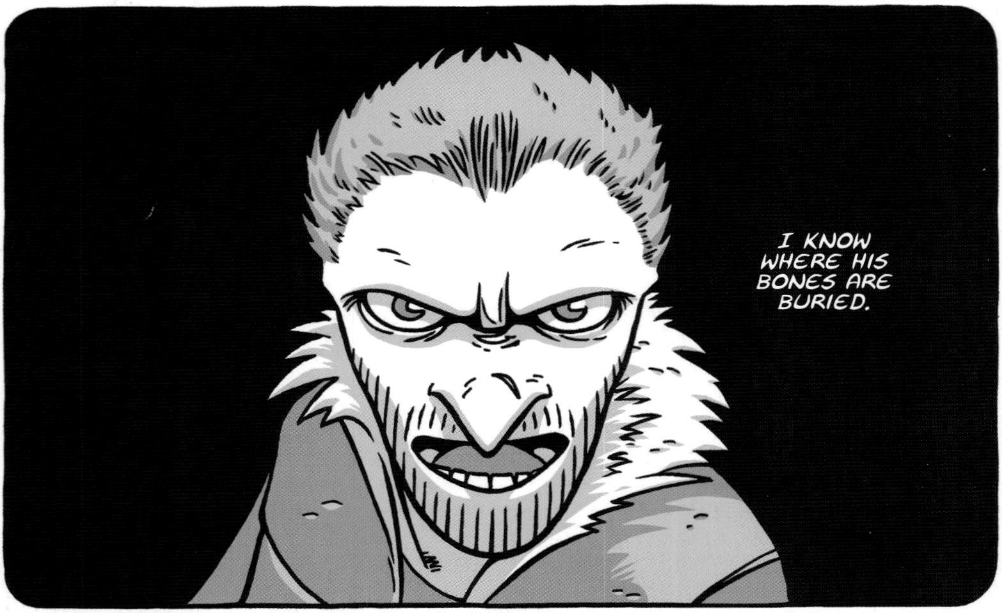
I KNOW WHERE HIS BONES ARE BURIED.

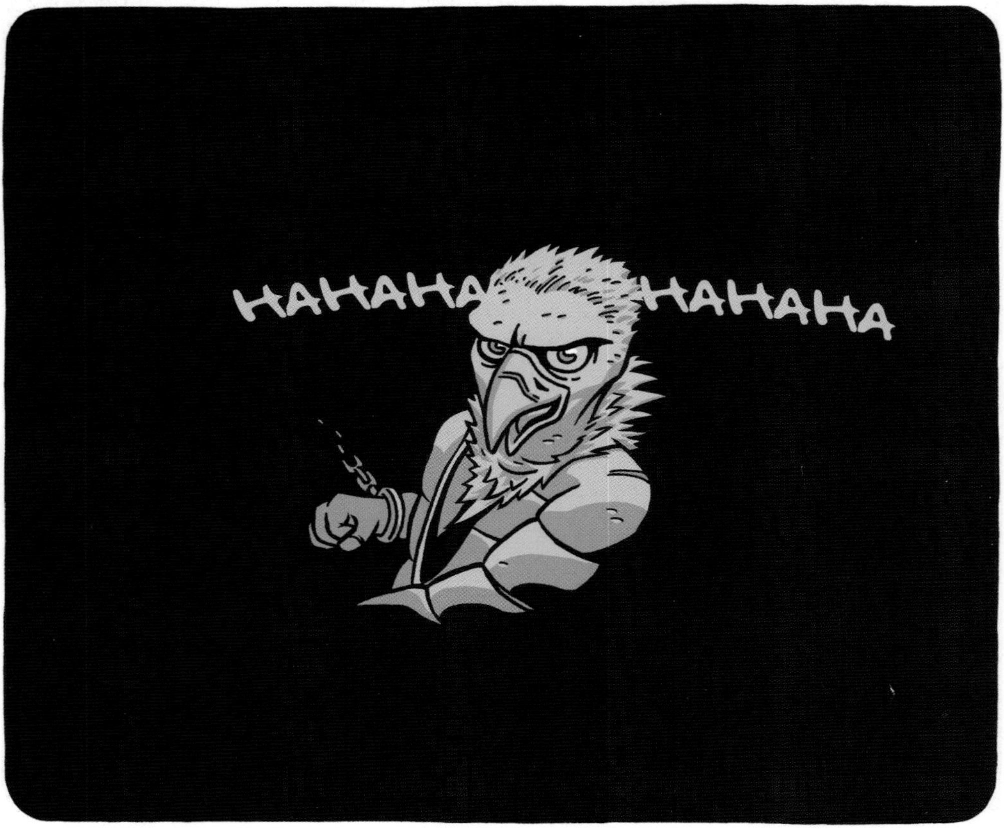
HAHAHA HAHAHA

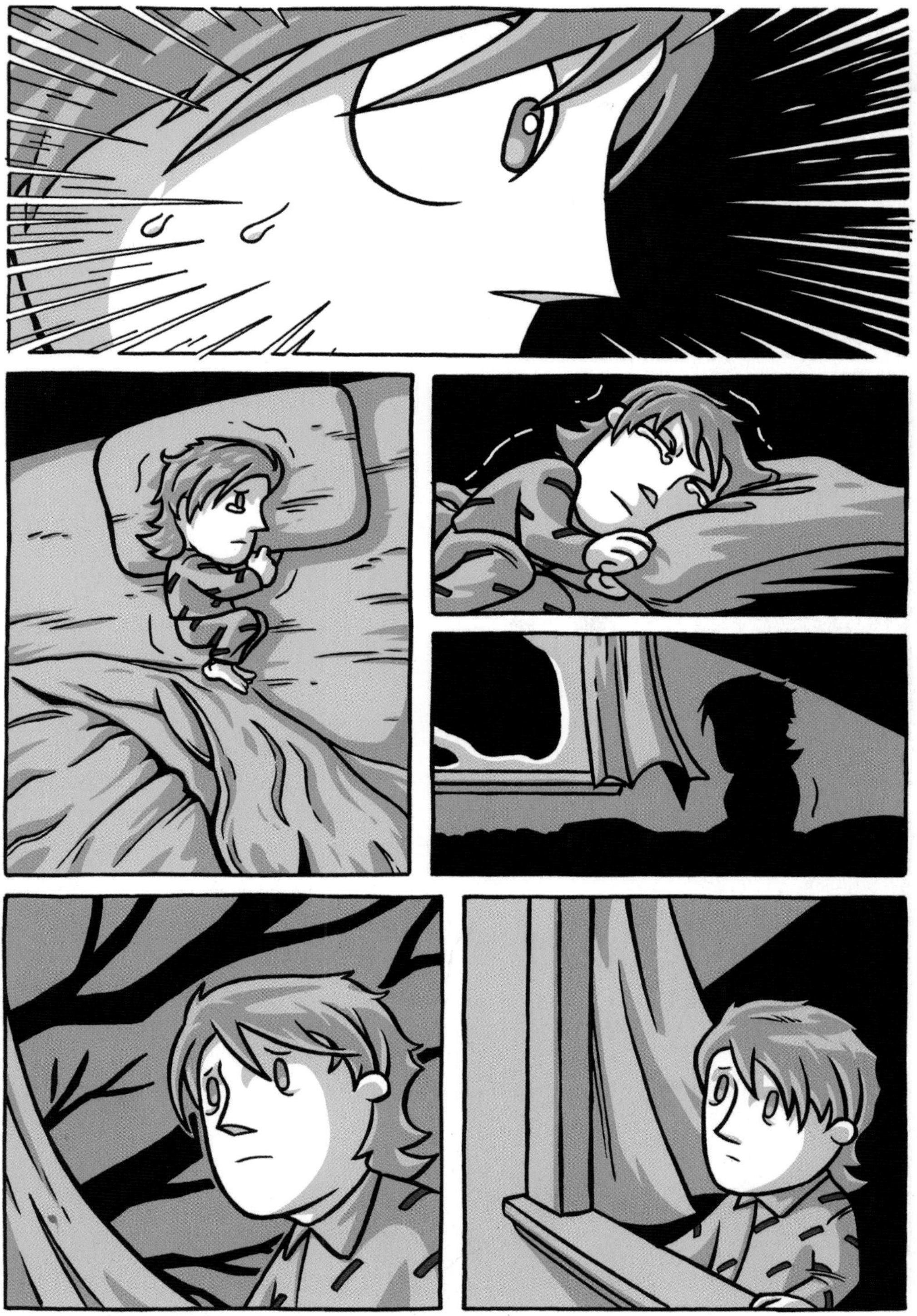

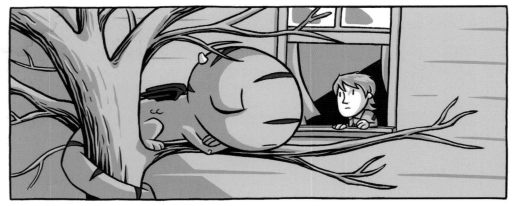

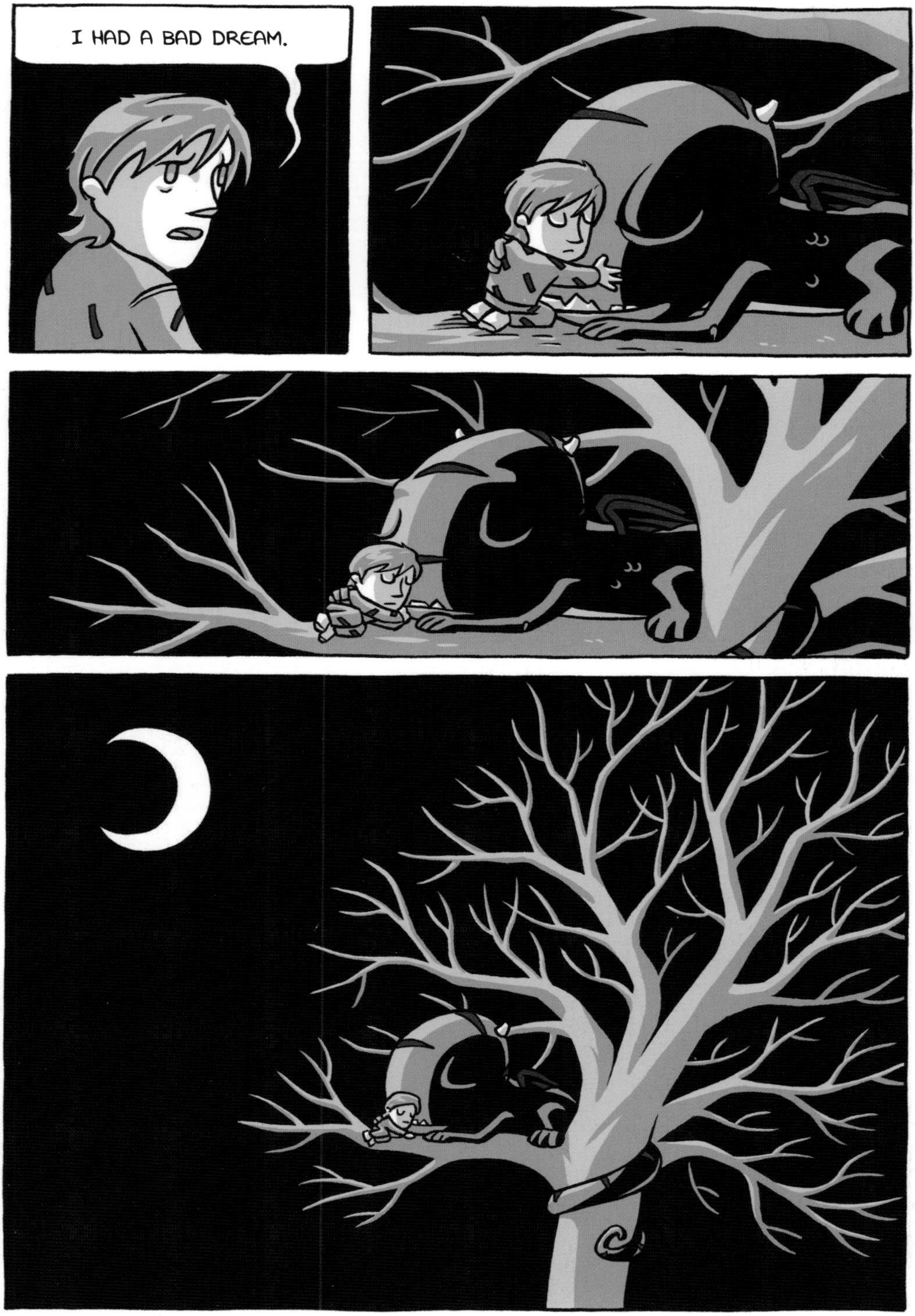
I HAD A BAD DREAM.

CHAPTER FIVE

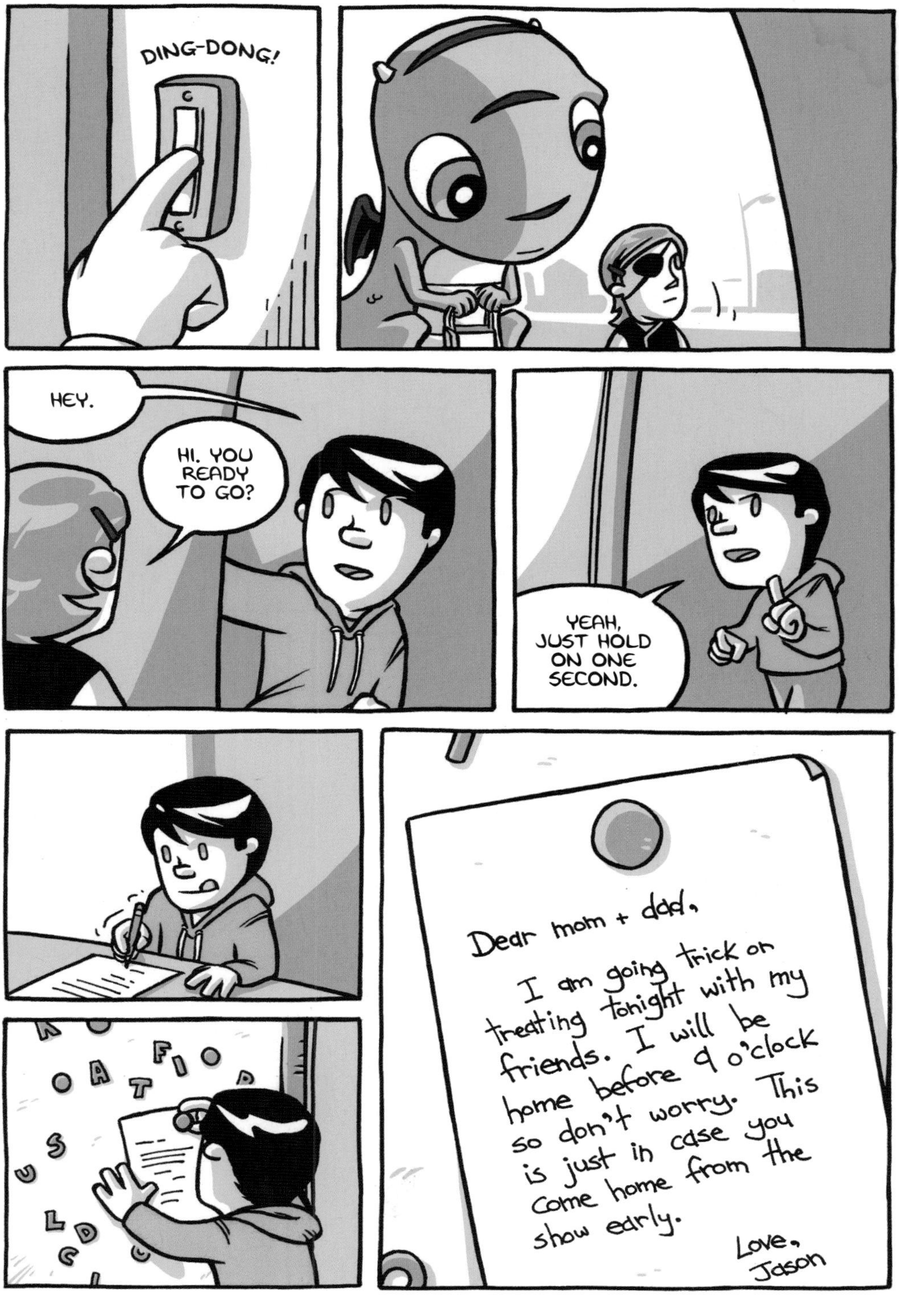
DING-DONG!
HEY.
HI. YOU READY TO GO?
YEAH, JUST HOLD ON ONE SECOND.
Dear mom + dad,
I am going trick or
treating tonight with my
friends. I will be
home before 9 o'clock
so don't worry. This
is just in case you
come home from the
show early.
Love,
Jason

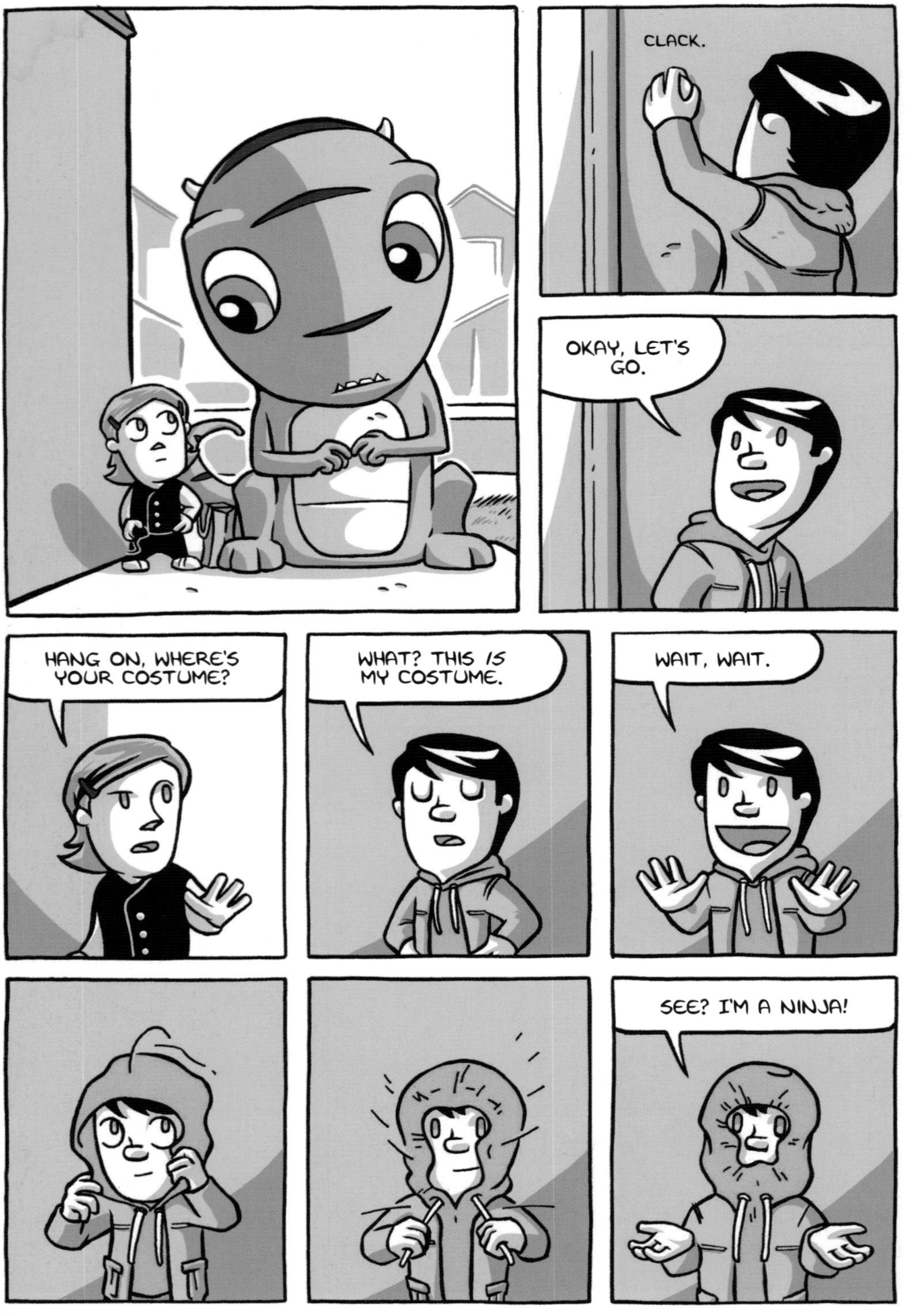
CLACK.
OKAY, LET'S GO.
HANG ON, WHERE'S YOUR COSTUME?
WHAT? THIS IS MY COSTUME.
WAIT, WAIT.
SEE? I'M A NINJA!

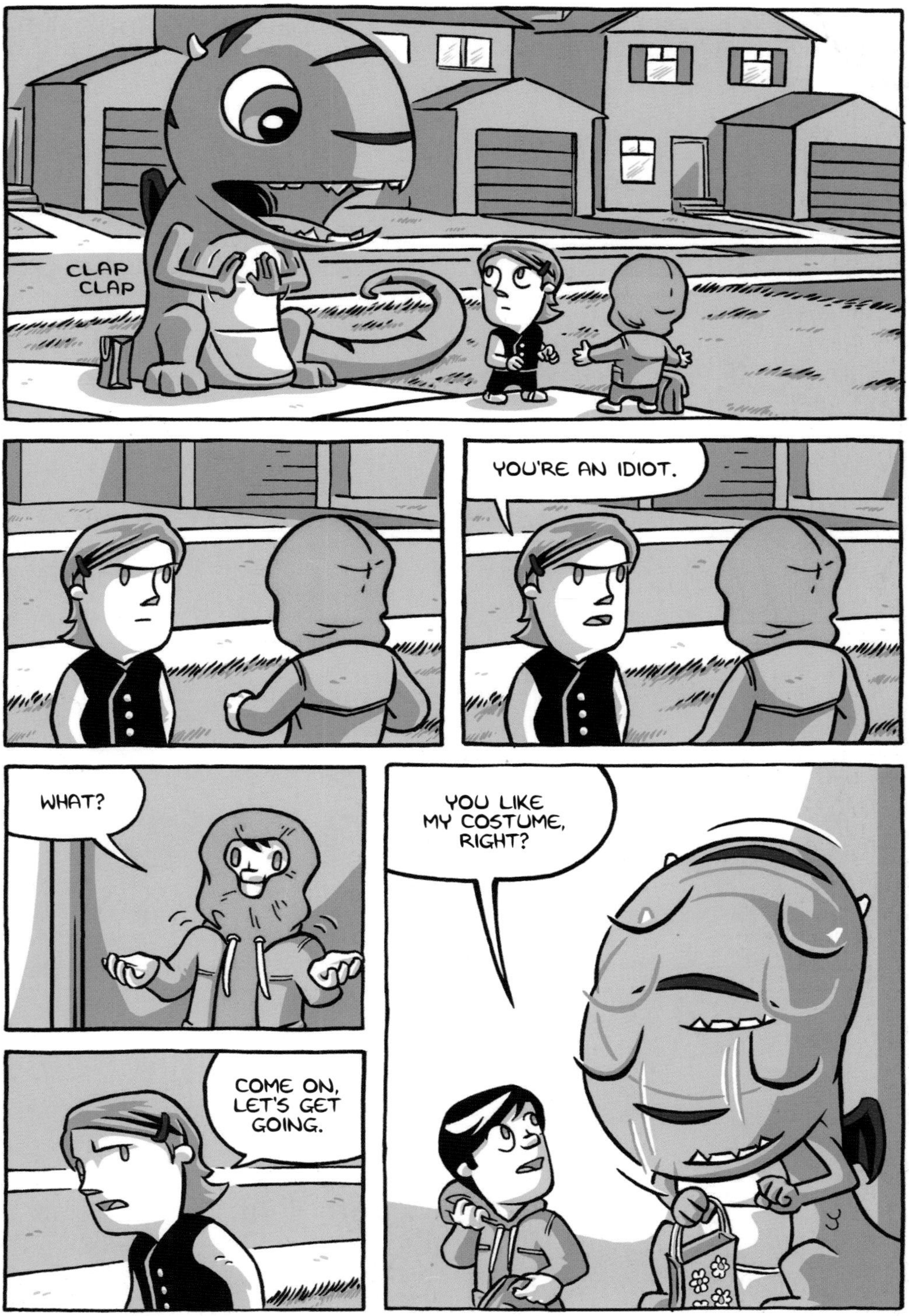
CLAP
CLAP
YOU'RE AN IDIOT.
WHAT?
YOU LIKE MY COSTUME, RIGHT?
COME ON, LET'S GET GOING.

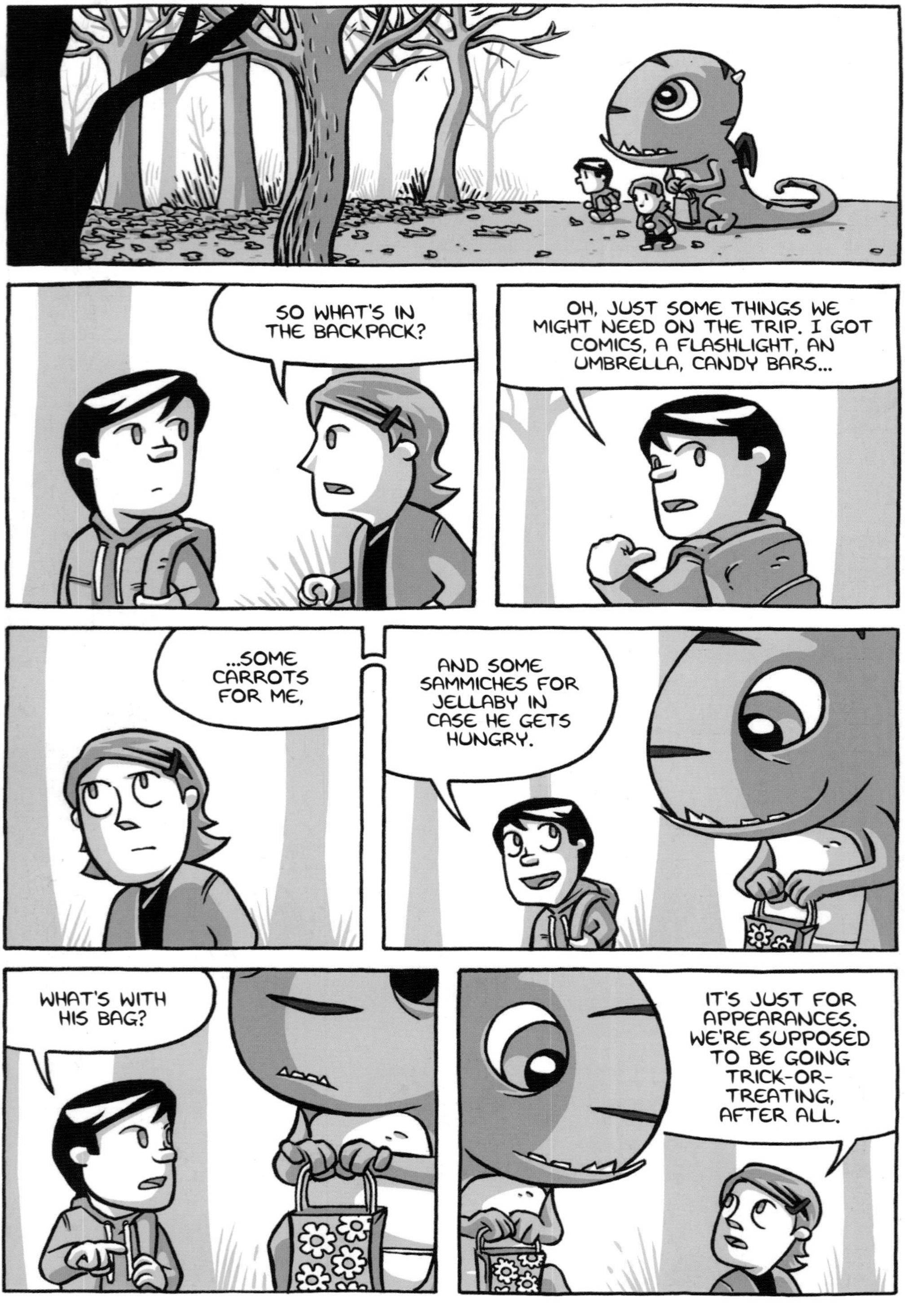
SO WHAT'S IN THE BACKPACK?
OH, JUST SOME THINGS WE MIGHT NEED ON THE TRIP. I GOT COMICS, A FLASHLIGHT, AN UMBRELLA, CANDY BARS...
...SOME CARROTS FOR ME,
AND SOME SAMMICHES FOR JELLABY IN CASE HE GETS HUNGRY.
WHAT'S WITH HIS BAG?
IT'S JUST FOR APPEARANCES. WE'RE SUPPOSED TO BE GOING TRICK-OR-TREATING, AFTER ALL.

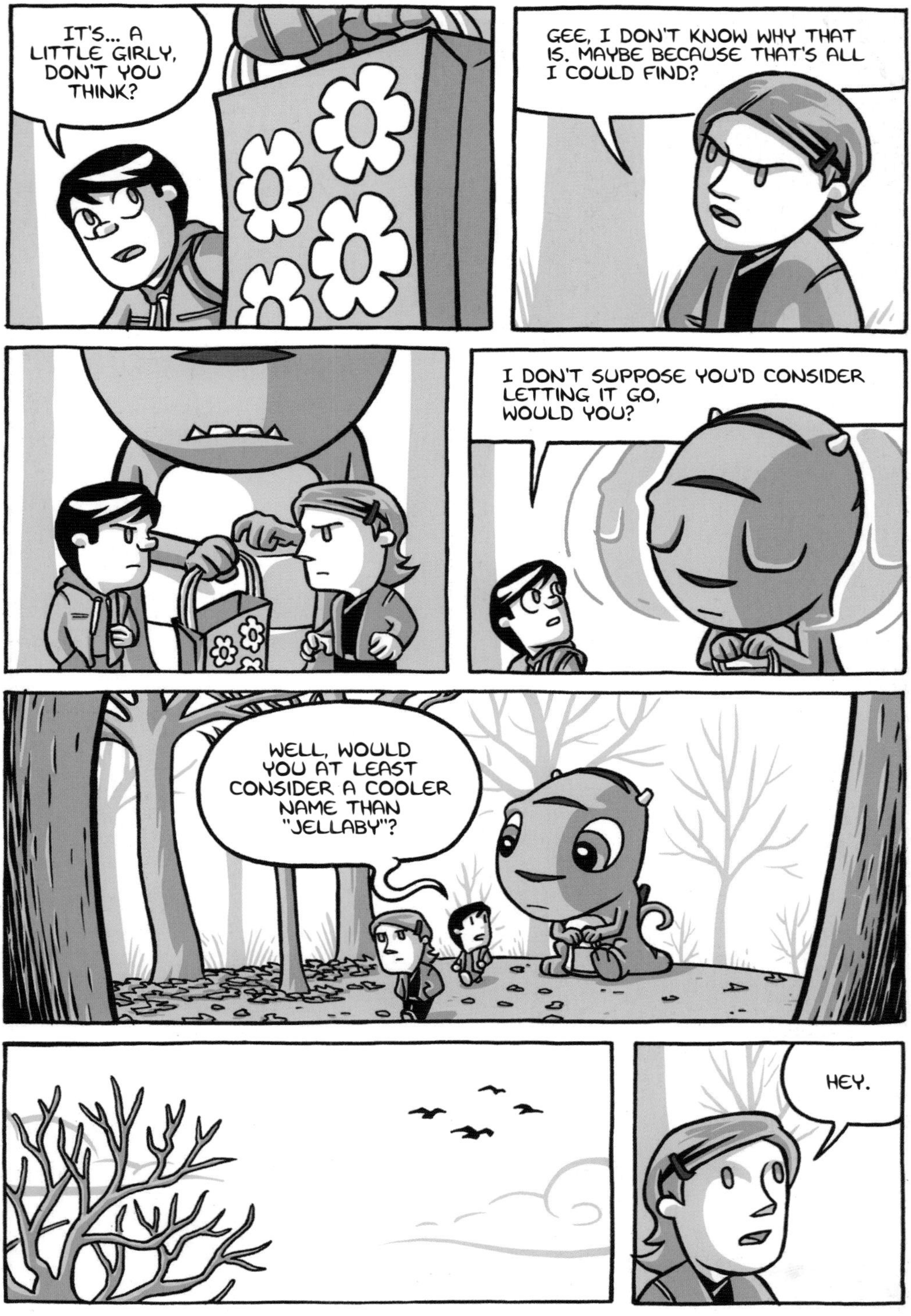
IT'S... A LITTLE GIRLY, DON'T YOU THINK?
GEE, I DON'T KNOW WHY THAT IS. MAYBE BECAUSE THAT'S ALL I COULD FIND?
I DON'T SUPPOSE YOU'D CONSIDER LETTING IT GO, WOULD YOU?
WELL, WOULD YOU AT LEAST CONSIDER A COOLER NAME THAN "JELLABY"?
HEY.

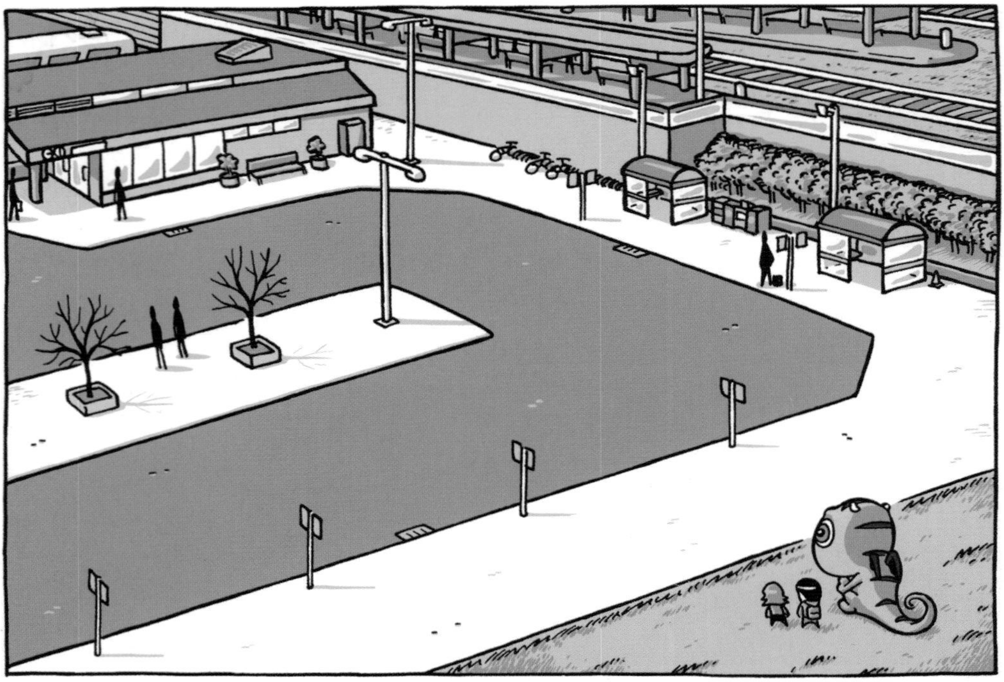

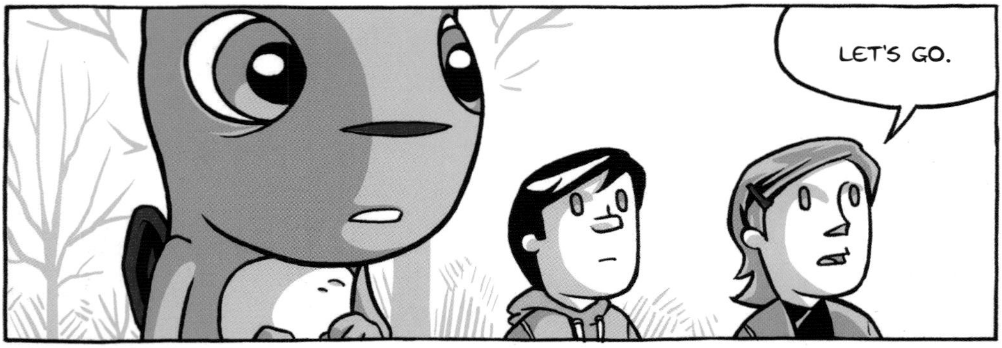
LET'S GO.

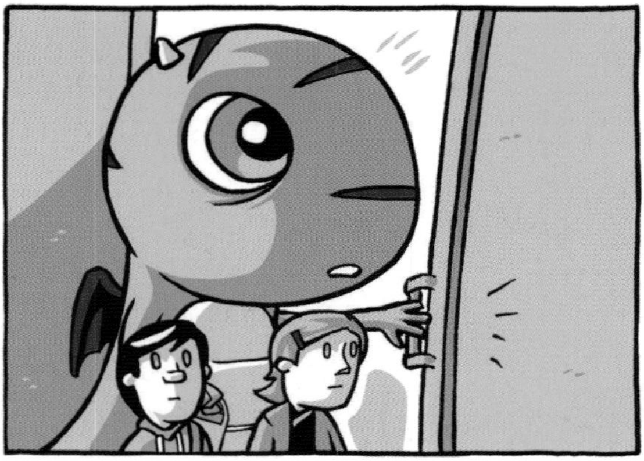

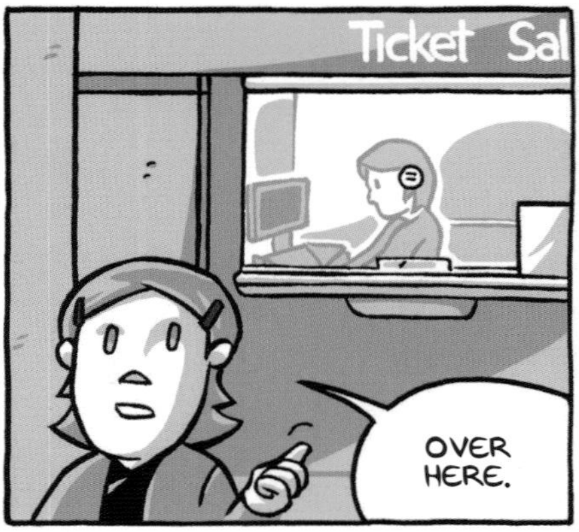
Ticket Sal
OVER HERE.

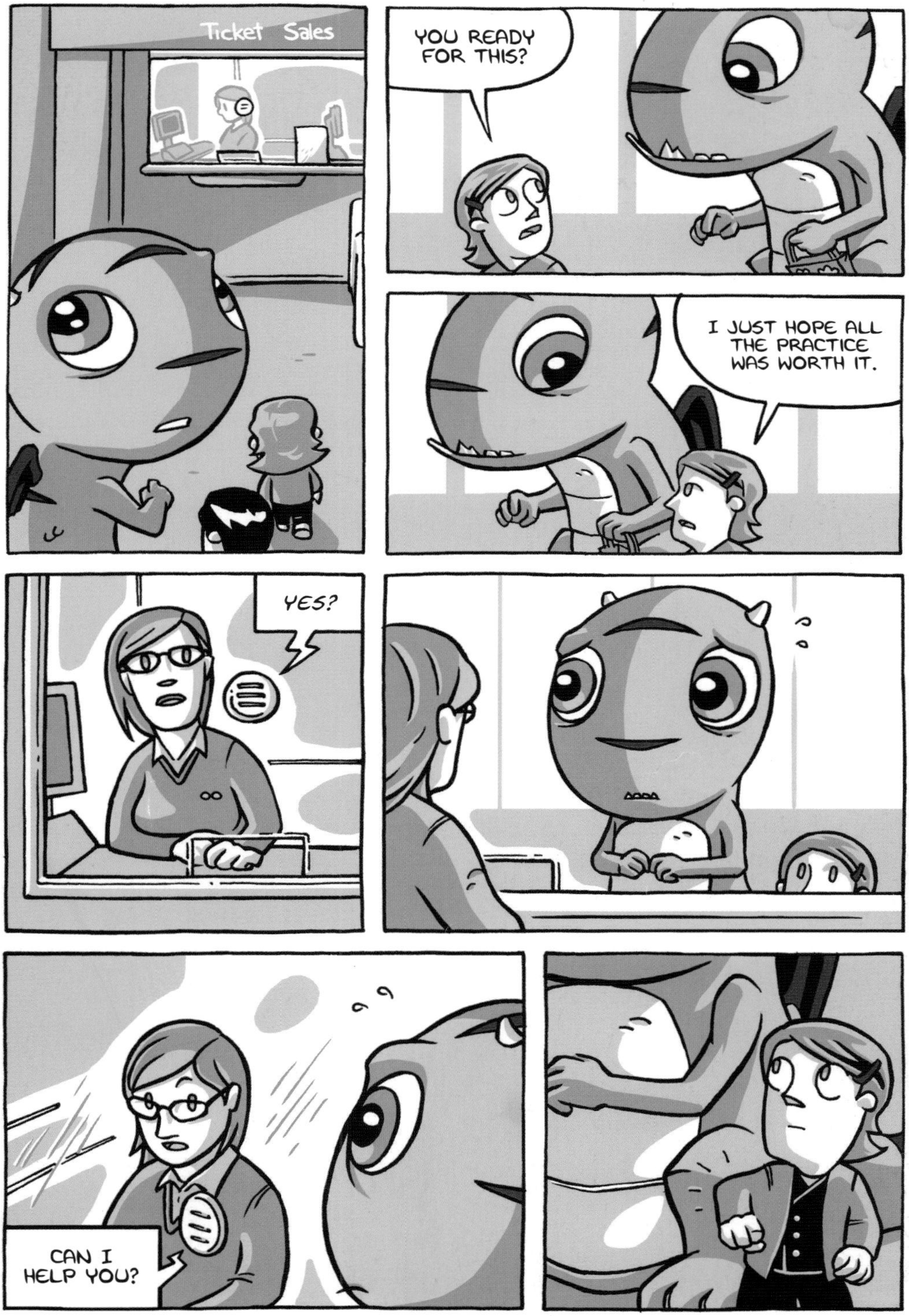
Ticket Sales
YOU READY FOR THIS?
I JUST HOPE ALL THE PRACTICE WAS WORTH IT.
YES?
CAN I HELP YOU?

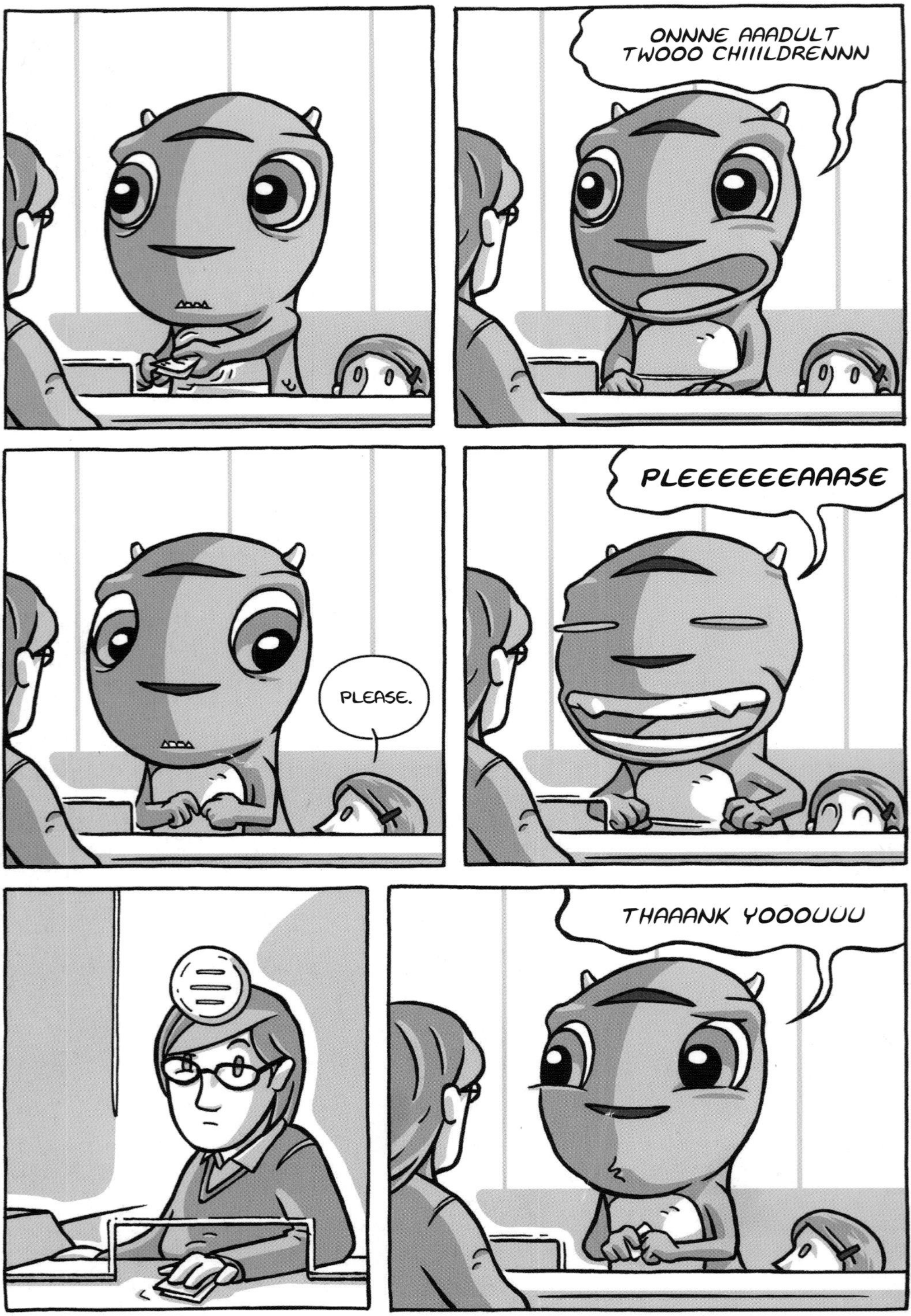
ONNNE AAADULT TWOOO CHIIILDRENNN
PLEASE.
PLEEEEEEAAASE
THAAANK YOOOUUU

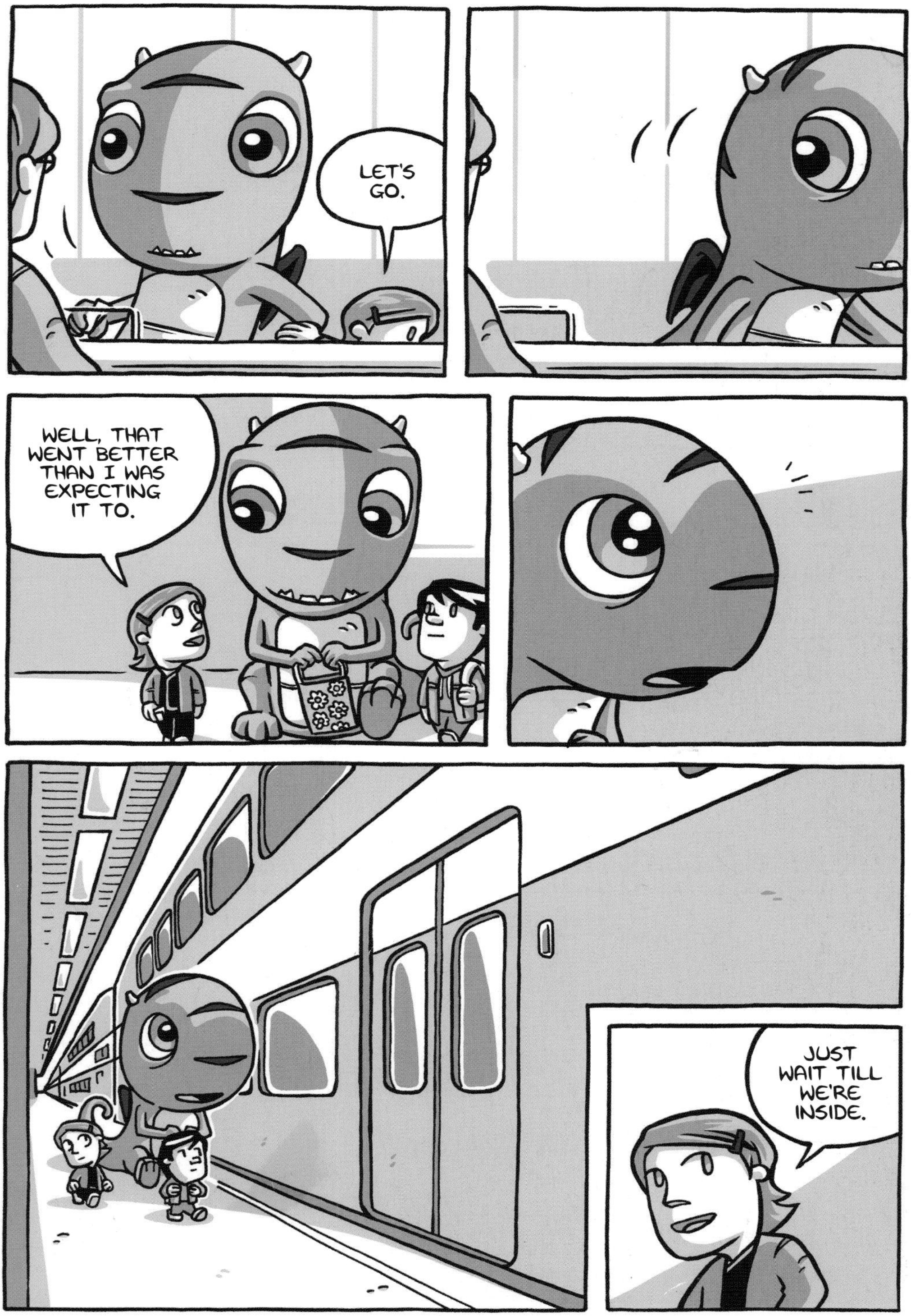
LET'S GO.
WELL, THAT WENT BETTER THAN I WAS EXPECTING IT TO.
JUST WAIT TILL WE'RE INSIDE.

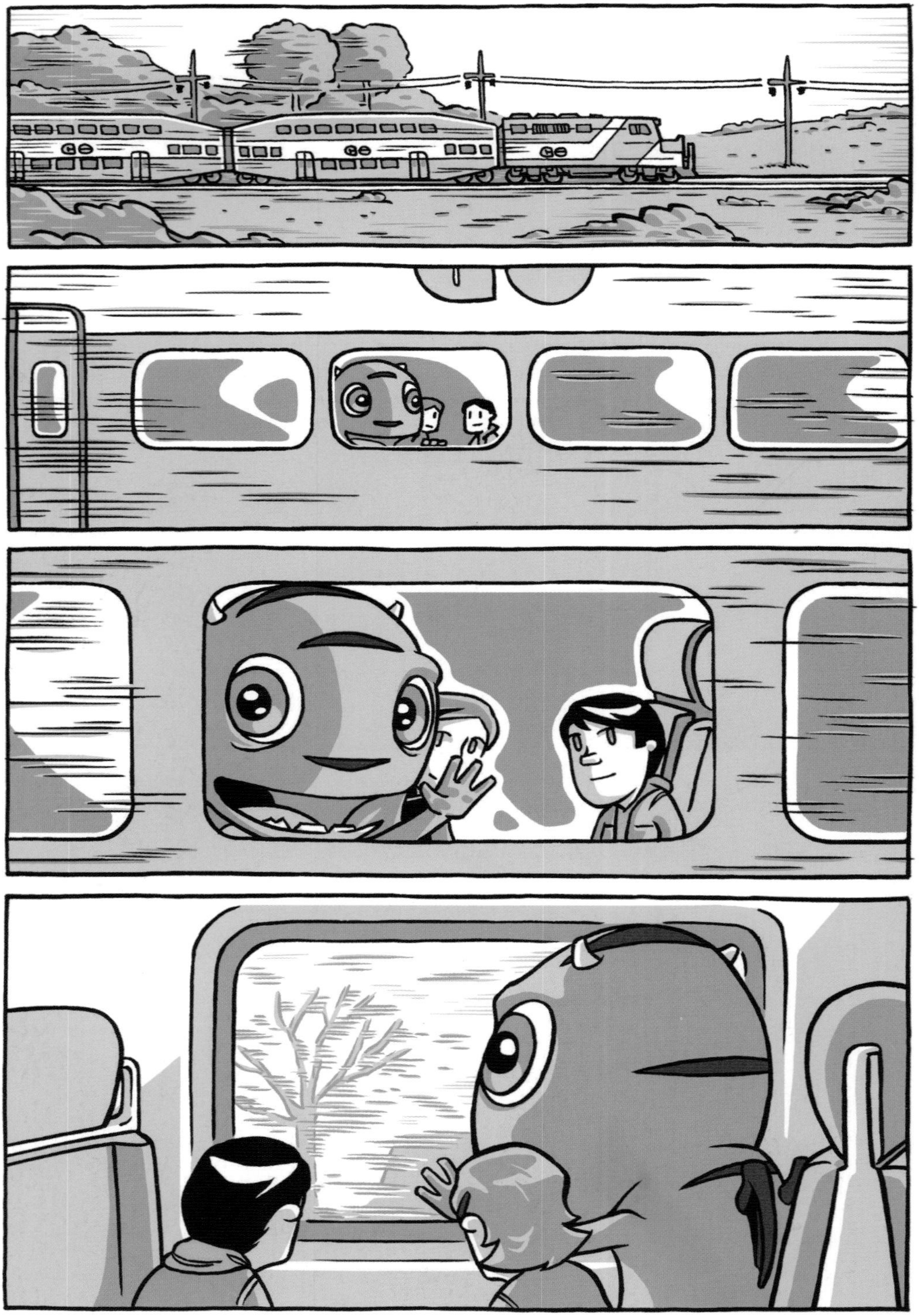

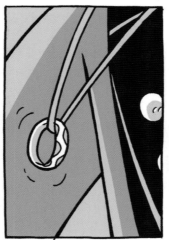

HEY, WHAT'S THAT?

THIS? IT'S JUST A LUCKY CHARM.

IT'S MY DAD'S.

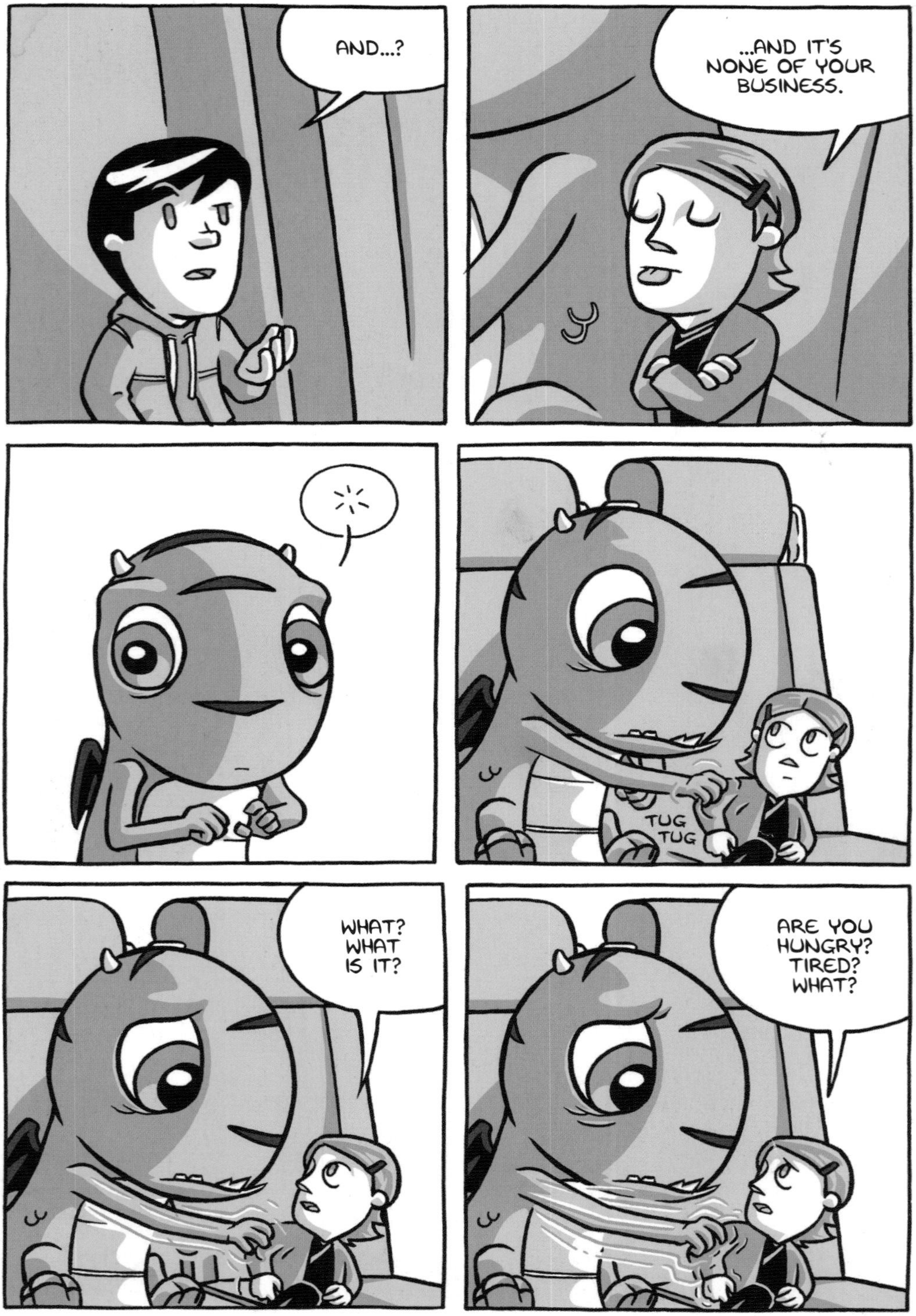
AND...?
...AND IT'S NONE OF YOUR BUSINESS.
TUG TUG
WHAT? WHAT IS IT?
ARE YOU HUNGRY? TIRED? WHAT?

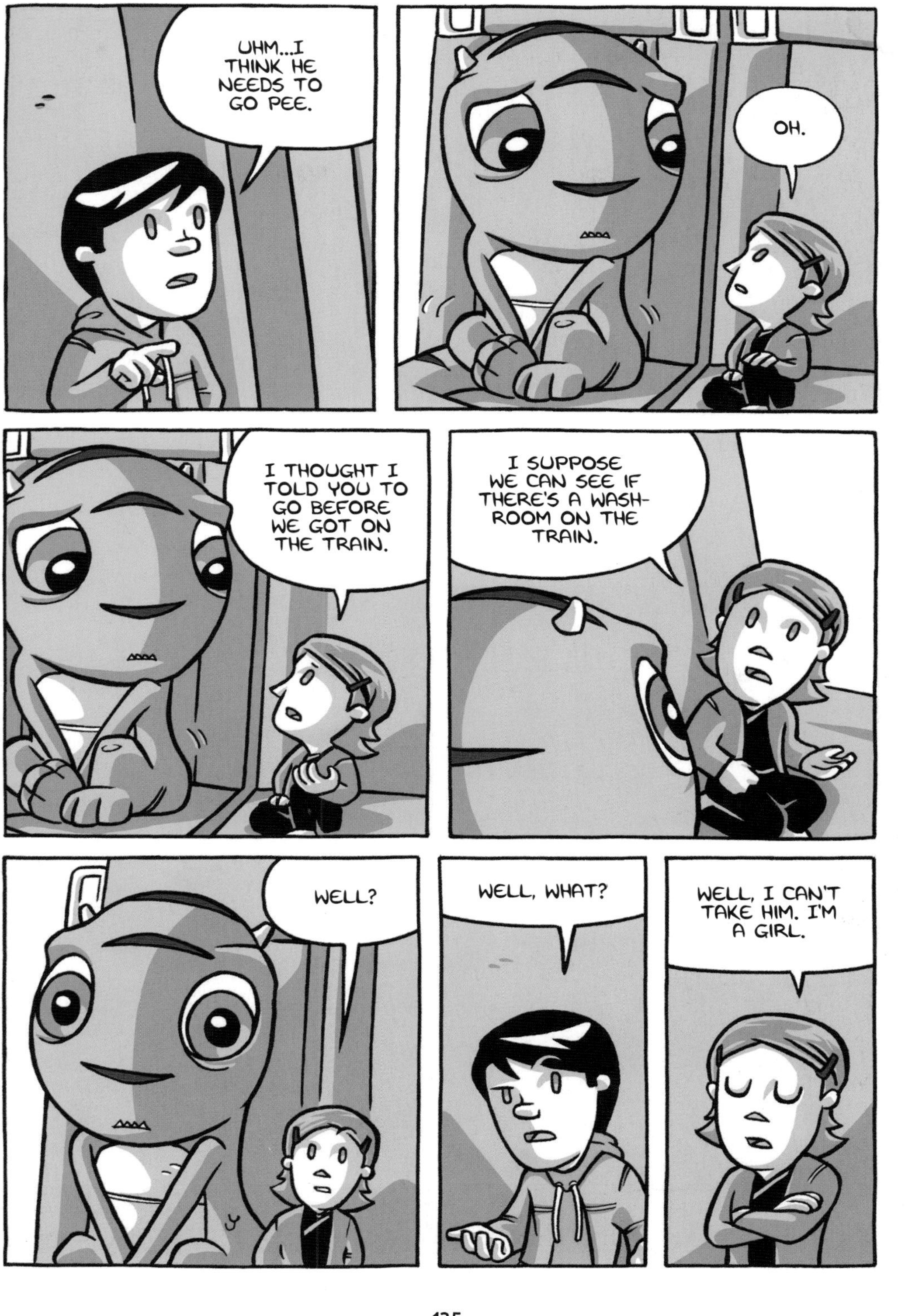
UHM...I THINK HE NEEDS TO GO PEE.
OH.
I THOUGHT I TOLD YOU TO GO BEFORE WE GOT ON THE TRAIN.
I SUPPOSE WE CAN SEE IF THERE'S A WASH-ROOM ON THE TRAIN.
WELL?
WELL, WHAT?
WELL, I CAN'T TAKE HIM. I'M A GIRL.

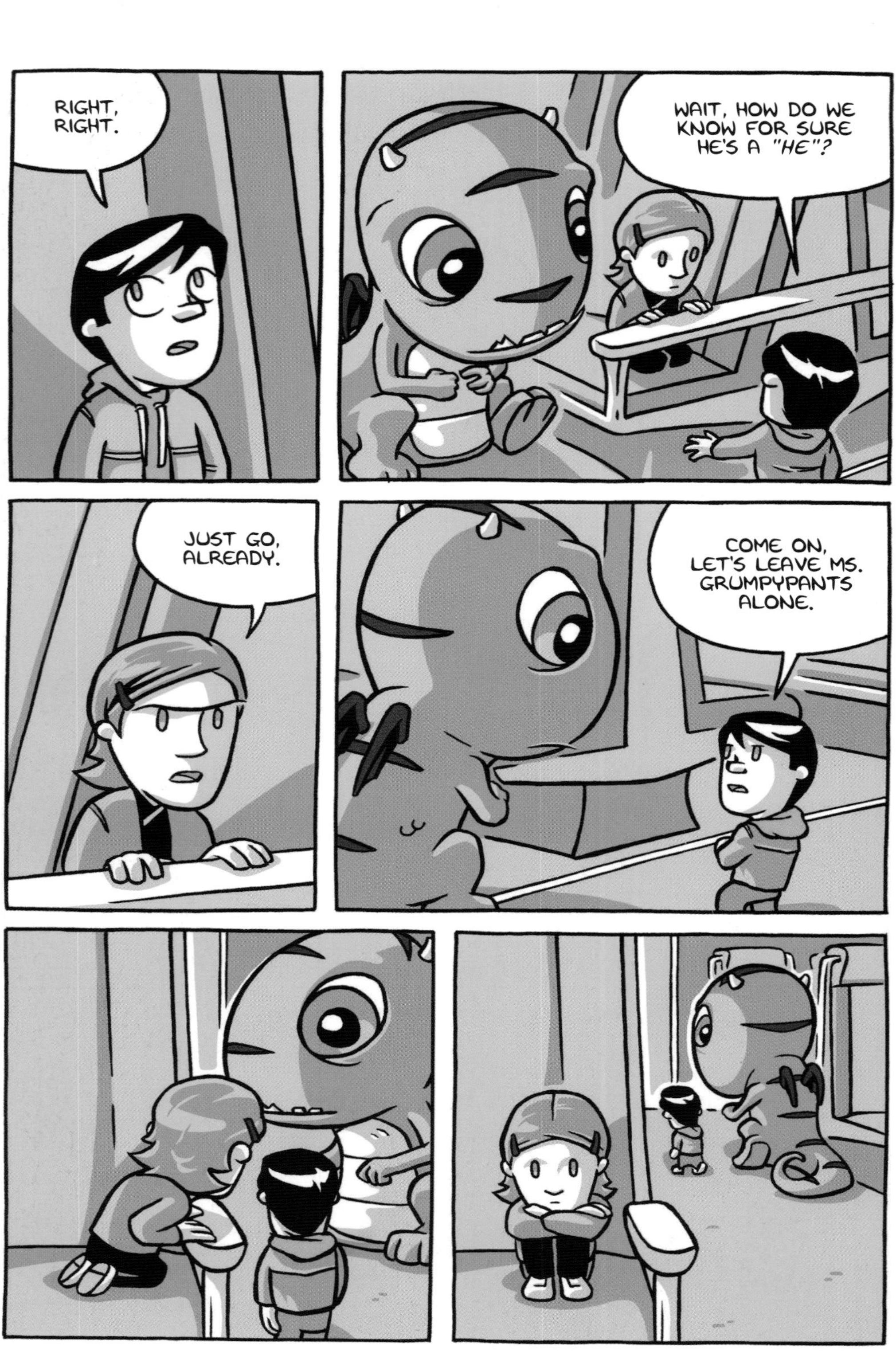
RIGHT, RIGHT.
WAIT, HOW DO WE KNOW FOR SURE HE'S A "HE"?
JUST GO, ALREADY.
COME ON, LET'S LEAVE MS. GRUMPYPANTS ALONE.

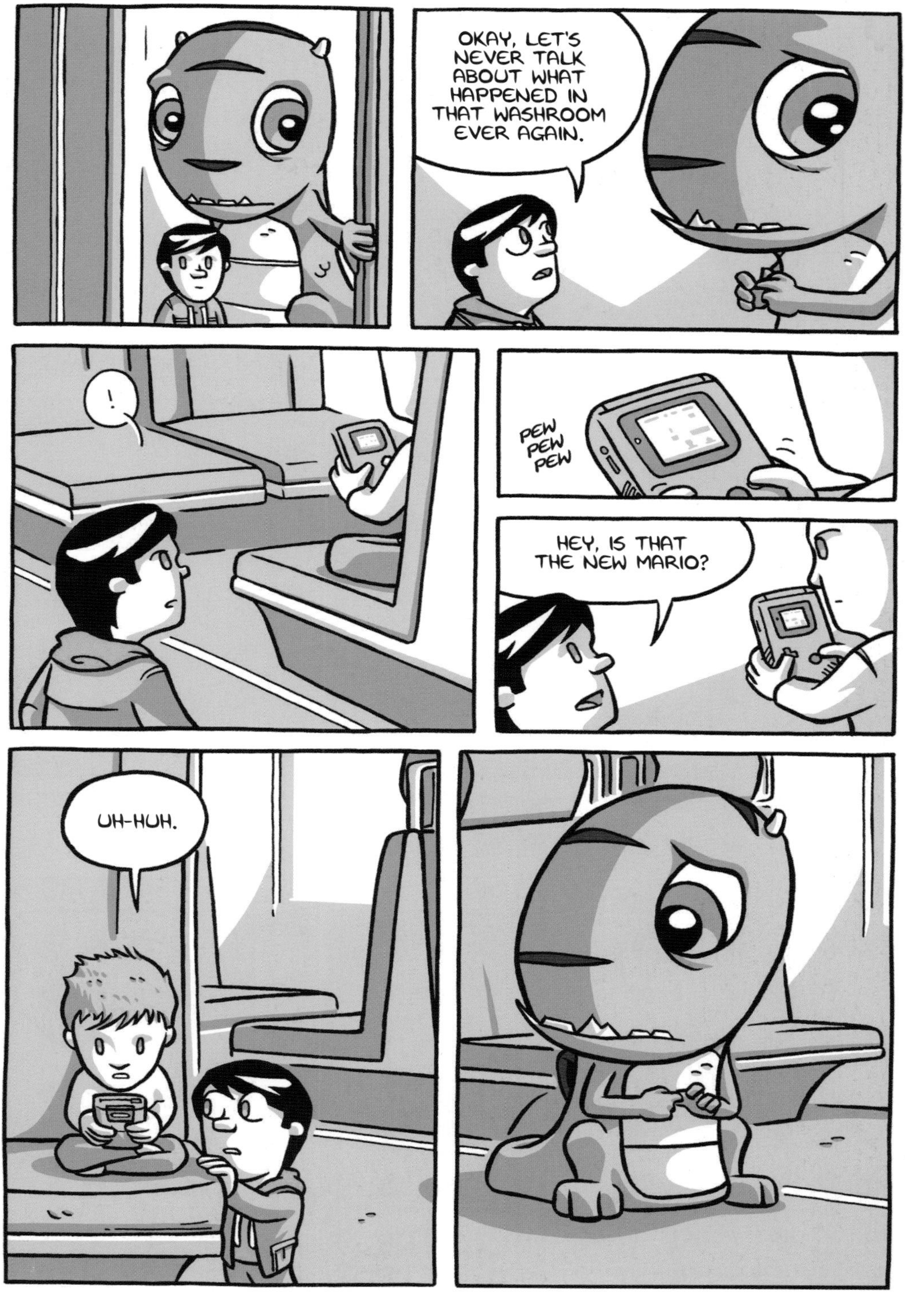

OKAY, LET'S NEVER TALK ABOUT WHAT HAPPENED IN THAT WASHROOM EVER AGAIN.
!
PEW PEW PEW
HEY, IS THAT THE NEW MARIO?
UH-HUH.

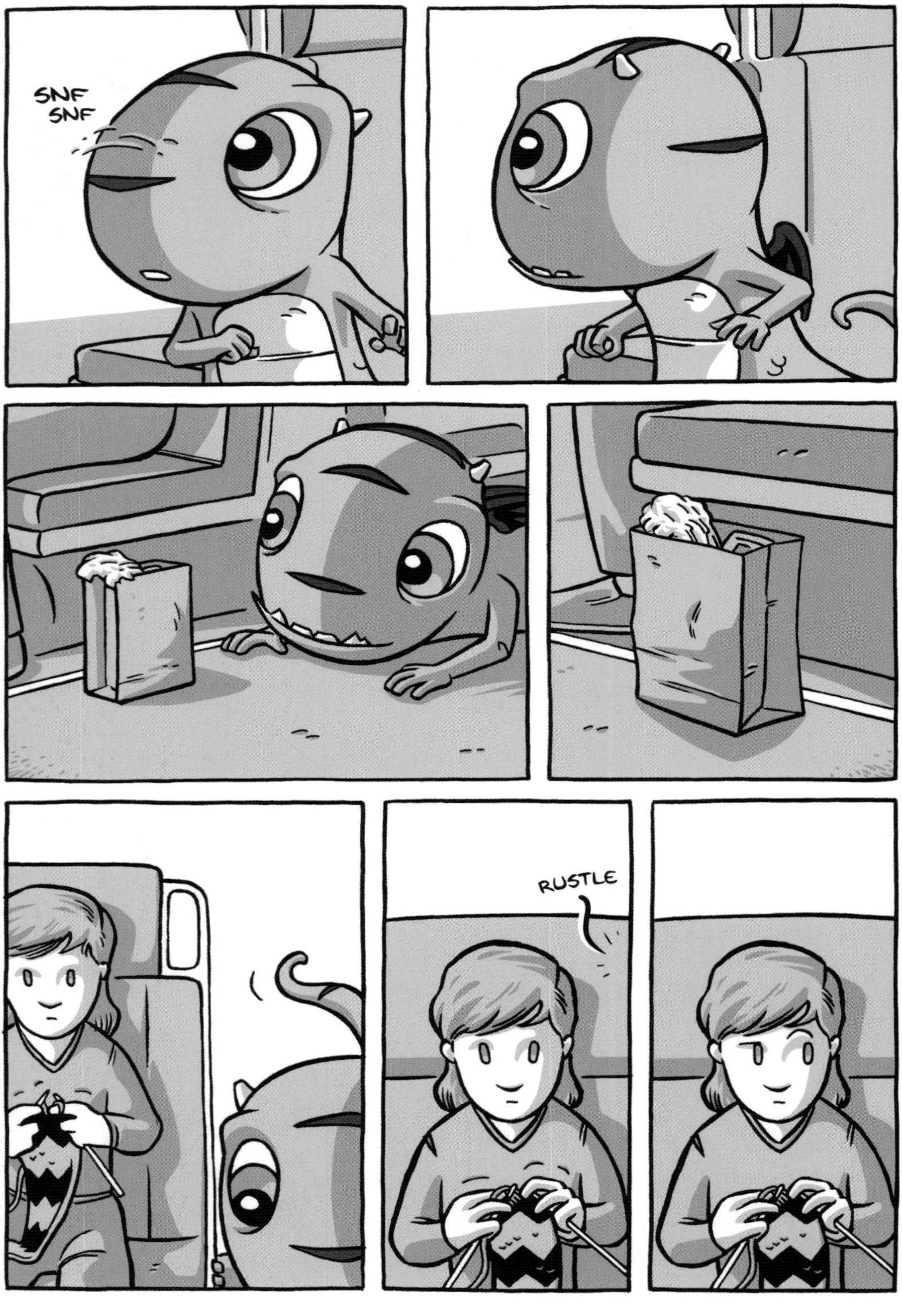
SNF
SNF
RUSTLE

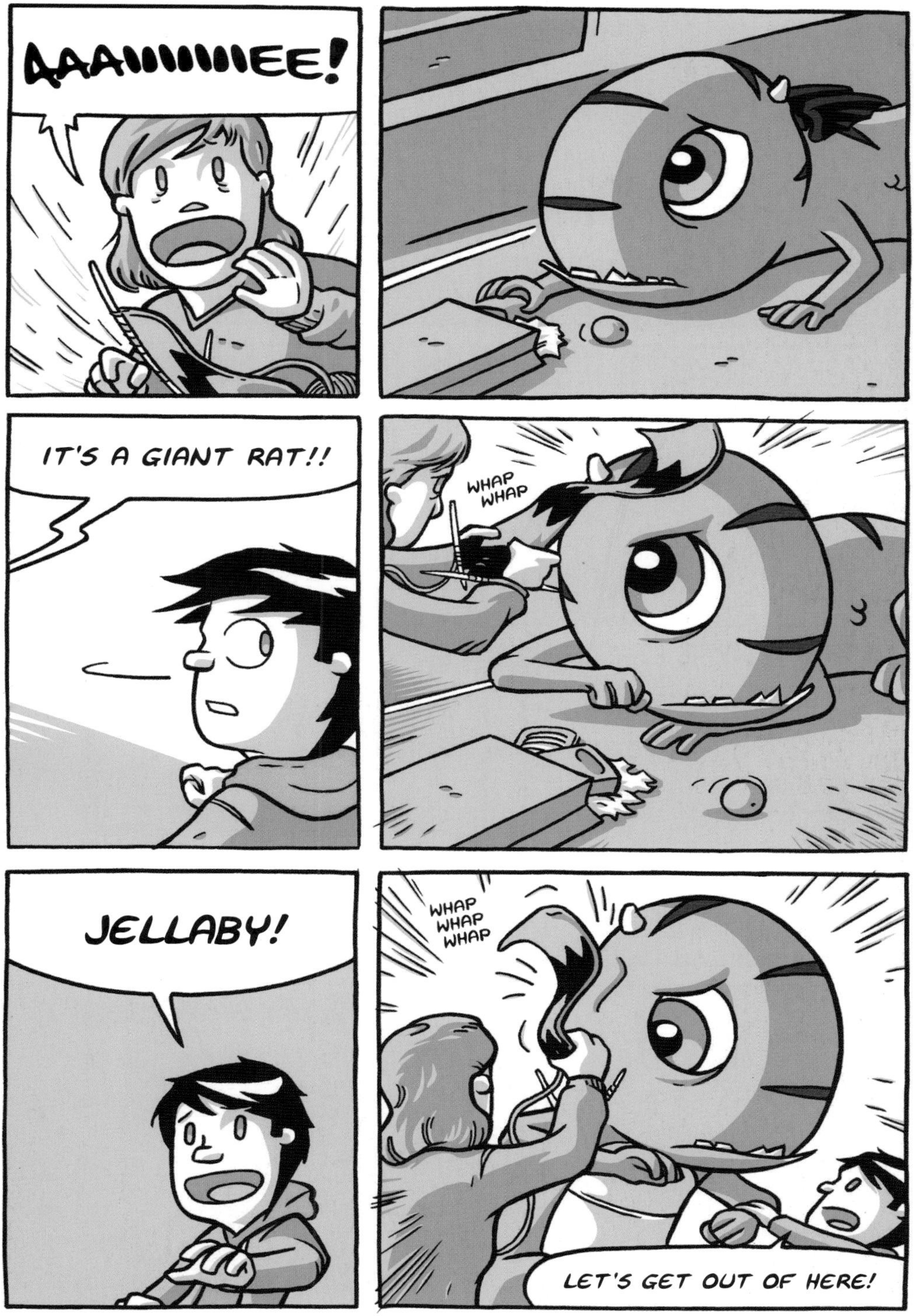

AAAIIIIIIIEE!
IT'S A GIANT RAT!!
WHAP WHAP
JELLABY!
WHAP WHAP WHAP
LET'S GET OUT OF HERE!

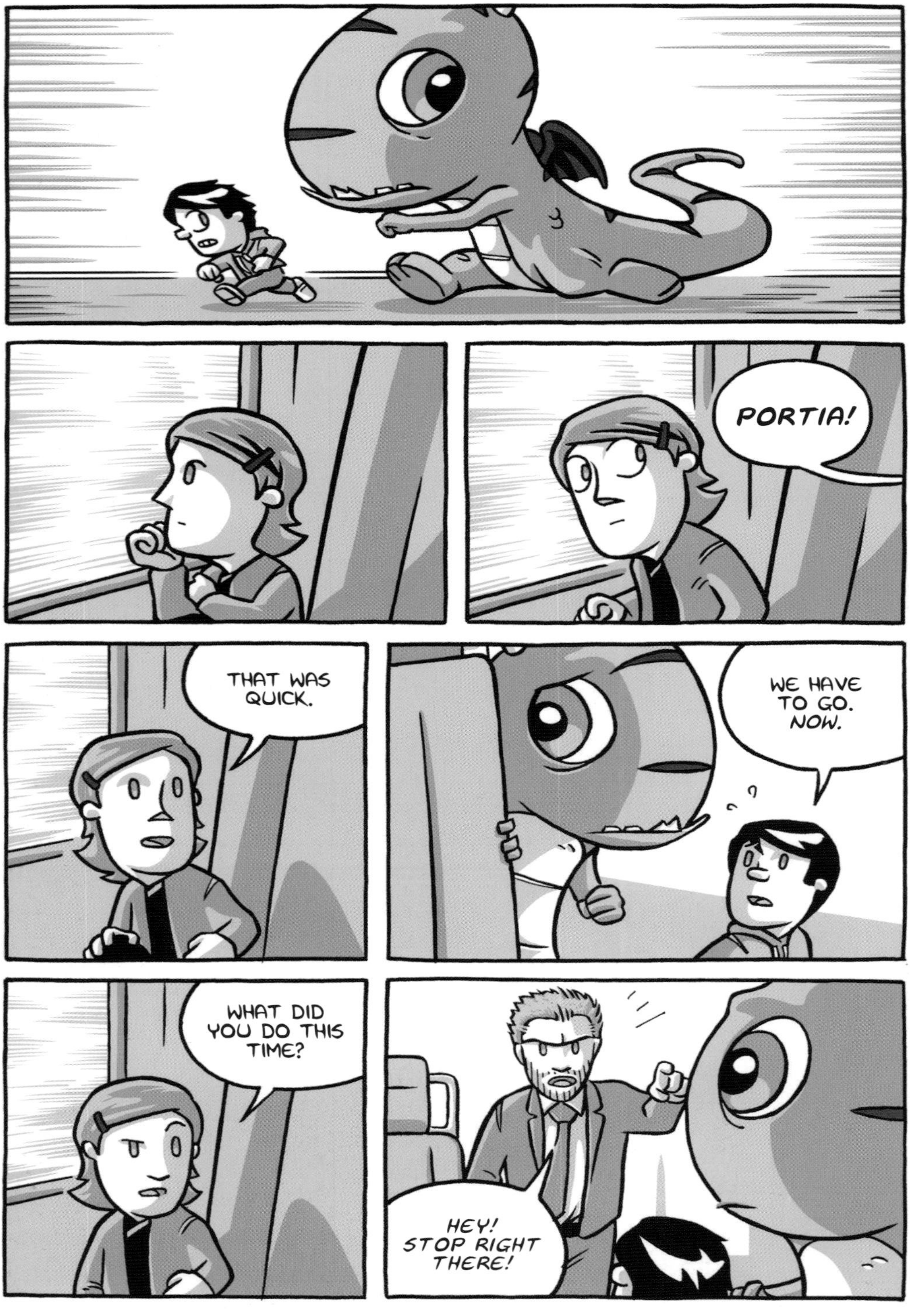
PORTIA!
THAT WAS QUICK.
WE HAVE TO GO. NOW.
WHAT DID YOU DO THIS TIME?
HEY! STOP RIGHT THERE!

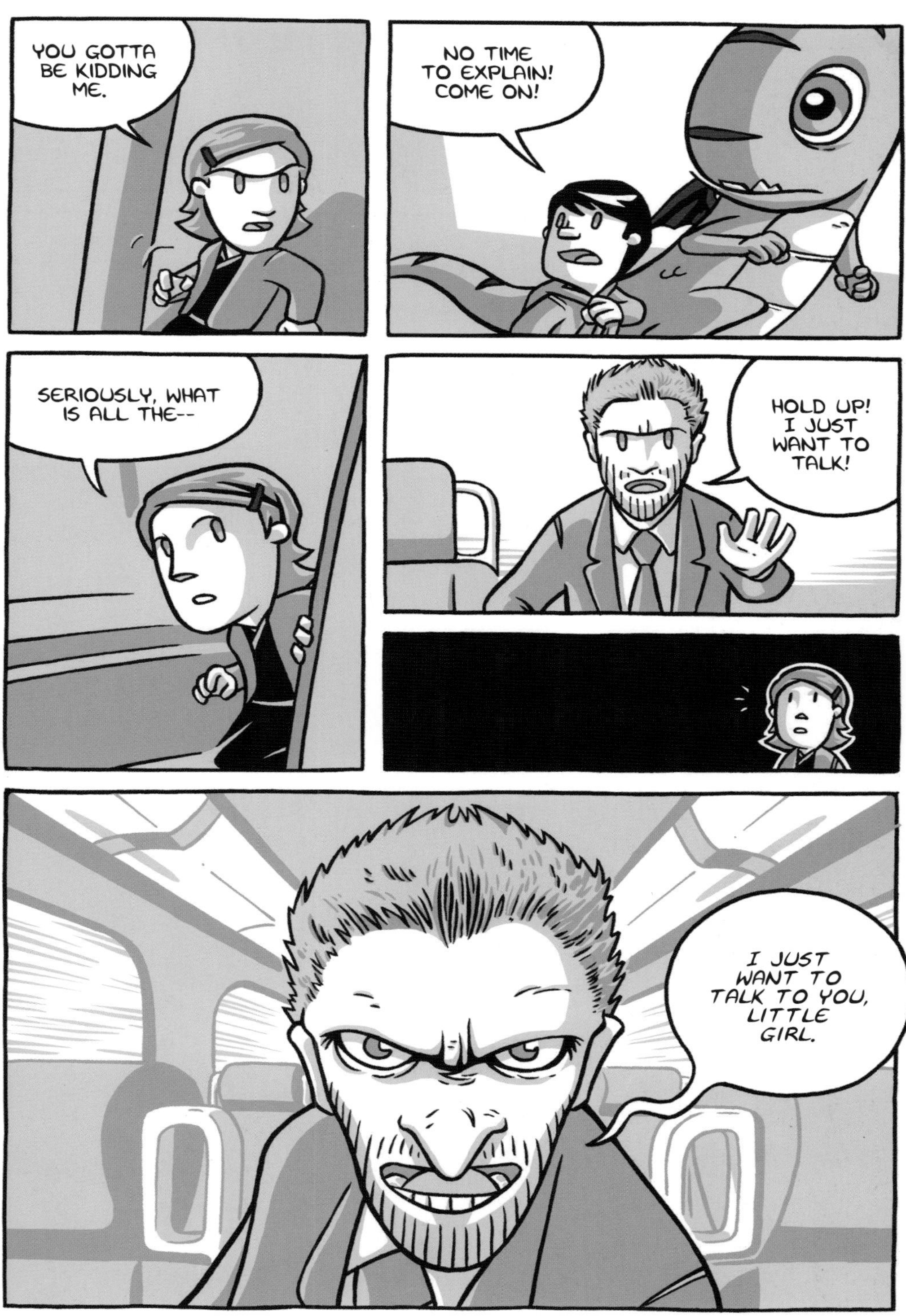
YOU GOTTA BE KIDDING ME.
NO TIME TO EXPLAIN! COME ON!
SERIOUSLY, WHAT IS ALL THE--
HOLD UP! I JUST WANT TO TALK!
I JUST WANT TO TALK TO YOU, LITTLE GIRL.

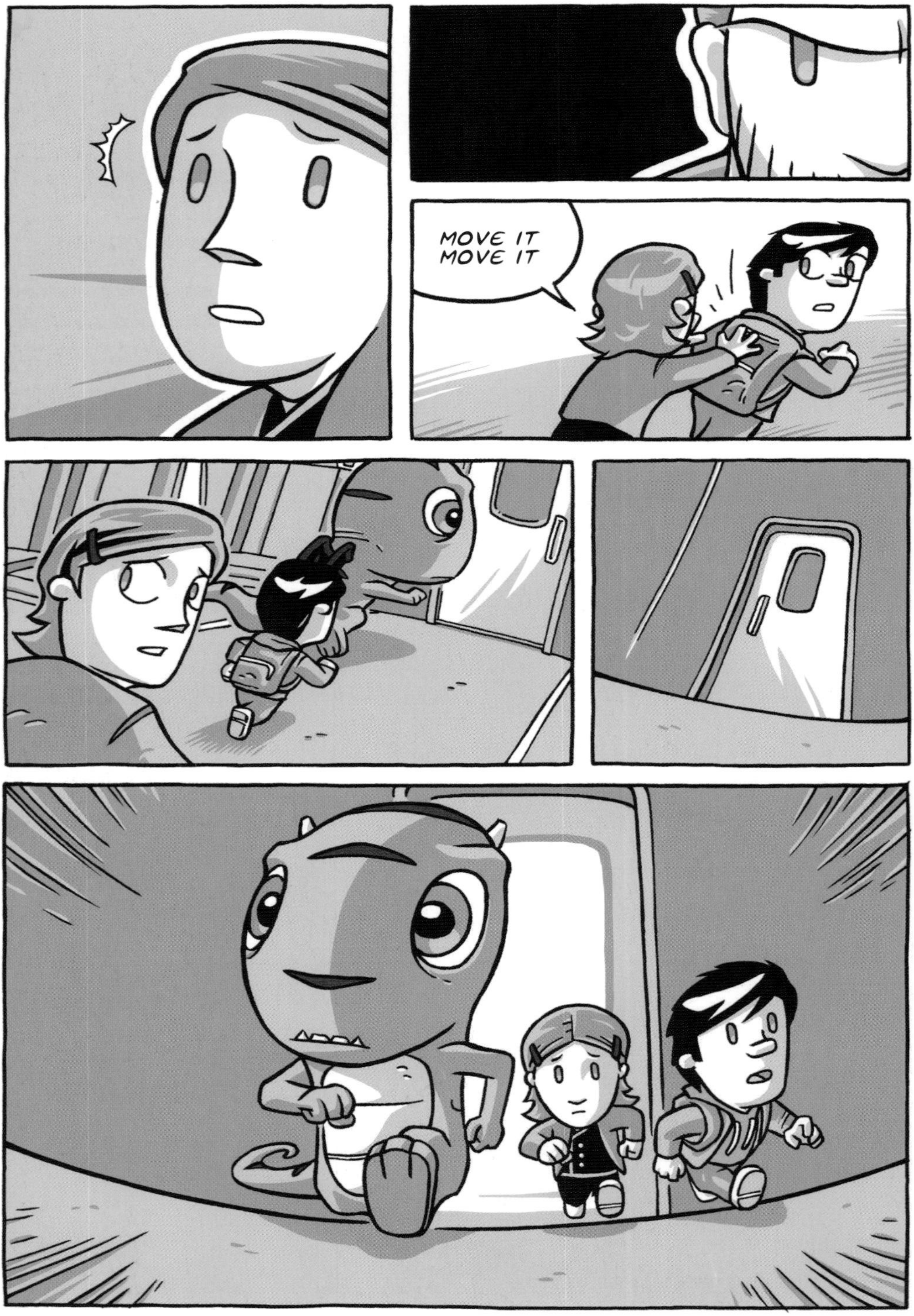
MOVE IT
MOVE IT

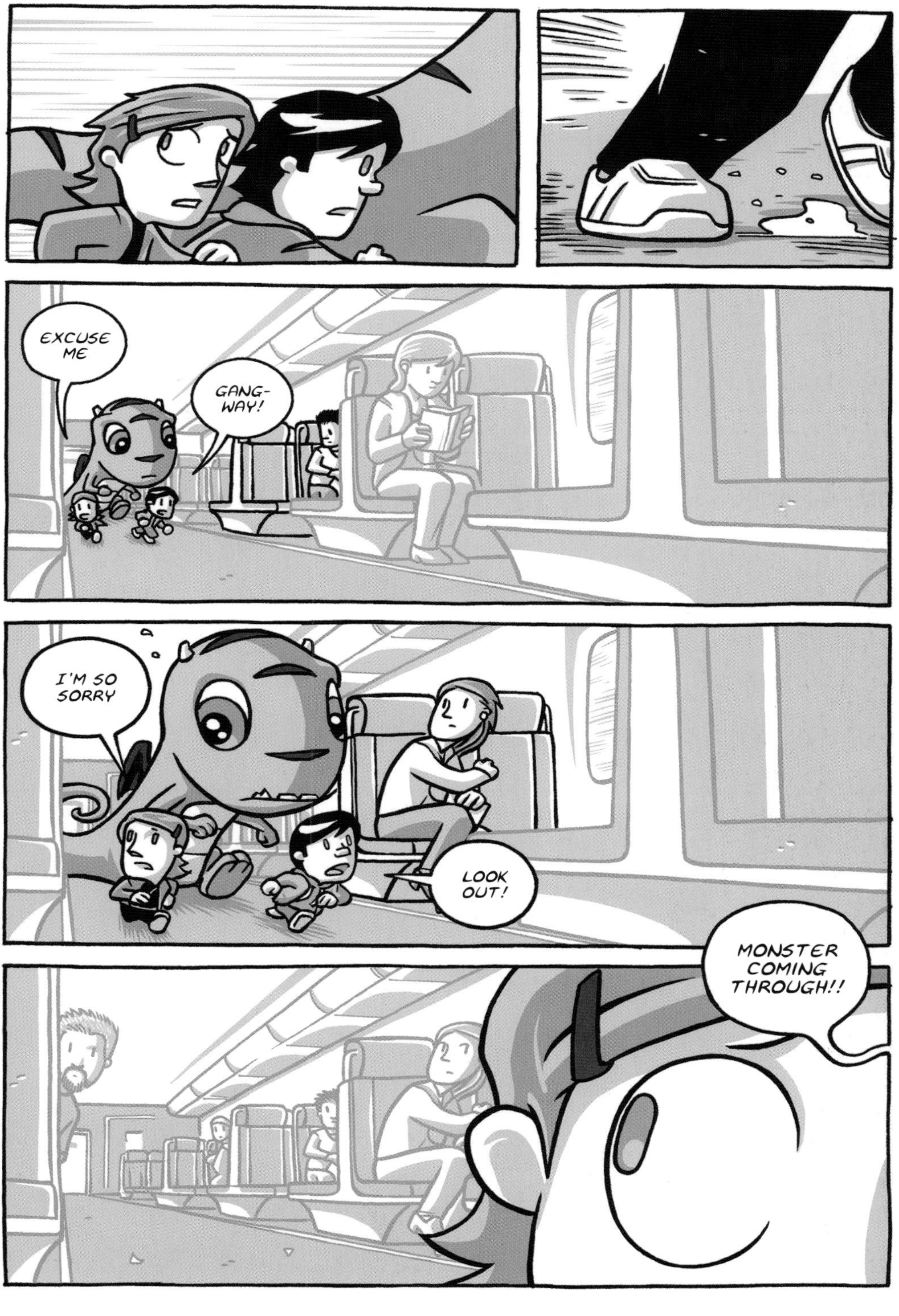
EXCUSE ME
GANG-WAY!
I'M SO SORRY
LOOK OUT!
MONSTER COMING THROUGH!!

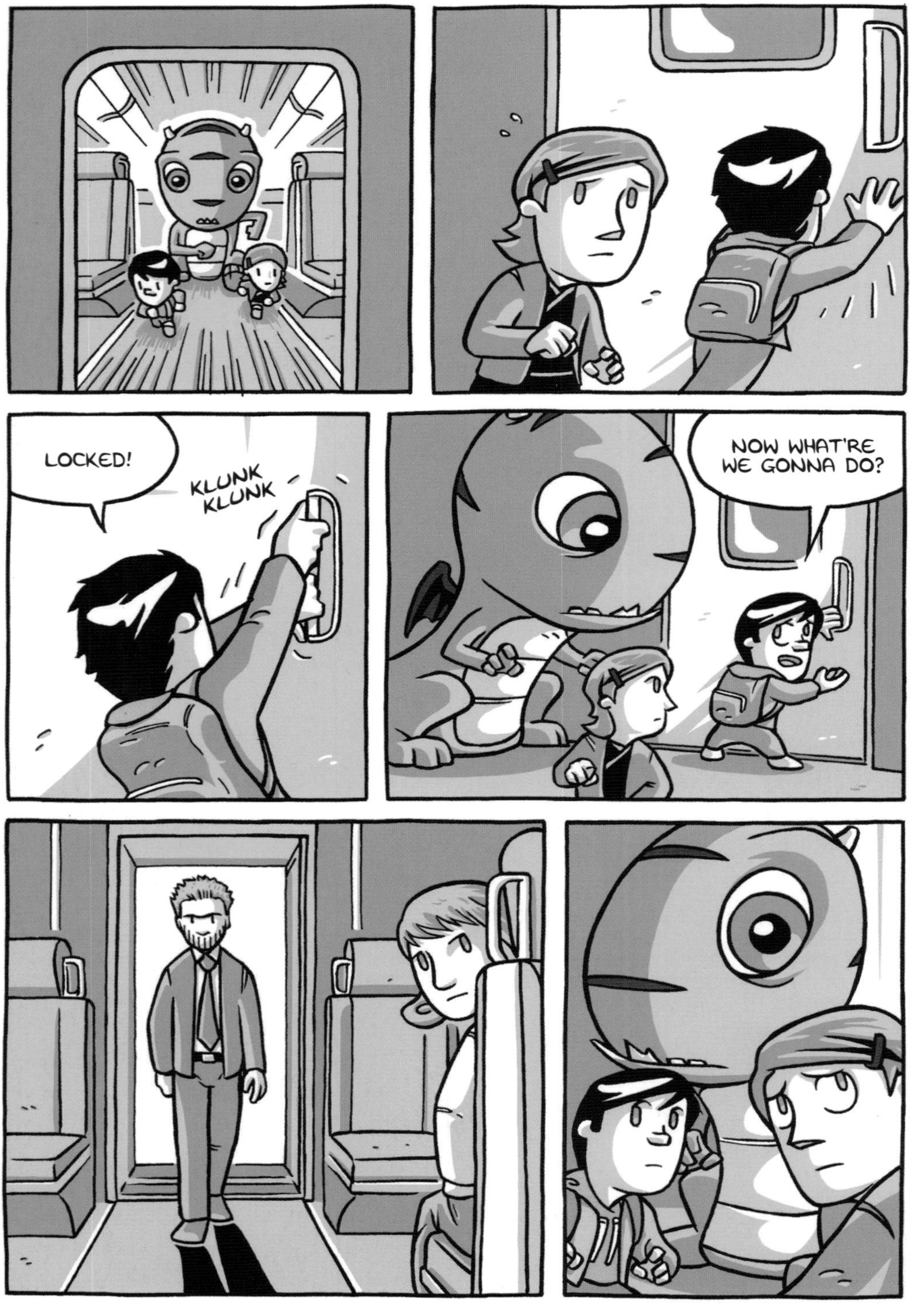
LOCKED!
KLUNK KLUNK
NOW WHAT'RE WE GONNA DO?

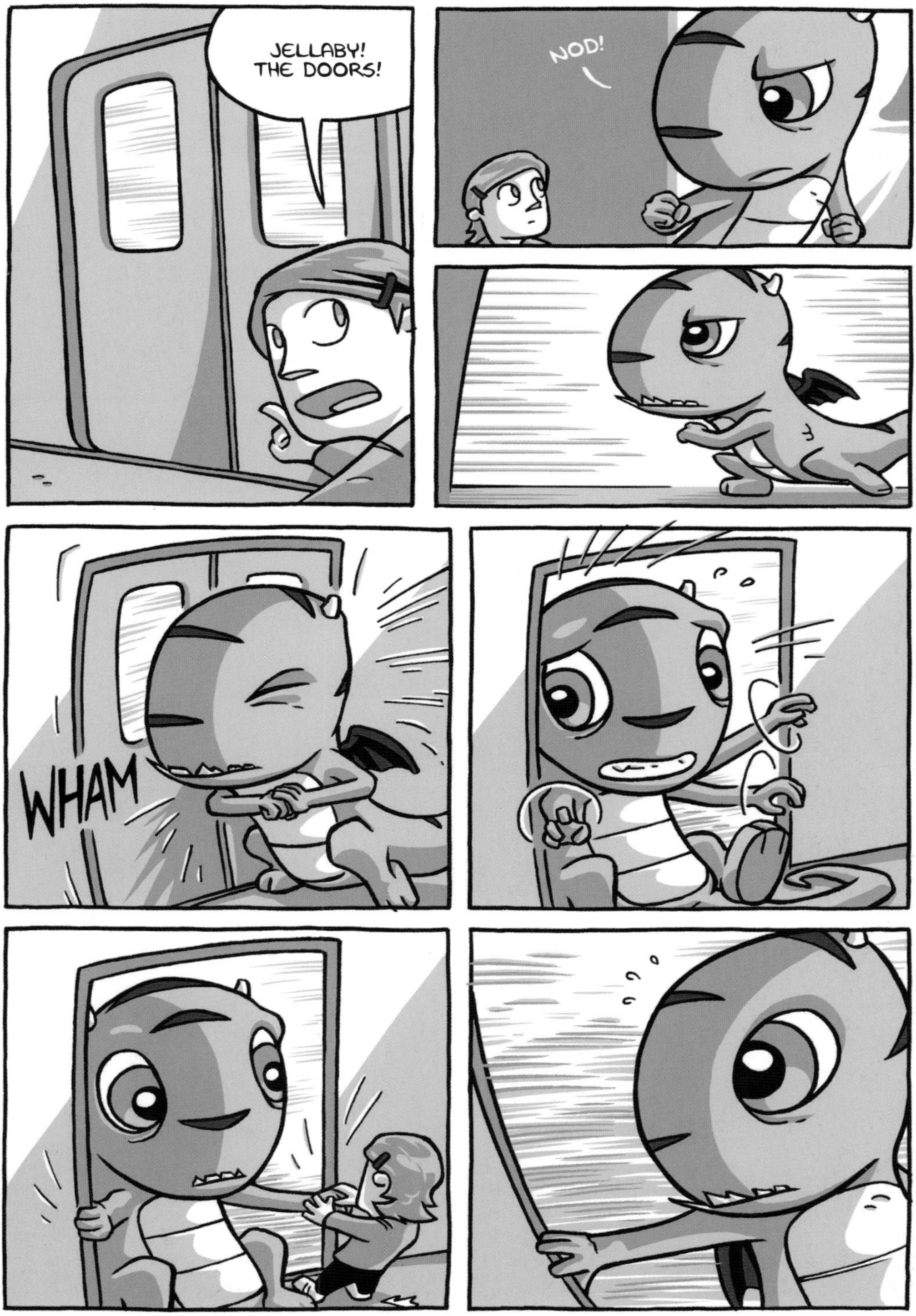

JELLABY! THE DOORS!
NOD!
WHAM

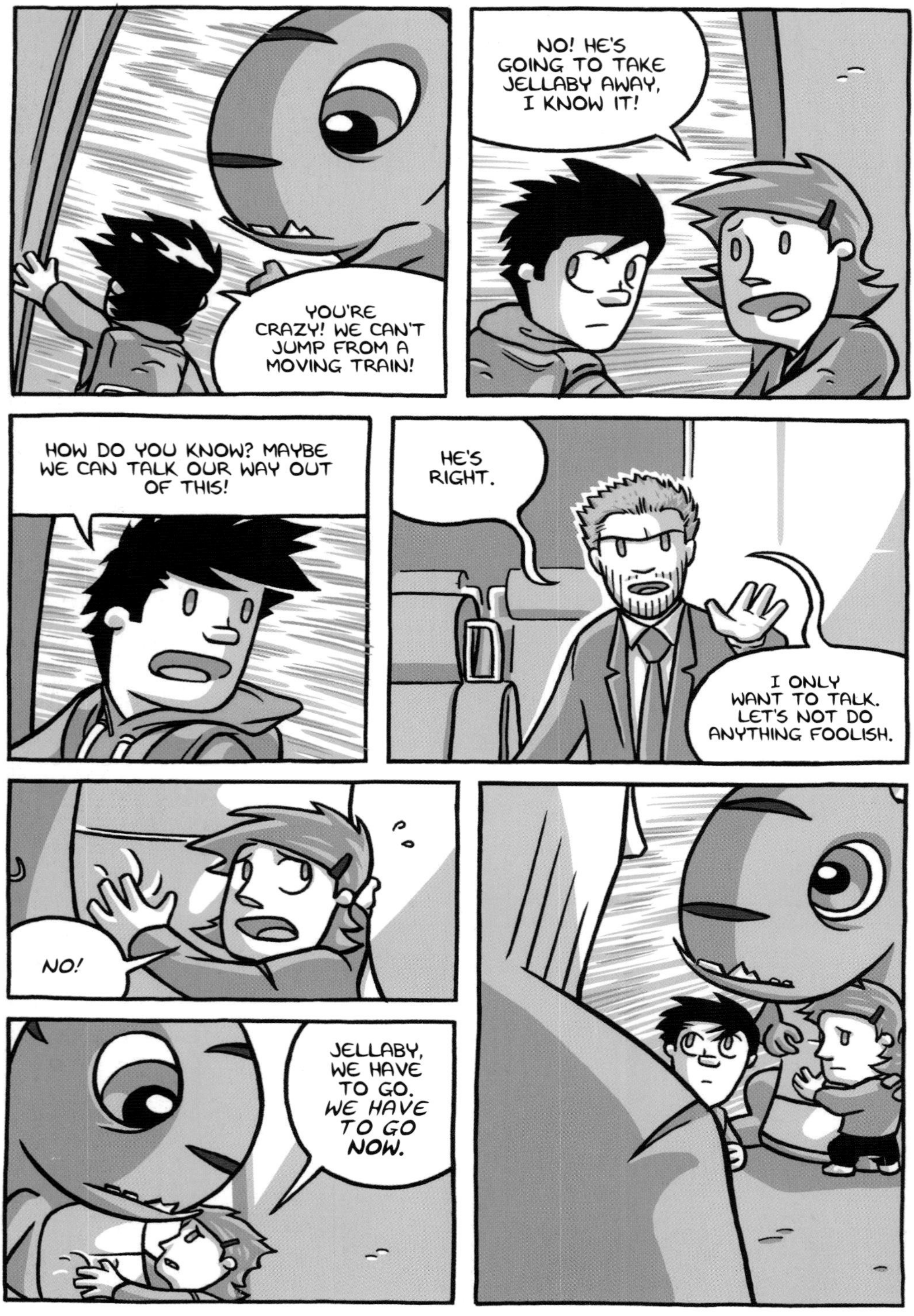
YOU'RE CRAZY! WE CAN'T JUMP FROM A MOVING TRAIN!
NO! HE'S GOING TO TAKE JELLABY AWAY, I KNOW IT!
HOW DO YOU KNOW? MAYBE WE CAN TALK OUR WAY OUT OF THIS!
HE'S RIGHT.
I ONLY WANT TO TALK. LET'S NOT DO ANYTHING FOOLISH.
NO!
JELLABY, WE HAVE TO GO. WE HAVE TO GO NOW.

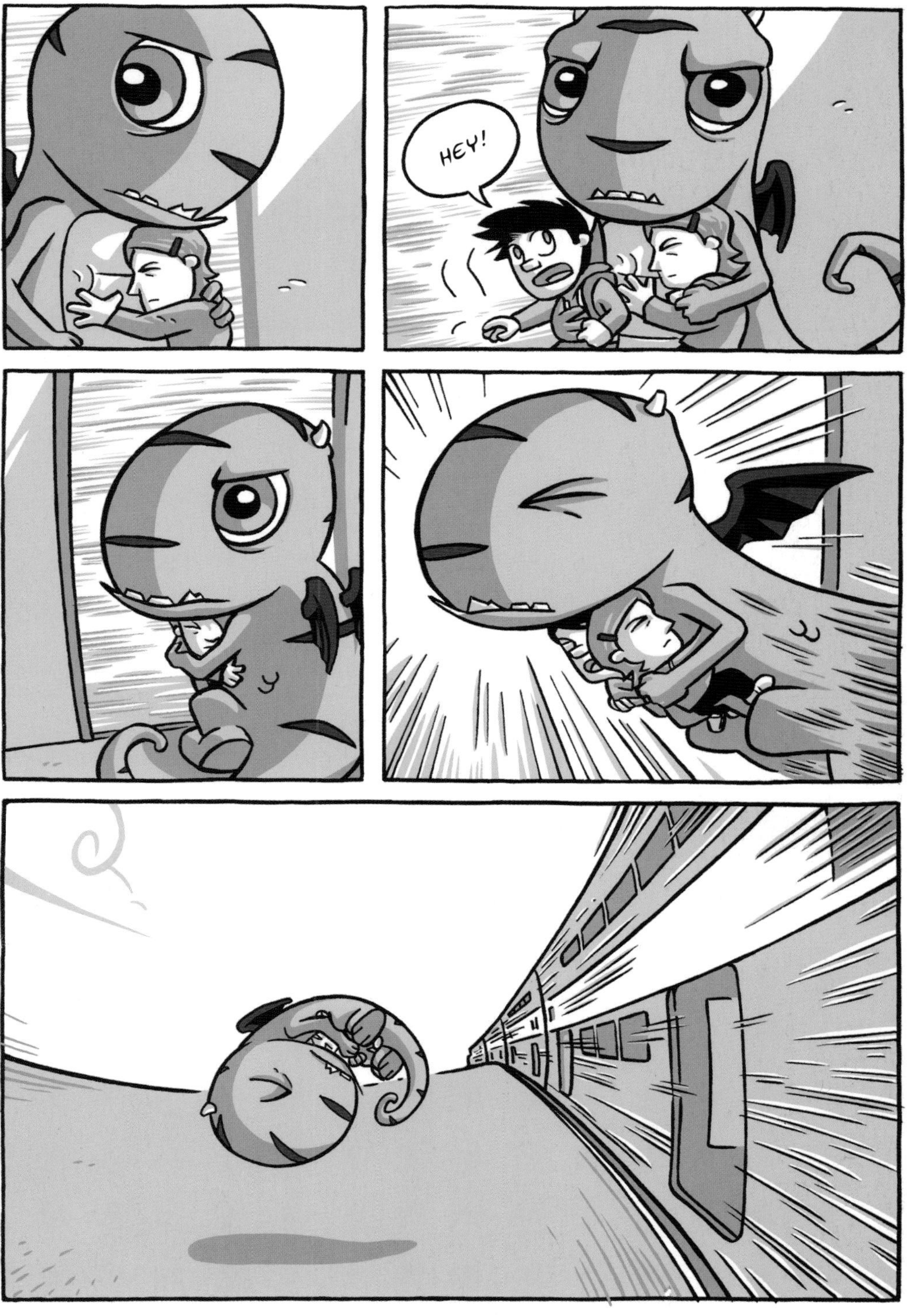
HEY!

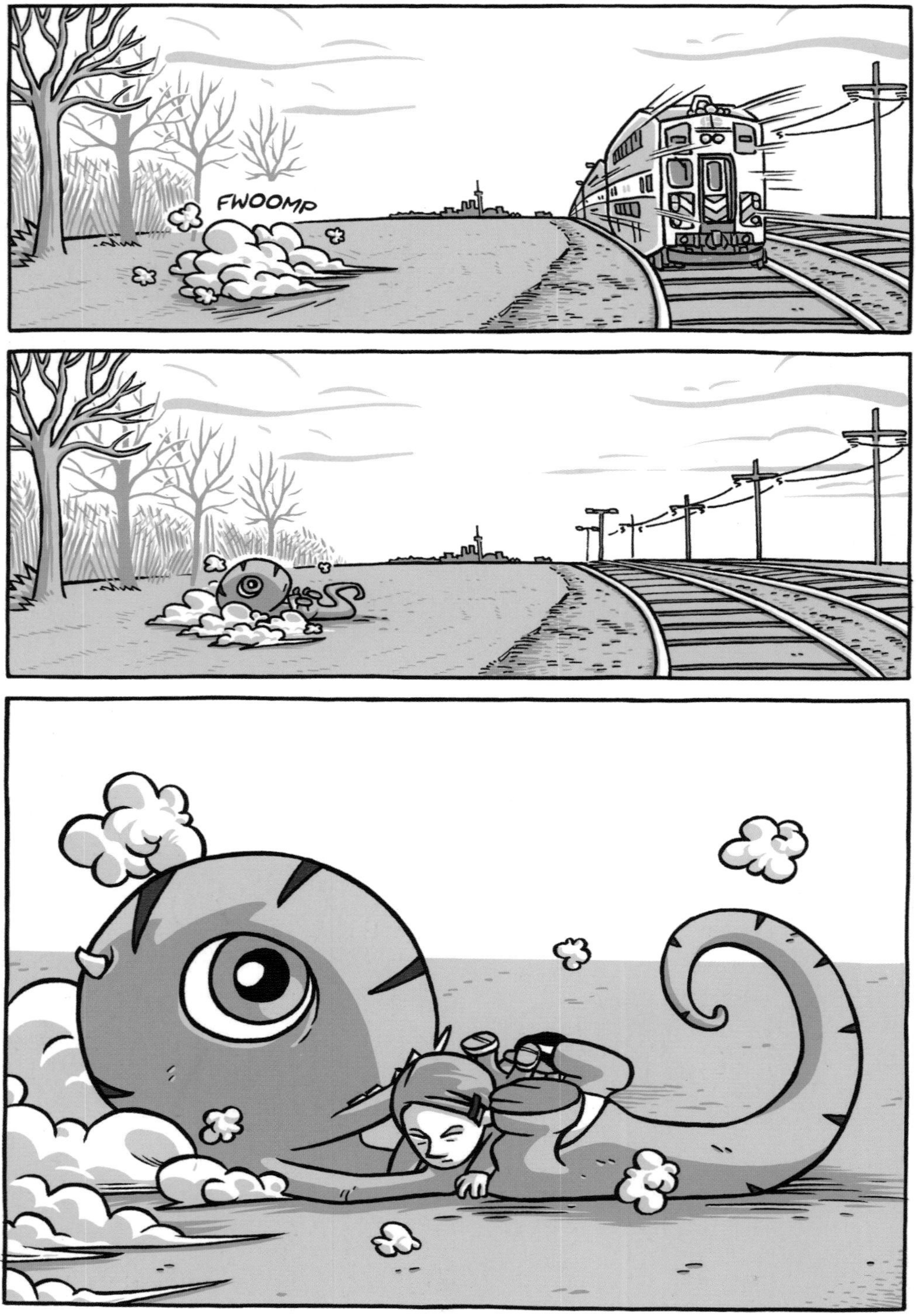
FWOOMP

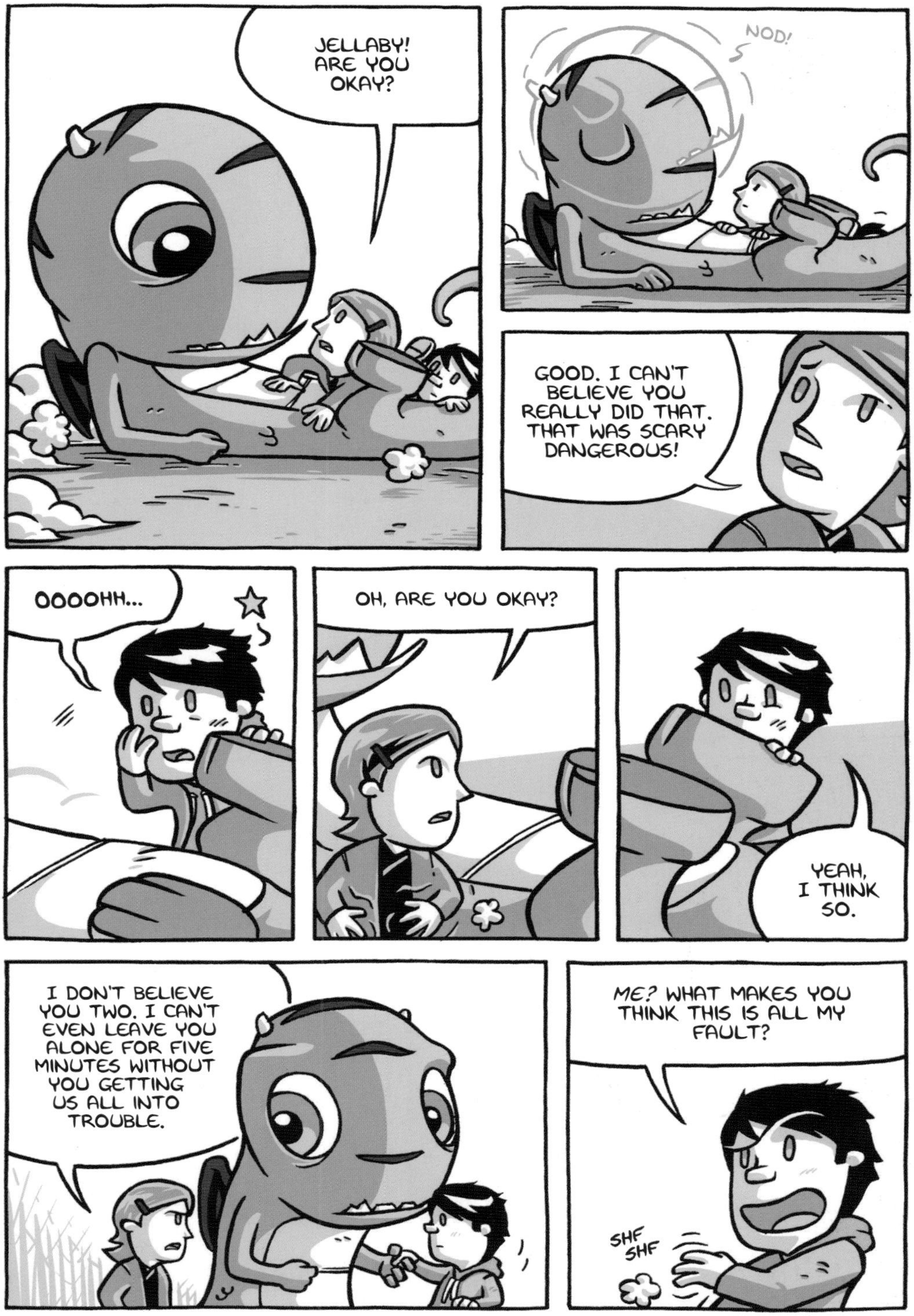
JELLABY! ARE YOU OKAY?
NOD!
GOOD. I CAN'T BELIEVE YOU REALLY DID THAT. THAT WAS SCARY DANGEROUS!
OOOOHH...
OH, ARE YOU OKAY?
YEAH, I THINK SO.
I DON'T BELIEVE YOU TWO. I CAN'T EVEN LEAVE YOU ALONE FOR FIVE MINUTES WITHOUT YOU GETTING US ALL INTO TROUBLE.
ME? WHAT MAKES YOU THINK THIS IS ALL MY FAULT?
SHF SHF

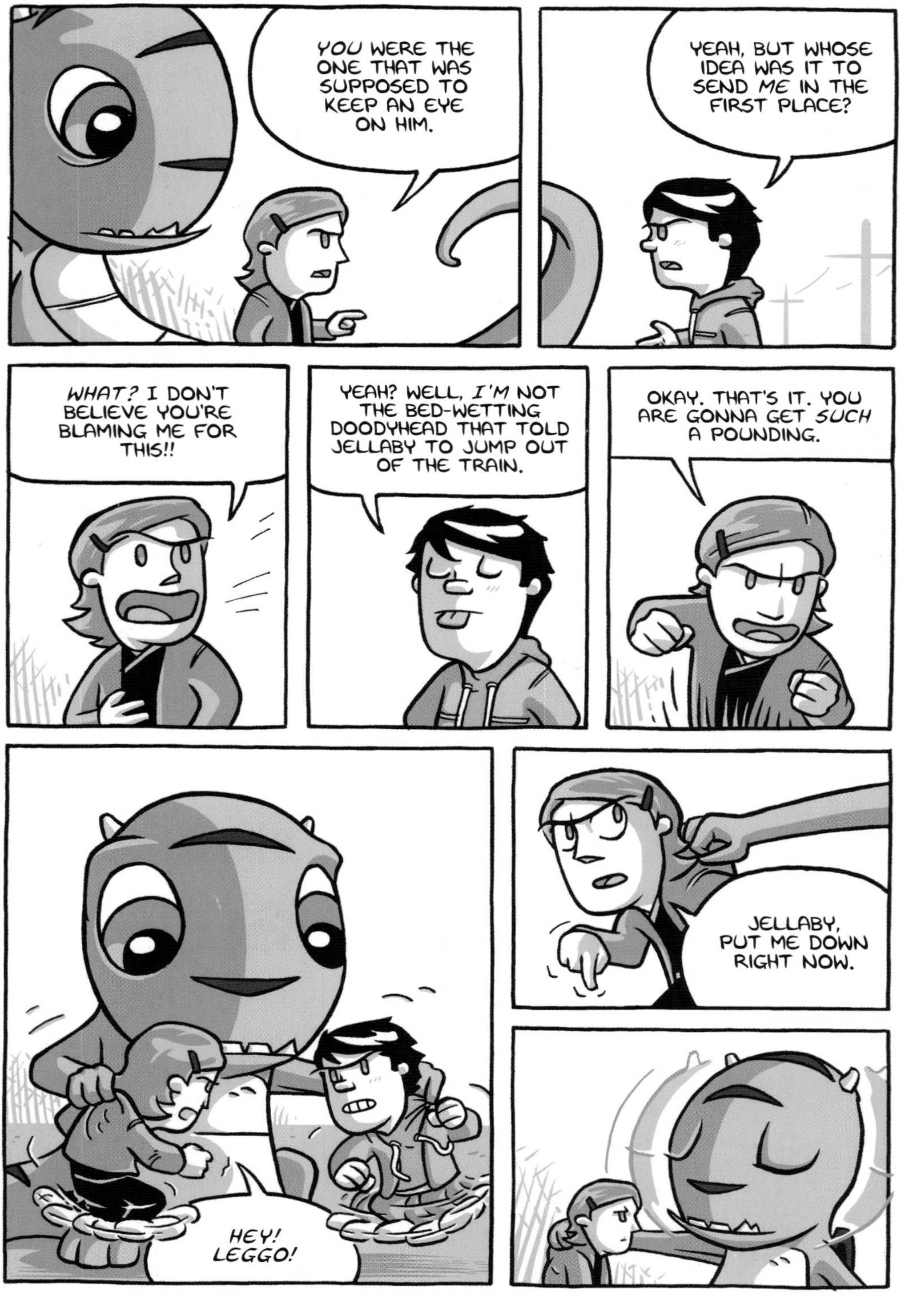
YOU WERE THE ONE THAT WAS SUPPOSED TO KEEP AN EYE ON HIM.
YEAH, BUT WHOSE IDEA WAS IT TO SEND ME IN THE FIRST PLACE?
WHAT? I DON'T BELIEVE YOU'RE BLAMING ME FOR THIS!!
YEAH? WELL, I'M NOT THE BED-WETTING DOODYHEAD THAT TOLD JELLABY TO JUMP OUT OF THE TRAIN.
OKAY. THAT'S IT. YOU ARE GONNA GET SUCH A POUNDING.
HEY! LEGGO!
JELLABY, PUT ME DOWN RIGHT NOW.

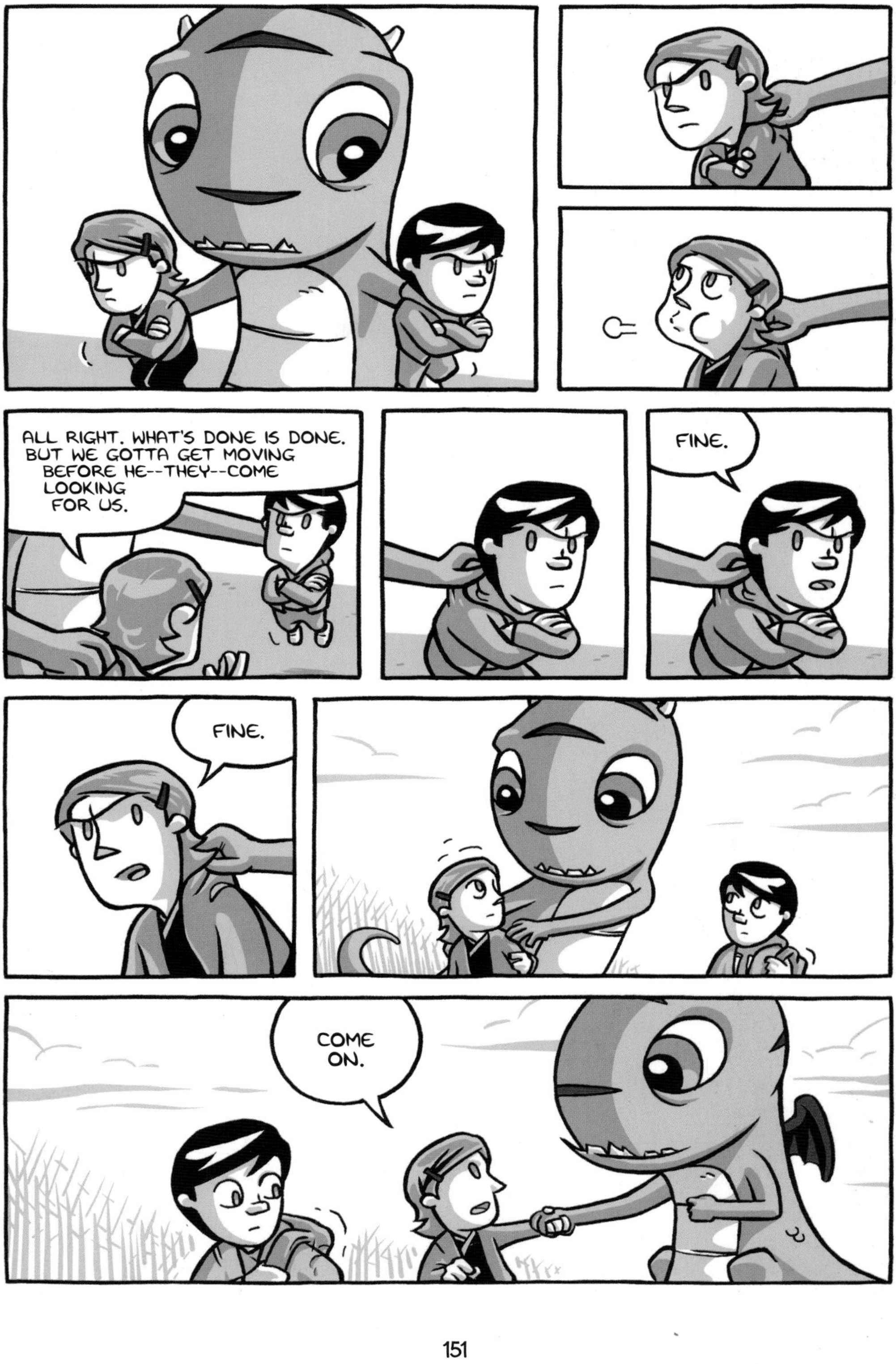
ALL RIGHT. WHAT'S DONE IS DONE. BUT WE GOTTA GET MOVING BEFORE HE--THEY--COME LOOKING FOR US.
FINE.
FINE.
COME ON.

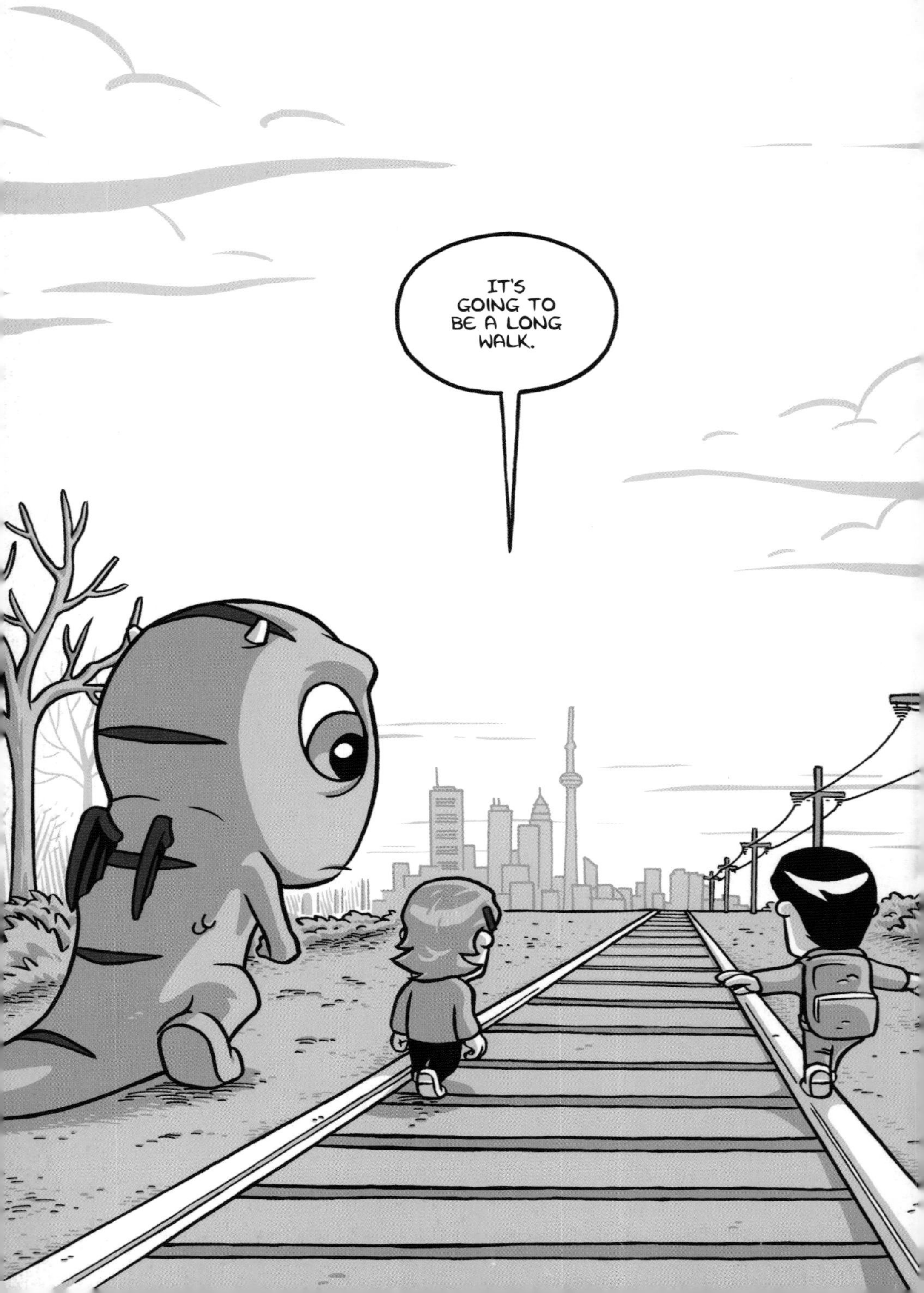
IT'S GOING TO BE A LONG WALK.

To be continued in...

JELLABY

Monster in the City

About the Author

Born in England and raised in Hong Kong, Kean Soo settled in Canada, where he planned to embark on a career in electrical engineering. However, he discovered that he'd rather draw comics instead. Kean began posting his comics on the Internet in 2002, and later became an assistant editor and regular contributor to the all-ages *Flight* anthologies. Kean was nominated for an Eisner Award and received a Joe Shuster Award for Best Comics for Kids for his work on *Jellaby*.

Kean likes carrots, but not nearly as much as he likes tuna sandwiches, usually with lots and lots of wasabi mayonnaise.

Portrait of the author by Phil Craven

Q&A with Kean Soo

Where did you get the idea for Jellaby?

The idea actually came from a single drawing in my sketchbook. At the time, I was trying to think of ideas for my first graphic novel, so in my sketchbook, I was just having fun drawing all the things I love to draw -- things like robots, monsters, and cars.

It was one of those drawings that really stood out to me: a little girl hugging a terrifying, grub-like monster. And because the monster was so terrifying, it made me wonder: why would these two be hugging each other? Why would they even be friends?

As I tried to answer these questions, it started raising more questions, and I wanted to find out more about these two. From there, the characters of Portia and Jellaby started to take shape, and the story naturally spun out of that.

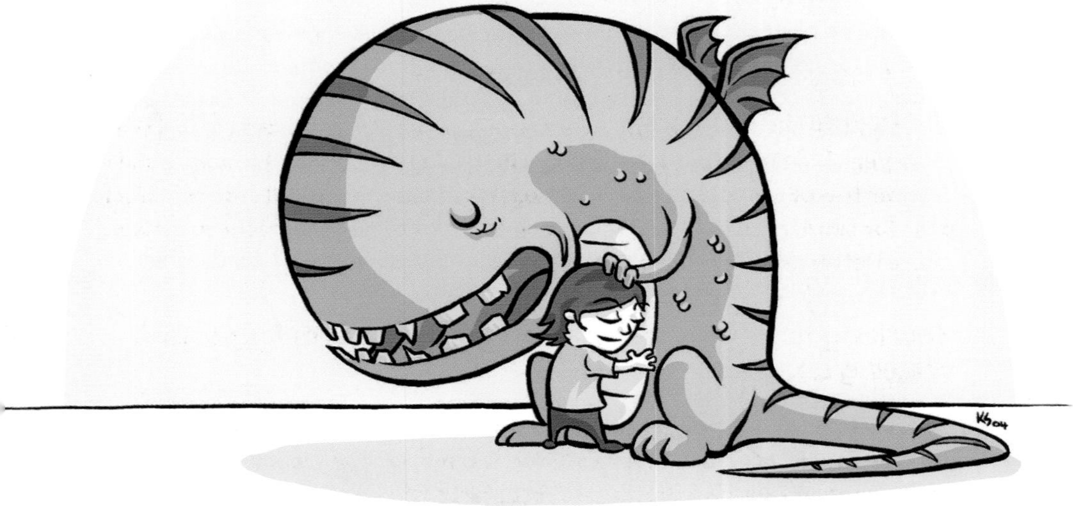

Above: The very first drawing of Portia and Jellaby. I had originally named the monster Cuddles, mostly because at the time, I thought it was a funny name for such a terrifying monster.

Why did you choose pink and purple for the colors of the book?

I had originally designed the book to be printed in black and white, but when I first started drawing Jellaby, I didn't have a publisher and I was just posting the pages online. Because it didn't cost anything extra to post color pages to the web, I decided to use pink and purple to make the pages a little more interesting, but those colors were also chosen because they could be easily converted back to black and white when the book was printed.

When a publisher did get in touch with me about printing the book, they liked the pink and purple colors so much that we ended up keeping them anyway!

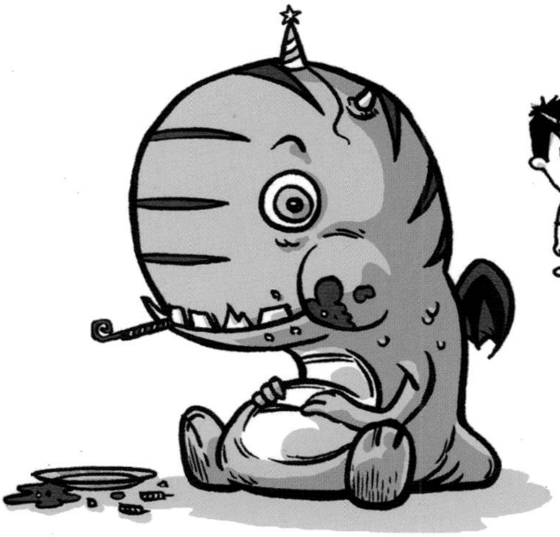

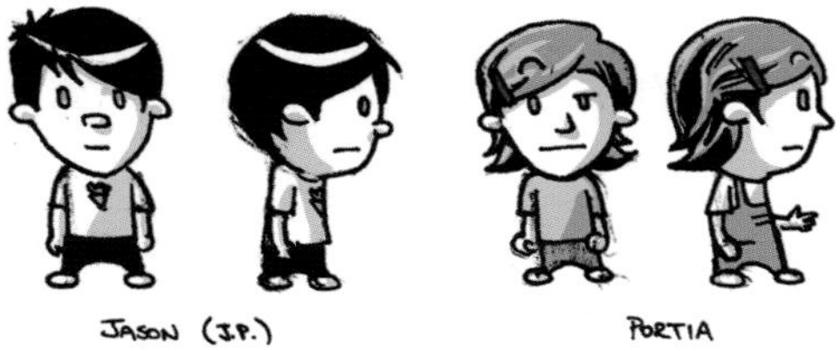
JASON (J.P.)
PORTIA

Above: The first color tests for the Jellaby characters.

What do you use to draw Jellaby?

I write and lay out my pages in my sketchbook with a regular HB pencil. I use that same pencil to draw the pages full size on 9" x 12" smooth bristol board, and I ink over top of those pencils using a Kuretake brush pen and Micron technical pens for smaller details. The finished pages are then scanned into a computer, where I letter and color the pages digitally.

How long have you been drawing for? When did you start drawing comics?

I've been drawing for as long as I can remember -- I specifically remember when I was around 4 years old, after watching the movie *Tron*, I would draw pages upon pages of light cycle battles. I didn't start making comics until I was much older, but I found that drawing a daily webcomic for almost two years really taught me a lot. In fact, I was still learning new tricks and techniques even while I was working on *Jellaby*.

Sketches

FIRST DAY OF SCHOOL

SHOOF SHOOF SHOOF

Above: More early sketches of Portia and Jellaby. Some of these sketches eventually made it into the final book (compare the sketch on the top right with Chapter Five's opening page).

Left: Sometimes I love a scene so much, I enjoy revisiting it when I'm warming up to draw. Here's another interpretation of Portia and Jellaby "shoofing" through the leaves from Chapter Two.

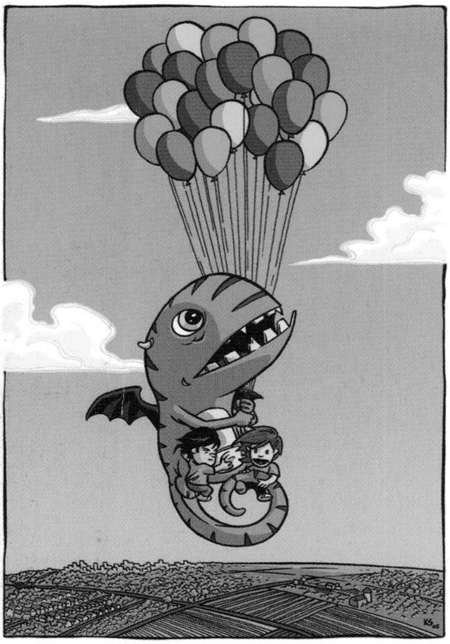

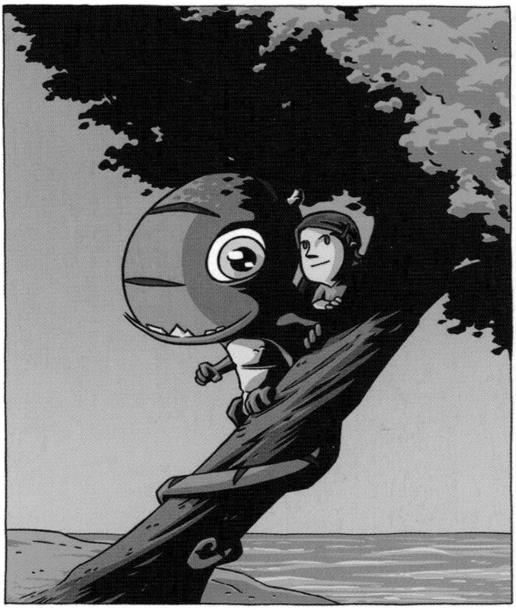

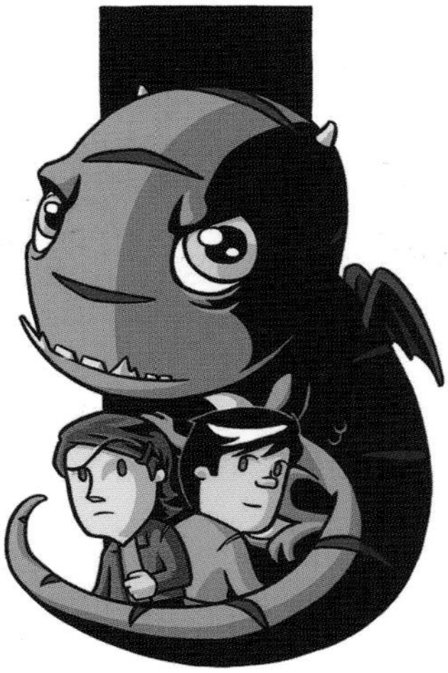

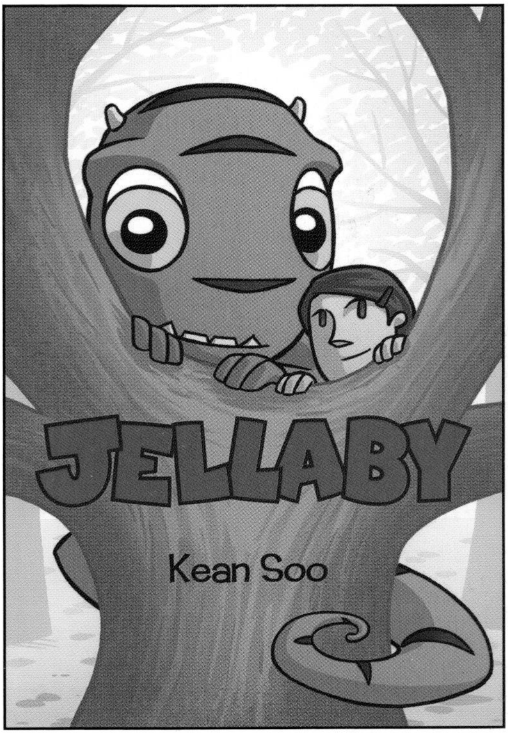
JELLABY
Kean Soo

Top: Art from various gallery exhibitions.

Above: Self-published Jellaby minicomic cover collecting Chapter Two.

Right: The original Jellaby cover, published in 2008.

Don't miss...

JELLABY

Monster in the City

Available only from...
Stone Arch Books
a capstone imprint

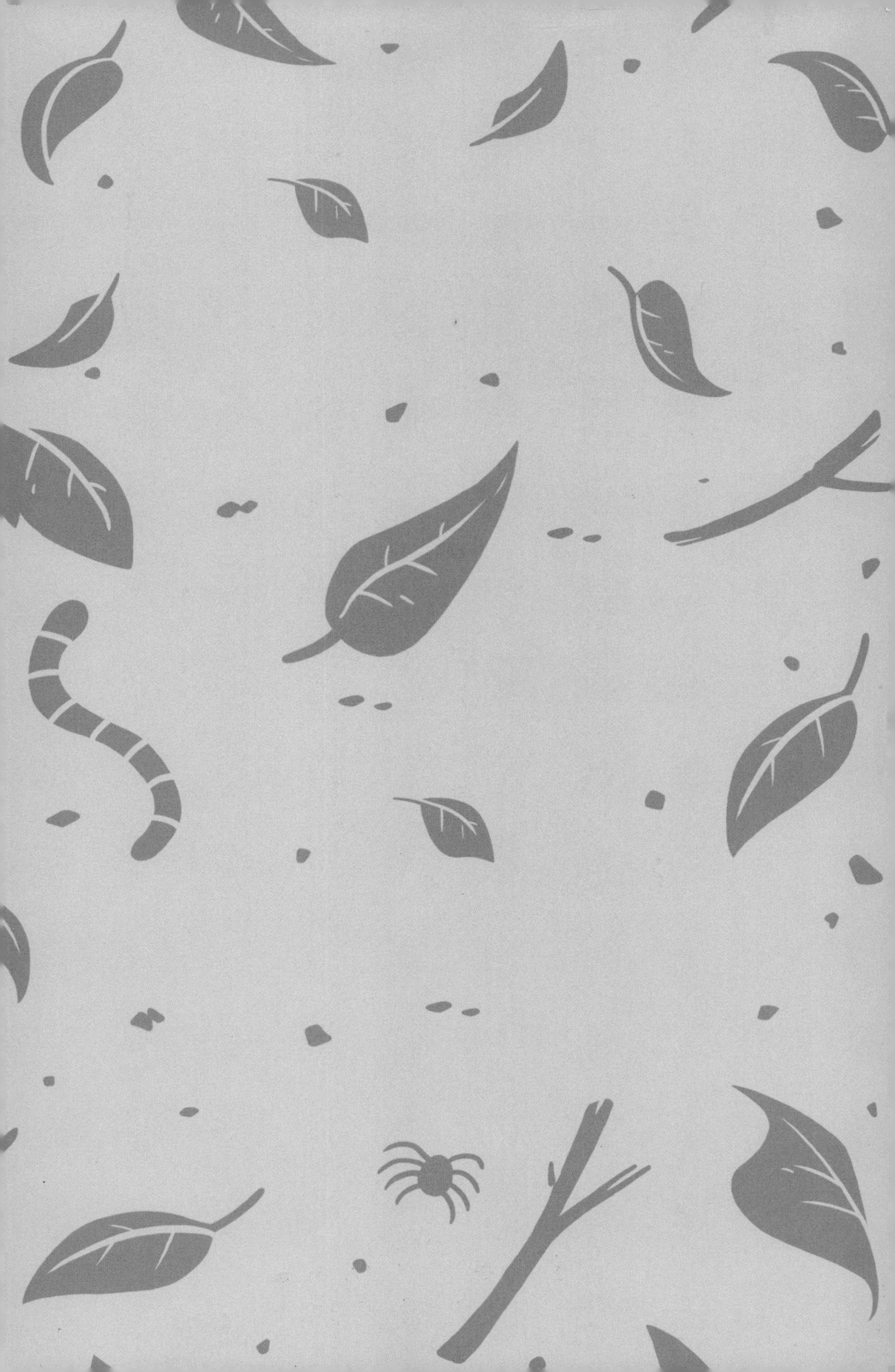

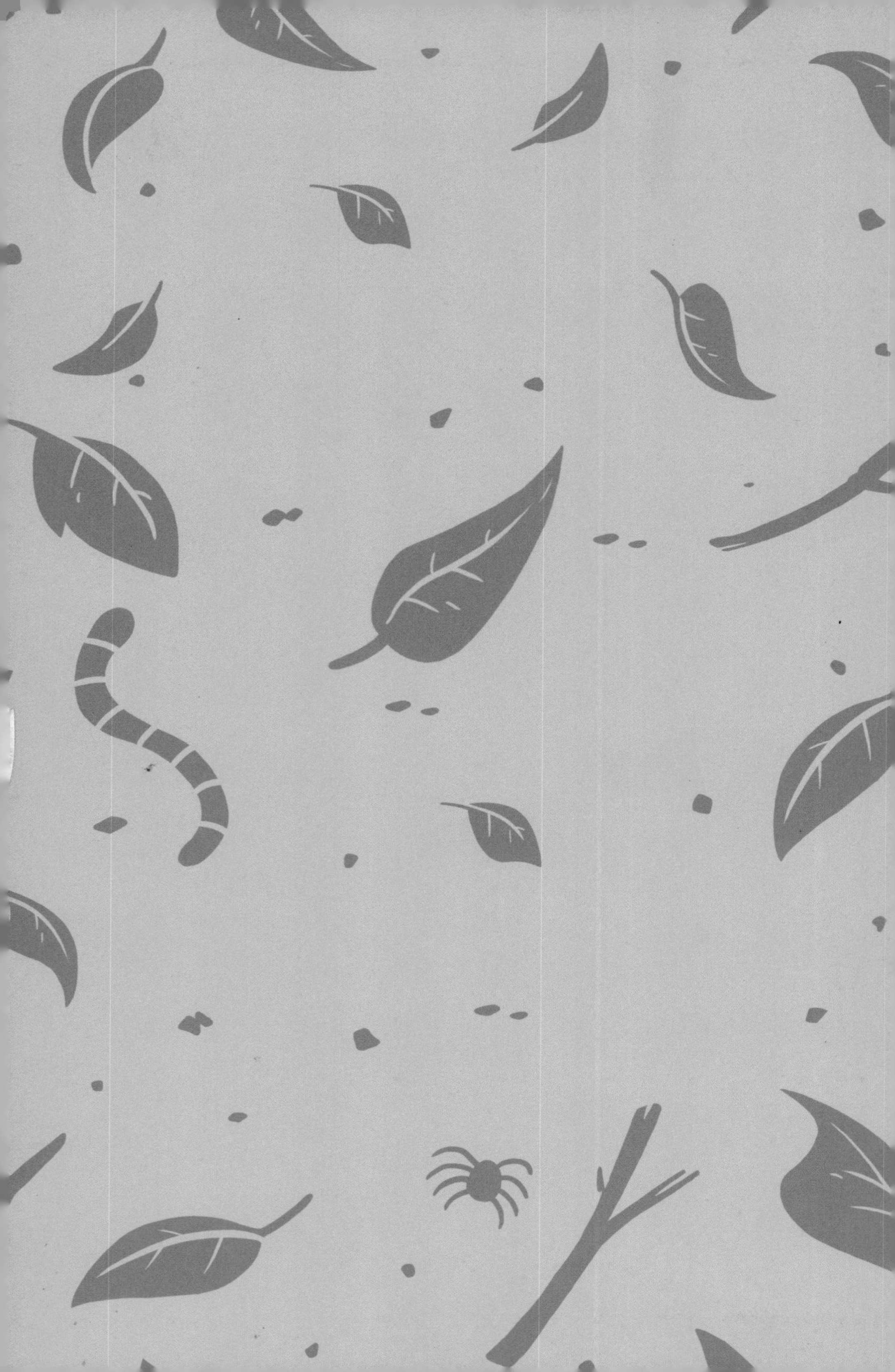